PENGUIN BOOKS

The Templar's Secret

The Templar's Secret

C. M. PALOV

Northumberland County Council	
3 0132 02233984 5	
Askews & Holts	Dec-2012
AF	£6.99

PENGUIN BOOKS

PENGUIN BOOKS

Published by the Penguin Group
Penguin Books Ltd, 80 Strand, London WC2R ORL, England
Penguin Group (USA) Inc., 375 Hudson Street, New York, New York 10014, USA
Penguin Group (Canada), 90 Eglinton Avenue East, Suite 700, Toronto, Ontario, Canada M4P 2Y3
(a division of Pearson Penguin Canada Inc.)
Penguin Ireland, 25 St Stephen's Green, Dublin 2, Ireland (a division of Penguin Books Ltd)
Penguin Group (Australia), 707 Collins Street, Melbourne, Victoria 3008, Australia
(a division of Pearson Australia Group Pty Ltd)
Penguin Books India Pvt Ltd, 11 Community Centre, Panchsheel Park, New Delhi – 110 017, India
Penguin Group (NZ), 67 Apollo Drive, Rosedale, Auckland 0632, New Zealand
(a division of Pearson New Zealand Ltd)
Penguin Books (South Africa) (Pty) Ltd, Block D, Rosebank Office Park, 181 Jan Smuts Avenue,
Parktown North, Gauteng, Johannesburg 2193, South Africa

Penguin Books Ltd, Registered Offices: 80 Strand, London WC2R ORL, England

www.penguin.com

First published 2012
1

Set in 12.5/14.75pt Garamond MT
Typeset by Palimpsest Book Production Limited, Falkirk, Stirlingshire
Printed in Great Britain by Clays Ltd, St Ives plc

ISBN: 978-0-241-95888-9

www.greenpenguin.co.uk

ALWAYS LEARNING   **PEARSON**

Ria Palov, *in memoriam*

Prologue

Chinon Castle, France

15 March, 1308

The king's henchman hefted the iron hammer, vigorously swinging his arm with unerring precision. In the next instant, an agonized scream rent the chill morning air, reverberating off the stone walls.

A lone Dominican, his face hidden by a hooded cowl, stood in the shadows observing the proceedings. On the other side of the cell, a second man, studiously hunched over a writing desk, sharpened an ink-stained quill.

'For the love of God! Make him stop!' the accused shrieked, having endured one blow too many.

Hearing that anguished plea, the apostolic inquisitor, Friar Raymbaud le Breton, stepped towards the wooden wheel that had been set in the middle of the dungeon. Wrinkling his nose, the stench unbearable, he inspected the torturer's handiwork. The bare-chested man who'd been lashed to the breaking wheel writhed in pain, his lower leg a bloody pulp of mangled flesh and splintered bones.

Satisfied that the accused Knight Templar had been sufficiently chastened, he nodded his approval. The henchman, hammer clutched in his fist, obediently stepped away from the wheel.

Thus far, Fortes de Pinós had steadfastly maintained his innocence, insisting that he had no direct knowledge of the Great Heresy and that he'd never been to Château Pèlerin. But if that were true, why had Brother Fortes made the perilous sea voyage to retrieve the ancient gospel known as the *Evangelium Gaspar*? *More importantly, why did he refuse to disclose the gospel's current whereabouts?*

Impatient to continue with the proceedings, Raymbaud picked up a sheet of parchment from the scribe's desk. He gave it a cursory glance before returning his attention to the accused. 'Fortes de Pinós, do you understand the charges that have been brought against you?'

'As I have repeatedly avowed, I am innocent of your despicable accusations,' the Templar hissed. Although he had fifty-four winters on his greying head, Brother Fortes had a surprisingly muscular physique that belied his age. His brawn was a testament to years of rigorous training, the warrior monks able to hold their own against any foe on the field of battle.

But this was not a battlefield. This was a damp dungeon in Chinon Castle.

The inquisitor handed the parchment back to the scribe. 'Brother Fortes, I grow impatient with the tiresome lies that spill from your lips with Lucifer's ease. In order to save your mortal soul, you must tell me where you hid the *Evangelium Gaspar*.'

'I will tell you *after* the Grand Master and the other Templar knights have been released from custody.'

'We both know that will never happen.' Raymbaud's belly growled with hunger. If not for this uncooperative Templar, he'd be in the refectory breaking his fast. 'Your

2

fate, and that of your brother knights, has been sealed.'

'Then I gain nothing by disclosing the gospel's whereabouts.' The gauntlet tossed, Fortes de Pinós glared at him, a haughty sneer on his blood-splattered face. The silent taunt affirmed what they both knew full well: any man, rich or poor, could become a Dominican friar, but only a man of noble birth could become a Knight Templar.

'In giving true witness, you gain the Lord's forgiveness. Or is that meaningless to an arrogant Knight Templar?'

'I will not testify to a hellhound in the employ of the Devil!'

The inquisitor flinched, the insult digging deep. Because of their sacred obligation to root out heresy, the Dominican Order were known as *Domini Canes*, the Hounds of the Lord. If not for their tireless sacrifice, Christendom would be overrun with heretics and idolaters.

'I demand that you reveal the location of the *Evangelium Gaspar*.'

'To see the house where Lucas dwelled, the faithful pilgrim sought the brother's way. Setting forth from the lion's castle, he dropped the French iron in the Spanish harbour,' the Templar recited in a wooden tone.

Raymbaud tamped down his ire. It was the same nonsensical riddle that Brother Fortes uttered each time the question was put to him.

Sighing resignedly, he motioned for the henchman to approach the wheel. 'Loosen his tongue.'

Frustrated by the Templar's refusal to make a full confession, Raymbaud stepped over to the loophole on the other side of the dungeon. In a surly temper, he glanced at the crudely scrawled symbol – the Seal of Solomon – that the Templar had incised into the soft limestone. *Yet another mystery that Brother Fortes had refused to explain.*

Turning a deaf ear to the pain-wracked bellows that ensued, he peered through the loophole. The new day had dawned, grey as chain mail, a snarl of wind lashing the weathered castle. Through the wisps of early-morning mist, he could see the fast-moving Vienne, the river curdled with chunks of ice that bobbed on the frothy rapids.

Behind him, the tortured screams intensified. Not even a stalwart Knight Templar could withstand an iron hammer wielded by one of God's own. Proving himself a wise pontiff, Pope Innocent IV had sanctioned the use of torture, stipulating that intense pain flushed the evil residue from a man's soul.

And how else can I pry loose the Templar's secret?

Once he had the *Evangelium Gaspar* in his possession, Raymbaud intended to use it to elevate his status within the Dominican order, fulfilling his long-held dream to become an abbot at a wealthy monastery. After his many years of service, he deserved to spend the rest of his days in comfortable ease, his earthly burdens alleviated.

Determined to put an end to the Templar's maddening truculence and uncover the gospel's whereabouts, he raised his hand, signalling the henchman to cease his ministrations. Approaching the breaking wheel, he was pleased to see that the Templar's white linen braies were stained crimson, several of his pelvic bones having been crushed.

'Again, I put the question to you: where can I find the *Evangelium Gaspar*?'

Blood-caked lips curved into a ghost of a smile. '*Go . . .*

to . . . the . . . Devil . . . Dominican!' the Templar rasped through a foaming gob of spittle.

'It does not profit your soul to –' Raymbaud stopped in midstream, horrified.

Without warning, the accused had begun to convulse, bucking wildly upon the wheel as his face turned an unnatural shade of blue.

Just as suddenly as the episode began, it ended, Fortes de Pinós's lifeless gaze set upon the heavens.

'No!' Raymbaud screamed, pounding his fist on the dead man's chest.

His fury was for naught. The Knight Templar had bested him, taking his secret to the grave.

PART I

'*Roma locuta causa finite est* . . . Rome has spoken and
that settles the matter.'

St Augustine

I

Lourdes Grotto, Vatican City

15 August, The Present Day

'We pray for our Mother, the Church upon earth,
And bless, dearest Lady, the land of our birth.
Ave, Ave, Ave, Maria! Ave, Ave, Maria!'

The chorus of male voices swelled before it fell into a respectful silence, the devotional hymn a paean to the one woman whom they all loved in common, the Blessed Virgin Mary.

The 'woman clothed with the sun'.

Or in this instance, given the lateness of the hour, garbed in the flickering flames of processional candles. Glancing at the attendant crowd that was cordoned off from the grotto and forced to celebrate the sunset Mass behind steel barricades, Cardinal Franco Fiorio wondered how many of the faithful knew that the salutation *Ave* had once been used by Roman gladiators to greet Caesar before they engaged in mortal combat: '*Ave, Caesar! Morituri te salutant!*'

'Hail, Caesar! Those who are about to die salute you!'

Somehow Franco doubted that the ragtag Christians who provided the gruesome opening act for the gladiatorial

9

games ever uttered those fateful words before they were mauled by hungry lions.

The Mass concluded, the recessional procession slowly filed past the grotto. Led by the cross bearer, the cavalcade included ruddy-cheeked altar servers holding crimson labara emblazoned with the Chi-Rho cross, solemn-faced acolytes carrying elongated candles and, finally, the Cardinal Camerlengo who had officiated.

Franco cast a last lingering glance at the cave-like grotto. The rocky lair was an artificial contrivance that replicated the famous shrine at Lourdes where, in 1858, a fourteen-year-old illiterate French girl had been visited by Our Lady. Making it a fitting location to celebrate one of the most important holy days on the liturgical calendar, the Feast of the Assumption of the Blessed Virgin Mary. Always celebrated on the fifteenth day of August, it was the day on which the Mother of God had been taken bodily into heaven. One of the sacred mysteries of the Church, the Assumption was still hotly contested in religious circles.

'Hogwash!' Protestants were always quick to decry, adamant that the devotional feast was another example of the Roman Catholic Church turning a pagan ritual into a high holy day. *Sola scriptura!* By scripture alone. If a 'sacred' event wasn't contained within the pages of the Bible, it never happened.

Taking his place in the recessional queue, Franco fell into line with the scores of cardinals who were similarly attired in ecclesiastical choir dress. When he was younger, he'd secretly despised the vestures, considering them overly fussy, making men of God look like clerical cross-dressers. His attitude had mellowed considerably with the passing decades as he'd come to embrace the inherent symbolism of the richly fashioned robes: the red cassock denoting a cardinal's willingness to give of his very blood to safeguard the Church; the white lace-trimmed rochet symbolizing his spiritual purity.

Moving in slow lockstep, the candlelit procession wound its way through the Giardini Vaticani, the fifty-seven acres of gardens and parkland that encompassed most of the Vatican Hill. With sparkling fountains, cleverly designed topiaries and artfully laid flowerbeds, the garden evoked the idyllic splendour of Eden. On the eastern horizon loomed Michelangelo's magnificent dome, the architectural tour de force bathed in a golden glimmer cast by the setting sun. Barely visible through the leafy bowers was the soaring defensive wall that had been built to keep out the enemies of the Church – of which there have always been many – and that now served as the international boundary for the Vatican City.

As they approached St Martha's Chapel, their procession was greeted by an overflow crowd comprised of devoted congregants and curious tourists. Like the cardinals, each and every one of them clutched a lit candle, creating a flickering sea of frail fireflies. But what should have been a joyous throng was visibly mired in grief, many openly sobbing, all grim-faced. More than a few held up photographs of Pope Pius XIII.

The recently deceased Pope Pius XIII.

The Vicar of Christ, the man who represented the Saviour here on earth, was dead, having succumbed to a massive coronary stroke four days ago during his private morning Mass. His unexpected death had plunged the

11

Holy See into a state of *sede vacante*, the pontiff's seat vacant. And it would remain vacant until the College of Cardinals met in conclave to elect St Peter's apostolic successor.

No sooner had the pope been officially declared dead than the Camerlengo, the papal chamberlain, had initiated a series of centuries-old rituals to safeguard against the unholy ambitions of scheming cardinals. The pope's ring, used to seal official documents, had been ceremonially crushed to thwart would-be forgers. The pope's private quarters had then been secured with wax seals to prevent the looting of the papal chambers. But as Franco knew full well, neither of those measures would deter an enterprising cleric.

Never was anything great achieved without danger, he mused as the procession of cardinals slowed to a halt, Machiavelli's sage advice as apropos in the twenty-first century as it had been during the Renaissance's back-stabbing heyday.

Unobtrusively slipping out of formation, Franco silently observed the various cliques. Heads bent, red-clad shoulders hunched, the same topic was being discussed in each tight-knit cluster. The soon-to-be-elected new pope, as the leader of more than a billion Catholics worldwide, would be an important figure in the religious and political arenas. If the right man were selected, he could become a game-changing figure on the world stage.

And so it had begun. The jockeying. The scheming. The arm-twisting. *You scratch my back, I'll scratch yours.*

Like his brethren, Franco was also planning for the upcoming conclave.

As the Prefect of the Archivo Segreto Vaticano – the Secret Archives of the Vatican – he'd examined the texts and codices safeguarded in the underground vaults and locked cabinets. In so doing, he'd fatefully happened upon the Templar trial records pertaining to the *Evangelium Gaspar*. An ancient gospel, it predated the four canonical gospels by several decades. Reason enough for a high-ranking Knight Templar named Fortes de Pinós to have embarked on an incredible sea voyage, searching for the *Evangelium Gaspar* in India, of all places. According to the Templar trial records, the *Evangelium Gaspar* contained 'The Great Heresy', a truth that was decidedly more profane than sacred. And one that, should it ever surface, would not only implode the Holy See, but change the course of human history.

During the Middle Ages, the Dominican inquisitors had tried, in vain, to unearth the gospel. But Franco, unlike the Dominicans, had the advantage of the digital age with a wealth of information at his fingertips. He also had something else – a cadre of men at his disposal who were far more ruthless than the fourteenth-century inquisitors.

A learned man who knew how to seize the initiative, not unlike Machiavelli's perfectly conceived prince, the Prefect knew that 'no enterprise is more likely to succeed than one concealed from the enemy until it is ripe for execution'.

Four days ago the bitter fruit had suddenly ripened – in that euphoric instant when his longstanding enemy, Pope Pius XIII, had unexpectedly thrown off the mortal coil.

2

Fort Cochin, India

17 August, 0806h

'It's not too late to apply to the London School of Economics.'

Anala Patel stared at her mother, flabbergasted by the suggestion. 'And then what? Become an investment banker?' Shaking her head, she defiantly folded her arms across her chest. 'In order to change society for the better, we have to change our political thinking. That's why I intend to do my graduate work at Oxford's Department of Politics and International Relations.'

'This might surprise you, but I don't particularly relish the notion of my daughter leading the charge to change the world.' Her mother punctuated the avowal by glancing pointedly at the black-and-white poster of Julian Assange that was taped to Anala's bedroom wall, her gaze zeroing in on a bright-red lipstick kiss plastered on his forehead.

'By the by, that happens to be my favourite shade, Chanel's Dragon Red,' Anala said cheekily. 'And you know what they say . . . lead, fight or get out of the way. Just so you know: I will live my life as *I* see fit. I'm no longer a child. I'm a twenty-two-year-old woman.' One who'd been coerced into spending the summer holiday, not in Europe with her mates sunbathing in the Greek Isles, but in the sweltering backwater of India. At her mother's insistence. Yet another reason for their strained relationship.

I am tired of playing the dutiful daughter to a woman who is clearly going through some sort of mid-life crisis.

Two years ago, for some unknown reason, Gita Patel had suddenly embraced her Indian heritage like it was a long-lost child. Accepting a job as head curator at the Kerala Cultural Museum, she moved from London to Fort Cochin, India. Why she did this, Anala had no idea; her mother had had an enviable job at the British Museum and the inexplicable relocation was a definite downgrade. Stranger still, though her mother was an Anglo-Indian – born, raised and educated in England – she'd gone completely native, now proudly wearing a sari and a bindi.

Anala stared at the small red bullseye that had been perfectly applied between her mother's hazel-green eyes. *This is not what I meant, Mummy, when I told you to 'get a life'.*

'You will always be my child, Anala. *Always.*'

'Oh, really? And here I was thinking that I was just your bloody retirement fund! That's the real reason why you want me to go into investment banking rather than politics, isn't it? Because then, with my Midas salary, I'll be able to take care of you in your old age.'

'How dare you!' Her mother physically recoiled, clutching her chest with her right hand as though she'd just been struck by a poison-tipped arrow to the heart.

Anala rolled her eyes. *Overreacting much?*

Convinced that what her mother really suffered from was a stab of conscience, Anala held her ground. 'No, how dare *you*? dictating what I will or will not study at university.

Like every Indian mother, you probably wish that you'd given birth to a son rather than a daughter.'

Hearing that, her mother gasped . . . just before she soundly slapped Anala across the cheek.

For several stunned moments they stood motionless.

Dazed, unable to speak, Anala gaped at her mother.

A few seconds later, snapping out of her fugue state, she put a hand to her cheek. *Blimey, I didn't see that coming.*

'We'll discuss this when I get home.' Clearly flustered, her mother glanced at her wristwatch. 'I . . . I need to get to the museum. And I'm very sorry that I slapped you.'

Anala snorted derisively at what she considered an obligatory afterthought. 'Sorry? I suspect you've wanted to do that for a long time. Nothing like exorcising one's demons, eh, Mum?'

Relieved to have her mother finally depart her bedroom, Anala strode over to her desk and flipped open her laptop, hitting the 'on' button. Although her cheek still stung, she refused to dwell on her mother's tantrum. *Really, sometimes I think that I'm the only adult in this household.* Despite the tiresome carping, as soon as Michaelmas term began in October, she intended to throw herself headlong into her thesis topic, 'Immigration and the Challenge of Social Justice'. At Oxford. At the Department of Politics and International Relations. Full stop. The end.

While she waited for the computer to boot up, Anala grabbed her iPod. Popping in the earbuds, she stood in front of the mirror and struck a stylized Bollywood dance pose. A few seconds later, hearing the hip-hop strains of 'Single Ladies', she gyrated her hips à la Beyoncé, dance moves that were *way* too provocative for the Hindi crowd.

She'd seen Beyoncé last summer at Glastonbury, the woman an absolute glamazon.

Sitting down at her desk, she quickly pulled up her article for the Liberal Conspiracy blog. A regular contributor, she thought the in-depth analysis of social media in the context of citizen journalists and their effect on public policy a timely topic. Although she'd finished the article last night, she was still playing around with various titles.

'How about "The Tweet Heard Round the World"?' she pondered aloud, giving it a test drive as she typed those six words above the body of text. She cocked her head from side to side. 'Ladies and gentlemen, I think we have a –'

Suddenly hearing something that sounded like the crisp *thrack!* of a willow cricket bat against a cork and leather ball, Anala yanked out the earbuds and glanced at the closed French windows.

Before her brain could register what was happening, the glass door flung open and a mustachioed man, dressed all in black, entered her bedroom. Spinning in her direction, he charged towards the desk. His narrowed gaze and harshly set facial features screamed malevolent intent.

Yelping with fear, Anala lurched to her feet. Too stunned to remember what she'd learned in her self-defence class, she grabbed her laptop and hurled it at the intruder. The man nimbly ducked to one side, completely avoiding the missile attack.

Not about to abandon the fight, Anala snatched the nearest items within reach – a lamp, a bronze elephant paperweight and a framed photograph – flinging them in quick succession. She scored two hits and one miss. None of which deterred the mustachioed interloper, the man simply raising his arm and deflecting the blows.

Quickly running out of ammo, she reached for her office chair . . . just as the intruder clasped her by the waist. Pinning her arms to her sides, he forcefully yanked her away from the desk. The chair toppled over as Anala frantically began to kick him in the shins.

'You bitch!'

'You bastard!' she screeched, lifting both her feet off the ground, *finally* recalling a self-defence tactic.

In the next instant the two of them hit the floor with a spine-jarring impact.

Managing to break free of the intruder's violent embrace, Anala scrambled to her feet and ran towards the bedroom door. No sooner did she reach for the doorknob than she was again seized, this time the brute cinching his fingers around her neck, slamming her against the closed door. As her vision blurred, her lungs screaming for oxygen, she instinctively clawed at his hands.

To her surprise, the assailant suddenly let go of her throat. Gasping for air, Anala felt a sharp, jabbing pain in her upper arm.

Rather than clearing, her vision immediately became more blurry, the room spinning off-kilter. Woozy, she opened her mouth to scream. Only to discover that –

She . . . couldn't . . . remember . . . how . . .

3

Paris, France

'. . . and I still think you should rename it "The Abduction of the Divine Bride". That's a much catchier title than "The Sacred and the Profane".'

'It's a PowerPoint presentation about the medieval Cathars,' the tall red-headed Englishman retorted, clearly appalled at the suggestion. 'Not a bloody romance novel.'

Getting up from the Edwardian sofa, Edie Miller wagged a finger at the man she teasingly referred to as her 'part-time paramour'. 'Yeah, but sex sells. Trust me, Cædmon. Change the title and you'll pack 'em in like sardines at the Avignon symposium.' She paused a moment before dangling a very enticing carrot. 'And it could boost your book sales.'

'So you think I should sex up my lecture, eh?' Having followed her into the hallway, Cædmon Aisquith cocked his head to one side and struck a thoughtful pose. 'Hmm . . . perhaps I could add a few naughty bits to the section on Isis Mystery cults. Although it'll require considerable rehearsal time with my research assistant,' he added, rakishly raising an auburn brow.

'I hate to douse your lurid fantasy, but rehearsal will

have to wait until I get some food in me. I'm utterly famished.' Edie pointedly looked over at her luggage still piled in the middle of the hall. Since she and Cædmon were leaving tomorrow for Avignon – and from there, heading to the Côte d'Azur – she didn't see the point of unpacking. 'They served Chicken Cordon *Blah* on the flight from Guatemala City. Two bites were all I could manage.'

'I've been meaning to ask: how did the photo shoot go?'

'Great pictures,' she told him with a satisfied nod. 'The women weavers at Santiago Atitlán are an inspiring example of girl power at its very best. On the downside, the poverty in Guatemala is heartbreaking.'

'A repeating refrain the world over, unfortunately.'

'All the same, it's still a painful tune.' As Edie was quickly discovering in her new gig with *National Geographic* magazine, having recently travelled to several third-world countries.

Five months ago an editor at the renowned monthly caught an exhibition of Edie's photography at a Washington DC gallery that specialized in African art. To her astonishment, the editor asked if she'd be interested in working as a freelance photographer. *Interested?* Dream come true. Although it meant that Edie now spent more time on the road than at her DC abode, squeezing in side trips to Paris when time permitted.

Cædmon glanced at his wristwatch. 'While it's a bit early for dinner, *l'heure de l'apéro* is fast approaching. Care to stroll down the street for an aperitif?'

Theatrically rolling her eyes, Edie said, 'Why don't you put on some French accordion music while you're at it?

Don't think for one instant, Big Red, that I don't see through your ploy. After plying me with alcohol, you intend to have your way with me,' she accused, the rebuke eclipsed with a puckish grin.

'If I'm that transparent, I've been out of the game far too long.' Chortling softly to himself, Cædmon retrieved his jacket from the library ladder that did double duty as a coat rack.

With its floor-to-ceiling bookcases, the expansive hallway put Edie in mind of the library from *Beauty and the Beast*. A reference that went right over Cædmon's head. At one time he had owned an English-language bookstore on the Left Bank. Soon after his debut tome *Isis Revealed* was published, he sold the shop but kept the inventory.

'Come, Miss Miller. A gastronomic adventure awaits us.' Invitation issued, Cædmon swung open the door to the flat, gallantly sweeping his arm towards the landing beyond.

A few moments later, after they descended to the ground floor in a rickety, old-fashioned lift, Edie allowed him to usher her out of the building.

When a religious zealot intent on finding the Ark of the Covenant had marked them both for execution, fate, quite literally, had hurled them together. Had it not been for that dangerous episode eight months ago, their paths would never have crossed.

While they were officially 'an item', because Cædmon lived in Paris and she was based in Washington, they saw each other irregularly, although they communicated nearly every day via Skype. Something of a commitment-phobe, Edie didn't mind ping-ponging across the Atlantic. Despite the fact that it was an unconventional relationship, she considered it the perfect distillation of romance, long-distance longing and shared passions. No wonder she was happier than she'd been in years.

'I thought that we could review our French Riviera itinerary over dinner,' Edie said as they made their way across the cobbled courtyard adjacent to the Beaux Arts apartment.

'This is the first that I've heard of a travel itinerary.' Putting a hand on the small of her back, Cædmon shepherded her through the stone archway that led to rue Saint-Benoît, a typical Paris street with upmarket boutiques at street level and elegant flats with wrought-iron balconies on the floors above.

'A holiday checklist is a must. If I let you do the planning, we'll spend our entire vacation traipsing through old castles and ancient ruins. When *instead* we could be hitting the nude beaches and über-hip discotheques.'

'Bloody hell,' Cædmon grumbled. 'Eight months into the relationship and I've become a predictable bore.'

'Anything but,' Edie was quick to assure him, unpredictability the key to Cædmon Aisquith's appeal. That and the fact that he was an incredibly smart man.

Soon after making Cædmon's acquaintance, Edie realized that he was addicted to knowledge. In a world of dangerous obsessions – drugs, pornography, online gambling – his was a harmless passion. And the fact that he exhibited such ardour when it came to cerebral pursuits was kinda sexy. But then she'd always been attracted to brainiacs, the mind being the sexiest organ bar none.

As they strolled leisurely down the street, arm-in-arm,

Edie was amused to catch sight of a woman in a passing taxi who gave Cædmon a wide-eyed second glance. At six foot three inches in height with a thatch of thick auburn hair, he definitely stood out in a crowd.

'Which of Paris's two venerable grandes dames would you care to patronize?' Cædmon asked when they reached Boulevard Saint-Germain.

Waiting for the traffic light to change, Edie surveyed the busy street lined with fashionable shops and leafy green trees, the thoroughfare bathed in a golden, only-in-Paris kind of light. Located within spitting distance of one another, the Café de Flore and Café Deux Magots were the belle époque 'grandes dames' in a city chock-full of sidewalk cafés. Long-time rivals, both were icons with a storied history that included some of the most celebrated artists, philosophers and literary giants of the twentieth century.

Edie contemplatively tapped her chin with her index finger. 'I think that I'm in the mood to channel my inner Simone de Beauvoir.'

'Café de Flore it is. Shall we sit outside on the patio?'

'Where else can we watch people from every walk of life go past?' Edie remarked as they headed towards the welcoming shade of a striped awning. Sidestepping a garçon decked out in a tuxedo jacket, crisp white shirt and a matching white apron, she suppressed an amused smile. It was the classic Parisian stereotype, and one that she loved. *Cue more French accordion music.* 'As I recall, the last time we were here we actually saw Karl Lagerfeld sitting a few tables away, sipping a glass of –'

'Hello, Cædmon.'

Hearing the unexpected greeting, Cædmon and Edie simultaneously turned round. Standing a few feet behind them was a lovely olive-skinned woman attired in a lightweight brown trouser suit, a leather messenger bag slung across her chest. Her long black hair was pulled into a serviceable ponytail, the fringe on her forehead accentuating a pair of red-rimmed hazel eyes. Either the woman suffered from severe allergies or she'd recently been crying. Belatedly, Edie realized it was the same woman she'd seen in the passing taxi who'd ogled Cædmon.

'I hope that . . . that you remember me,' the dark-haired woman stammered nervously.

Cædmon recoiled slightly, clearly surprised. 'My God . . . Gita. Of course I remember. What a delightful surprise.' Quickly recovering, he gestured in Edie's direction. 'Allow me to introduce you to my companion, Edie Miller. Edie, this is Gita Patel. Gita and I were chums at Oxford.'

Smiling politely, Edie extended her hand in the other woman's direction. Still resembling a deer caught in the headlights, Gita returned the courtesy, murmuring the familiar 'pleased to meet you' rejoinder.

'Has it really been more than twenty years since we last saw one another?' Not giving Gita a chance to reply, Cædmon went on, 'I take it that you're in Paris on a holiday?'

'Um, actually I'm here on a matter of great urgency. And I apologize for not ringing ahead, but I – I've just arrived.'

'Do you mean to say that this urgent matter involves *me*?' Cædmon's brow furrowed in obvious confusion.

Suddenly picking up on a very strange vibe, Edie glanced anxiously between the two former Oxford 'chums'.

'Y-yes . . . it does involve you,' Gita croaked, her voice cracking with emotion. 'Your daughter has been abducted.'

'Obviously, there's been some mistake,' Cædmon replied matter-of-factly. 'I don't have a daughter.'

'I'm sorry . . . I wasn't clear . . . *Our* daughter has been abducted.'

4

In a twilight state, Anala Patel blinked several times as the room came into focus. The thump of her heart against her breastbone gave testimony that she was still among the living and not stuck in some afterlife limbo.

My head is about to split wide open, she brooded, wondering why someone didn't take a hammer and chisel and finish her off. Utterly decimated, she decided that she was hungover, suffering from a severe case of brown-bottle flu. Although, for the life of her, she couldn't recall any of the party particulars.

Parched, she tried to lick her lips, but couldn't do that either. That was when she belatedly realized that there was a strap of tape across her mouth.

Hmm . . . that's odd.

She tried to decipher the reason for her unusual predicament, but it proved an impossible undertaking. Her brain was functioning at a frustratingly sluggish speed, unable to do much of anything other than note the fact that she was in a dismally ugly room. Panelled in dark wood, there was only one window, near the ceiling, and no furniture save for a metal camp bed and a plain wooden chair. Heavy-limbed and heavy-lidded, she fought the urge to close her eyes and return to the Land of Nod.

I can't go to sleep. I need to go to the loo.

Determined to follow through on what she considered

a very good idea, she moved to get off the bed. Only to fall back upon the lumpy mattress, her hands bound behind her back. Peering down at her legs, she could see that her ankles were strapped together as well with grey duct tape.

Panic-stricken, Anala struggled to come out of her stupor, a host of images flashing across her mind's eye – a mustachioed brute, a violent struggle and then a total blackout.

I've been abducted!

By who? And why?

She'd obviously been tranquilized. Whatever drug had been administered, the after-effects were gruelling, as though she'd been lashed to the wheel and forced to withstand the mother of all storms. Grimacing, she rolled her tongue over the back of her teeth, her mouth tasting like the bottom of a baby's pram. Wondering if she'd been given a date-rape drug, she glanced at her garments, relieved to see that her sleeveless cotton shirt was buttoned and her cropped cargo trousers were properly fastened. Her feet, though, were bare, someone having removed her trainers. Puzzled, she wondered why someone would have taken her trainers but left her clothes on?

Work, brain, work!

She had to figure out why she'd been kidnapped. Had to gather her thoughts and –

Suddenly realizing the reason for the abduction, her stomach lurched.

Feeling the sting of tears, she squeezed her eyes shut . . . *She'd been nabbed by sex traffickers.* Who else would brazenly kidnap a woman right out of her own home? Every day, all across India, females were seized and forced into brothels.

Shock, horror and fear hit her in equal measure.

I have to escape! Now!

Refusing to become another sex statistic, she squirmed clumsily into a seated position. From there, she wiggled her bum to the edge of the bed. She then bent at the waist and examined the bed frame. Espying a raised screw head, she twisted, positioning her bound wrists over the top of the metal protuberance.

Her only hope of escape.

5

A daughter!

Christ. The sky was falling.

The blood drained from Cædmon's head so rapidly, it nearly felled him in its nauseous swoop. He opened his mouth to speak, but the words skidded to a silencing halt, his vocal cords paralyzed with shock.

Edie, glancing nervously between him and Gita Patel, gestured to a nearby café table. 'Um, maybe we should all sit down and, you know, regroup?'

Cædmon managed a half-hearted nod. Pulling out a chair, he perfunctorily motioned for Gita to sit down. Then, still on auto-pilot, he performed the same courtesy for Edie before gracelessly plonking his own arse in a less than sturdy café chair. The ridiculously small table, no more than twenty inches in diameter, was designed for an intimate duo rather than an impersonal trio, forcing the three of them to huddle awkwardly around it.

Still processing Gita's bombshell, Cædmon tried to wrap his mind around the fact that twentysomething years ago he'd fathered a child. Out of wedlock and seemingly out of the blue.

Her expression one of deepening concern, Edie put a hand on his shoulder. 'Cædmon, are you all right?' she asked in a lowered voice.

He nodded weakly once more. Better to lie than confess to the truth – that he was far from all right.

A weighty silence ensued, not one of them knowing what next to say.

An aproned waiter stepped over to their table. '*Désirez-vous un apéritif?*'

Taking charge, Edie asked Gita what she would like to drink. She then glanced expectantly in Cædmon's direction. His thoughts jumbled, he shrugged. He didn't want a drink; he wanted to climb into a hole. And a deep, dark, bottomless pit at that.

'. . . *et une tasse de thé, s'il vous plaît,*' Edie told the waiter, finishing the order with a strained smile.

Rudderless, Cædmon stared at the blurred flash of motorists and pedestrians moving back and forth along Boulevard Saint-Germain. Stage props in a dream from which he could not wake.

The fact that he had a daughter a few years older than he'd been when he dated Gita Patel at Oxford was unbelievable to him. He wasn't the father to a gurgling baby in nappies. He was the father of a full-grown woman. *How is this even possible?* And why the bloody hell did Gita wait all these years to tell him?

Navigating his way across unfamiliar terrain, Cædmon struggled for the right words to convey his utter shock at learning that her daughter – no, *their* daughter – had been abducted. 'Of course, Gita, I'll help in any way that I can, but I'm at a complete loss to understand how –'

'I couldn't tell you that I was pregnant,' Gita interjected, having somehow intuited his train of thought.

Hearing that, he exhaled a shaky breath, realizing that

he was in the dark about a great many things. 'Since I seem to have come into this at the denouement rather than the intro, I would appreciate hearing the story from the very beginning.'

Gita gnawed anxiously on her lower lip before saying, 'There's not a great deal to tell. When I left Oxford at the end of Trinity term, I discovered that I was pregnant. My father was concerned that –' She broke off in midstream, an anguished look in her hazel eyes. In that suspended instant, Cædmon could see that she was facing down her demons. 'My father was afraid that my *predicament* would adversely affect his political career. Which is why he forbade me to contact you.'

'He was the Labour MP from Ealing Southall as I recall.'

She gave a terse nod. 'Determined to keep my pregnancy under wraps, my father hastily arranged a marriage for me, paying the groom and his family a small fortune to turn a blind eye.'

Cædmon frowned, incensed – not at Gita, but at a man he'd never met. 'Said groom was a Hindu, I take it?'

'A computer engineer newly arrived from Delhi.' Gita punctuated the comment with a slight shudder. 'Needless to say, it was a disastrous union, one that barely lasted four years. When I divorced Dev Malik, I took custody of Anala, retook my maiden name, and moved on with my life.'

Anala. His daughter's name was Anala. For some reason, it'd not occurred to him to ask.

Lost in thought, Cædmon stared at Gita Patel, culling from his memory banks that brief interlude at Oxford when they'd been inseparable, raging hormones and a shared love of history the glue that held them together. He had tried once or twice to contact her, but assumed the returned letters meant that, unbeknownst to him, the relationship had officially ended. In the decades since, he'd not given her a single passing thought. Even now, all he could recall with any certainty was that she was the product of a mixed marriage, she had an unnatural fear of spiders and that her academic field had been Oriental Studies. Meaning that, for all intents and purposes, the woman sitting across from him was a virtual stranger.

'So that would make our daughter –' Cædmon did a quick mental calculation – 'twenty-two years of age. And her name is Anala, is that correct?'

'Yes. Just a moment . . . I brought a current picture.' Fumbling with the leather messenger bag still slung across her chest, Gita retrieved a wallet from which she removed a colour photograph. Clearly nervous, she handed it to him.

Equally nervous, Cædmon raised the photograph to his face.

An instant later, his jaw slackened. *Un-bloody-believable.*

Barely able to breathe, let alone move, he stared at the photo, taken aback by the image of a brown-haired, blue-eyed young woman.

'I never knew my mother . . . she died in childbirth. That said, the resemblance in the face and eyes is uncanny,' he rasped. So similar, it was as though he was peering at a ghost.

Afraid that he'd lose what little emotional control he still had, Cædmon quickly shoved the image of his long-dead mother back into the mental lockbox that held all of his sepia-toned memories. Those things best forgotten or too painful to call to mind.

God Almighty. When am I going to wake up from this nightmare?

Leaning towards him, Edie looked over his shoulder at the photo.

'Anala is a lovely young woman,' she said to Gita.

His hand visibly shaking, Cædmon set the photo in the middle of the table. 'Does she know about me?'

The question caused Gita to blush furiously. Unable to look him in the eye, she gazed down at the table. 'Anala thinks that my ex-husband is her biological father.'

'I see.' Now it was Cædmon's turn to stare at the table, feeling very much like a man who'd just been stomped and kicked when he was down.

His belly tightened painfully. *I have a daughter who doesn't even know that I exist.*

He took a deep breath, trying desperately to keep his emotions in check. 'What can you tell me about the abduction?' he said abruptly, his voice noticeably hoarse.

'Anala was kidnapped two days ago from our home in Fort Cochin, India,' Gita informed him. Pausing a moment, she tightly clasped her hands together. Presumably to stop the palsied tremble. 'There was a message scrawled on her bedroom mirror in lipstick . . . "Don't call the police or she dies."'

'Oh my God,' Edie gasped, clearly horrified.

Equally horrified, Cædmon sat silent. He was listing so badly, he feared he might not be able to keep afloat.

Out of the corner of his eye, he saw their waiter

approach, a tray expertly balanced on his fingertips. A blasé expression plastered on his Gallic features, he set down a glass of chilled rosé for Edie and a small stainless-steel pot of hot water with a cup and saucer for Gita. Then, with a flourish, he placed a Dubonnet Rouge in front of Cædmon, who was very tempted to tell the aproned bastard to save the theatrics for another customer.

Cædmon waited until the waiter had departed before he cleared his throat and said, 'Excuse me for being indelicate, but do you need money for a ransom?'

'The captors don't want money.'

'If not money, then what the bloody hell do they want?'

Gita's bottom lip began to quiver. 'They want an ancient gospel called the *Evangelium Gaspar*.'

Hearing that, Cædmon stared at her, uncomprehending. *The kidnappers want an ancient gospel?* It made no sense. He shook his head, wondering if he'd heard correctly.

Edie turned to him. 'Are you familiar with the *Evangelium Gaspar*?'

Floundering, he searched his memory banks for anything pertaining to the *Evangelium Gaspar*. To no avail. Other than the fact that *Evangelium Gaspar* was Latin for 'Gospel of Gaspar', he drew a blank.

Think, man, think!

'I'm afraid that I've never heard of it,' he said at last, not a single bell having tolled.

Hazel eyes welled with tears as Gita openly gaped at him. 'But I . . . I was so certain that you'd be familiar with the *Evangelium Gaspar*.'

'And why would you think that?' Befuddled, he returned her stare.

'Because the Knights Templar went to India in 1307 to retrieve it.'

'The Knights Templar!' Cædmon spat out the exclamation like a cherry pit, one that he was very close to gagging on. '*In India?!*'

6

'Yes, India,' Gita Patel reiterated. 'According to your author website, you wrote your Masters' thesis on the Knights Templar.' This was the very reason why she'd travelled five thousand miles to see Cædmon Aisquith.

How could he not know about the Templar's voyage?

'I also wrote my dissertation on those blasted knights, but that's another story.'

'Are you *absolutely* certain that you have never heard of –'

'If the Knights Templar ever sought a relic known as the *Evangelium Gaspar*, I'm unaware of it,' Cædmon interjected. Shrugging apologetically, he said, 'While they did have the largest standing navy in medieval Europe, as far as I know they never sailed to India.'

Refusing to retreat, Gita hurriedly opened the flap on her leather bag and removed a compact computer notebook. 'I can prove to you that they *did* sail to India.'

As she waited for the laptop to boot up, Gita stole a quick sideways glance at Cædmon. Although she'd recognized him immediately when she'd caught sight of him on the street, at closer range she could see that he'd changed considerably in the last twenty-three years. At Oxford he'd been a lanky, loose-knit teenager. Somewhere along the line, he'd grown into his height, his shoulders, chest, even his face, broader now than in his youth. Befitting his age, there were horizontal lines on his brow and vertical lines bracketing his mouth. Only the head of deep auburn hair was unchanged; that, and the faint smattering of freckles on the back of his hands. Or, more precisely, on the back of his right hand; his left was marred with raised criss-crossing scar tissue and a ragged surgical incision.

Realizing that she was staring at Cædmon's ravaged hand, Gita hastily averted her gaze.

In retrospect, she supposed that she should have apologized for not telling him about his daughter. Yes, she had regrets, too many to enumerate, but after so many years an apology seemed like a paltry atonement. Though if he required an apology, she'd go down on bended knee. Grovel, if that's what it took to secure his cooperation, her pride be damned. Over the last two decades, she'd given up everything for her daughter: family, friends, her youth. Humbling herself to the man seated across from her seemed inconsequential compared to all of that.

Self-consciously aware of two sets of eyes quizzically peering at her laptop, Gita hurriedly opened the computer file labelled 'Maharaja Plate'. The file contained two digital photos, front and back, of an engraved copper plate that measured six by nine inches; approximately the size of a large reporter's notebook. She spun the computer around so that Cædmon and Edie could see the two side-by-side images.

Squinting, Cædmon leaned forward slightly. 'What am I looking at?'

'Three months ago, this 700-year-old copper plate was uncovered during an excavation at the ancient port of Muziris, which is located on the Malabar Coast of India.

It's a Royal Grant issued by the Maharaja in the year 1307,' Gita informed him, watching closely for his reaction. 'As you can plainly see, it's scribed in the Tamil language.'

'What exactly is the, um, Maharaja granting?' Edie Miller enquired, cutting to the chase.

'The Maharaja is granting a Knight Templar named Fortes de Pinós, who's listed as the designated emissary of the Grand Master Jacques de Molay, official permission to seek out the St Thomas Christians in Malabar regarding a gospel written by someone named Gaspar in the year 52 AD.' Gita underscored the statement by pointing to several lines of highly decorative script.

Cædmon glanced up from the computer screen. 'How did this Maharaja Plate come to be in your possession?'

'Forgive me . . . I th-thought I told you already,' she stammered. 'I'm the curator at the Kerala Cultural Museum.'

'I see.' A long silence followed as Cædmon continued to examine the digital photos. Finally, frowning at the screen, he said, 'The oldest known gospel manuscript dates to 125 AD. Not only is it a fragment, it's a copy of a copy. That said, if the *Evangelium Gaspar* actually exists, it would be the oldest original gospel ever written. Bloody hell . . . those damned Templars.'

Nerves frayed, uncertain whether she could count on Cædmon to lend his expertise, Gita picked up the wrapped tea bag that the waiter had earlier set down in front of her. Fumbling with the small paper packet, she tried, unsuccessfully, to open it.

Without uttering a word, Edie reached across the table and eased the packet from her trembling hands. Extricating the tea bag from the packet, she dunked it in the pot of hot water. 'Slow deep breaths,' she said with a sympathetic smile.

Grateful, Gita shyly nodded her thanks. 'Afraid that I'm all thumbs.'

'Perfectly understandable given the circumstances.'

Taller than average, with long curly brown hair, Edie had a decidedly Bohemian air about her. However, her deep-set umber-brown eyes and straight brows gave her a serious mien at odds with the colourful attire and cork-screw curls.

Earlier, when Gita had followed Cædmon and Edie down rue Saint-Benoît, it had been abundantly clear to her that they were quite enamoured. In fact, they'd seemed so enthralled – touching, laughing, sharing glances – that for one hideous, gut-wrenching moment, she feared Cædmon would spurn her overture. After all, he had a flourishing career, a happy relationship – *why should he care about a daughter he didn't even know existed?* Had the situation not been so dire, Gita would never have approached him.

'Do you mind if we backtrack a moment?' Edie said, tapping her index finger on the computer screen. 'There are two things that I'm curious about. First of all, who are the St Thomas Christians? And, secondly, who's Gaspar?'

'St Thomas was one of the original twelve apostles,' Gita replied as she attempted to raise her teacup to her lips without sloshing the contents.

'Better known as "Doubting Thomas",' Cædmon clarified in a quick aside. 'I believe it was in the Gospel of John that he famously poked his finger into the risen Lord's side.'

'Oh, *that* Thomas.' Connection made, Edie slowly nodded her head.

Gita set her teacup on the saucer; to her dismay, the two pieces of porcelain rattled noisily. 'According to the Indian legends, the Apostle Thomas arrived at the port city of Muziris in the year 52, whereupon he immediately began to convert the locals to Christianity. The descendants of those early converts are still known to this day as the St Thomas Christians; though they refer to themselves as the Nazrani. As for Gaspar . . .' Gita gave an apologetic shrug. 'Being a Hindu, I'm afraid that my knowledge of Indian Christianity only goes so far. Perhaps Gaspar was one of Jesus' disciples who accompanied Thomas to India.'

'Makes perfect sense,' Cædmon concurred with a nod. 'I can't imagine Thomas setting off on the Silk Road without an entourage. Safety in numbers and all that.' To Gita's surprise, he suddenly reached over and placed a hand on her wrist. 'In case we can't find the *Evangelium Gaspar*, I have contacts within Her Majesty's government who can –'

'No!' she exclaimed vehemently. Putting the kibosh on Cædmon's suggestion, Gita slid her hand free. 'I was expressly warned not to mention the abduction to the authorities. I shouldn't even be here, but . . . I'm desperate, Cædmon. These people won't return my daughter until I find the *Evangelium Gaspar*.'

'*Our* daughter.' Correction made, Cædmon continued to examine the digital photos of the Maharaja Plate.

Although she should have been pleased that Cædmon so readily acknowledged paternity, for some inexplicable reason the fact that he did made her acutely uncomfortable.

Ill at ease, Gita turned her head and stared listlessly at the nearby streetscape. She'd always wanted to travel to Paris, but had never got beyond the initial dreaming stage. Paris was a city for lovers. Not a lone woman, map in hand, trying to find the Louvre.

'I'll need a list of everyone who has knowledge of the Maharaja Plate.'

Hearing that, Gita glanced back at Cædmon. The late-day sun slanted across the pavement, throwing his face into shadow.

'It's not a very long list,' she told him. 'Although I should mention that soon after the plate was brought to the museum, I contacted the Vatican Secret Archives.'

'You did *what*?!'

7

Anala ripped the strip of duct tape binding her wrists, having used the metal screw head to cut through the restraint.

Hands freed, she yanked the piece of tape from her mouth and gulped in a mouthful of musty air. Not that she minded the poor air quality. It was better than no air – which is what she'd be breathing in the grave. Bending forward, she removed the straps of tape from her ankles. Unshackled, she was ready to make a prison break. While she had no idea where she was or how long she'd been unconscious, she only knew that she *had* to escape before the mustachioed kidnapper returned to the room.

She glanced at the slanted beam of dust-laden light that shone through the dirty panes of glass; the window was set approximately six feet above the floor.

Good. She preferred to escape in broad daylight rather than dead of night.

Ready to leave, Anala surged to her feet. Only to sway unsteadily, hit simultaneously with a dizzy undertow and an excruciating burst of pain radiating from her skull. Grasping the bed frame, she refused to give in to the siren's call to lie back down on the lumpy mattress.

She waited a few seconds for the lightheaded hubbub to diminish. Hobbled by aching joints and a walloping headache, she put a hand to the panelled wall. Holding on to it for support, she moved gingerly around the perimeter of the room towards the exit.

A few seconds later, she reached for the doorknob. *Damn!* It was locked from the outside.

Frustrated, she leaned her head against the door. Of course it was locked from the outside. She'd been a fool to think that it would actually have been unlocked. Why would anyone have gone to so much trouble to abduct a woman from her home, only to deposit her in an unlocked room?

Angry that she'd wasted valuable time – worried that the warden would return at any moment – Anala shuffled back to the metal-framed cot. Gritting her teeth, she dragged it several feet, flinching at the harsh grating sound that ensued. It took several determined tugs for her to manoeuvre the bed under the window. But the effort cost her. Panting from exertion, she bent at the waist and promptly vomited a stream of watery stomach bile on to the linoleum floor.

Straightening, Anala spat out a mouthful of acidic residue before wiping her mouth with the back of her hand. At that moment, she'd gladly have given her back teeth for a gulp of fresh water.

Needing to quicken the pace, she snatched the grungy-looking pillow and wadded it over her right forearm and hand. She then stood on top of the cot and bashed her padded fist through the window pane, shattering the glass on contact.

She peered through the opening, taken aback by the lavish vista of verdant scenery. *Lush trees. Rolling hills. Flowering shrubs.* She blinked, her ocular nerve overloaded with every imaginable shade of green – hunter, forest, fern, pine and shamrock. At a glance, she could see that it wasn't the tropical green of India.

More like the bucolic green of England.

Dumbfounded, she scanned the horizon, unable to see a house or building. Or any structure that suggested human habitation.

The warm sunshine heated her face, inciting a second wave of nausea. She waited a few seconds for the queasy roiling to abate before she began to hurriedly extract jagged pieces of glass out of the frame. She needed to remove all of the remaining pieces before she shimmied through the window. Otherwise, she'd cut herself to ribbons.

'Sod it!' she muttered under her breath, pricking her thumb.

About to wipe away the crimson blob, she instead kept plucking shards and flinging them on to the plush carpet of grass on the other side of the window frame.

Stay focused and finish the job!

Tossing aside the last piece of glass, she put her hands on the frame. Ready to hoist herself through the cleared opening, she suddenly heard the door open.

'What the fuck are you doing?' a deep voice snarled in English.

Before Anala could react, she was grasped by the waist and yanked backwards, the irate captor flinging her on to the mattress. She caught only a blurred glimpse of a dark-skinned, dark-eyed man before she saw the balled fist that, in the next instant, painfully connected with her jaw.

The assault happened so quickly, there was no time to scream, let alone fend off her attacker. Anala was hurled into an enveloping darkness.

8

'If you must know, I had a very good reason for contacting the Vatican Secret Archives,' Gita Patel retorted in a defensive tone of voice. 'The only information that I could find on the internet pertaining to Fortes de Pinós was an official prisoner list of Templar knights held at Chinon Castle in France. And that list merely indicated his name and the date that he was arrested.'

Hearing that, Cædmon asked the obvious. 'Which was?'

'March the eighth, 1308.'

'Mmmm ... interesting. Given that the Knights Templar were arrested en masse on October thirteenth, 1307, Brother Fortes obviously wasn't caught in Philippe le Bel's original dragnet.'

'Perhaps he was still in India on that particular date,' Gita conjectured. Reaching for the stainless-steel pot, she poured the remains into her teacup, Cædmon was relieved to see that the trembling in her hands had steadied considerably. 'According to the Maharaja Plate, Fortes de Pinós was in Muziris during the latter part of 1307.'

Having yet to touch his own drink, Cædmon stared morosely at the yellow bit of lemon peel that jockeyed for position with the melting nuggets of ice.

Those damned Templars.

There had been a time, many years ago while he was at Oxford, when he'd been thoroughly enamoured with the white-robed warrior monks. In his dissertation he'd asserted that the Knights Templar had been exposed to ancient esoteric rites; an exposure that coloured their Christian beliefs. To his horror, the head of the history department at Queen's College denounced his hypothesis as little more than an unfounded fairy tale. Realizing that his advanced degree would not be conferred, he left Oxford, mortified by the very public put-down.

Whereupon he'd promptly been recruited by MI5, Britain's security service.

As fate would have it, MI5 actively sought men like him, defrocked academics keen to prove their worth. Grateful to have a job, he'd spent eleven years in Her Majesty's Service before returning to his first love, history. No longer concerned with how his peers might react to his controversial theories, he'd written *Isis Revealed*. And though many critics disagreed with the book's premise – that the medieval Cathars of the Languedoc had been an Isis Mystery cult – Cædmon had seen the proof of it with his own eyes.

'Assuming that Fortes de Pinós returned to France some time in early 1308, he would have learned that his brother knights had been arrested soon after he docked at the Templar naval harbour at New Rochelle,' Cædmon said thoughtfully. Then, frowning, he posed the obvious: 'So why didn't Brother Fortes pull up anchor and elude capture while he still had a chance to save himself?'

'I wondered the same thing,' Gita replied as she opened

46

a paper packet and dropped a sugar cube into her teacup. 'That's the reason why I contacted the Vatican Secret Archives. Since the archives are only open to scholars and researchers, I used my museum credentials to make an official request for the Inquisition records pertaining to Fortes de Pinós.'

'In your request, did you happen to mention the Maharaja Plate or the *Evangelium Gaspar*?'

In the process of raising the cup to her lips, Gita instead lowered it to the table. 'I mentioned both of them at length,' she informed him, her brows drawing together.

'Back up a minute,' Edie said, inserting herself into the conversation. 'If the archives are secret, how can someone request, let alone examine, the records?'

Shifting his hips slightly, Cædmon turned in her direction. 'The name is misleading. Although the Archivo Segreto Vaticano is the repository for all records pertaining to the Holy See, it's merely "secret" in the medieval sense of the word, meaning that those records are the personal property of the pope. In fact, the archives have been opened to scholars since the late nineteenth century.' He returned his attention to Gita. 'Did anyone at the Vatican Secret Archives answer your request?'

'Not exactly.' A strange look crept into her eyes. 'While I did receive the requested Inquisition records, they weren't sent by anyone at the Vatican. They were forwarded by an unaffiliated person named Irenaeus.'

Cædmon took a moment to consider the admittedly odd twist. 'A tongue-in-cheek alias, I'll warrant. St Irenaeus was the early Church Father who decreed which gospels would be included in the official canon. He believed, rightly or wrongly, that because there were four corners of the earth, there could only be four authentic gospels. All other gospels, of which there were scores, were condemned as "heretical".' His jaw tightened. In the aftermath of that sweeping ban, books were burned and whole libraries destroyed. 'And I wouldn't jump to the conclusion that the records weren't sent by someone at the Vatican,' he added, wondering if the Church was still trying to root out the Templar heresy. If so, it meant the clerics in Rome not only had a long memory, but a very long reach.

Just what the hell was contained in the *Evangelium Gaspar*?

'When did you receive the Inquisition records?'

'The records were sent to me on the same day that Anala was abducted.' Tears welling in her eyes, Gita wrapped both hands around her teacup, the trembling having recommenced. 'The email stated that Anala was being held for ransom and that she wouldn't be released until I found the *Evangelium Gaspar*.' Sniffling softly, she snatched a paper napkin from the table and swiped at an errant tear.

'Did you bring the Inquisition records with you?' Cædmon asked in a neutral tone, hoping to put a wet flannel on Gita before she combusted.

Still sniffling, she said, 'I have them on my laptop. Irenaeus sent both the Latin original and a translated copy.'

'What a considerate bastard. Did you reply to his email?'

Gita nodded shakily. 'I informed Irenaeus that I couldn't possibly locate the *Evangelium Gaspar* based on the Inquisition transcript that he sent to me.' She spun the notebook computer in her direction and pulled up a new file. 'Although I begged him to send additional information, he sent only a five-word reply: "Find it or she dies." Which is when, out of sheer desperation, I immediately booked a flight to Paris.'

'Right. Let's see what we've got.' Cædmon swivelled the computer so that he and Edie could read the transcript.

Chinon Castle, 15 March, 1308

In the name of the Lord and by the mercy of God, I, Raymbaud le Breton, cleric of the diocese of Soissons, declare this a truthful account of the enquiry ordered by our most Supreme Pontiff Clement into the grievous matter pertaining to violations of sacred trust committed by Brother Fortes de Pinós, grand commander of the Paris preceptory of the Order of Knights Templar.

When asked if he had been ordered by Jacques de Molay, Grand Master of the Order of Knights Templar, to lead an expedition by sea to the princely state of Muziris on the coast of Malabar, Brother Fortes did confess that he undertook such a voyage which was a year in duration.

When asked if the purpose of this voyage had been to find the sacrilegious text known as the Evangelium Gaspar, the prisoner confessed that he had been commissioned by the Grand Master to determine if such a text did exist. He further confessed to discovering the whereabouts of this text which he said was scribed upon three copper plates in a language unfamiliar to him.

When asked if he transported the Evangelium Gaspar to France, he replied that he did so upon the order of his Grand Master.

When asked if he knew the current whereabouts of the Evangelium Gaspar, Brother Fortes gave the following reply: To see the house where Lucas dwelled, the faithful pilgrim sought the brother's way. Setting forth from the lion's castle, he dropped the French iron in a Spanish harbour.

When asked to explain his nonsensical reply, Brother Fortes refused to answer the question put to him.

When asked if he had attempted to secure the release of his brother knights through an unlawful act of subornment with the king of France, Brother Fortes did confess to offering the illustrious sovereign King Philippe the Evangelium Gaspar in exchange for the imprisoned Templars.

When asked why he had carved the Seal of Solomon on to the wall of his cell, Brother Fortes claimed that he had been contemplating the wisdom of that great king which he believed to be a precursor to the wisdom that our Lord Jesus Christ imparted to his twelve disciples.

When asked if he had knowledge of any relics pertaining to our Saviour that had been safeguarded at Château Pèlerin, Brother Fortes replied that he had never been to that Templar commandery.

At the conclusion of the enquiry, Brother Fortes did denounce in our presence all acts of heresy and, standing on his knees with his hands clasped in prayerful pose, he did swear that he had spoken naught but the truth and he begged the Almighty Father to strike him dead if he had uttered a single falsehood. Answering the disingenuous prayer of this most blasphemous of knights, our Heavenly Father did strike him dead on the spot.

Raymbaud le Breton, Ordo Praedicatorum
Huon Villeroi, cleric of Beziers, notary of apostolic power
Baldewyn Hainault, a pious seneschal of Chinon

'Whoa,' Edie murmured when she reached the end of the document. 'I didn't see that coming. Talk about being struck down by God's "terrible swift sword".' Clearly rattled, she reached for her wine glass and took a quick swig.

'While Fortes de Pinós may have been felled by a sword, I doubt very much that God wielded the blade,' Cædmon grated between clenched teeth. 'More than likely the poor bloke was tortured to death. And I now know why De Pinós didn't escape from France; he had hoped to use the *Evangelium Gaspar* that he'd just uncovered in Muziris to bribe King Philippe into releasing his brother knights.'

'A plan that tragically backfired,' Edie remarked before downing the last of her rosé. 'Although it appears that he covered his rear and hid the *Evangelium Gaspar* so that it wouldn't be confiscated by the inquisitors.'

'So it would seem.' Cædmon stared at the translated riddle, having yet to decide if Fortes de Pinós had been a remarkably brave man or a knight on a fool's errand. 'The riddle was obviously devised for the benefit of his fellow knights rather than the Inquisitor. Since the Templars' trial had recently begun, De Pinós may have thought that the Grand Master, Jacques de Molay, or some other high-ranking officer who knew about his mission to India, would be exonerated.'

'At which point, they could then use the riddle to find the *Evangelium Gaspar.*'

'Precisely,' Cædmon verified with a nod. 'What De Pinós didn't know was that Jacques de Molay and the other high-ranking officers would eventually be burned at the stake in front of Notre-Dame cathedral.'

Gita leaned in his direction, her anguish plain to see. 'Given that you're so well-versed in the Templars and their history, I came to Paris in the hope that you could decipher the riddle.'

On the verge of informing Gita that she was asking the impossible, Cædmon instead read aloud the pertinent passage in the transcript. 'To see the house where Lucas dwelled, the faithful pilgrim sought the brother's way. Setting forth from the lion's castle, he dropped the French iron in a Spanish harbour.' As he pondered the cryptic lines of text, an apprehensive silence ensued, two sets of eyes, one brown and one hazel, anxiously glued to him.

Finally, refusing to hold out hope where none could be had, he shrugged and said, 'Other than the obvious reference to dropping a ship's anchor at a Spanish port, I'm at a loss to know what it means.'

Edie, kicking him under the table, shot him a chastising glance. 'What Cædmon means to say is that he needs some time to hit the research books before he can decipher the clue,' she told Gita, cementing the assurance with a consoling pat to the hand.

'So, you will try to find the gospel?'

Deflecting Gita's query, Cædmon feinted in a different

direction. 'Have the kidnappers set a deadline for the delivery of the *Evangelium Gaspar*?' he asked, returning his gaze to the computer screen.

'Irenaeus gave me exactly ten days to find it. Since three days have already lapsed, there are seven days remaining. The ransom deadline is set for next Sunday at twelve noon.'

Hearing this, Cædmon's head instantly whipped in Gita's direction.

Surely she wasn't serious! If the Roman Catholic Church had been unable to locate the gospel in the last seven centuries, how could he possibly find it in a mere seven days?

His anxiety soaring to new heights, Cædmon reached for his untouched aperitif. As he gulped a mouthful of the now tepid Dubonnet, he wondered how best to inform Gita that weeks, perhaps months, of research would be required to decipher the cryptic riddle. And that was assuming the *Evangelium Gaspar* was still where Fortes de Pinós had left it in the year 1308.

In other words, finding the long-lost gospel would be nothing short of a titanic feat.

On the verge of delivering the bad news, Cædmon glanced at Gita, who stared at him beseechingly. He next peered over at Edie, who smiled encouragingly, silently conveying a confidence in him that wasn't in the least merited.

And then there was the woman who wasn't present, Anala Patel. He could only imagine the expression on her face. Undoubtedly, it would be one of stark terror because in one week's time, if he hadn't found the blasted gospel, she would be summarily killed. A defenceless young woman,

Anala was at the mercy of a ruthless bastard who had resorted to drastic and brutal means to glean the Templars' dark secret.

Christ. They're going to kill my daughter.

No sooner did the thought cross his mind than Cædmon's heart painfully thumped against his breastbone. The first throes of heartache.

Thrown off-kilter by the sudden burst of pain, he dejectedly stared at the Chinon transcript.

I have to find that damned gospel.

No, he silently amended a split second later. *I WILL find that damned gospel.*

Mind made up, Cædmon pushed out a deep breath. 'Rest assured, I will move heaven and earth to find the *Evangelium Gaspar*,' he told Gita.

If need be, even make a pact with the devil.

9

The lone man sitting a few tables away slowly lowered his *Le Monde* newspaper from his face.

Getting up from the table, Hector Calzada stretched the kink out of his back before slapping some euros on the table to pay for his espresso. His arms ached from holding the newspaper in place. But his balls ached more from watching all the French asses in tight skirts stroll past.

No doubt about it. Paris is for fuckers.

As he approached the vacated table, his mouth gaped open and Hector let loose with a head-shaking, killer yawn. The jet lag was most definitely catching up with him.

Three days ago he'd made the round trip from India to New York, he and his homie Roberto Diaz having successfully smuggled the Patel girl out of the country on a medical transport flight. A stupidly simple operation. The bitch had been unconscious the entire flight, oblivious to the fact that she was in the care of her 'brother' Hector and her 'male nurse' Roberto. Because India was a hub for medical tourism, people getting facelifts and heart transplants on the cheap, medical transport flights were readily available. And since he'd nabbed the girl's passport from her bedroom when he'd abducted her, no one batted an eye or gave them a second glance. The personnel on medical transport airlines were used to seeing unconscious passengers with IVs stuck in their arms, strapped on to gurneys. That's why they were in business.

Hector didn't know why the Indian girl or her mother were so important. He didn't need to know. He'd taken a vow to never question the authority of the man whose orders he was following. And a homie never broke a blood vow. If he did, he paid for it *with* his blood.

Strolling over to the table where the trio had been sitting, Hector nonchalantly slid the credit card receipt out from under a saucer so he could read the scrawled signature. It took several seconds of studied squinting before he could make out the name 'Cædmon Aisquith'.

Now, that is one fucked-up name.

But, on the upside, since it was such an odd name, it would be an easy one to Google.

I should have no problem getting a hit and finding out who the hell I'm dealing with. The guy didn't look like he'd prove much of a threat. Too fair-skinned. Not enough blood to burnish his skin a deeper shade. Blood is what made a man. Like the blood of Hector's Aztec ancestors. *The blood of his father. The blood of his enemies. The blood of Jesus Christ dying on the cross.*

Before turning to leave, Hector reached for the half-empty wine glass. Plucking the piece of lemon peel from the glass and flinging it aside, he then gulped down the rouge-tinted drink. Not liking the taste of it, he violently spat a mouthful on to the pavement.

'Hey! What are you looking at?' he snarled, catching sight of a wide-eyed café patron indignantly staring at him. Then, grinning luridly at the long-faced woman, he grabbed his crotch as he clicked his tongue against the back of his teeth.

Hey, chiquita! Eyeball this!

Cackling at her shocked response, Hector jauntily made his way down the street, keeping a discreet distance from the trio up ahead. He hoped something happened soon because he was getting bored following the Indian woman. *Maybe the three of them will get it on.* Woman on man on woman. What the French called a *ménage à trois*. Yeah, that might be interesting to watch. Exciting even. He needed something exciting to occur, something to get his blood pumping. Make his pecker stand on end.

Once upon a time he used to live a very exciting life. Shaking down shopkeepers for 'protection money'. Peddling crack cocaine. Hanging out with his homies at strip joints. Drive-by shootings. Close-up shootings. Gangland executions. But those days were gone. *Adiós.*

Sighing wistfully, Hector Calzada grazed his hand over the Beretta M9 that was shoved under his shirt.

Nothing like a little bang-bang to add some piquant spice to a man's life.

10

*Sanguis Christi Fellowship,
Dutchess County, New York*

Why do the heathen rage . . . ?

Whatever the reason, Anala Patel could rant and rage all she wanted. *It won't alter the situation*, Gracián Santos thought grimly as he cast a last glance at the unconscious woman sprawled on the metal-framed bed. No one will hear the Hindu's cries for help, her tortured laments, or her desperate pleas for mercy.

This was one instance where he could show no clemency towards a helpless individual. Despite the fact that it niggled his conscience, a desperate man rarely had the luxury of compassion. Instead, such men were often driven by circumstances beyond their control to commit heinous acts. Steal a car. Rob a convenience store. Pull a trigger. Or, in this case, abduct an innocent woman.

The means, cruel though they might be, were wholly justified.

The man currently on sentry duty peered up from his laptop computer. Seated on a plain wooden chair within close proximity of the bed, he'd been ordered to keep an attentive eye on the captive woman who'd shown a surprising amount of gumption.

'Don't worry, G-Dog. She's not going anywhere.' Flashing Gracián a cocky smile, the sentry then stated the obvious: 'She's down for the count.'

While most people would be taken aback that anyone would deign to call a Catholic priest 'G-Dog' – considering it a sign of disrespect – Gracián knew that the opposite was true. In gang parlance, a 'dog' was a loyal individual who would defend you through thick and thin. In calling him 'G-Dog', the young men and women in his gang ministry paid Gracián the highest compliment.

It's for you, my children, that I have done this despicable thing.

'Let me know when she regains consciousness,' he instructed before departing the room.

Guilt-ridden, Gracián Santos trudged down the deserted corridor. A few moments later he exited the building. Built in the late nineteenth century, it resembled the famous Greek Parthenon, albeit on a much smaller scale. *An architectural folly.* He supposed it was called that because the outrageous structure had never served a practical purpose. A rich man's ode to antiquity, it was once the site of lavish parties thrown during that decadent period of American history known as 'the Gay Nineties'. Given its current derelict condition, several columns missing, others haphazardly scattered about, it had been many years since the well-heeled had frolicked in their Greek togas and laurel wreaths. He'd chosen the folly as a suitable place to stow the captive because it was remotely located, situated nearly a half mile from Mercy Hall.

Climbing into the golf cart that was parked outside the folly, Gracián turned the ignition key and headed back across the green dales.

As he crested a grassy knoll, a sprawling 200-room

historic mansion came into view. *Mercy Hall*. A magnificent Tudor-style estate with a cobblestone foundation, leaded-glass windows, stone terraces, numerous gables and several turrets, it was prominently sited on top of a small hillock. Several years ago, Gracián's non-profit ministry, the Sanguis Christi Fellowship, had purchased Mercy Hall, a former women's college, and the surrounding three hundred acres.

It was a sight that normally engendered a swell of pride. But not this day.

As executive director of the co-ed charter high school and vocational training centre, Gracián's burdens were too great to feel anything other than dread fear. One of the largest gang intervention programmes on the East Coast, his ministry not only educated former gang members, but gave them two years of vocational training and job placement assistance.

Over the years, the Sanguis Christi Fellowship had taken in members from New York City's more fearsome gangs: the Latin Kings; the Bloods; the DDP; and the most notorious of them all, *Los Diablos de Santa Muerte*. The Demons of Saint Death. For these scarred, tattooed and hard-hearted young men, in particular, the saving message of 'God not guns' did not come easily. Most of the Diablos had been indoctrinated into the cult of violence at a tender age and were considered beyond redemption. Not only had society-at-large written them off as expendable, but their own families had turned their backs, unwilling to waste the energy or resources to save these tormented youths from a life of mindless violence. Oftentimes a short life at that.

But Gracián could not bring himself to reject the Diablos, certain that they *could* be reformed.

I am the living proof that it can be done.

But the road to salvation was never an easy one, many of the Diablos having packed their bags and returned to New York City. To the old familiar life of drive-by shootings and gang slayings. A handful, however, had remained at the Fellowship, having shifted their loyalties from the Diablos to Gracián. It was a first step. The next would be to shift their allegiance from Gracián to God.

And we know that God causes all things to work together for good to those who love God.

Unfortunately, it wasn't working fast enough, the Sanguis Christi Fellowship was teetering on the precipice.

Several years ago Gracián had taken out a $3-million-dollar short-term commercial loan to completely renovate Mercy Hall with separate boys' and girls' dormitories and updated classrooms, and to construct from the ground up – his pride and joy – the Vocational Training Centre.

No sooner had the Sanguis Christi Fellowship opened its newly painted doors than the worldwide financial markets imploded in 2008.

In the ensuing meltdown, the stock market crashed, the housing market tanked, and several of Gracián's big-money donors suddenly went belly-up, more than a few of them losing their shirts in a now infamous Ponzi scheme that had rocked New York's wealthy elites. The years that followed weren't any kinder, with foundation money, which had always been a dependable source of funding, quickly drying up. And in a particularly bitter setback, his ministry had recently lost their annual donation from the Catholic Charities network.

He was now two years behind on the loan payments, the First New York Loan and Trust Bank having initiated legal proceedings to seize the entire compound. In what turned out to have been a foolish financial move, Gracián had used Mercy Hall and the surrounding three hundred acres as collateral to secure the loan. With the big-money donations having plummeted, he had just enough cash trickling in to cover minimum operating expenses. If he didn't come up with the $2.2-million-dollar loan payment by 31 August, they'd all be thrown out on the street.

Bleary-eyed, Gracián parked the golf cart in front of the school chapel where, in recent weeks, he'd spent many sleepless nights praying, *begging*, for a miracle.

Just when he'd abandoned all hope, the 'miracle' happened: the former Archbishop of New York, Cardinal Franco Fiorio, having learned of the Fellowship's dire financial predicament, contacted Gracián, generously offering to pay off the entire $2.2-million-dollar bank loan.

Provided that Gracián first secure a heretical gospel known as the Evangelium Gaspar.

According to the cardinal, the ancient text would destroy the Roman Catholic Church if it were ever leaked to the public. '*As Defenders of the Faith, it is our sacred duty to ensure that never happens,*' the cardinal had emphasized.

Desperate for the money, Gracián had reluctantly entered into a pact with Cardinal Fiorio, even complying with his request to use former members of *Los Diablos de Santa Muerte* to carry out the plan.

'*No harm will come to your little savages,*' the cardinal had assured Gracián when he'd expressed concern about the young men's safety. '*And they will gain rewards in heaven for answering the Lord's call to safeguard His Church.*'

But Gracián *did* worry, having done little else since Hector, Javier and Roberto – the three Diablos – had departed for Fort Cochin. Even though Anala Patel had been successfully smuggled out of India on a medical transport plane, he'd had second and even third thoughts about the whole scheme.

As he entered the chapel sanctuary, Father Gracián Santos dipped his fingers into the marble stoup. Cool water dripped from his fingers as he reverentially blessed himself. He then stepped over to a wooden pew and sank to his knees. As he gazed at the crucifix mounted behind the altar, he tightly clasped his hands together, his emotions in a tumult. Anxious. Nervous.

Scared to death.

PART II

'These are the picked troops of God . . . each man sword in hand, and superbly trained to war.'

St Bernard of Clairvaux

I I

Over the Arabian Sea

Wednesday, 22 August

Removing the black satin sleep mask, Edie peered out of the window of the Airbus passenger jet. 'Wow. The jewel in the crown,' she marvelled, awestruck.

Thirty thousand feet below, the golden shoreline of India's Malabar Coast was bracketed on one side by the iridescent blue Arabian Sea and, on the other side, by fecund green rice paddies. In the far distance, the Western Ghats rose in striated bands of russet and ochre. Even from that elevated distance, it was a blatantly exotic locale.

Still slightly groggy, she yanked off the courtesy blanket and slid her leather recliner into the upright position. 'Now, that's a stunning sight to wake up to, wouldn't you agree?'

Cædmon, seated across from her, made no reply other than an inattentive 'Humph'. Intently studying the research notes on his laptop computer, Edie wondered if he'd got any sleep at all. Other than the basics – 'Are you hungry?', 'Excuse me, I'm going to the loo,' and 'The flight's on time, thank God' – he'd been uncharacteristically reticent. Every thought turned inwards, he was clearly determined to unlock Fortes de Pinós's cryptic riddle regarding the whereabouts of the *Evangelium Gaspar*.

Because he'd had no luck finding historical data pertaining to the long-lost gospel or De Pinós's 1307 voyage to Muziris, Cædmon had decided to travel to the source – India – to glean what he could from the St Thomas Christians. '*It may well be that the bloody gospel is still in India.*'

Over the course of the last forty-eight hours, the proverbial clock ticking far too quickly, they'd gone from the love nest to the cuckoo's nest, scurrying to get the proper tourist visas, book air flights, cancel the Avignon lecture and indefinitely postpone their French Riviera holiday. Although Cædmon had suggested that Edie remain behind in Paris, she'd been adamant about accompanying him. Since it'd taken two days just to get the necessary travel visas, he now had only five days to find the *Evangelium Gaspar*.

'We'll be landing in a few minutes,' a pleasant-faced steward informed them. 'I'm afraid, sir, that you'll have to stow the laptop computer.'

'Right,' Cædmon muttered, clearly peeved by the intrusion. Frowning, he reached for his computer bag.

Edie once again pondered her secret worry that the *Evangelium Gaspar* might be a phantom relic, like Veronica's Veil or the True Cross, that existed only in the medieval imagination. Even the oh-so-knowledgeable Cædmon acknowledged that he'd never heard of the gospel.

Keeping her doubts to herself, Edie said, 'Given that the Knights Templar had been accused of heresy, don't you think it's odd that Fortes de Pinós would undertake an epic sea journey to find a lost gospel?'

Cædmon made no immediate reply. Instead, he slid open the plastic window cover and gazed pensively at the patchwork landscape below. A few moments later, sighing deeply, he shut the cover. 'I suspect that the heresy charges stemmed from the fact that it's rare to find a depiction of the Crucifixion in a Templar church. The few extant renderings of Jesus at Templar sites usually depict him as a teacher rather than a god-like Saviour. And, speaking of Templar sites, I'm perplexed by the reference in the Chinon transcript to Château Pèlerin.'

Shifting her hips slightly, Edie smoothed a fold of bunched fabric. Attired for comfort, she wore a lightweight summer dress. Cædmon, also casually attired, was outfitted in khaki trousers and a blue short-sleeved polo shirt. 'As I recall, the inquisitor asked Fortes de Pinós if he knew about any relics that had been warehoused at Château Pèlerin and he replied "no".'

'That's not precisely the answer he gave,' Cædmon pointed out. 'De Pinós prevaricated, stating that he'd never been to that particular Templar commandery. I keep wondering *why*, of all the hundreds of Templar castles and commanderies, did the inquisitor want to know about Château Pèlerin?'

'Excuse me for being late to the party, but where exactly is Château Pèlerin located?'

'It was situated in the Holy Land, just a few miles southeast of Mount Carmel. A massive fortress, the Knights Templar constructed it to withstand a long-term siege.' Bracketing his chin on his thumb, Cædmon lightly tapped a finger against his upper lip. 'Curiously enough, Château Pèlerin is French for "Pilgrim Castle".'

'I take it that's an important –' Edie snapped her fingers, suddenly making the connection. '"To see the house where Lucas dwelled, the faithful pilgrim sought the brother's way. Setting forth from the lion's castle, he dropped the French iron in a Spanish harbour,"' she said excitedly, quoting from Fortes de Pinós's riddle in the Chinon transcript. 'Are you thinking what I'm thinking, that the word "pilgrim" is some sort of clue as to the gospel's whereabouts?'

'While I don't want to jump to an erroneous conclusion, there may possibly be a link between the *Evangelium Gaspar* and Château Pèlerin,' Cædmon remarked in a circumspect tone of voice. 'Amidst all the sensationalism, people tend to forget that the Knights Templar were originally founded to protect Christian pilgrims in the Holy Land, and Mount Carmel was one of the more popular sites on the pilgrimage route.'

Dutifully obeying the audio announcement, Edie buckled in for the landing. 'Well, I know why Jerusalem was a must-see holy site, but what was the big deal about Mount Carmel?'

'Its significance has more to do with the Old Testament than the New,' Cædmon said as he, too, reached for his seatbelt. 'Part of a coastal mountain range in northern Israel, Mount Carmel has a storied history as a religious sanctuary. When the medieval crusaders first explored Mount Carmel in 1150, they discovered a group of monastic holy men living there. Modern biblical scholars now believe that these holy men were, in fact, the descendants of an obscure Jewish sect known as the Essenes.'

'They were the ones who hid the Dead Sea Scrolls at Qumran, right?'

Cædmon nodded. 'They also maintained a sanctuary at

Mount Carmel. According to the ancient Jewish historian Flavius Josephus, the sect flourished during the 300-year period between the Second Century BC and the First Century of the common era.' Unstrapping his watch, Cædmon popped out the crown with this thumbnail and proceeded to reset his timepiece. 'Additionally, Josephus recounts that the Essenes maintained an extensive library at Mount Carmel where they preserved the secret teachings of the ancient prophets.'

Another piece of the puzzle, albeit a small one, suddenly snapped into place. 'So, if Mount Carmel was a sacred destination, there could have been untold relics and ancient texts stashed away in mountain hidey-holes that were discovered by the Knights Templar and taken to Château Pèlerin,' Edie speculated. 'Maybe the Templars found something at Mount Carmel that, in turn, caused them to set sail for India in search of the *Evangelium Gaspar.*'

Cædmon concurred with a brusque nod. 'It would explain why the Knights Templar fought so desperately to hold on to their seaside bastion at Château Pèlerin. Most historians incorrectly cite Acre as the last Templar stronghold in the Holy Land to fall to the Saracens, but, in actuality, Château Pèlerin has that distinction.'

As the plane made its approach to Cochin International Airport, they both grasped their armrests.

'The problem with the bloody Templars is that there aren't any surviving records,' Cædmon continued, his voice tinged with ire. 'Nearly every document pertaining to the order was destroyed by the Church or hidden by fugitive Templars. All that remains is a 700-year-old mystery.'

What Cædmon didn't say, but Edie knew he had to be

thinking, was that if he didn't solve the mystery, his daughter, Anala Patel, would be executed. For him, solving the Chinon riddle and finding the *Evangelium Gaspar* was more than an academic exercise.

Moments later, the fuselage shuddered as the Airbus jet skidded to a stop on the runway.

'We can deduce from the information engraved on the Maharaja Plate that the *Evangelium Gaspar* was in the custody of the St Thomas Christians when Fortes de Pinós arrived in Muziris in 1307,' Cædmon said once the signal flashed to unbuckle their seatbelts. 'Let us hope that their descendants can shed some light on the matter.'

'Hope *and* pray,' Edie silently amended.

Galleri delle Carte Geografiche, The Vatican

'. . . and though some of you may be disappointed that the exhibition won't include the love letters of Henry the Eighth to Anne Boleyn, I'm pleased to announce that Pope Clement's official correspondence to the English parliament regarding the king's marriage to Catherine of Aragon will be on display,' the Cardinal Secretary informed the press corps.

Sitting at the end of the dais that had been set up in the Galleri delle Carte Geografiche – the Gallery of Maps – Franco Fiorio silently fumed. The journalist's question had been directed to the Prefect of the Secret Archives *not* the Cardinal Secretary of State. The Secretary of State, who was given to self-important airs and held a position that was often described as papal prime minister and foreign secretary rolled into one, had had no direct involvement in the upcoming exhibition, 'World Treasures of the Vatican's Secret Archives'.

However, given the way that he was monopolizing the press conference, an outside observer would think the highly anticipated exhibit was Cardinal Thomas Moran's brainchild when, in fact, it was Franco who'd spent two hectic years working with Vatican officials, archivists and *scrittori* to curate the exhibition. Highlighting rare documents from the eighth through to the twentieth centuries, it would be the first time that the general public would be able to examine the historically significant pontifical letters and correspondence.

Annoyed by Cardinal Secretary Moran's showboating, Franco couldn't help but wonder if the hastily planned press conference wasn't a contrived opportunity for the Cardinal Secretary to get his name and photograph into the international papers. *Yet again.* The announcement – that the 27 August opening for the exhibition would be temporarily delayed until after the new pontiff had been elected – could have been given in a Vatican press release. Even the choice of venue, the magnificent Gallery of Maps, was suspect. One hundred and twenty metres in length, the gallery boasted forty wall frescoes depicting topographical maps of sixteenth-century Italy. Commissioned by Pope Gregory XIII, the detailed maps were remarkably accurate given the fact that Friar Ignazio Danti, the Dominican cosmographer who'd overseen the commission, had devised his charts using a compass, gnomon and an astrolabe. The Cardinal Secretary had, rather conspicuously, positioned himself directly beneath the map of the city of Rome.

The press corps, cordoned off from the dais behind a velvet rope, was taking turns passing a microphone to various members. Having just been handed the mic, a youthful-looking reporter wearing an ill-fitting suit jacket cleared his throat, the harsh sound reverberating throughout the gallery.

'Matt McCracken from the *Baltimore Sun.*' The shaggy-haired young man held his press badge aloft, as though his credentials were in dispute. 'It's my understanding that there are reams of information contained in the archives pertaining to the, um – I don't know how to put this delicately.' Again, he cleared his throat. 'Pertaining to the, um, perverted pontiffs that reigned during the Middle Ages and the Renaissance. Will any of those documents be included in the exhibit?'

A startled hush immediately fell over the map room. It was the question that every reporter in the gallery had undoubtedly wanted to ask, but all had lacked the courage to pose. Save for the clearly nervous American.

Not missing so much as a half-beat, Cardinal Secretary Moran waved a hand in Franco's direction. 'Since our esteemed Prefect hails from the fair city of Baltimore, I'll turn the question over to him.'

Franco bit back a tart reply, incensed that Moran had so effortlessly assigned him latrine duty. Slowly twisting his gold cardinal's ring, he considered how best to respond.

For whatever reason, the lurid history of the papacy still fascinated long centuries after the fact. And because it was so lurid, Franco wasn't going to quibble with the reporter over semantics. Those pontiffs had been perverted. Disgustingly so. Having read some of the more 'steamy' entries, he'd often wondered why the papal Curia hadn't consigned the files to the flames long centuries ago. Did historians *really* need to know that Benedict IX engaged in bestiality and threw bisexual orgies; that John XII, who became pope at the tender age of eighteen, turned the papal residence into a brothel; or that Julius II had sexual relations with cardinals, pages and any comely male that caught his fancy? Although to the man's credit, the degenerate Julius did manage to coerce a very reluctant Michelangelo into painting his greatest masterpiece on the ceiling of the Sistine Chapel.

The American journalist was also correct in that records existed, carefully archived for posterity. *Would they be included in the exhibit?* Absolutely not. While sex sold, under no circumstance would the Vatican expose its dark history for the price of admission.

For a Bishop must be blameless, as the steward of God.

Gathering his dignity as best he could, Franco replied, 'As you know, the Archives contain more than thirty miles of shelving –' he forced a smile on to his face – 'all tied with the legendary red tape. Not only is the history of the Church contained in those files, but that of Western civilization as well. This pivotal aspect, the role the Church has played in world history, will be the focus of the upcoming exhibition.' Answer given, Franco reached for his water bottle, silently signalling that he wouldn't entertain a follow-up question.

The microphone was next handed to a leggy blonde who was dressed in head-to-toe Armani.

'Sylvia Marsden with the *Sun*. This question is directed to the Cardinal Secretary,' the stunning reporter announced, speaking with a plummy English accent. 'Your Eminence, as you know, the election of the next pontiff is a matter of grave importance. Are you aware of the fact that the William Hill international gambling service currently has you listed as the hands-down favourite for becoming the new pontiff at nine-to-four odds?'

The question elicited more than a few shocked gasps,

Franco was aghast that anyone had the effrontery to pose such a cross enquiry. The upcoming papal election was not a game of chance, of wagers being placed with a backroom bookie.

'I am a man of God, Ms Marsden, not a betting man,' the Cardinal Secretary answered smoothly, not the least bit ruffled by the rude query. 'The election of the Vicar of Christ has always been conducted in secrecy and I think it best that we continue that solemn tradition. Besides, we wouldn't want to spoil the surprise, would we?' As he spoke, Cardinal Thomas Moran grasped his gold pectoral cross in his right hand. A particularly annoying affectation; as though he was channelling the crucified Christ. 'This concludes our question and answer session. The Prefect and I look forward to seeing each and every one of you when the exhibition opens.'

Rising to his feet, the Cardinal Secretary walked around the dais and strode towards the cordoned press area.

Franco, utterly disgusted that he'd been hoodwinked into participating in Moran's little publicity stunt, collected his press folder. Despite his protestations to the contrary, Cardinal Thomas Moran knew full well that his name was being bandied about as 'the heir apparent' to Peter's throne. Franco, whose name was never mentioned, suspected that his own odds were somewhere in the neighbourhood of sixty-to-one. A *very* dark horse, indeed.

Getting up from the table, Franco glanced over to where the Cardinal Secretary was now holding court with the group of eager reporters. Attired in formal house dress – a black cassock piped in scarlet worn with a short pellegrina shoulder cape – the Chicago native cut a striking figure. For good reason, Thomas Moran was known as the 'camera-ready cardinal' with Vatican observers, particularly those of the fairer sex, often remarking that he possessed movie-star looks. 'Charisma' and 'charm' were also inevitably used whenever Moran's name came up in conversation.

To the best of Franco's knowledge, no one had ever used such flattering terms in regards to *him*. Because of the two years he'd spent as the head of the Congregation for the Doctrine of the Faith, the Curia office responsible for maintaining Catholic *dogmata*, he was usually described in more pejorative terms. *Cunning. Secretive. Ruthless.* To name just a few. He took no offence, assuming the dark dye had to do with the fact that the CDF was more popularly referred to as the Office of the Inquisition.

Despite the fact that Franco had made great strides in reorganizing the CDF, turning it into a 'lean, mean fighting machine', the late pontiff had summarily given him the boot. No sooner did Pius take the papal seat than he'd cleaned house, removing conservative cardinals from prestigious positions within the Curia and replacing them with his liberal-leaning allies. It was during the shake-up that Thomas Moran, one of the pontiff's favourites, and an unapologetic liberal, was given his very high-profile position.

And the Church has been floundering ever since.

The Church's Neo-Modernist wing, as the liberals were sometimes called, believed that dogma could evolve over time, shape-shifting and morphing with the tides of history. Even more outrageous than that, the liberals wanted to circumvent those Church teachings that they found burdensome and replace them with new strictures that were easier to bear. *Weaklings!* Their dangerous views had already undermined Church authority to such an extent that it was on the verge of becoming irrelevant.

Franco was well aware that the Cardinal Secretary and his liberal cronies secretly referred to the conservative standard bearers within the Church as 'Taliban Catholics'. A profoundly disgusting insult that denigrated those who maintained the supremacy of orthodoxy. In another day and age, one in which *dogmata* was strictly adhered to, Thomas Moran would have been condemned as a heretic, excommunicated and burned at the stake in front of St Peter's. His blackened bones would have then served as a vivid aide-memoire to the faithful as to what happens when one strayed from Church doctrine.

There could be no evolution of dogma!

No updating of Catholic morality. No repackaging of the Faith.

A casualty of Pius's liberal reshuffle, Franco unexpectedly found himself in charge of the papal archives. Publicly, Pius had stated that it was a suitable post given Franco's impressive academic credentials and interest in ancient church history. However, privately, the late pontiff had delighted in the fact that he'd effectively neutered the cardinal once known as 'the Church's attack dog', turning the ex-head of the CDF into a *topo de biblioteca* – a library mouse who scurried, out of sight, in the Vatican's dark recesses.

'*Let Cardinal Fiorio apply that towering intellect to the pressing problem of how best to safeguard the archives from mould and mildew,*' Pius had liked to quip.

Although he never mentioned the humiliating 'demotion' that he'd suffered three years ago at the hands of the

79

late pontiff, Franco had yet to recover the loss of face, his rage still burning bright.

As he moved away from the crush of reporters gathered around the Cardinal Secretary, a young seminary student who worked in the archives offices approached.

'This just arrived for you. I was instructed to hand-deliver it,' the seminarian said as he gave Franco an unmarked manila envelope.

'Thank you.' Taking the envelope, Franco tucked it under his arm. 'It's the budgetary report for the next fiscal quarter,' he added, not wishing to arouse the young man's curiosity. Although he no longer had the resources of the CDF at his disposal, Franco still maintained a close relationship with several operatives in the Servizio Informazione del Vaticano, the Vatican's secret service.

Needing to find a private place, Franco took his leave of the seminarian and headed for a locked door at the far end of the gallery.

Little did the late pontiff know when he'd condemned Franco to the dark recesses of the archives that the library mouse would uncover an explosive secret.

One that could change the odds considerably.

13

Fort Cochin, Kerala, India

'Could you please turn the radio down,' Cædmon requested, raising his voice to be heard over the tinny Indian music blaring from the taxi's audio system.

The driver, a shaggy-haired bloke who spoke a minimum of English, bobbed his head enthusiastically. 'Yes, nice town.'

'*Down*, not – Oh, bloody hell.'

Swearing softly under his breath, Cædmon turned his head and peered out of the grimy window. Once an English stronghold – the prized harbour town wrested away from the Dutch, who, in turn, pried it from the Portuguese – Fort Cochin had an old-world patina. Nestled amidst the lush foliage and tropical flower gardens were Portuguese arches, Dutch verandas and English bungalows. Normally, he would have been charmed by the bygone beauty of the dilapidated colonial architecture. But not today.

Annoyed by the heavy traffic, he glanced at his watch – 1:32 p.m. *Christ.* The day was fast escaping him. Short on time, he'd left Edie at the hotel to see to their reservations while he quickly checked in with Gita. He and Edie had a 3:30 p.m. appointment with a historian at the St Thomas

Seminary in Kottayam and he didn't want to be late. With only five days until the ransom deadline, every hour counted.

Winding down his window, Cædmon let the sea air ruffle the hair on his forehead, the heat stifling. As he sat roasting, he rubbed his clammy palms against his trouser legs. His great-grandfather, who had served in the Royal Scots Greys, used to say that there was no hell worse than being stationed in India during the summer swelter. The old man obviously never had to listen to what sounded like a Bollywood soundtrack whilst languishing in the Bengal heat, an even more fiendish circle of hell.

'Right house for you?' the driver enquired as the taxi came to an abrupt stop on a tree-lined residential street.

Because the house in question was obscured by an eight-foot-high stucco wall and there wasn't an address plate in sight, Cædmon couldn't rightly say.

'We'll soon find out,' he muttered, hitching a hip and removing his wallet from his trouser pocket.

Getting out of the cab, he handed the driver a twenty-rupee note and nodded obligingly, unable to comprehend the man's pidgin English. As he walked towards the mahogany gate, an older woman attired in a plain cotton sari and holding aloft a dusty black umbrella strolled past. Wiping the back of his hand across his beaded brow, Cædmon thought the makeshift parasol a damned good idea.

Dismayed to find the gate unlocked, he pushed open the heavy double-doors, disturbing a scrawny three-legged cat that had been napping on the other side of the entry. The cat arched its back and hissed its displeasure before scampering off, the motley beast astonishingly nimble.

In a hurry, Cædmon strode down a pathway that wound

through a manicured garden. A two-storey colonial bungalow painted a decidedly feminine shade of coral pink with white trim was situated at the end of the cobbled path. A massive banyan tree provided welcome shade. Frowning, he could see that its tangled branches also provided an easy means for an intruder to climb onto the upper balcony and trespass undetected.

Taking a deep breath, he approached the front door. In lieu of a knocker, there was a domed bell attached to one side of the door frame. He reached up and yanked on the leather strap that dangled jauntily, the resounding clamour causing him to grit his teeth. While he waited for the summons to be answered, he spotted a pair of women's sandals on a mat near the door.

'When in Rome,' he murmured, toeing off his leather monk shoes, not bothering with undoing the buckle. Bending at the waist, he snatched off a sock and stuffed it into a shoe. Just as he was about to remove the second sock, the front door swung wide open.

'Afraid that you've caught me in a state of déshabillé,' he deadpanned. Still bent over, he glanced up, taken aback to see that Gita was garbed in a traditional sari. He was even more surprised to see the small red bindi dot between her eyes. He'd never seen her in anything but Western-style clothing.

'How was your flight?' she asked, stepping back and motioning him inside the house.

'Er, fine.' Not altogether certain how one should greet the estranged mother of one's child, he put a hand on her shoulder and gave her the obligatory French *faire la bise*.

Clearly taken aback by the cheek kiss, Gita smiled nervously. 'Would you like something to drink? I could put on the kettle and make some –'

'Nothing for me,' he interjected with a wave of the hand. 'I grabbed a cup of coffee at the airport.' As he spoke, Cædmon glanced around the dimly lit hall, his gaze drawn to a corner of the reception area where there was a bronze statue of Shiva set into a large niche. A trio of votary candles cast flickering shadows on to a framed photograph of Anala that was set in front of the cosmic dancer.

Tearing his gaze away from that distinctly morbid display, he said, 'Have Anala's abductors made contact with you since we last spoke?'

'A man who refused to identify himself rang me yesterday and enquired if I'd made any progress in finding the *Evangelium Gaspar*. I assured him that I was doing everything in my power to locate the lost gospel. Then, as you instructed in Paris, I asked for proof of life.' Stepping over to an ornately carved side table, Gita picked up a mobile phone. 'This is what he sent me,' she said in a barely audible voice as she handed the mobile to Cædmon.

Bracing himself, Cædmon examined the small LCD screen. Even in miniature, the photo of a young woman, sitting on the edge of a metal-framed bed, bound and gagged, was sickening. In that instant, his belly painfully cramped as though some sadistic bastard had just clamped a pair of red-hot pincers around his intestines.

Only one other time in his life had he experienced the same sort of palpable, existential horror; that was five years ago when his lover, Juliana Howe, had been killed in a RIRA bomb attack on a London tube station. That incident, and its brutal and bloodthirsty aftermath, had caused a downwards spiral that was best forgotten, his battle with the bottle still ongoing.

'Did the caller permit you to speak to Anala?' Cædmon asked in a businesslike tone as he returned the mobile to Gita.

She wordlessly shook her head, the bleak despair in her eyes almost too painful to bear.

'Right.' Grateful for the muted lighting, he coughed into a balled fist, trying desperately to suppress his swelling emotions. 'You mentioned that Anala was abducted from her bedroom, is that correct?' When Gita, again, mutely nodded, Cædmon glanced at his wristwatch and said, 'I've just enough time to examine the room before I have to depart for Kottayam.'

'This way.' Turning, Gita headed towards the staircase on the other side of the hallway.

A few moments later, stopping in front of a closed door, Gita turned the handle and pushed the door ajar. Cædmon followed her into Anala's bedroom, taken aback by the ransacked debris. Smashed lamps; apparel, bedding and curtains flung haphazardly; an overturned bedside table; pictures ripped from the wall and smashed underfoot.

Staring at the wreckage, he could feel his self-control disintegrating. Unless he was greatly mistaken, Anala had fought her abductor. Tooth and nail, by the looks of it.

Suddenly feeling the sting of bitter tears, Cædmon closed his eyes and breathed deeply, fighting for control. Accidentally stepping on a framed photograph, he bent down and retrieved it. For several moments, he stared pensively at the picture of Anala standing beside Gita in front of Balliol College at Oxford. For one brief, forbidden moment, he imagined himself standing on the other side of his daughter.

'You didn't tell me that she was a student at Oxford,' he said in a ragged voice, the disequilibrium expanding. Like a metastasizing cancer.

'There's a great deal that I didn't tell you,' Gita replied with a guilty blush. 'I was only in Paris for a few hours and –' She waved away the explanation. 'Anala has a first-class honours degree in PPE and has been accepted at the Department of Politics and International Relations.' Taking the framed photograph from him, she turned it upside down, broken shards of glass falling on to the bed covers. She then removed the photo from the frame and handed it to him. 'You should have a picture of her.'

Wordlessly, Cædmon slipped the photograph into his trouser pocket. More affected than he wanted to be, he strode over to the window.

'Cædmon, are you all right?' Joining him at the window, Gita put a solicitous hand on his forearm.

'I'm fine,' he said automatically. Turning his head, he looked directly into Gita's eyes. The dark half-moons that shadowed her lower lids indicated that she'd been getting little to no sleep.

Unwillingly, Cædmon recalled that when he was nineteen years old, he fell in love with Gita Patel's eyes, going weak at the knees when he used to gaze into her hazel orbs. He also remembered how, in the pre-dawn light, he would dash from Gita's Oxford digs, the cobbles slick with rain, the scent of her still clinging to his person.

How did I get from there to here?

As the seconds slipped past, neither spoke. Probably because neither of them knew what to say.

He redirected his gaze out of the window, the long-ago remembrances making him distinctly uncomfortable.

On the other side of the stucco wall, he saw a group of boys playing cricket on a cleared field with youthful abandon, their childish shouts carried on the breeze. About to turn away from the window, Cædmon caught sight of a dark-skinned man attired in a black T-shirt and baggy jeans. Loitering near a red motorbike, his gaze was fixed on Gita's house. Although he stood in the shadows, Cædmon could see that the lone figure had a moustache and closely shaved dark hair.

Suffering a faint dyspeptic twinge, he suspected that whoever abducted Anala had assigned a 'watcher' to keep tabs on Gita and report on her movements, to ensure that she didn't go to the authorities.

He stared at the dodgy-looking fellow for a few seconds longer. Then, glancing down, he noticed a milky palm print on the glass pane. Curious, he went down on bent knee.

'Were you aware of the fact that there's a print on this pane of glass?' he asked Gita, certain that the window had been the abductor's point of entry into the house.

'I had no idea,' Gita said, her brows drawn worriedly together.

Cædmon scrutinized the distinctive print – 'distinctive' because it clearly indicated that Anala's abductor had a

Chi-Rho cross branded on his right palm, the tell-tale image now stamped on to the glass.

A symbol dating back to the reign of Constantine the Great, it was actually a monogram composed of two superimposed Greek letters. More importantly, it was a symbol long associated with the Roman Catholic Church. A damning signpost.

'Bloody hell,' he muttered under his breath.

It was what he'd feared all along.

14

Bored out of her wits, Anala Patel wondered if it was possible to die from unrelenting ennui, her brain withering on the vine.

Sitting cross-legged on the narrow bed, she closed her eyes, the harsh glare of the bare light bulb that dangled from the ceiling inducing a headache. By her reckoning, she'd spent three days in her wood-panelled dungeon, her life reduced to the most banal of bodily functions: eating, sleeping and using the loo.

Sighing, she opened her eyes and glanced at the dour-faced guard who sat on the wooden chair a few feet away playing a video game. There were three different guards who rotated shifts, taking turns watching her. Because of the constant surveillance, her only privacy was the few minutes each day that she was escorted to a grungy toilet. Oddly enough, while all three men spoke Spanish amongst themselves – which Anala didn't speak – they addressed her in accented English.

She still had no idea in which country she was being held, the guards refusing to divulge any details. None the less, she'd been able to glean a few dribs and drabs, fairly certain that the men holding her captive weren't sex traffickers. Much to her relief. For the time being, at least, her captors didn't want her dead. Merely docile.

Despite the fact that meek had never been her MO,

Anala had quickly assumed the role of mild-mannered captive. The last thing she wanted to do was antagonize her jailers who, after the failed escape attempt, had manacled her wrists with plastic Flexicuffs rather than duct tape. The upgrade meant that she didn't have a hope of breaking free of the restraints. However, on the plus side, they'd cuffed her hands in front of her waist, enabling her to feed herself and tend to more personal matters, albeit it rather awkwardly.

Suffering a twinge of pain in her hip, Anala shifted her weight, the metal bed frame creaking loudly.

The guard immediately glanced up from his video game, brows drawn in a fierce frown.

'No need for alarm,' she hastened to assure him. 'I'm just trying to find a more comfortable position.' Two days ago she'd asked permission to pace the room, explaining that she desperately needed some exercise. The request had been denied.

Frown dissipating, the guard held up a water bottle, silently offering her a drink. Very tempted to tell him to 'piss off' – he'd been the bastard who'd stopped her from pacing – Anala, instead, nodded her head, refusing to let her pride dictate her actions.

Taking the bottle from him, she murmured her thanks.

This is what my life has come to. Not quite the end of the world. But I can definitely see it from here.

As a despondent wave washed over her, she rested her head on her bent knees and stared at the dingy linoleum.

Which is when she caught sight of a piece of glass glittering on the floor about eight feet from the bed. Obviously someone had missed it when they'd swept the floor after her failed escape, the window having been boarded over with planks of wood.

I can use that piece of glass to cut through the plastic cuffs!

No sooner did the thought take root than Anala turned her head in the other direction, keeping her expression as neutral as possible. Seeing that jagged piece of glass, a small flame of hope had flickered. Not a bright flame. But enough of a glow for her to immediately think about how she might go about retrieving it.

She didn't need to hang around until the closing credits to know how the movie was going to end. It was going to end badly. *Very badly.* Unless she did something to rewrite the script.

15

La Torre dei Venti, The Vatican

The Prefect of the Secret Archives peered over his shoulder, verifying that no one lurked in the vicinity.

Stuffing a hand into his cassock pocket, he removed a silver key on a nondescript ring and quickly inserted it into the door lock. La Torre dei Venti – the Tower of the Winds – was closed to the public. The reason why it was his favourite retreat. Reclusive by nature, he adjourned to the tower whenever he needed a bit of privacy. Or to escape from prying Vatican eyes.

In a hurry, Franco made his way down a passageway that led to a small elevator.

A few moments later, the old-fashioned lift shuddered to a stop. Exiting, he strode down a dimly lit corridor that dead-ended at the Tower of the Winds.

As he rushed down the corridor, Franco barely gave the flaking frescoes that covered the walls a passing glance, whimsical personifications of the seasons and vividly imagined biblical scenes streaming past his peripheral sight line in a colourful blur.

Piled against those forgotten masterpieces were bins full of bound indexes, the tower used as an overflow storage area for the Archives. Here, some of the greatest secrets of papal history were safeguarded, with much of the diplomatic correspondence scribed in secret code due to the sensitive nature of the communiqués. Often confused with the Vatican Library, which was the repository for books, texts, codices and manuscripts, the Archives contained all of the papers pertaining to the internal workings of the Church, much of it political in nature.

On the far side of the storage room there was a spiral staircase. Lifting his cassock with his left hand, Franco ascended. Halfway up, huffing, his chest burning from the exertion, he came to a gasping halt.

Bracing a hand on the wall, Franco continued up the corkscrewed stairs. *Well worth the effort*, he thought as he reached the top and entered the beautifully decorated Meridian Room, the only area in the tower that contained no book bins.

Still trying to catch his breath, Franco set his gaze upon the anemoscope at the top of the ceiling, an instrument that never ceased to fascinate. Designed by the same Dominican friar responsible for the topographical maps in the Galleri delle Carte Geografiche, the anemoscope had a pointer attached to an outdoor weather vane that indicated the movement of the wind.

Oddly enough, it was the anemoscope that had inspired Franco to use the alias 'Irenaeus' when he'd contacted the Patel woman. One of the early Church Fathers, Irenaeus was instrumental in creating the Gospel canon, weeding out the heretical gospels that had proliferated in the ancient world.

'*Because there are four corners of the universe and there are four principal winds, therefore there can only be four gospels that are authentic.'*

No surprise that liberal-leaning biblical scholars refused to countenance Irenaeus's assertion and actively sought heretical gospels, wasting an inordinate amount of time traipsing around the Middle East peering into bat-infested caves. When the Nag Hammadi Library of ancient Gnostic texts was unearthed in the mid-twentieth century, rogue scholars were downright orgiastic about the discovery.

Standing in the white marble meridian circle that was embedded in the middle of the floor – part of a zodiacal diagram orientated to the movement of the sun – Franco opened the manila envelope that he'd received from the Vatican secret service. Although the airy enclave lacked electrical lighting, there was a small hole near the ceiling through which streamed a beam of natural light. It provided enough illumination for him to read the two typed sheets of paper; the dossier he'd requested on one Cædmon St John Aisquith.

He gave the photograph of a middle-aged auburn-haired man a cursory glance. According to the dossier, Aisquith had attended Oxford University and had an advanced degree in medieval history. Which he had clearly put to deviant use, having authored a work of conspiracy history entitled *Isis Revealed*. The sort of tripe that would have garnered a visit by the Grand Inquisitor several hundred years ago.

Franco reread the particulars, disturbed by the fact that there were nearly twelve years, from 1995 to 2006, missing from Aisquith's biographical data. As though the man had temporarily disappeared off the face of the planet. He was also uncertain what to make of the fact that Gita Patel had contacted the Englishman.

Perhaps they had known one another at Oxford.

'Yes, no doubt that's it,' he murmured. Given that Aisquith and the Patel woman were the same age, the explanation was entirely plausible. Since Aisquith was a medieval scholar, Franco assumed that she'd consulted him to assist in deciphering Fortes de Pinós's cryptic riddle.

Stuffing the two sheets of paper back into the envelope, Franco strode towards a closed door that led to an outdoor terrace. Like his lavishly designed tower, the little patio was another perk that came with the job.

After his humiliating ouster from the Congregation for the Doctrine of the Faith, Franco had made the best of the situation, undertaking his new duties overseeing the Secret Archives with due diligence and devotion. His humility was soon rewarded when he began to peruse long-forgotten files pertaining to the Knights Templar that had been stashed in a locked *armadi*, the closet tucked away in the section of the Archives that was often referred to as *terra incognito*.

Like Minerva's owl spreading 'its wings only with the falling of dusk,' the Templars' dark secrets had been unfathomable during their 200-year history. The Church only knew that they *had* secrets. Even the inquisitors could only wring from them hints and vague allusions. '*The knights at Château Pèlerin discovered something in the caves of Mount Carmel.*' '*The Grand Master was hiding a relic at the commandery on Cyprus.*' '*There was a secret ritual performed beneath the preceptory in Paris.*' Never anything *specific*. Just enough information to induce the inquisitor to loosen the screws and lessen the pain.

Although he had no proof, Franco believed that the Templars' demise had nothing to do with their insufferable arrogance or blind ambition, as was so often claimed, but rather their fall from grace had to do with a great secret. One that harkened to the very dawn of Christianity. A secret that was contained in the *Evangelium Gaspar*.

Fascinated by this bit of unknown Templar history, Franco had begun to comb through the archive indexes in search of all the files pertaining to the Templar Order. No easy task given that the archival records weren't maintained in alphabetical or even date order. Instead, the voluminous records were indexed by narrow topics.

It had taken three years of committed research to finally locate Fortes de Pinós's inquisition transcript.

Having had no luck deciphering De Pinós's riddle, Franco had nearly given up all hope of ever finding the ancient gospel when, quite unexpectedly, a historian from India contacted the Vatican Secret Archives requesting information regarding a Knight Templar named Fortes de Pinós. The politely worded missive was a godsend, Franco nearly swooning on the spot when he'd first read it, certain that Dr Patel knew far more about the *Evangelium Gaspar* than she revealed in her email.

While Franco had been considering his next move, unsure how to coerce Dr Patel into spilling her golden beans, Pope Pius XIII, who'd always enjoyed excellent health, had suddenly died.

The fact that those two unforeseen incidents occurred within a twenty-four-hour period convinced Franco that the invisible Hand of Providence was at work, the Almighty giving him the means and the opportunity to rebuild His Church.

However, he'd been given a very narrow window to do so. In order to execute the plan, he had to get his hands on the ancient gospel *before* the College of Cardinals went into conclave. Once the papal election was underway, it would be too late to act.

Inserting a key into a lock, Franco opened the door that led to the terrace. The second-highest point in the Vatican City, the tower provided a breathtaking view of the Cortile del Belvedere. When the weather permitted, he often took advantage of the private terrace to escape the maddening crowds, if only for a few brief moments. Between the throngs of tourists and the army of black-robed clerics, he sometimes felt as though he were trapped in an overcrowded ecclesiastical prison.

Inhaling a deep breath, Franco admired the lovely courtyard enclosed at the far end with a soaring exedra wall. A light breeze, blowing across the Tiber, ruffled the deep folds on his cassock. He reached up and removed his red zucchetto, the skullcap worn by cardinals, and tucked it under his arm to prevent it from skittering across the terrace. He then retrieved a slender box of wood-tipped cigarillos from his pocket. Every priest had his vice. His was tobacco. *We are, after all, men not gods.*

Lighting up, he blew a hazy plume into the air. To his surprise, Franco caught sight of Cardinal Secretary Moran rushing along a pathway that separated the grassy courtyard parterres below.

He frowned, his pleasant respite instantly spoiled.

No different than Satan, Thomas Moran and his liberal ilk constituted a dark menace.

'I'm not interested in preserving the status quo; I want to overthrow it,' Franco murmured, Machiavelli's advice ringing with pitch-perfect clarity. And he had the perfect secret weapon with which to launch his offensive. Tucked away in the hinterlands of upstate New York.

Needing an update, he removed his mobile phone from his cassock pocket. Father Gracián Santos and his cadre of not-so-reformed gang-bangers were Franco's secret weapon. Not even our Lord and Saviour could convert the impenitent thief who was crucified alongside of him, for some men were spawned from an evil seed.

Beyond redemption.

16

India might be a hell hole, but it only took a little *baksheesh* – bribe money – to buy heaven. *Guns. Women. Dope.* It was all there for the rupees.

In the last few days, Hector Calzada had bought all three. The pussy and hashish he could have done without, but the gun was absolutely essential. Particularly since Cædmon Aisquith had earlier arrived in Fort Cochin. Although G-Dog had been adamant about exercising restraint – *'follow but don't engage'* – Hector was starting to get a bad feeling about the red-headed Englishman.

Leaning against the trunk of a massive banyan tree, he trained his gaze on the pink stucco house situated on the other side of the privacy wall. As he dreamt of all the ways that he could alleviate his boredom, he absently rubbed the stippled gun grip that protruded from his waistband. *The best kind of hard-on that a man could have.*

Acquiring a gun was never a problem for Hector; the world was bloated with them. His old gang, *Los Diablos de Santa Muerte*, like most Latino gangs, had gone global with 'branches' in all of the major cities in Western Europe. India, however, was a little trickier since there were no Latino gangs on the subcontinent. *Yet.* But because Indians had a gun obsession – a whole cottage industry having sprung up with illegal backroom factories – he'd actually been able to buy a gun in the bazaar. Like it was some kind of bronze trinket. Granted, it was a piece of Indian shit, but as long as it ejected a bullet when he pulled the trigger, Hector would be willing to overlook the inferior design.

Sweltering, he smoothed a hand over his moustache before swiping at several beads of perspiration that trickled down his face. He wiped his clammy palms against his jeans, the sweat causing his right palm to itch. Turning his hand over, he lightly scratched the scarred flesh. His stigmata. He relished the story behind the Chi-Rho cross – '*In this sign, conquer!*' – the brand reminding him of his heritage: Hector was descended from a long line of warriors that went all the way back to the ancient Aztecs.

Not only had his father and all of his uncles been modern-day warriors, i.e. gang-bangers, their small apartment in Spanish Harlem had been used as a flop house for drug dealers and fugitives. Raised to follow in their footsteps, while Hector was still a young boy his male relatives took him to cock fights, let him smoke weed and even, on occasion, allowed him to play with their guns. They also taught him the rules of the street, the code that they lived by. If a man broke the code, any part of it, justice would be swiftly administered. Also, a real man must avenge all insults. *Never turn the other cheek*, his father had emphasized when he gave Hector a beautiful switchblade for his thirteenth birthday. Three months later, Hector used the knife to cut off a classmate's ear, the white boy having called Hector a 'wetback'.

Because that particular incident had occurred on school grounds, Hector had been subjected to a full battery of exams and psychological testing. No one in his family had the education to understand the densely worded report that ensued. 'Lack of empathy.' 'Violent predisposition.' 'Sociopathic tendencies.' *What the hell did it mean?* Other than the fact that Hector could no longer attend school, his parents were at a loss, although they were canny enough to know that the Calzada family had been gravely insulted by the white gringos on the school board.

Unfortunately, Hector's father was gunned down by a rival gang member before he could avenge the slight.

Having suddenly become the man of the family, not only did Hector take care of the school superintendent, using a stolen .357 Magnum to blow away the fucker while he was walking his dog, but he also took care of his father's killer.

You don't mess with a Calzada.

The kills earned Hector a fearsome reputation as a *depredador* – a predator who, like a shark prowling the ocean deep, would kill anyone who failed to give him the proper respect. When he snuffed out an enemy, he didn't just kill that one man; he killed his woman, his children, the neighbours and even the family dog.

Pulling a trigger always made Hector feel strong. Potent. *Alive.* In truth, he never felt more alive than when he took the life of another, as though he'd captured the dead man's very soul and had made it his own. Something the school board forgot to put in their report.

When he was seventeen years old, Hector had racked up enough kills to have the skeletal *Santa Muerte*, Saint Death, tattooed on to his chest. The ghoulish image served as a constant reminder that Lady Death ruled the world, a scythe in one hand, a globe in the other. And like the best cocaine money could buy, she gave sweet succour to those who worshipped her.

The Englishman didn't know it, but he was the walking dead. Once the ransom was delivered, Hector would personally see to it that the red-headed fucker was sacrificed to *Santa Muerte*.

He grinned, savouring the gory image, imaging how he would slice the other man wide open and remove his still-beating heart from his chest cavity.

Blood lust. There was no feeling like it. Not even a good fuck could compare.

While Saint Death guided Hector during his waking hours, Our Lady of Guadalupe protected him while he slept, *la Virgen* tattooed on to his back. Although he couldn't see the beautiful tat, Hector rested easy knowing that the Queen of Heaven kept a vigilant eye. Some might call it conflicted loyalties, but that's because most people didn't understand that *Santa Muerte* and Our Lady were two sides of the same street. That's why he was able to worship the one and revere the other. *Good and evil.* The nature of the beast.

Folding his arms over his chest, Hector watched as his homie Roberto Diaz approached on foot. The other man grinned foolishly, flashing a gold-plated front tooth.

Somebody's been smoking a little too much hashish.

In addition to being Hector's first cousin, Roberto was an initiated member of *Los Diablos de Santa Muerte*. Last year, the two of them had run afoul of a tough-talking Diablo crew leader who'd accused them of skimming drugs and extortion money off the top. Big mistake on their part as they'd belatedly discovered. Roberto, who'd been dragged out of his girlfriend's bed in the middle of the night, had his tongue cut out, although he'd managed to escape before the crew leader took the knife to his throat.

Fond of his tongue, and all his other body parts, Hector had turned to Father Gracián Santos, begging the priest to give him and Roberto safe sanctuary. G-Dog had initially expressed reservations, worried that they might not have the inner strength to go straight. Desperate, he and Roberto each had a Chi-Rho cross branded on to the palm of their right hand. A badge of fidelity and a show of good faith. And while he was still leery, G-Dog agreed to give them safe haven in upstate New York. Hector owed Father Gracián big time, the man, literally, saving his life.

'I want you to stay here and watch the Indian bitch while I keep an eye on the Englishman,' Hector told his cousin.

Roberto grunted his assent; the only form of communication that he was capable of making. It was a language of sorts, and Hector was actually able to understand what various grunts meant. From time to time, he'd even caught himself answering his cousin in like manner.

Nature of the beast.

17

'Moreover, Constantine's cross was superimposed with the rallying cry *"In hoc signo vinces"*,' Cædmon iterated, pointing to the Chi-Rho cross that he'd drawn on the sheet of blank paper. 'In this sign you shall conquer.'

Edie rolled down the cab window, beginning to suspect that there was some sort of official regulation banning air conditioning in all Indian taxis. Somewhat revived, she tapped her finger against the monogram of an 'X' overlaying a skinny 'P'. 'As I recall, chi and rho are the first two letters of the Greek word *Kristós*.'

Cædmon nodded. 'Which makes the symbol a christogram rather than a true cross. Immediately after the Emperor Constantine had his vision of the Chi-Rho, he ordered his soldiers to affix the symbol on to their battle standards. Said action famously resulted in Constantine's triumphant victory at the Battle of Milvian Bridge.'

'And so began a long tradition of Christians slaughtering their enemy in the name of Jesus Christ,' Edie retorted sarcastically, the subject one that never failed to raise her ire. 'Having read the New Testament, I am fairly convinced that JC would have been the first to condemn that sort of brutal carnage.'

'I daresay the Prince of Peace would not have approved.' Frowning, Cædmon rubbed his eyes with his thumb and middle finger.

Like Cædmon, Edie wondered at the significance of Anala's abductor being branded with the ancient symbol. The fact that anyone would purposefully mutilate their flesh indicated a cultish devotion. *But to what? Or who?*

As she pondered the bizarre twist, Edie peered out of the window, her attention drawn to the passing streetscape. While many, if not most, of the old colonial buildings were in a sad state of negligent decay, it somehow lent Fort Cochin a decrepit sort of beauty. Rising above the town's red-tiled rooftops were Islamic minarets, Christian steeples and the gleaming metallic finials of Hindu temples. It bespoke a tolerance that was sadly absent in many of the places she'd recently visited while on assignment for *National Geographic*.

A lively coastal town, the streets teemed with vehicles of every description, the adjacent pavements jam-packed with tourists, vendors peddling their wares and the occasional farm animal. The latter was taken in stride by the locals. Not to mention their taxi driver who suddenly swerved into the oncoming lane, circumnavigating an emaciated bovine aimlessly wandering in the middle of the road.

'The Chi-Rho handprint on Anala's bedroom window reiterates that someone affiliated with the Catholic Church masterminded her abduction,' Edie remarked.

Cædmon concurred with a nod. 'And, according to the Chinon transcript, the Roman Catholic Church had been very keen to find the *Evangelium Gaspar*.'

'Yeah, seven hundred years ago,' she countered, pointing out the obvious.

'No institution survives as long as the Papal See without having a long memory. I suspect that the *Evangelium*

Gaspar contains some damning revelation that contradicts traditional Church teaching. If it were merely a recitation of what's already contained in the four canonical gospels, Anala's abductors wouldn't have gone to such extreme lengths to retrieve it.'

'Hopefully, the historian at the St Thomas Seminary can shed some light on the matter.' As she spoke, a bead of perspiration broke free from her brow and rolled down Edie's right temple. Opening her basket-weave satchel, she retrieved a paper fan. Glad that she'd had the foresight to toss it in her bag, she unfolded the gilded fan, swishing it back and forth in front of her face.

Their driver, applying the horn with great aplomb, abruptly swerved – this time to the left – bypassing a stalled lorry loaded with burlap sacks full of produce. Edie grabbed hold of the hand strap to avoid being hurled on to Cædmon's lap. In front of her, the dangling glass beads that separated front and rear passenger seats noisily clattered. Having left Fort Cochin, they were now headed southeast on a rural two-lane highway fringed with coconut palms. To the east were the green foothills of the Western Ghats, home to Kerala's fabled tea plantations, coffee estates and cardamom groves. To the west were the region's fertile rice paddies.

Realizing that the backs of her calves were stuck to the vinyl upholstery, Edie briefly considered reaching down and unsticking them, but couldn't summon any enthusiasm for the task. Because they had an appointment at a religious seminary, she'd purposefully worn a plain white dress with a high décolleté. Big mistake – beads of sweat were trickling down her cleavage. The ponderous humidity and high temperature were a debilitating combination, the miasma so thick that she was forced to take small measured breaths. Although her brain knew better, she secretly feared that if she inhaled too deeply, the muggy air might clog her lungs and asphyxiate her.

Having retreated into silence, Cædmon stared pensively at the Chi-Rho symbol that he'd drawn in his journal.

'You never did say how you and Gita met,' Edie ventured timorously.

To her surprise, Cædmon's lips curved into a faint smile – the first in days. '"The clouds methought would open, and show riches ready to drop upon me, that when I waked I cried to dream again."' Then, just as quickly as it appeared, the smile vanished. 'We were in the same Oxford thespian troupe,' he said by way of explanation. 'I played Caliban to Gita's Miranda in *The Tempest*.'

Edie quickly searched her memory bank. 'Miranda was Prospero's daughter and Caliban was the freckled monster who tried to rape her, wasn't he?'

'Er, yes. But I can assure you that my actual feelings were of a more tender nature, Gita Patel my first love.' The admission caused two ruddy splotches to instantly materialize on his cheeks. Clearly embarrassed, he turned his head and stared out of the window.

Having suspected as much, Edie made no comment. She certainly didn't begrudge Cædmon the relationship; the boom and blush of love's first rush was one of life's more poignant chapters.

'My father, as you know, was a stern taskmaster,' he continued in a low voice, his gaze still focused on the rice paddies in the near distance. 'Gita possessed a gentleness that had been lacking in my youth and . . . she was incredibly empathetic.' Slowly turning his head from side to side, Cædmon rubbed the back of his neck, giving Edie the distinct impression that speaking about the past was a painful exercise for him. 'Shamefully, I never questioned why Gita left Oxford so abruptly. When she returned my letters unopened, instead of pursuing the matter, I shrugged it off and blithely traipsed on to the next love. I assumed the relationship was over and that was that. But I should have pressed harder. Should have gone down to London and –' He broke off abruptly, leaving the thought unfinished.

'You have no reason to feel guilty,' Edie told him, sensing that was the root cause of Cædmon's distress. 'You didn't commit any misdeed or transgression.'

His jaw tightened. 'You can't absolve me of my sins. I *am* blameworthy in this tragedy.'

Stymied by Cædmon's heartfelt conviction, Edie cast her glance downwards; she'd had no idea that he felt so culpable. Having unexpectedly stepped on a verbal landmine, she nervously fiddled with her fan. Guilt, like jealousy or mistrust, was one of those emotions that carnivorously gnawed at the inner core.

'You were a nineteen-year-old kid,' she pointed out in a renewed attempt to reassure him. 'Hardly an experienced man of the world. And it's not as if you knew that Gita was pregnant and then turned your back on her and the baby.'

'No, that would have been unforgivable. A better man than that, I was merely a despicable coward,' he rasped in a mocking voice. Folding his arms over his chest, Cædmon leaned his head against the back of the vinyl seat and closed his eyes. Effectively ending the conversation.

The fact that he'd opened up at all was something of a miracle; Cædmon rarely spoke of his past, particularly his childhood. But, to be fair, neither did she. Once, early on in the relationship, he'd revealed that his father, Neville, resented the fact that his wife had died in childbirth, wrongly blaming Cædmon. In return, she'd confessed that when her mother Melissa died of a heroin overdose, she'd been forced to spend two years in a sexually abusive foster home. But that's all that they'd shared with one another, their respective pasts hermetically sealed as an emotional safeguard to protect the living. Edie sometimes worried that they were so well insulated, it might harm their burgeoning relationship.

A few minutes later, the taxi slowed as they approached the congested streets of Kottayam, verdant fields giving way to an urban hustle-bustle. Directly ahead of them, spewing dark plumes of oil-laced carbon monoxide, was a dilapidated red bus that had clearly seen better days. Those days being the 1950s from the look of it. Not only were there at least a dozen men 'riding shotgun' on the roof, there were four scrawny men clinging precariously to a metal rack mounted on the rear. Presumably installed for that very purpose. No sooner did the bus slow than 'passengers' began to disembark by leaping over the side.

'I don't know why that reminds me of lemmings jumping off a cliff. Probably because it's an inherently dangerous activity,' Edie mused as she watched them.

'Mmmm . . .' Clearly uninterested, Cædmon peered in the other direction.

Up ahead, traffic had inexplicably come to a standstill.

'There's a festival today,' their driver said, jutting his chin at the stalled gridlock.

Muttering under his breath, Cædmon glanced at his watch.

Edie, hoping to put the delay to good use, unfolded the tourist map that she'd picked up at their hotel. Trying to determine her eastings from her northings, she caught sight of a red motorbike in the driver's wing mirror.

The skin on the back of her neck instantly prickled.

Craning her head, she peered over her left shoulder at the press of cars, rickshaws and motorbikes idling directly behind their taxi, the red two-wheeler in the middle of a dusty pack about twenty feet back.

'Is something the matter?' Cædmon enquired.

'I just had the strangest feeling that –' Shaking her head, she snorted self-consciously at her overblown fear. 'Forget it.'

'Forget what?' he pressed, eyes narrowed.

Worried that she was going to sound paranoid, Edie relented and said, 'I glimpsed a red motorbike that I think I may have seen back in Fort Cochin. But I'm sure it's probably –'

'There was a sentry with a red motorbike posted outside of Gita's house,' he interjected.

Flabbergasted, Edie's jaw slackened. 'And you were going to tell me this *when*?! For crying out loud, Cædmon! What did this sentry look like?'

'He was olive-skinned with dark hair.'

Great. A description that fitted nearly every man in Kottayam. Including the guys who'd just jumped off the bus.

'Oh, yes, and he had a moustache.'

Oh, God. Edie reflexively grabbed the vinyl seat to steady herself.

'The guy on the red motorbike has a moustache,' she whispered hoarsely.

Hearing that, Cædmon immediately leaned forward and said to the driver, 'We're getting out here.'

18

Cædmon hastily ushered Edie to the kerb, peering first in one direction and then the other.

Along the bustling artery conveyances of every imaginable description choked the thoroughfare. An endless stream of honking vehicles belching dark plumes of noxious exhaust. A few feet away, a trio of untethered goats nonchalantly grazed on a pile of rubbish. One of them lackadaisically raised its head, stuck out its tongue and greeted them with a quavering '*Blaaaa.*'

'Great. We're actually sharing the kerb with the Three Billy Goats Gruff.' A few seconds later, lowering her voice, Edie said, 'Here he comes.'

Slowly passing them, the moustachioed brute on the red motorbike craned his head in their direction. Leering malevolently, he lifted his right hand off the handlebar. Purposefully showing them the telltale brand on his palm.

The mark of Cain.

Visibly flinching, Edie grabbed hold of Cædmon's arm.

'As you'll undoubtedly recall, Gita was warned not to go to the authorities,' he told her.

'But you're not the authorities. You're Anala's biological father. Which, I know, sounded *way* too clinical. Sorry.'

'Clinical or not, the abductors have no idea that I'm her father. They may have erroneously concluded that Anala hired a private detective.'

'But that doesn't explain why – Oh, Lord Shiva!' Edie shrieked as the two of them dodged to the far side of the pavement, narrowly avoiding a collision with a blue Tata lorry, richly decorated with Hindu symbols, fresh flowers and dangling beads. At the back of the open lorry there was a large elephant in tow, the animal painted in vivid shades of green, yellow, pink and purple. A gargantuan coat of many colours.

'Our cab driver said that there was a festival going on,' Edie remarked, wide-eyed. 'He didn't say anything about the circus being in town.'

'My understanding is that Hindu religious festivals are rather like a circus.' As he spoke, Cædmon glanced at his watch. 2:45 p.m. Ample time to make their three-thirty appointment at the St Thomas Seminary. If they faded into the festival crowd, they could then double-back and hail another taxi, losing the moustachioed brute in the process.

Cuffing a hand around Edie's elbow, he quickened the pace.

With her free arm, Edie swiped at her brow. 'And I thought that DC in August was brutal; this heat is debilitating. I feel like a wrung-out sponge.'

'Just be grateful that we're not here during the monsoon season,' Cædmon rasped irritably, the noise, the soaring temperature and the branded bastard all having a disagreeable effect on him.

Up ahead, the lane opened on to a large grassy square jam-packed with lorries, elephants, bare-chested musicians and a milling mob of excited onlookers. A rambunctious kaleidoscope of Indian culture, it was a different world entirely, the air thick with a palpable, frenetic energy.

Closer at hand, an Indian swaddled in a white cotton *mundu* was in the process of unloading a decorated elephant from a lorry, the animal's forehead majestically caparisoned in a glittering golden *nettipattam*.

'Mind your step,' Cædmon cautioned, guiding Edie around a far less majestic sight – a puny wrangler holding a plastic-lined rubbish bin to a pachyderm's wrinkled haunches.

'Sorta like cleaning the kitty litter box, huh?' Edie wrinkled her nose. 'Although I'm guessing that's not the most enviable job at the circus.'

'Obviously, we've stumbled into the elephant holding area. We need to –' Suddenly hearing the sound of a deep-throttled engine, Cædmon peered over his shoulder.

At the far end of the lane, the branded bastard calmly sat on his idling red motorbike. Raising his right hand, he grinned and waved . . . before loudly revving the engine.

Several wranglers glanced nervously around, the elephants becoming noticeably agitated. Just then, one of the behemoths raised its trunk, hurling a loafing lorry driver to the ground. Hollering in a foreign tongue, the man nimbly rolled out of the stomping beast's path. In a whirl of motion, the keepers scrambled to keep their charges calm, rightfully worried that the tuskers might suddenly stampede.

Revving his engine one last time, their adversary suddenly zoomed towards them. Animal handlers hollered. An elephant roared. All three sounds were near deafening.

'Is he out of his freaking –'

'Yes!' Cædmon interjected, that being the short reply. Having no time to brief the troops, he grabbed Edie's hand and charged towards the throng of festival-goers in the square.

Glancing behind him, Cædmon glimpsed the motorcyclist as he zipped around a parked lorry, forcing a wrangler to leap out of harm's way. The manoeuvre caused several pugnacious pachyderms to indignantly bellow.

Christ!

Just ahead of them, a large group of spectators, realizing they were at the forefront of a potentially dangerous scene, surged forward into the milling crowd, inciting a frantic chain reaction. A ferocious jangle of sight and sound.

Cædmon veered to the right, the two of them dashing past a drum and trumpet troupe, the music reaching a riotous crescendo even as the festival-goers charged hither and yon. Over the noise of the crowd, he heard a distinctive motorized rumble.

'Where to now?' Edie asked as they shouldered their way into the wild crush. Red-faced, her chest heaved with each ragged pant.

Good question.

Cædmon hurriedly surveyed the environs: to one side of the open square was an ornate Hindu temple; to the other, a line of buildings, the rooftops brimming with festival spectators.

Perfect.

He and Edie charged past a small circle of men twirling sequinned parasols in the air. Cædmon tuned it all out – the clanging cymbals, the thunderous shouts, the colourful costumes – his attention fully focused on the line of buildings on the square's perimeter.

Breathless, they reached the edge of the square, their passage blocked by a line of cars parked bumper to bumper. Letting go of Edie's hand, he leapt on to the bonnet of the nearest vehicle. He then spun on his heel and, with an outstretched arm, hauled Edie on to the car. Her white dress flared behind her hips like a ship's sail.

Together, they jumped to the pavement.

As if on cue, the motorcyclist thundered forth from the frenzied midst. Heedless of the turmoil he'd left in his wake, he braked to a halt, the long line of parked auto-mobiles an obstacle he couldn't roar through or whiz around. The perfect barricade.

At least until the relentless bastard disembarked and continued to follow them on foot.

'Keep moving,' Cædmon ordered gruffly.

Edie pointed to a narrow opening tucked between two buildings. 'I see an alley!'

'Right.'

A few seconds later, they cannonballed through the opening. At the other end of the dimly lit passage, Cædmon saw scores of people with shopping bags looped on their arms.

It was an open-air marketplace.

Emerging from the alleyway, he steered Edie into a gaggle of sari-clad women. 'Run as fast as you can!' he ordered.

Edie obeyed without argument. Grabbing hold of her skirt, she dashed hurriedly through the crowded market.

As they raced past a table laden with Hindu icons, a merchant, clearly mistaking them for customers, rushed forward. 'For you, good price!' he importuned.

'No, thank you!' Cædmon told him. 'We're not interested!'

Refusing to take 'No' for an answer, the merchant followed them for several feet. 'Special sale for you!'

'*Illa! Illa!*' Cædmon said forcefully. Hearing the Malayalam word for 'No', the merchant finally retreated.

Seconds later, they left the marketplace, making their exodus at a busy intersection. Assaulted by honking horns, darting motorbikes and blasts of foul-smelling diesel fuel, Cædmon feared they'd reached the proverbial end of the road, not a taxi in sight.

Edie peered over her shoulder. 'He's about twenty-five yards back!'

Just then, a dusty red coach, lumbering at a more sedate speed than the other vehicles on the road, rolled past.

'Hurry!' Rushing after the coach, Cædmon leaped up and grabbed the metal railing attached to the back end of the conveyance, hauling himself onboard. He then extended an arm towards Edie.

Their fingers grazed.

Then pulled apart.

Edie ran faster, inciting the bevy of Indian men riding on top of the bus to yell raucous encouragements.

Worried that she wouldn't be able to leap aboard, Cædmon was about to jump off the coach when Edie jettisoned forward. Snatching hold of her wrist, he pulled her on to the narrow steel platform.

As the coach picked up speed, he stared at their pursuer who now stood on the corner glaring at them.

Still panting, Edie clung to the railing. 'We left him in the dust. Mission accomplished,' she said breathlessly.

At least for the time being.

19

Mar Thoma Seminary, Kottayam

'Please accept our apologies for being a few minutes late,'
Cædmon said to the heavily bearded priest. 'We met with
an unexpected delay.'

Having cordially welcomed them to the seminary, the
Reverend Doctor Geevarghese Mar Paulos waved away
the apology. Attired in a white cassock that perfectly
matched his chest-length white beard, the elderly historian was also bedecked in a peaked navy-blue cap with
red trim and adorned with the crux quadrata. Other
than the colour – which Cædmon assumed was a con-
cession to the heat – the clerical outfit bore a striking
resemblance to that worn by Eastern Orthodox priests.

'Shall we adjourn to the library? It's much cooler
there.'

Exhausted by their foot race through Kottayam, Cædmon smiled gratefully. 'By all means.'

As they strolled under a covered arcade, he peered at
Edie who'd donned a long grey scarf, which she'd wrapped
around her shoulders and upper arms. The earlier incident had sobered her considerably. Indeed, the episode
had been a grim reminder that the men who kidnapped
Anala were not bound by laws. Or scruples. Or ethics.
And while they had managed to elude the moustachioed

Bête Noire, he was still out there, *somewhere*, roaming the streets of Kottayam.

Glancing about, Cædmon appreciated the fact that the seminary compound was a tranquil oasis. Certainly, it was a marked contrast to the frenetic energy outside the walled enclosure, the grounds exuding an air of spiritual seclusion accentuated by the strains of liturgical music echoing softly across the cloister.

'The Mar Thoma Seminary choir is practising for an upcoming concert,' Dr Paulos informed them, gesturing to a nearby building.

'I'm curious about the name "Mar Thoma". What exactly does it mean?' As she spoke, Edie adjusted her scarf, ensuring that she was modestly covered.

'Mar Thoma is Aramaic for Saint Thomas. We are also known as the Nazrani,' the older cleric replied as he ushered them into the library, a high-ceilinged enclave with wooden tables and chairs uniformly placed amidst numerous bookcases. Tall windows, shaded with intricately carved *jali* screens, cast exotic filigree shadows on to the floor.

Dr Paulos motioned them to a table. 'As I understand it, Mr Aisquith, you're writing a book about early Christianity.'

Suffering a momentary twinge of guilt, Cædmon nodded, that being the fabrication he'd used to garner the appointment with the eminent church historian. As he held out a chair for Edie, he shoved guilt to the wayside, embellishing on the lie. 'I'm particularly interested in the Apostle Thomas and his missionary work in India.'

'The story is simple enough,' Dr Paulos began, taking a

seat across from them. 'Thomas arrived in Muziris in the year 52 AD whereupon he immediately founded seven churches and converted hundreds, if not thousands, of people.'

A young man with a neatly trimmed beard, presumably a seminarian, carried a tray into the library. Smiling shyly, he set three glasses of fragrant chai tea on to the table, taking his leave without a word.

Cædmon accepted the proffered spiced tea, the mingled scents of cardamom, cinnamon and ginger perfuming the air. 'I presume that the Apostle Thomas was converting Brahmin Indians to Christianity.'

Shaking his head, the bearded cleric said, 'On the contrary. Thomas came to India to preach to the resident Jewish population.'

'Jews? In India? I had no idea.'

'Most westerners are unaware that a large contingent of Zadokite Jews emigrated to the Malabar Coast in the second century BC in the wake of the Maccabean Uprising,' Dr Paulos informed them. 'Although those early emigrant Jews referred to themselves as the "Sons of Zadok", they are nowadays better known as the Essenes.'

Hearing that, Cædmon and Edie immediately glanced at one another. Earlier in the day, the Essenes had popped up in a discussion about the Knights Templar and Château Pèlerin, the knights having discovered an enclave of Essene descendants at nearby Mount Carmel.

'Eventually, Thomas's Essene converts came to be known as the Nazrani.' As he spoke, Dr Paulos smoothed a withered hand over his beard.

'Is the word "Nazrani" of Malayalam derivation?' Edie asked politely, wading into the conversation.

Again, the older man shook his head. 'The word "Nazrani" derives from two Hebrew root words: *nazir*, meaning 'consecrated', and *notsrim*, meaning "The Keepers of the Secret".'

How very intriguing, Cædmon thought. He had speculated that the Templars may have discovered something at Mount Carmel that had led them to the Nazrani in India. He was now convinced of it.

'This might be off base, but is there a connection between the words Nazrani and Nazareth?' Edie enquired of their host. 'I'm thinking specifically of Jesus of Nazareth.' Her remark was not only germane, but spot-on, the two words remarkably similar.

The old cleric's lips twitched as though he were amused by the question. 'Surely you know that "Jesus of Nazareth" is a fictional persona?'

Edie's eyes opened wide, her shock plainly evident. 'I beg your pardon?'

'According to biblical archaeologists, the town of "Nazareth" didn't exist prior to the third century of the common era,' Dr Paulos explained in a more serious tone. '"Jesus of Nazareth" is a third-century mistranslation from the original Greek. "Jesus the Nazorean" is the correct translation.'

The mystery deepening, Cædmon wondered if 'Nazorean' wasn't a linguistic fusion of 'Nazrani' and 'Essene'. While tempted to ask, being short on time, he got right to the gist. 'In the course of my research, I've come across several references to a long-lost gospel known as the *Evangelium Gaspar*.'

Setting his tea glass on the table, the white-bearded cleric folded his hands over his chest. 'I see.'

'Furthermore, it's my understanding that a Knights Templar by the name of Fortes de Pinós was granted custody of the gospel in the early fourteenth century.'

'You are ill-informed.' Gaze narrowing, Dr Paulos shot Cædmon a penetrating stare. 'The Nazrani bishops did not give Fortes de Pinós the *Evangelium Gaspar.*'

'They didn't?' *Shite.* Cædmon gulped reflexively, on the verge of losing his tea. His search for the long-lost gospel was premised on the assumption that the Knights Templar had acquired the ancient text.

'Taking advantage of his Nazrani hosts, that unscrupulous knight *stole* the *Evangelium Gaspar* from the sanctuary in Palayoor,' Dr Paulos continued. 'That, incidentally, is the site of the very first church founded by St Thomas, making the Templar's crime all the more reprehensible.'

Cædmon's shoulders slumped with relief.

'Would you happen to know in what language the *Evangelium Gaspar* was scribed?' he next enquired, hoping to glean a few more details about the mysterious gospel.

'It was written in Aramaic, the liturgical language used by the Nazrani until the twentieth century.'

Aramaic. The language spoken by Jesus and the original apostles.

Assuming a bland expression, Cædmon glanced at the nearby bookcases. 'Does your collection include a copy of the *Evangelium Gaspar* that I could peruse?'

The older man's brows drew together; the makings of a disapproving scowl. 'In the year 1542, a group of Jesuit priests arrived in Malabar. Their mission, simply put, was to coerce the Nazrani to adopt Roman Catholic orthodoxy. To that end, they initiated what has come to be known as the Goan Inquisition. Accusing the Nazrani of heresy, the Jesuits pilfered our churches and burned our sacred Aramaic texts, including all of our copies of the *Evangelium Gaspar*.' Dr Paulos's scowl finally relaxed, replaced by a more placid expression. 'By God's grace, we managed to shake off the Roman yoke in the middle of the seventeenth century.'

Leaning back in his chair, Cædmon rested his chin on his steepled fingers, pondering the meaning of the very informative history lesson. The Nazrani could rightfully lay claim to being one of the oldest Christian churches in the world. Even more astounding, the Nazrani were the Aramaic-speaking descendants of Essenes who'd sought religious sanctuary in India more than two thousand years ago.

The Sons of Zadok. The Keepers of the Secret.

'Given everything that you've told us, I assume that Gaspar, the author of the stolen gospel, was an Essene convert to Christianity,' Cædmon remarked in passing.

'Since I've never read the *Evangelium Gaspar*, I can't rightly say if that's true.' Smiling apologetically, Dr Paulos shrugged. 'Like so many legendary personages in the Bible, the myth may not accurately reflect reality.'

Cædmon sat up straighter in his chair. 'Gaspar? A legendary figure, you say?' He wondered if the Nazrani adhered to a different Bible than the King James version that he'd been raised upon.

'But I thought you already knew.' The bearded historian glanced first at Cædmon, then at Edie. 'Gaspar was one of the Three Wise Men.'

'*What?!*' Not only did Edie's jaw visibly drop, but the tea glass nearly slipped from her fingers. 'As in "We Three Kings of Orient Are"?'

The old cleric's eyes twinkled merrily. 'None other.'

20

'I'll be honest with you, Cædmon; I'm having a difficult time wrapping my mind around the idea of one of the Three Wise Men writing a gospel account,' Edie remarked, reaching for her glass of Kingfisher beer. Although she wasn't necessarily in the mood for alcohol, Cædmon insisted that they drink bottled beer rather than tap water.

Having returned to Fort Cochin a short while ago, they'd found a café near the harbour with air conditioning, the noise of which aggressively competed with the Hindu music blaring from the sound system. From where they sat, near the oversized plate-glass window at the front of the café, Edie could see the red-tiled *godown* warehouses where spice merchants plied their trade. Just outside the window, rickshaw *wallahs*, attired in their khaki uniform shirts, were huddled around a board game while they waited for the next paying customer.

Cædmon poured himself a glass of beer. 'While a gospel scribed by a Wise Man is seemingly odd on face value, I suspect Gaspar and his two cronies, Melchior and Balthazar, were actually Jews.'

'But in the Nativity story, they're depicted as three *exotic* men from foreign locales.'

'Which doesn't preclude their being Jews,' Cædmon insisted. 'As you undoubtedly know, the Three Wise Men are only mentioned in one gospel, that being Matthew, with the entire story relayed in a mere twelve verses.'

'Making it the most famous short story ever written.' Never tiring of the tale, Edie needed no coaxing. 'The Three Wise Men from the East see a star in the night sky foretelling the birth of a king, prompting them to throw a few things in an overnight bag, hop on their camels and journey to Jerusalem. Whereupon they immediately inform King Herod that they're searching for the new-born King of the Jews. After consulting the ancient prophecies, Herod's high priests point them in the direction of Bethlehem.'

'Being a heartless bastard, Herod summarily orders the execution of all baby boys under the age of three to eliminate a rival heir to the throne,' Cædmon said, continuing the story where she'd left off. 'Although there's no mention of it in the Bible, I'm certain that the Three Wise Men were descendants of the Hebrew Zadokite priest-hood.'

Just then, the waiter returned to their table with a tray laden with fragrant dishes. Her stomach rumbling, Edie watched as he laid out a sumptuous feast for two. In the mood for some fiery cuisine, she'd ordered the vegetarian *thali* – a potpourri of curried dishes, red-streaked rice and assorted chutneys – served on a large banana leaf. Always adventuresome when it came to ethnic food, she intended to dine like the locals and eat with her fingers. Playing it safe and sticking to a milder repast, Cædmon had ordered a tuna steak cooked in a coconut masala. His meal, unlike hers, included cutlery.

'In 586 BC when Nebuchadnezzar destroyed the Temple in Jerusalem, he forced the entire Zadokite priesthood, along with a large contingent of upper-class and educated Jews, into Babylonian exile,' Cædmon continued once the waiter had taken his leave. 'Many of the Zadokite priests, still retaining their belief in Yahweh, became part of a mysterious sect known as the Magi.'

'I'm guessing that the Magi were ancient magicians.' Ravenous, Edie broke off a piece of *parotta* bread. Using the piece of bread in lieu of a fork, she took a mouthful of lentil *dhal*.

'Not exactly. The Magi interpreted dreams, served as court advisors and, as we know from Matthew's account, plotted the stars in the night sky.'

Having just swallowed a mouthful laden with green chillies, Edie hurriedly snatched her beer glass, taking an unladylike gulp. Fire extinguished, she said, 'Was Gaspar a Wise Man or a Magi then?'

Always the gentleman, Cædmon refilled her glass. 'Technically, he belonged to the latter group. Because the Early Christian Church condemned astrology as a demonic pursuit, the Magi were re-branded as the Three Wise Men. A more seemly occupation.'

Using the fingers of her right hand, Edie mixed yogurt and steamed root vegetables into a thick slurry. As she did, she stole a quick glance at Cædmon, who was observing the proceedings, clearly aghast. She bit back an amused smile. 'So if the Three Magi were the descendants of the Zadokite priesthood, maybe, like so many Jews in the first century, they'd actually been waiting for the prophesied Messiah. Whaddya think?'

Brows drawing together, Cædmon surprised her by saying, 'What I think is that our trip to India has been a colossal waste of time. With the ransom deadline fast approaching, I'd hoped that –' He shook away the thought. His expression having suddenly turned bleak, he finished his beer.

'The trip hasn't been a total waste,' Edie said quietly. 'We now know who authored the gospel and we've verified that Fortes de Pinós did, in fact, take the *Evangelium Gaspar* to Europe.'

'And in case it's slipped your notice, neither of those details has brought me any closer to finding the *Evangelium Gaspar*. Christ! I feel like Sisyphus pushing the bloody boulder up the hill.'

Unsure how to leaven Cædmon's spirits, Edie peered around the lively restaurant, her gaze drawn to a statue of a portly Indian god with four arms and a sweetly smiling elephant head. *Ganesh*. The Remover of Obstacles.

'I've always wondered why the Hindus put so many arms on their gods,' she said conversationally, purposefully changing the subject.

'That damned bastard!'

'Who? Ganesh?'

Blue eyes narrowing, Cædmon jutted his chin at the window. 'The Bête Noire with the Chi-Rho brand on his palm. I just caught sight of him standing in the shadows across the street.'

21

Cædmon slapped a 500-rupee note on to the table. 'That should pay for the meal and your taxi to the hotel,' he said, stuffing his wallet back into his trouser pocket.

'Where in God's name are you going?' Edie, clearly aghast, stared at the note as though it were contaminated.

'I mean to have a word with the moustachioed Bête Noire.'

'Are you crazy?' she squawked. 'He could kill you!' Fear writ large in her brown eyes, Edie reached across the table and grabbed hold of his wrist. 'Please, Cædmon . . . just stay put.'

Biting back an acerbic retort, he refrained from telling her that such timidity would only spell Anala's doom. 'I mean to introduce myself as Anala's father and broker a détente with the kidnappers.' When Edie refused to relinquish her hold, Cædmon none too gently pried his wrist free. 'They need to understand that I won't be able to meet their bloody ransom demand if I'm hampered by someone scurrying in my shadow.'

'Then I'm coming with you.'

He put a staying hand on Edie's shoulder, preventing her from rising to her feet. 'I would have thought you'd had enough hair-raising harum-scarum for one day. You're to go straight away to the hotel and remain there until I return.' Orders issued, Cædmon bent down and hurriedly kissed her on the forehead, softening the blow.

Without a backwards glance, he strode towards the café exit.

Emerging on to the busy lane, he slowly, methodically, studied the busy streetscape. Just as he'd feared, the Bête Noire was no longer in sight, having moved to a different location. Undeterred, Cædmon shaded his eyes with his hand and searched for the one person in the chaotic scene who didn't belong.

Chai wallahs, rickshaw drivers, street pedlars, beggars, tourists. They were the very people that one would expect to see on a boisterous Indian street corner. And then he saw him – a male of average height and build with close-cut dark hair and a thick moustache, dressed entirely in black. The odd man out, he stood beneath a weather-worn awning near an outdoor café located on the other side of the street.

Deciding on a brazen course of action, Cædmon purposefully crossed the thoroughfare. No sooner did he reach the other side of the street than the Bête Noire's head whiplashed in his direction.

'You there!' Cædmon called out. 'A word if I may!'

Perhaps fearing an assault, the Bête Noire spun on his heel and took off running.

Shite!

Giving chase, Cædmon charged through the crowded outdoor café. Accidentally bumping into several tables, he knocked a glass of water into one chap's lap and sent a plate crashing to the pavement – minor catastrophes that merited a shrill shriek from a few of the female patrons. The burly fellow with the wet lap thrust his right hand into the air, flipping Cædmon the *digitus infamis*.

There being no time to apologize, he zigzagged around the clustered tables.

Bloody hell! Where did the jackal go?

Cædmon swivelled his head, scanning the hectic environs. Catching sight of a black blur dodging into an alley, he sprinted in that direction. When he reached the corner, a large aluminium disc came soaring through the air, the object whirling towards his head at a dizzying speed. Cædmon reflexively recoiled to one side, the disc hurtling past his ear and crashing into the side of the building with a deafening clatter.

That was when he belatedly realized that he'd nearly been decapitated with the lid from an aluminium dustbin.

Sodding bastard!

Refusing to surrender, Cædmon dashed down the alley, his black-clad foe having already exited at the other end of the dank passageway.

Worried that another airborne missile might fly in his direction, he slowed his speed at the terminus and tentatively peered around the corner. Verifying that the coast was clear, he left the alley and entered an eerily deserted marketplace. A faded, hand-painted sign – written in English – indicated that he'd just entered Fort Cochin's fabled spice bazaar. A tight cluster of pastel-coloured warehouses flanked either side of the street; all with the same red-tiled roof; all in a similar sad state of dilapidation.

On high alert, he wended his way down the lane, primed and ready for the tough guy to burst out of the shadows.

Many of the warehouses had already closed for business, their windows and doors shuttered for the night. Many, but not all, Cædmon passed an entryway painted an eye-catching shade of turquoise blue. Glancing inside, he saw bags of spice – cloves, cardamom, ginger, pepper, anise – stacked to the rafters. A stoop-shouldered man hunched over an open newspaper gave Cædmon a disinterested glance. Two wiry blokes loading jute sacks on to the back of a truck ignored him entirely.

He wrinkled his nose, the combined scent from all those spices creating a noxious bouquet.

The brute was here, *somewhere*, amidst the ginger and anise.

'*Where in that nest of spicery they shall breed . . .*'

A few seconds later a small brindled nanny goat scampered out of a doorway, the bell around its neck merrily tinkling. *Got you!*

Cædmon immediately headed in that direction, certain the skittish goat had been frightened by a moustachioed intruder.

Warily he approached the deserted warehouse, the elaborately carved door softly swinging on its hinges. Cædmon's adrenalin instantly spiked. Taking several deep breaths, he tried to countermand the hormone's effect, his heart thumping much too rapidly.

Stiffening his resolve, he stepped through the doorway. A beam of light slanting through an open window hit him full in the face. He moved out of its path, keeping to the shadows as he surveyed the otherwise murky interior. Spartan, it was an open space with a wooden table, a set of old-fashioned scales, two handcarts, a forklift and towers of stacked spice sacks. Hearing a tell-tale creak, Cædmon glanced towards the ceiling.

Someone is prowling about on the second floor.

He strode over to the stairwell, certain that his quarry had gone upstairs.

The wooden steps groaned under his weight. *Ready or not, here I come*, he silently grated, unable to muffle his footfall.

At the top of the staircase, he paused. The dimly lit environs were little more than an attic storage space, packing crates full of spice sacks lining one entire side of the gloomy expanse.

He took a few cautious steps.

A creaking floorboard and a sudden rush of air was the only warning Cædmon had before he saw a flash of metal slashing in his direction.

No time to think, he automatically spun to one side.

But not in time, a steel pole battering into his left shoulder.

The blow sent him careening off-kilter. Crashing into a stack of crates, he smashed several packing boxes on impact. A sack of cloves split open, brown nubbins spilling on to the floor in a noisy rattle.

Heaving in pain, he staggered to his feet. *Bruised all the way to the marrow, I'll warrant*. Still determined to speak to his adversary, Cædmon turned towards the other man, who stood at the ready, capably grasping a five-foot-long pole. Hoping that actions spoke louder than words, Cædmon held out both hands, palms upwards. The age-old gesture that he meant no harm. That he wanted to call a temporary truce.

'We need to talk. *Please*,' he implored. 'I have vital information to convey to you.'

Sneering, the Bête Noire hissed, 'After I crack open

your skull, you can tell it to the devil, English!' Holding the five-foot pole in a two-handed grip, the brute swung high.

Cædmon ducked low, the pole slicing through the air above his head and missing its intended target by a scant inch. *Too damned close for comfort.*

Still bent over, Cædmon charged his opponent, ramming his head into the other man's lower belly. Ploughing forward, he didn't stop until he'd hammered his foe's backside against the wall. Wood splintered and cracked. Pinned in place, the Bête Noire slammed the metal pole against Cædmon's upper back, knocking the wind out of him.

Gasping for breath, Cædmon managed to hook first his right hand, then his left, on to the pole. For several seconds they violently grappled for control of the weapon.

I need to end this. Now!

Cædmon pushed with all his might, thrusting the horizontal pole into the other man's torso. A low grunt ensued. Then a harsh groan. That being his cue, Cædmon straightened his spine and viciously ripped the pole from the other man's grasp.

Furious, he hurled the pole across the warehouse, embedding the rod into a sack of spice. As he took the Bête Noire's measure, their eyes made contact. There was no mistaking the rabid hatred in the other man's narrowed gaze.

Bull-like, the moustachioed brute snorted through flared nostrils. '*Tú eres un cabrón!*'

'Yes, I'm a right fucking bastard,' Cædmon retorted impatiently, not in the mood for any macho posturing. 'Be that as it may, I can assure you that what I have to say is crucially important.' He swiped at a wet ribbon of blood that coursed down the side of his face from an open gash on his temple.

The Bête Noire glanced at the pole protruding from the burlap bag. 'You should have held on to that, English.' Admonition issued, he grabbed his crotch and sneered . . . just before he sprinted towards the stairs.

God almighty!

His energy dissipating, Cædmon staggered after the fleeing man, refusing to call retreat. Hands braced on either side of the stairwell, he pounded down the flight of rickety steps, determined to catch his opponent.

'Wait! I have a message for Irenaeus!' he shouted in desperation as he neared the bottom of the stairs. 'It's imperative that you –'

Just then, the sole of his leather shoe punched through a weakened stair tread. Unable to stop his downwards momentum, Cædmon was propelled forward. One foot stuck in the shattered tread, the other one slid out from under him.

Collapsing on the floor in a contorted sprawl, he screamed in agony.

'Christ! I've broken my ankle!'

22

'Cædmon is chasing down a lead and, well, I'm not exactly sure when he'll be returning to the hotel,' Edie hedged, shading the truth so that she wouldn't unduly worry Gita Patel.

Recalling the fierce look on Cædmon's face before he'd charged out of the café, Edie's own fear mushroomed anew. The moustachioed 'Bête Noire', as Cædmon referred to him, had obviously followed them back to Fort Cochin.

'That's why I'm here,' Gita said, clearly excited about something. Unsnapping her leather messenger bag, she removed her laptop computer. 'I've also been chasing down a lead. Quite by accident, I discovered additional information about the Knight Templar, Fortes de Pinós.' Prying the computer open, she hit the 'on' button.

Encouraged by the other woman's enthusiasm, Edie scooted her chair a few inches closer to the laptop.

Having run into each other several minutes ago in the lobby, the two of them were now seated at a small table on the veranda of the Old Lighthouse Hotel, a white stucco remnant from the British colonial period. The out-door lounge, shaded by spatula-leafed peepal trees, was surrounded by the hotel's magnificent grounds. Just beyond the lush ferns and flowering plants, the hotel's private beach was visible, the Arabian Sea sparkling in the late-day sun.

'I just need to boot-up and log on to the Internet,' Gita said, sliding a pair of sunglasses on to the top of her head; her hair, dark and shiny as a crow's wing, was pulled into a no-nonsense bun.

Attired in a traditional unbleached Keralean sari with woven bands shot through with golden thread and a red bindi dot between her brows, Gita was certainly different-looking to when Edie first met her in Paris, the change from West to East startling. The only thing that hadn't changed were the swollen hazel eyes rimmed with dark circles. *Too many tears and not enough sleep*, Edie thought.

A waistcoated server approached. With a crisp economy of motion, he placed two napkins, an iced latte and a cup of chai on the table.

Edie immediately reached for the latte. 'I know. It's a sacrilege to be drinking coffee in a country famous for its tea, but jet lag is about to get the better of me.'

Nodding sympathetically, Gita said, 'I understand. For the last five days, I've been subsisting on chai and cigarettes.'

'You smoke cigarettes?' Edie tried to visualize it, but couldn't bring the image to mind. Somehow it didn't jive with the sari and bindi dot.

'Although it's still something of a taboo in India for women to smoke, I picked up a few packs at Charles de Gaulle airport,' Gita confessed, her cheeks flushed with colour. 'I'd read somewhere that cigarettes calm the nerves.' She raised the teacup to her lips and took a measured sip. 'Maybe I'm not smoking enough.'

In all honesty, Edie didn't know how the woman was coping emotionally, unable to fathom the torment that

Gita had been made to endure since Anala's abduction. *Whatever gets you through the night . . .*

Sugar being her drug of choice, Edie reached for the bottle of flavoured syrup, adding a sweetened spurt to her beverage.

As they waited for the computer to boot up, Edie decided to throw caution to the Indian wind and ask a question that had been niggling since Paris. 'I'm curious . . . what was Cædmon like when you knew him at Oxford? He rarely talks about his past.'

Gita lowered her teacup. For an infinitesimal second, her brow wrinkled before again smoothing out. 'Cædmon would probably cringe to hear me say this, but he was sweetly demonstrative. The snobbery at Oxford could, at times, be breathtaking, yet he possessed none of the conceited pretensions of his peers. In that bastion of conformity, he was very much his own person.' Her lips curved ever so slightly. A ghost of a smile. 'Do you by any chance know what the name "Anala" means in Sanskrit?'

Curious, Edie shook her head. 'I have no idea.'

'It means "fire". I used to tell Cædmon that he had red hair because he burned with an inner fire. After I became pregnant, my father prohibited me from mentioning his name,' she confessed in a hoarse tone of voice, one tinged with sadness. 'Naming our daughter Anala was my clandestine way of giving her –' Clearing her throat, Gita waved away the thought. 'Twenty-two years is a lifetime. What's he like now?'

The other woman having deftly turned the tables, Edie smiled, more than happy to return the favour. 'He's still an iconoclast. And, yes, he still has an inner fire, but it's tempered with the courage of conviction.' Although tempted, Edie refrained from mentioning that on occasion the 'fire' burned out of control. As it did earlier when Cædmon charged out of the café. 'And just so you know, Cædmon has book smarts *and* street smarts,' she added, to reassure herself as much as Gita.

'When I first discovered that Anala had been abducted from the house, I . . . I didn't know who else to turn to,' Gita whispered, hazel eyes welling with tears.

Hearing that, Edie intuited that Gita Patel also had no one to turn to emotionally; that she'd been going through this hellish nightmare all alone. Suddenly feeling a deep connection to the dark-haired, teary-eyed woman in the beautiful sari, Edie reached across the table and pressed Gita's hands between hers.

'Trust me. Cædmon *will* do everything in his power to find the *Evangelium Gaspar*.' Giving Gita's hands a consoling squeeze, Edie wordlessly handed her a clean napkin.

'Forgive me . . . I'm a mess.' As she wiped her cheeks, Gita smiled weakly, clearly embarrassed that she'd lost control of her emotions.

'No need to apologize. In fact, I'm impressed with how well you're keeping it together.'

More composed, Gita began tapping away on the computer keyboard. 'It won't take a moment for me to pull up the file.'

'Great. I'm interested to see what you found.' Leaning forward, Edie peered at the computer screen and read through the particulars. Finished, she glanced over at Gita and grinned. 'Ohmygod . . . you hit the jackpot.'

23

'It's your lucky day, *cabrón*,' the Bête Noire rasped. On the verge of swinging an old-fashioned metal scale at Cædmon's head, he instead flung the heavy device aside. He then glanced dismissively at the two Indian men who, hearing Cædmon's agonized scream, had rushed to the scene. Sneering at the pair, the brute stormed out of the spice warehouse.

'But not so lucky for you,' Cædmon muttered, still sprawled at the bottom of the stairs.

The ruse having worked, he gratefully allowed the two men to assist him to his feet. Brushing the dust off his trousers, he thanked each man in turn before rushing outside. Worried that he wouldn't be able to overtake the Bête Noire, when his shoe lodged in the stair tread he'd impetuously feigned a broken limb. It seemed the most expedient way to pursue without all of the huffing and puffing. He could now surreptitiously follow the other man to his lair while conserving his energy for the next bout.

Keeping to the shadows, Cædmon hurried down the lane that ran through the middle of the spice bazaar, the Bête Noire approximately fifty metres ahead of him. Arms swinging, torso listing in a macho swagger, the Spanish-speaking tough was blithely unaware that Cædmon had risen from the deep and now followed in his wake.

The fact that the man *did* speak Spanish, as well as heavily accented English, was an inexplicable but nagging detail.

Still concealed in the umbra, Cædmon rounded the corner and continued to follow his quarry through a marketplace. Closed for business, the stalls were shuttered and locked. Only a few loiterers ambled along the pavement. Completely taken in by Cædmon's ploy, the cocky bastard didn't once turn and peer in the opposite direction.

It's that sort of smug hubris that can get a man killed, Cædmon mused.

Passing a derelict truck parked on the kerb, hanks of green and red beads dangling from the windows, he stepped over to the rear passenger bumper. Hope springing, he reached under the grimy protrusion. With his arm extended, he rummaged around and – *perfect!* – slid a blackened tyre iron out of the metal rings securing it to the vehicle's underside. Weapon at the ready, he picked up the pace, the Bête Noire having veered on to a cross street.

By the time he reached the intersection, the bruiser was nowhere in sight.

Bloody hell.

Worried the fish may have escaped the trawl, he hurriedly made his way down the litter-strewn lane that was framed on either side by wooden shanties; derelict structures that he suspected had never seen better days. India's squalor was not for the faint-hearted, the stench enough to make a weaker man bend over and retch. As it was, he had to put the back of his free hand to his nostrils to block out the smell of the alley which was a putrid effluvium awash in raw sewage, rubbish and the odd animal carcass.

The Jewel in the Crown, my arse.

Day fast fading, murky grey shadows materialized. Sensing something in the gloaming, he raised the tyre iron.

Only to lower it an instant later when two pathetically thin, doe-eyed boys scampered out of a doorway.

The taller of the two lads whipped out an accordion-style souvenir book. 'Very nice. Very nice. Only twenty rupees,' he informed Cædmon, holding the book up for inspection. 'Good buy!'

'I'll give you the twenty rupees, but first you must answer a few questions.'

'You American?' the second boy enquired.

Tucking the tyre iron under his arm, Cædmon reached for his wallet. 'I'm English,' he replied, extracting the stipulated amount plus another twenty. Both boys' eyes lit up with an entrepreneurial gleam. 'There's twenty for each of you, but only if you tell the truth. Did a man with a moustache pass through here a few moments ago?'

In concert, the boys eagerly nodded.

'What was he wearing?' Cædmon next asked, the question a set-up to gauge the pair's veracity.

'Black clothes,' the shorter one said.

'Just like his friends,' the other one supplied, unasked.

'Ah! So the man with the moustache has a few friends, does he? Do you know how many?'

The taller boy held up two fingers.

Alarmed to learn of an unholy trinity, Cædmon asked

the follow-up: 'By any chance, did he meet his two friends just now?'

The question elicited simultaneous shakes of the head.

'And, lastly, do you know where the man with the moustache is staying?'

Again, it was the taller lad who took the lead. 'Follow me.'

Cædmon did, the boys navigating a labyrinth of winding lanes and narrow alleys. The maze ended at a two-storey guest house. A dilapidated colonial vestige, the building featured two covered patios on the ground floor and two balconies above. Without being asked, the taller boy silently pointed to one of the patios.

Got you, you bastard!

Their fee earned, Cædmon handed each boy twenty rupees.

'Good buy!' the smaller one enthused.

'Indeed.'

Cædmon waited until the two urchins had disappeared back into the maze before approaching the patio. His senses tightly calibrated, he soft-shoed towards the tawdry guest house. As he did, he eyed the peeling paint, mismatched curtains and rotting garbage. *My compliments. Lovely accommodations.*

In the far distance, a pair of dogs contentiously barked. In the near distance, he heard muffled footsteps. Someone scurrying home while there was still a bit of daylight left. In a matter of minutes the sun would conclude its westwards glide, twilight waiting in the wings.

Moving with a predator's slow, deliberate gait, Cædmon stepped over the low railing that bordered the patio and took up a position near the French windows. The lights were on inside the room, enabling him to peer into the jackal's lair. At a glance, he could see that there were two unmade beds and a narrow camp bed. Empty beer bottles and containers of takeaway were scattered about. An unidentified dark-skinned man was sprawled on one of the beds, a plastic shopping bag clutched in his hand.

A door suddenly opened on the other side of the shabby guestroom, spilling garish light as the Bête Noire stepped out of the bathroom. He glanced at the prone man's plastic bag and frowned. 'I told you not to drink the water.'

'Fuck you, Hector. My belly aches from the food not the water.' Wincing, the other man gingerly sat up. 'Shit, man! Everything I eat now turns to water.'

Hector.

At last Cædmon had a name; the irony of which made him smile humourlessly. *Had anyone ever been so inappropriately christened?* Hector, the firstborn son of King Priam, had been ancient Troy's most stalwart warrior, famed for his courage and honour. During the Middle Ages, Hector was esteemed as one of 'The Nine Worthies', a legendary figure who personified the chivalric ideal.

'So, where the hell have you been anyway?'

'That English *cabrón* ambushed me,' the misnamed brute informed his crony.

Arms moving in a herky-jerky motion, Hector spewed a venomous litany, going into great detail about the 'ambush'. Most of his soliloquy was in English with the odd word of Spanish. Cædmon had been to Gibraltar where a similar mash-up of English and Spanish was occasionally spoken. But these two men weren't Europeans. The idioms and macho body language strongly suggested that they were Americans. Probably first or second generation, their families having immigrated from Mexico or Central America.

An uneasy dread gripped Cædmon's lower belly, none of the puzzle pieces fitting together. *How did these two thugs find out about the* Evangelium Gaspar? By no stretch of the imagination were they academics. Hired muscle, more than likely.

Still fuming, Hector peeled off his T-shirt and tossed it on to the floor. When, an instant later, he turned round to retrieve a duffel bag, Cædmon's eyes opened wide – the man's entire back, from his waist to shoulders, was covered in an elaborate and colourful tattoo of Our Lady of Guadalupe, the patron saint of Mexico. Impeccably rendered, the Virgin was garbed in a bright green cloak and limned in a brilliant halo of golden light. Crowned with roses and a ghoulish *calavera*, a Mexican skull, she stood atop a twining serpent. A New World variation of 'a woman cloaked with the sun' from the Book of Revelation.

Seeing the religious icon was further confirmation that the Catholic Church was somehow involved in Anala's kidnapping.

'Jesus, my gut is killing me,' the unnamed man groaned. Clutching his belly, he flopped backwards on to the bed.

Showing a noticeable lack of sympathy, Hector snatched a bottle of deodorant from the dresser and, removing the cap, slathered each armpit. He then tugged a dark brown T-shirt over his head. Retrieving a leather wallet from his hip pocket, he took a quick tally. 'That should be enough.'

The other man raised his head off the mattress. 'Where you going, homie?'

'There's a whorehouse down the street. *Mi chorizo* needs a lil' curry sauce,' the lout snickered, cupping his crotch. It was an affectation that Cædmon found annoyingly tiresome. A vulgar twist on girding one's loins.

'Hey, man, you promised G-Dog that you'd control yourself.'

G-Dog? Cædmon's ears instantly pricked. An alias, obviously, he wondered if G-Dog was the mastermind behind the abduction. *If so, were G-dog and Irenaeus, the individual who sent Gita the ransom demand, one and the same?*

'I only promised G-Dog that I would play it safe.' Shoving a hand into his jeans pocket, Hector pulled out a length of wrapped prophylactics. 'Never leave *la casa* without them, *amigo*.' He grinned, proving that he was one of those beasts who actually enjoyed wallowing in the mire. 'Bitches are the same the world over. They lie on their back and show me their crack and usher me to paradise.'

'After which, you pay them the going rate,' the other man said pointedly.

Still grinning, the bastard shrugged and said, 'Heaven doesn't come cheap. Although I bet the blue-eyed Sanskrita that we bagged for G-Dog would have given it to me for free.'

The blue-eyed Sanskrita. Did he mean Anala?
The bastard!

Licking his lips, Hector smashed a balled fist into an open palm while he humped the air with his hips.

Watching the lewd pantomime, an incendiary rage surged up Cædmon's spine. In that molten instant, images flashed across his mind's eye: Anala's ransacked room; Anala's 'proof of life' photo, bound and gagged; Gita's tear-stained face. Images that blurred around the edges. Congealing into a stone-cold fury. The kind of fury that incited a savage desire to slay one's enemy. To kick in the French windows and inflict blood-drenched bodily harm.

He drew a ragged breath. Then another. *I need to stay calm. To collect as much intelligence as possible. To learn the enemy's strengths and weaknesses before launching an attack.*

The man sprawled on the bed gestured to the laptop computer on the nearby table. 'We're supposed to Skype G-Dog in a little while.'

'Stop nagging. It's just gonna be a quick fuck-and-go. I don't particularly like dark meat, but a man needs his sustenance,' Hector said over his shoulder as he headed for the door.

'*Qué cabrón,*' the bedridden man muttered sourly as the door slammed shut.

Unmoved, Cædmon watched as the other man suddenly sat up and vomited into his plastic bag. The weak animal in the herd, he had no idea that a predator lurked. Waiting to take him down.

Cædmon slid his hands over the tyre iron.

He knew right from wrong. Knew how tenuous the sliver of space between them could be.

Was he willing to cross that line to save a child he'd never met?

Yes. Absolutely.

'Well, that's that,' he whispered, ready to make his move.

24

Cædmon waited until the lone man went to the bathroom.

Seizing his chance, he used the tyre iron to pop the lock on the French windows. Hurriedly, he slipped across the threshold, the loud blare from the television in the neighbouring guest room muffling the break-in.

At a glance, he could see that the accommodations were even more dingy and cramped than they'd appeared from the other side of the glass, the walls covered in a grey, dirt-laden veneer. As with any cheap hotel, the beds sagged and the amenities were almost non-existent, consisting of only a scarred wooden table and two chairs. Surveillance photos of Anala and Gita were tacked haphazardly on to the wall adjacent to the table. Momentarily stopped in his tracks, Cædmon stared at the dozen or so photographs.

Seething, the bile rose in his throat.

Securing a hand around each end of the tyre iron, he stormed over to the closed bathroom door. On the other side, he heard a prosaic flush. Now wasn't the time to debate the situational ethics of the intended act. Now was the time to act.

With that thought in mind, he kicked in the flimsy door.

The round-faced man stood in front of the sink, the water still running. In that split second when the door flew open, their gazes met in the mirror.

Brown eyes opened wide. The shock absolute.

'Who the fuck –'

Cædmon rushed forward, squelching the query mid-stream. Looping the tyre iron over the shorter man's head, he yoked it around his neck. He then pulled with all his might, yanking the man backwards. Legs spread wide, he pulled the other man against his chest. With the iron pressed to his windpipe, he proceeded to cut off the lout's airflow.

Grabbing at the iron, violently twisting and turning, the other man tried to break free. Cædmon refused to let go. Teeth bared, he tightened his grip. The tiled bathroom was barely large enough to turn round in, let alone wage gladiatorial combat. Flailing wildly, his adversary grabbed the only weapon within reach – the metal towel rack – and yanked it free of its moorings, sending chalky wads of plaster flying through the air.

Weapon in hand, he tried to clout Cædmon in the head, swinging the chrome length over his shoulder.

Cædmon instinctively recoiled, the makeshift bludgeon missing the mark. Worried the other man might actually knock him out, he released his left hand from the tyre iron. At the same time, he forcefully swung his right arm downwards, smashing the iron into his adversary's shins.

The jackal bleated, instantly crashing to his knees.

He kicked the towel rack out of his opponent's hands, the metal length clattering against the shower stall. Then, for good measure, he struck his foe in the kidneys, causing the man to bleat even louder.

His demons barely restrained, Cædmon grabbed the man by the head and – straddling his shoulders – slammed his face into the toilet bowl. Water sloshed liberally in every direction. An obstinate brute, the man braced his hands on the porcelain rim, endeavouring to heave upwards, trying to hurl Cædmon off him.

In an uncharitable mood, Cædmon pushed down that much harder. Refusing to waver.

'If you don't cease and desist, I *will* send you to a watery grave,' he grated. Ultimatum issued, he shoved his knee-cap against the man's tenderized kidney and applied painful pressure.

Burbling into the water, the other man – *finally!* – sagged against the porcelain bowl.

Cædmon released his grip and stepped back, giving the man enough room to rise to his feet. Worried that the surrender might be short-lived, he menacingly raised the tyre iron, ready to pummel his adversary into full submission.

To his surprise, the other man suddenly lurched back towards the toilet, retching violently.

'Which merely proves that there are no swans in the cesspool,' Cædmon muttered dispassionately.

A few moments later, panting, barely able to draw breath, his conquered foe glared at him. A wet rodent put to rout, water sluiced off his temples, ears, nose and chin.

'*Condenado!*' he hissed in a strained whisper. Raising a hand, he rubbed his bruised windpipe.

Cædmon didn't bother pointing out that he'd already been consigned to the ranks of the damned. Years ago, in a dark alley in Belfast, when he pulled the trigger and killed the Irish terrorist who'd masterminded a bomb attack on a London tube station. A soul-sucking 'eye for an eye'.

Instead, he snarled, 'Be grateful that you still have a voice.' Snatching hold of the man's right wrist, Cædmon twisted it. *Hard.* Like his cohort, the man had a Chi-Rho cross branded in middle of his palm. *In hoc signo vinces.* In this sign, you shall conquer.

Like bloody hell!

Cuffing a hand on his adversary's upper arm, Cædmon yanked the man out of the bathroom.

'I'm not alone,' his prisoner insisted. 'The others will be back . . . *soon!*'

'You're not the only one who's engaged in surveillance activities,' Cædmon informed him. With his free hand, he grabbed one of the wooden chairs from the scarred table and dragged it to the middle of the room. He then shoved his hostage on to it.

'I don't know what you're talking about, you pasty-faced *pendejo*!'

Ignoring the insult, Cædmon said matter-of-factly, 'I happen to know that your cohort Hector is at the local bordello with his trousers, presumably, around his ankles. Pity the poor prostitute,' he added, jabbing the end of the tyre iron into the man's chest, a silent warning to remain seated. 'As for the third member of your triad, he's more than likely sitting outside Gita Patel's house, keeping an eye on her comings and goings.'

Eyes narrowing, the man opened his mouth to protest, only to think better of it at the last. Clamping his jaw closed, he sullenly folded his arms over his chest.

Hostage subdued, Cædmon snatched the duffel bag that the Bête Noire had earlier rummaged through. Tucking the iron under his arm, he unzipped the bag and unceremoniously dumped the contents on to the table. Keen to uncover actionable intelligence, he rifled through the various articles of clothing and sundry toiletries. Popping the lid on the aspirin bottle, he shook three tablets loose, his shoulder and ankle aching from the earlier fracas at the spice bazaar. Not about to drink the tap water, he chomped down with his teeth, mashing the pills into a paste before swallowing.

The other man stared, bug-eyed. 'You crazy motherfucker!'

'Yes, unfortunately for you, they gave me a day pass from the asylum.'

'You're such a sick fuck, I actually believe it.'

Tuning out the litany of foul-mouthed complaints that ensued, Cædmon removed a US passport and airline ticket from the interior pocket of the duffel bag. He flipped open the blue cover and quickly scanned the particulars. *Name: Hector Calzada. Age: 21. Place of birth: New York City.* Tossing it on to the pile, he next examined the airline ticket. Also issued to Hector Calzada, it was an open ticket from Mumbai to Newark International Airport in New Jersey.

It made him wonder if Anala had been taken to the US. *Christ! Could the situation get any worse?*

Shoving that dread thought to the wayside, he grabbed the next piece of luggage off the floor. A dog-eared bible thumped on to the table, the initials RSV-CE stamped on the leather cover. *The Revised Standard Version Catholic Edition.* Beneath that was the Latin phrase *Sanguis Christi.* The Blood of Christ. Disinterested, he shoved it aside and reached for the blue US passport. It was in the name of one Javier Esteban Aveles who, like Calzada, had been born in New York City.

He cast a glance at his seated captive. 'I take it that you're Javier.'

'*Hah-vee-air!*' the man spat out, pronouncing his name with a soft 'h' instead of a hard 'j'.

Cædmon smiled insincerely, having purposefully butchered the name. 'Please accept my apologies.' He snatched the third and last duffel bag, upending its contents. This one belonged to a 22-year-old New Yorker named Roberto Diaz. The last man in the unholy trinity.

'Hey, man, just take my wallet and get the hell out of here.'

Cædmon spared Javier a quick glance. 'I don't want your money. I do, however, wish to have a little chat. But not with you.'

He'd already determined that the three banditos were simply hired muscle, the reason why Hector refused to speak to him at the spice bazaar. If he was to convey his message, he had to converse with their handler, G-Dog. To that end, he dragged the other chair over to the bureau and sat down in front of the laptop computer. Taking it out of sleep mode, he accessed the Skype feature and clicked on the phone directory, dismayed to see that there were no contact numbers listed.

Hefting the computer in his left hand, he walked over to Aveles and set it on his lap. 'Call G-Dog.'

'Go to hell!' Aveles retorted, quick-fire. 'I don't know his phone number.'

As he considered his options, Cædmon lightly smacked the tyre iron against his left palm. Clearly, the man had drawn a line in the sand; one that he refused to cross. *So be it.* He would be only too happy to usher Javier Aveles over the great divide. To inflict enough bodily harm to ensure full cooperation.

Intending to decimate Aveles's slavish devotion to his master, he said, 'Make the fucking Skype call or I *will* crack your skull wide open.'

Muttering in Spanish, Aveles clicked out a long string of digits on the keypad. As he committed the number to memory, Cædmon recognized the international calling code for the United States. The number dialled, Cædmon grabbed the laptop and strode back to the bureau. Reseating himself, he waited as the computer beeped and chirped, noisily processing the connection.

Several moments later, a face materialized on the screen – a middle-aged man with even features, thick pewter-coloured hair and an olive complexion. Visible from the chest up, Cædmon could clearly see that he wore a black shirt and clerical collar.

'Yes?' the other man intoned, a quizzical expression on his face.

Not altogether surprised that G-Dog was a Catholic priest, he spoke in a clear, concise tone of voice. 'My name is Cædmon Aisquith and I'm calling in regards to my daughter, Anala Patel.'

The man on the other side of the world was clearly horror-struck. '*Ay, Dios mío!*'

'Let's leave God out of this, shall we?' Not giving the other man a chance to respond, Cædmon continued and said, 'Do you prefer to be called G-Dog or Irenaeus?'

'Wh-who's Irenaeus?' the priest stammered.

Cædmon hid his surprise. 'He's the author of the third-century classic *Adversus Haereses*. But it matters not. We can't all be biblical scholars. That, of course, is the reason why you kidnapped Anala; so that someone more knowledgeable could unearth the *Evangelium Gaspar*. Since I'm a Templar scholar, I am that person.'

The priest shook his head, the confusion having yet to clear from his eyes. 'No one has mentioned a father. We were informed that . . . that there is only the mother.'

His remarks caused a dull ache to settle behind Cædmon's breastbone. He wanted very much to reach through the computer screen and strangle the iniquitous priest. He didn't want to engage in this sham civility.

'Being a priest, you may not have great experience in these matters, but I can assure you that it does take both a man and a woman to produce a child. Barring, of course, the one notable exception,' he added sarcastically. 'As I stated already, I will meet your ransom demand, but I want you to call off your three watchdogs. And one last thing . . . is it possible to get an extension on the deadline?'

Vehemently shaking his head, the priest said, 'The deadline has been set and cannot be changed.'

Cædmon frowned. The man had to know that finding the *Evangelium Gaspar* would prove a daunting task.

'And what happens if I can't find the *Evangelium Gaspar*?'

Unable to meet his pixilated gaze, the priest bent his head and muttered, 'You'll never see your daughter again.'

Hearing the threat verbalized caused Cædmon to suffer a pain so precise, it nearly cleaved him in two.

'Rest assured. I *will* find your blasted gospel,' he said in an even enough tone, refusing to let any doubt or uncertainty creep into his voice.

'I'm pleased to hear it.'

The bill of particulars delivered, he disconnected the call. Getting to his feet, Cædmon strode towards the French windows, intending to exit the guest room the same way he entered.

'Shit, man! Are you telling me that you shoved my head in the john just so you could make a fucking phone call?' Aveles screeched.

Cædmon shot the young thug a disparaging glance. 'Count your blessings, Javier . . . I very much wanted to kill you.'

25

Sanguis Christi Fellowship, Dutchess County, New York

Unnerved by the silence, Father Gracián Santos got up from his desk, walked over and turned on the radio. It was set to a pop music station, his secretary, Bernadette Dombrowski, a fan of 'the oldies'.

Since Bernadette wasn't there and Gracián couldn't stomach the syrupy sounds of the Beach Boys, he turned the dial to a Spanish language station. While the *banda* music was far from soothing, the Mexican-style polka tune helped ameliorate the palpable silence, the music drowning out the sound of his ragged breathing.

He didn't like being alone. Never had. It caused him to think dark thoughts. Made the old memories resurface.

And was there anything lonelier than being the only person inside sprawling Mercy Hall?

Like a man condemned to a strange, surreal sort of hell, Gracián had spent the last couple of days rambling aimlessly in the empty 200-room mansion. Peering into unoccupied classrooms. Peeking into vacant dormitories. As with any father who missed his children, he was anxious for the tour buses to return to the Fellowship grounds and unload the boisterous passengers.

It would, however, be another week and a half before the student body returned to the Fellowship. Bernadette and several other staff members had taken everyone on a two-week Catholic retreat in the Catskills Mountains, Cardinal Fiorio having used his influence to arrange for the all-expenses-paid trip.

With the students' departure, the only souls now prowling the 300-acre estate were Gracián and the three Diablos who were guarding the Patel girl. Gracián implicitly trusted the three former gang-bangers. Although much younger than him, they were 'blood brothers', the bond extending across the generations. Forged on the dark and dangerous streets of New York City's *El Barrio*.

Uncertain what to make of the latest development, Gracián walked over to the Tudor-style window. Seeing his own worried reflection, he frowned. The fear that the Englishman wouldn't be able to find the ancient gospel caused the muscles in his belly to instantly cramp.

No! It WILL happen, he was quick to assure himself. *I am the living proof that insurmountable odds can be beaten.* Certainly, no one would have ever dared to think that a blooded member of the notorious *Los Diablos de Santa Muerte* gang could become a Roman Catholic priest. At least no one in his Spanish Harlem neighbourhood would have thought it possible.

Born in the Puebla region of Mexico, Gracián immigrated to New York City with his family in the early 1980s. The Santos family quickly settled into one of the block-style tenements that housed so many of the Spanish-speaking immigrants who'd crossed the border in search of a better life, although many native-born Americans might question how good a life could be with a family of six crammed into a small two-bedroom apartment.

To help with the family coffers, Gracián had taken a part-time job after school at the corner bodega. A decision that would change the course of his life.

While many youths joined a gang because they mistakenly thought that it was a thrilling, even glamorous, way to live one's life, Gracián accidentally wandered into it. It happened late one afternoon when he was on bended knee stocking the shelves. Three swaggering tattooed males entered the bodega; at which point, the owner, an older man from Guadalajara, became visibly nervous. Without uttering a word, the owner opened the cash register and handed one of the teens a wad of cash. A second teen strolled over to Gracián.

'Do you want to make some real money?' the belligerent youth had asked.

Thinking the question asinine – as though any intelligent person would ever say 'No' – Gracián had shrugged and said, 'Who doesn't?'

With that reply, Gracián Santos was recruited into *Los Diablos de Santa Muerte*. No application required. However, as he quickly learned, there was an unwritten handbook full of rules that had to be strictly obeyed. On pain of death.

To an outsider, those rules harkened to a patriarchal Latin culture that idealized the notion of machismo. And Gracián admitted that you couldn't get more macho than the Diablos initiation, one common to all Latino gangs – 'jumping in'. It was a savage rite of passage, with new members forced to endure a brutal beating administered by three to six gang members. Vicious kicks. Full-face punches. A merciless barrage of flesh pounding on flesh. After which, if you survived the ordeal without crying out, the gang members would help the bloodied piñata to his feet and offer him a warm and hearty congratulation. *'Now you're a homeboy! One of us. A real man.'*

At first, Gracián enjoyed the back-slapping camaraderie and partying with his homies. Like all of the Diablos, Gracián *never* backed away from a stare or backed down from a challenge. And though he felt guilty about dealing drugs and extorting cash from hard-working Latinos, he never raised an objection for fear of crossing Felipe Torres, his crew leader. Unquestioning obedience was the Diablos' first unwritten rule.

Which is why, when Felipe handed Gracián a serrated knife and ordered him to 'silence' a rival gang member – and bring back the proof – Gracián was forced to commit the most gruesome act he could have ever imagined. When he'd first joined the Diablos, he knew that the gang motto *'Blood in, blood out'* wasn't an empty expression. He'd always accepted that the day would come when he'd be forced to kill someone to prove his unswerving fidelity. He'd just assumed that his initiation kill would be something impersonal, like a drive-by shooting. A murderous act that happened in a speeding blur and could be easily forgotten.

Terrified that he wouldn't be able to follow through on Felipe's order, an act of cowardice that would lead to his own execution, Gracián smoked enough crack cocaine to desensitize him to what he was about to do.

But, as he'd discovered, nothing can desensitize a man

to hearing a victim's hideous shrieks. Or to feeling the warm blood that splattered on to his cheeks as he 'silenced' the rival gang member by severing his head from his neck.

The guilt that ensued in the weeks and months that followed was like a festering wound that wouldn't heal, Gracián plagued by nightmares and night sweats. He desperately wanted to quit the gang, but couldn't. Membership was for life. *Blood in, blood out.* The only way to leave was in a pine box.

Too late, he realized that he'd thrown in his lot with a pack of maladaptive psychopaths who collectively suffered from a dangerous sense of entitlement, the homies all bloodthirsty maniacs who would beat, maim or kill with a disturbing lack of remorse. While they proudly considered themselves 'warriors', the Diablos were little more than feral animals.

A few months after his grisly initiation kill, Gracián was arrested and charged with being an accessory in an armed robbery. Although he was only sixteen years of age, he was tried as an adult and sentenced to five years at Sing Sing, the maximum security prison in Ossining, New York.

It was there – behind the high concrete walls and razor-wire fences – that his life would again change dramatically in an unforeseen way.

'She says that she doesn't eat meat because she's a Hindu. What do you want me to do, G-Dog?'

'Hmm?' Hurled out of his dark reverie, Gracián turned away from the window, surprised to see Jacko Maciel standing in the doorway of his office.

Jacko was one of the six former Diablo gang members

who worked in the Fellowship's maintenance department. Because of their criminal records, no other employer would hire them, but Gracián was unable to turn his back on the young men. Despite their protestations to the contrary, he suspected that the only reason the Diablos remained at the Sanguis Christi Fellowship was because they'd been placed on some crew leader's hit list and sought safe haven in Dutchess County.

Having taken on the role of father figure, Gracián was hopeful that, in time, the Diablos would repent their heinous sins and open their hearts to the Lord.

However, given all that had transpired in the last week, he was no longer certain that a religious conversion was on the horizon. The stain was too dark.

26

Biting back a joyful yelp, Edie watched as Cædmon unlimbered his tall frame from the motorized rickshaw.

'Cædmon! I'm over here!' she hollered, waving an arm in the air to get his attention. She'd been sitting at the pool for the last two hours waiting for his return.

Overcome with relief, she leapt from her poolside deckchair and ran across the dimly lit hotel lawn towards the front veranda, heedless of the fact that she was attired in a red bikini, a colourful sarong wrapped around her waist. While it was perfectly proper attire for the pool, it wasn't so proper for the rest of the hotel, Indians being a modest bunch.

She met Cædmon on the circular drive in front of the lobby entrance. About to hurl herself at his chest, she pulled up short.

'Oh my god! Where have you been?' Horrified by his battered appearance, she gently touched his face, shocked to see dried blood on his temple and smeared all over his shirt front.

'The correct question is, "Where haven't I been?" A trip to hell and back would have been an easier jaunt.'

'Let's go sit by the pool and you can tell me what happened,' she said, taking him by the arm. As she led him across the lawn, she wondered if he had any idea how worried she'd been. Having spent the last several hours on tenterhooks, she'd been on the verge of contacting the local authorities when the rickshaw pulled up to the hotel.

Grunting softly, Cædmon eased himself into a deck-chair.

In nursing mode, Edie snatched her water bottle and a clean napkin. Soaking the cloth, she used it to clean the gash on his temple. 'The next time that you go off the reservation, I'd appreciate a phone call or text message –' she glanced pointedly at the mobile phone in plain view on the tabletop –'*anything* to let me know that you're okay.'

'Why are you so upset? It's not as though we're joined at the hip. Furthermore, I'm perfectly capable of taking care of myself.' As if to prove that very point, he shoved her hand aside.

'Well and good, but I still worry about you.' The reason why she'd called him, *repeatedly*, finally abandoning the effort when she surmised that he'd turned off his mobile.

To Edie's surprise, Cædmon suddenly reached for the hand he'd only just spurned. 'I'm sorry, love. You're right. I should have called with an update,' he said contritely. 'Ever since Gita showed up in Paris, my gut's been twisted in a Gordian knot.'

Hoping to mitigate the awkward interlude, Edie slid a plate of fresh fruit in front of him. She'd ordered the mangos, melons and bananas a short while ago, but had barely touched the plate, too upset to eat. 'So, tell me what happened. Did you speak to the guy with the moustache?'

Cædmon forked a cube of mango. 'Ah! You're refer-ring to Hector Calzada.'

'You found out his name. That's great!' she enthused,

relieved that he'd made some progress. 'What else did you learn?'

'I learned a great many things.' For several long seconds, Cædmon stared at the palm fronds that rimmed the edge of the pool before saying, 'Anala was abducted by three young Latin-American men, all of whom hail from New York City. Moreover, they're working under the tutelage of a Catholic priest.'

'So then the bad guy really does dress in black.'

'No surprise there. The history of the Catholic Church is saturated with blood and gore. The stuff of legends.' Scowling, he speared a piece of watermelon on to the end of his fork. 'And though it took a bit of coaxing, I managed a Skype call with the duplicitous priest.'

'Did you ask him for an extension on the deadline?'

'I did. And the request was promptly denied.'

Hearing that, Edie shook her head, baffled. 'I don't get it. The Catholic Church has been searching for the *Evangelium Gaspar* for the last seven hundred years. Now, suddenly, they have to have it in four days' time.'

'A fact that makes me sick to the back teeth.' Finished with the fruit plate, Cædmon shoved it aside.

'I also have an update,' Edie said, reaching for her iPad. 'Earlier today, Gita stopped by the hotel to share some very interesting research pertaining to Fortes de Pinós.'

Cædmon sat up straighter in his chair. 'Enlighten me. Please. I'm in dire need of some uplifting news.'

Happy to comply, Edie pulled up the genealogy chart that Gita had discovered online. 'It turns out that our fourteenth-century Knight Templar has a twenty-first-century direct descendant: a Spaniard named Luis Fidelis de Pinós, who happens to be the twelfth Marqués de Bagá.'

'How could Fortes de Pinós have a direct descendant? The Knights Templar were a celibate order.'

Sliding her chair a few inches closer to his, Edie showed Cædmon the genealogy chart. 'As you can see, in the year 1272, when he was eighteen years old, Fortes got married. He and the missus then had four children. Ten years later, his wife died. At which point in time, he joined the Knights Templar.'

Cædmon stared pensively at the iPad. 'Since widowers were allowed to join the order, it does explain how a man who took a vow of celibacy could have a direct heir.'

'Funny that you should mention the word "heir",' Edie replied, pulling up the next computer file, a news article from the English language edition of *El País*, a leading Spanish newspaper. 'According to this article, the Marqués de Bagá runs an organization headquartered in Madrid called the Sovereign Order of the Temple.'

His lips twisted into a sarcastic sneer. 'Fancy themselves to be latter-day Knights Templar, do they?'

'Do they ever,' she said with a vigorous nod, having spent several hours online researching the group. 'Not only do the members of the Sovereign Order of the Temple claim to be the rightful heirs of the medieval Knights Templar, they recently filed documents in the Spanish court system to sue the Vatican for return of all property and valuables stolen from Spanish Templar preceptories in the wake of the fourteenth-century *auto-da-fé*. Assets which the Marqués claims are worth twenty billion euros.'

'Even if Jesus Christ himself adjudicated the case, the Sovereign Order of the Temple will never win their case,' Cædmon said. 'The Vatican has an army of canon lawyers at their disposal; legal sharks who'll ensure the Holy See doesn't relinquish one euro of their ill-gotten gains. While it makes for a headline-grabbing news story, I suspect the Marqués de Bagá is nothing more than a Spaniard looking to make an easy haul.'

'Not necessarily,' she countered. 'The Marqués has publicly stated that he has no desire to financially ruin the Vatican. He merely wants to bring to the public's attention the maniacal plot instigated against the Knights Templar in 1307 which culminated in the order's ignominious downfall. Personally, I think it's highly significant that this man is a descendant of Fortes de Pinós.'

Staring at the iPad, Cædmon pushed out a deep breath. 'I agree. Even if the Marqués de Bagá has no knowledge of the *Evangelium Gaspar*, he may be able to provide us with some useful information regarding his ancestor.'

'My thinking exactly. So, let's go to Madrid and put the screws on him. Figuratively speaking,' she amended a split second later, her gaze darting to Cædmon's bloodstained shirt. 'I already checked the airline schedule. There's a flight that leaves for Madrid in four hours' time.'

'Although a Spanish aristocrat thirty generations removed is a bit of a dark horse, at the moment it's the only nag in the race.' Placing a hand on each arm of the chair, Cædmon wearily pushed himself to his feet. 'If you'll excuse me, I'm going up to our hotel room to take a shower before we leave for the airport.'

'I think I'll stay out here a bit longer.'

'Right.'

Her heart in her throat, Edie watched as Cædmon made his way to the hotel's front entrance. Stoic though he might be, he was going through an emotional crisis.

One that she feared would tear him asunder.

27

Porta Sant'Anna, The Vatican

'Rome, sweet Rome,' Cardinal Franco Fiorio muttered under his breath as he sidestepped the cluster of jabbering, finger-pointing tourists who blocked his path.

Wrinkling his nose at the noxious fumes belched by a passing motorbike, he crossed Via di Porta Angelica and headed towards the Borgo. Not only did all roads lead to the Eternal City, but they were often congested with a jostling mix of the faithful, bibles and rosaries in hand; wide-eyed tourists; and the increasingly rude rabble. The thundering herd, as Franco secretly referred to them.

Despite the fact that Roman Catholics around the world were in the midst of the *novemdiales*, the official nine days of mourning that began after Pope Pius XIII's Requiem Mass, the lively crowds appeared far from bereaved. Last week's grief had clearly dissipated, replaced with a flurry of anticipation over the upcoming conclave.

That air of expectancy had invaded the papal city as well, turning it into a viper's nest of jockeying cardinals working their 'constituency'. All very subtle, of course, no one wanting to be accused of campaigning for the papacy. None the less, Vatican City was abuzz with whispers. Rumours. Spies everywhere. Plotting and scheming how best to position their candidate.

A lone wolf, Franco didn't trust anyone within the Leonine Walls.

Slipping a hand into his breast pocket, he removed a pair of dark-tinted sunglasses. To the casual observer, he was a short, stocky, balding priest, dressed in a black clerical suit with a Roman collar. But to those with a more attentive eye, the pectoral cross that hung from the chain around his neck was the telltale clue that Franco Fiorio was, in fact, a Prince of the Church. One who'd left the castle grounds for an early-evening stroll down Borgo Pio, a narrow cobblestone lane teeming with cafés and family-owned businesses. Like several other prelates, he chose to reside in the Borgo rather than the papal city.

Feeling his mobile phone vibrate, Franco unclipped it from his waist and checked the display screen. Annoyed that the Vice-Prefect had sent a text message regarding a misplaced engineering memo, Franco deleted it. He'd hoped that it was another status report from Father Gracián Santos. Earlier, he'd received a most enlightening update – the medieval scholar Cædmon Aisquith was the abducted girl's father. A thrilling turn of events that convinced Franco that the Hand of Providence was orchestrating events. He'd promptly ordered Father Santos to question the girl and ascertain if she knew anything about the Knights Templar or the *Evangelium Gaspar*.

As he made his way to his favourite café, Franco passed two young Roman women garbed in what, fifty years ago, would have been considered suitable attire for a pair of streetwalkers. While more than a few clerics slyly enjoyed the bouncing, jiggling displays, Franco was disgusted with the short skirts and cleavage-bearing tops worn by so many women. Ever since the sweeping mandates of Vatican II went into effect in the 1960s, untold numbers of Catholics had succumbed to a moral depravity. And because the Church had, for all intents and purposes, turned a blind eye, Catholics in ever-increasing numbers were using birth control, getting divorced and eschewing the sacraments with apathetic regularity.

Too many Catholics lack the ardent faith of the Church Fathers.

Shoulders slumped with fatigue, Franco seated himself at a vacant table shaded by a white canvas umbrella, setting his attaché case on an empty chair. No sooner had he removed his sunglasses than a waiter garbed in a vermillion gold waistcoat placed a glass of sparkling Prosecco on the table. The management knew his daily routine and always took care to have his preferred table and his favourite aperitif ready for him.

'Will there be anything else, *Excellenza*?'

'No, that will be all. Thank you, Giovanni.'

Sitting at the café and savouring a glass of Prosecco was the only part of his day when, for a few brief moments, Franco could be, not a man of God, but a man of the people. Able to enjoy the fabled *dolce vita*.

Raising the glass to his lips, Franco took an appreciative sniff. By no stretch of the imagination was this the life that he'd dreamed about as a boy growing up in Baltimore, Maryland. His father, Sal, a second-generation Italian-American, had proudly fought in the 'Big One', as he called it, with the US Fifth Army. While stationed in southern Italy, he fell in love with sixteen-year-old Rosella de Luca, convincing the young beauty to marry him. Even though Rosella ran off with the spindly-legged corporal, she never made a secret of the fact that she had big dreams. Big American dreams. But as the years passed and those dreams remained unfulfilled, Rosella was forced to take matters into her own hands.

A devout Catholic, his mother belatedly realized that the Church could provide their working-class family with the social status she so fervently desired. Soon it wasn't enough to attend early-morning Mass *every* morning. Her two sons had to become altar boys at Fourteen Holy Martyrs Church, her husband had to take on a leadership role within the Knights of Columbus, and Rosella, who overcame the acute self-consciousness that she suffered because of her broken English, became heavily involved in local Catholic charities.

To Rosella's unmitigated delight, 'Campaign Piety', as Sal had dubbed it, was entirely successful. In no time at all, Father McCarty was coming round for dinner on a regular basis and, even more significant, Monsignor Hellerman would occasionally stop by for coffee. And, joy of joys, his mother was invited to join Our Lady of Perpetual Help Rosary Club, a small group of Catholic ladies who gathered once a week to pray, drink coffee, eat sugary pastries and make rosaries for Catholics in Third-World countries.

Between daily Mass and entertaining parish priests, the Fiorios lived a typical Roman Catholic existence. Until the *miraculous* event occurred. One that would forever change their lives and have a far-reaching influence.

The unexpected event happened on a Saturday morning in mid-May while Rosella was outside planting a bed of petunias in their postage-stamp of a backyard. It was there that she was blinded by a flash of bright light. Although the day had started out clear and sunny, she was suddenly shrouded by a vaporous mist infused with the scent of roses. A beautiful woman, garbed in an immaculate white robe, her head modestly covered with a long blue veil, appeared in the mist. Rosella, awestruck, was rendered speechless. Several seconds later, the diaphanous lady abruptly vanished, smoke and all.

The only thing that remained was the lingering scent of Damask rose.

Awestruck, certain that she'd been the recipient of a divine visitation by the Blessed Virgin Mary, Rosella excitedly regaled everyone at Fourteen Holy Martyrs Church.

Much to the parishioners acute discomfort.

A few of the women in the Rosary Club even went so far as to intimate that the 'vision' may have been a figment of Rosella Fiorio's vivid Italian imagination.

Fearing suddenly that the divine visitation would invite disdainful gossip, Franco's mother immediately made a large withdrawal from the family savings account and used the money to purchase a four-foot-high painted plaster statue of the Blessed Virgin Mary. The statue was prominently installed on a pedestal in the front hallway. Rosella then nagged Sal into building a small altar in front of the statue so that she could illuminate Our Lady with devotional candles set into little red glass holders. It was all part of his mother's heartfelt attempt to lure the Blessed Virgin into making another appearance. Which she obligingly did, eight months later.

The second visitation happened late one night as Rosella was praying the rosary in front of the statue. His mother claimed later that she'd involuntarily fallen asleep and was suddenly awakened when she fell off the velvet kneeler. In the next instant, the beautiful lady, cloaked in radiant beams of light, appeared near the stair landing.

Several moments passed in enraptured silence. Then, extending her right hand in Rosella's direction, the beautiful lady said, in a soft melodic voice, 'My Son and your son.'

Message delivered, the lady dematerialized in a quick flash of light, leaving behind thirteen red rose petals scattered on the stair landing. The fact that it was the middle of January convinced their parish priest, Father McCarty, that a blessed event had indeed occurred. '*The white roses in Paradise all blushed red when kissed by the Virgin Mary*,' he had informed everyone in a hushed, reverential tone of voice.

Vindicated, his mother became something of a local celebrity. At least in Roman Catholic circles.

Not exactly certain what to make of his mother's visitation, Franco, along with his father and brother Angelo, were baffled by the message given to Rosella – 'My Son and your son.'

What did it mean?

Rosella Fiorio wasn't the least bit confused by the divine communication. She knew *exactly* what it meant. And as Franco was soon to discover, those five fateful words would have momentous consequences for the entire Fiorio family.

Finished with his Prosecco, the Prefect of the Secret Archives set his glass on the table, signalling to the waiter that he was ready to take his leave.

Even now, fifty-four years after the fact, those five words still reverberated.

Continually reminding Franco that he was the chosen one. A Defender of the Faith. Commissioned by God to save His Holy Church here on earth.

28

'*The Knights Templar!*' Anala Patel exclaimed. 'Are you daft?'

Squinting her eyes, she peered at the dark silhouette barely visibly behind the bright lamp. A few moments ago, the strange man, whom the guard called 'G-Dog', had entered the panelled room and begun to question her.

'What would make you think that my mother knows *anything* about the Knights Templar? Her field of expertise is Indian culture. Obviously, you kidnapped the wrong daughter,' Anala added, beginning to suspect that she was the victim of a horrible blunder.

But as horrible as her predicament was, she couldn't even imagine the emotional tumult that her mother was suffering. All because some idiot had abducted the wrong person.

How could this have happened?

As her mother's image took shape in her mind's eye, Anala unwillingly recalled their last heated argument, her eyes quickly filling with remorseful tears. Drawing her knees to her chin, she bent her head and sniffled, embarrassed that the quiz master was witnessing her teary-eyed moment of weakness.

'It would seem that your mother is keeping secrets from you.'

Hearing that, Anala raised her head and stared into the gleaming light, the man's meaning so opaque as to be incomprehensible. The fact that she couldn't see G-Dog's face only added to her confusion.

Step out where I can see you, you bloody coward! I'm a defenceless woman. What are you afraid of?

'Earlier I spoke to your father and he informed me that he's a Templar scholar.'

'*What!?*' Anala practically screeched, the interrogation having just taken a very bizarre turn.

Does my abduction actually have something to do with Dev Malik?

Even as she thought it, Anala instantly ruled out the possibility. She hadn't seen her father in nearly twenty years, the man having turned his back on her and her mother.

Certain now that the abduction was a case of mistaken identity, Anala said, 'Dev Malik is a computer engineer. As I said, you've abducted the wrong person.'

'No mistake has been made,' G-Dog retorted in his slightly accented voice. 'The resemblance between you and Cædmon Aisquith, particularly in the eyes, is too strong to be a mere coincidence.'

'First of all, I don't know anyone named Cædmon Aisquith. Secondly, lots of people have blue eyes, none of whom I am related to. And, thirdly, I would be flabbergasted to discover that Dev Malik knows *anything* about the Knights Templar.'

'Stop lying to me,' the disembodied voice snapped. 'According to your father's web page, he has a graduate degree in medieval studies from Oxford University where, I presume, he met your mother.'

'How could my parents have met at Oxford? Dev Malik

attended the Indian Institute of Technology in New Delhi and –' . . . *and he has dark brown eyes.*

Anala's mouth gaped, sails slackened.

Granted, she'd always wondered how she'd ended up with baby blues since neither of her parents had blue eyes. She'd just assumed that it was a freak accident of nature. Even though, according to a biology course she once took, it was genetically impossible for a woman with hazel-green eyes and a man with brown eyes to produce a blue-eyed offspring. While her maternal grandmother, an Englishwoman, was blue-eyed, her father would still have had to contribute a dominant gene for blue eyes.

Ergo, Dev Malik cannot be my father.

Instead, some bloke she'd never heard of named Cædmon Aisquith was her biological parent.

Can that actually be true? she wondered, stunned. If the answer to that question was 'yes', it would explain why Dev Malik had disowned her.

Turning his back on her because she was some other man's child.

Shaken to the core, Anala stared at the glaring light.

'It would seem that your mother is keeping secrets from you.'

From where she sat, it was the mother of all secrets.

29

Too tired to shave, Cædmon padded out to the bedroom, the hot shower having done little to revive him.

A deluxe accommodation, their hotel room boasted teak furnishings, canopied bed, luxurious fabrics and a set of French windows that opened on to a balcony with a sea view. Lovely amenities that he didn't have the time to enjoy or appreciate.

Gritting his teeth, every moment laden with pain, he proceeded to get dressed. Although tempted to lie down and take a catnap, it was an indulgence that he couldn't afford. Particularly since he had little to show for his day's labour other than G-Dog's phone number and the name of Fortes de Pinós's twenty-first-century descendant, the Marqués de Bagá. The phone number he intended to run past his old Group Leader at MI5. If he could get an actual name and location for the duplicitous cleric, he would be able put a rescue mission into play.

Grunting softly, Cædmon eased a clean polo shirt over his head, his shoulder still throbbing from the earlier attack in the spice bazaar. Finished dressing, he sat down at the writing table. Nothing that he'd discovered over the course of the interminably long day had brought him any closer to deciphering Fortes de Pinós's enigmatic riddle and finding the *Evangelium Gaspar*.

Pen and paper in hand, he proceeded to scribble the riddle on to the sheet of paper.

'*To see the house where Lucas dwelled, the faithful pilgrim sought the brother's way. Setting forth from the lion's castle, he dropped the French iron in a Spanish harbour.*'

'What the bloody hell does it mean?' he muttered, De Pinós having crafted a medieval conundrum. A brain teaser, to use the modern parlance.

He assumed that the word 'pilgrim' had something to do with Château Pèlerin in the Holy Land, a famous pilgrimage site. But that was merely an academic hunch without any tangible evidence.

Damn you, Fortes de Pinós.

Staring at the sheet of paper, he had the nagging suspicion that there was something important, some clue, some tidbit in the day's potpourri that he'd overlooked. But he had no idea what that 'something' might be.

Think, man!

As though he were shrieking at a corpse, the admonition rang hollow, the jet lag having taken its toll. He should have slept on the flight to Kerala, but he'd been too anxious. Too overwrought. Too afraid that he wouldn't be able to solve the damned riddle by Sunday's deadline.

'Hannibal crossing the Alps, elephants in tow, might well prove an easier feat than finding the *Evangelium Gaspar*,' he muttered.

And then there were the three banditos, Hector, Javier and Roberto. Their presence was a chilling reminder that the danger was very real, reiterating that he now had less than four days to save Anala Patel's life.

A drowning man will catch at a straw, the Proverb well says.

Truth be told, he was willing to grasp at anything to rescue Anala, decency be damned; the moral high ground was out of reach to a drowning man.

In dire need of a pick-me-up, Cædmon got up from the desk and strode over to the kitchenette that was tucked into an alcove on the other side of the room. Having yet to recover from the heat of the day, he grabbed a bottle of Kingfisher beer out of the miniature refrigerator. As he did, it occurred to him that he'd had his first taste of Kingfisher beer more than two decades ago. With Gita Patel, of all people. They'd gone to an Indian restaurant in Oxford. Café Masala. Or some similarly named eatery. His palate not nearly as cultivated in his youth, he'd ordered the mildest dish on the menu, palak paneer. But even the mashed spinach and curd cheese proved too much for his virginal taste buds, Gita laughing uproariously as he'd gulped his Kingfisher to put out the fire. *The follies of youth.* Although, strangely enough, from that day forward, Kingfisher was always his beer of choice.

That he could still recall details of his relationship with Gita with any specificity frankly surprised him. It made him think that the relationship's denouement had been far more painful than he'd owned up to at the time. That he had, as with so many of the painful episodes of his life, shoved it into a mental lock box and promptly thrown away the key. Which is not the same thing as wiping the memory slate clean.

Hit with a lacerating pain, his eyes filled with tears.

Christ, Gita! Why didn't you tell me twenty-two years ago that I'd fathered a child?

He shuddered as he experienced the sudden terrifying sense of falling through the floor. Except there was no crash landing. Instead, he kept smashing through to the floor below. Over and over and over again.

Taking several deep breaths, Cædmon waited for the moment to pass. He wanted very much to shove it all – the pain, the fear, the anger – into the box.

But he couldn't.

'Damn you, Fortes de Pinós.'

With no small measure of irony, it occurred to him that the name 'Fortes' was derived from the Latin word *fortis*, meaning steadfast courage. An appropriate name for a Knight Templar. *For the craven and depraved need not apply* – as Philippe le Bel discovered when he attempted to join the order, the Templars shunning the black-hearted French monarch. The king, of course, wanted all of the glory of knighthood, but none of the privation that came with living by monastic rule. That the Templars voluntarily renounced whoring, pillaging and gambling – the hallowed pastimes of the knights of old – made them living legends, enabling them to pick and choose from the cream of European manhood.

'No Kingfisher beers for the valiant knights in white,' Cædmon deadpanned, raising the bottle to his lips and taking a noisy slurp.

And then there was the physical danger inherent with being a Knight Templar, warfare in the Middle Ages a harsh and brutal undertaking. Forbidden to call retreat unless the enemy had at least a three-to-one numerical advantage, many a Templar met his death on the field of battle.

Ironically, those were the same odds that Cædmon now confronted.

'Except I can't call retreat.'

Grimly he acknowledged that he had only one option available to him.

With my shield or on it.

PART III

'Behold, I show you a mystery; We shall not all sleep, but we shall all be changed.'

Corinthians 15:51

30

El Barrio de la Latina, Madrid, Spain

Thursday, 1405h

Shuddering, Edie peered at the imposing building. '*That* is incredibly daunting. And not in a good way.'

'As it was intended to be,' Cædmon remarked. Taking hold of her elbow, he ushered her past the fortress-like Capilla del Obispo, the Bishop's Chapel. 'Medieval churches were purposefully designed to induce a bum-clenching terror in the flock. That dread fear kept the communicants in line and, more importantly, ensured that they coughed up their ten per cent tithe to the bishop. This particular building is where Spanish peasants deposited their bundled hay tithes. The barred windows and prison-like entryway enabled the Church to secure their ill-gotten gains.'

'Back in the Church's *hey*day when a person could actually buy their way into heaven,' she wisecracked as they veered on to a narrow lane.

'Mmmm, indeed,' Cædmon murmured distractedly, the pun failing to produce a chuckle, much less a smile. Coming to a standstill, he pulled out the city map that he'd earlier purchased at the Madrid-Barajas Airport.

Edie stood silent while he checked their coordinates;

navigating the labyrinth was no easy feat. Like an elaborate spider web, cobblestone lanes radiated out from the Plaza de la Paja. A district of blocky Gothic-style buildings and ornate Baroque residences, the centuries-old edifices were all crammed together in a claustrophobic maze. For this reason, they'd parked their hire car several blocks away on a much wider thoroughfare. Located somewhere within the warren was Casa de Pinós, the seventeenth-century residence of the Marqués de Bagá.

Fending off a wide-mouthed yawn, Edie dutifully trudged onwards as Cædmon led the way down an eerily deserted street. While large businesses remained open during the traditional afternoon siesta, the smaller shops were shuttered, creating a distinctly somnolent air.

Disorientated from having crossed too many time zones in too few hours, she glanced at her wristwatch. While there wasn't much to cheer about, circumstances being what they were, they did gain an extra four and a half hours. Time that they intended to put to good use questioning the Marqués de Bagá about his Templar ancestor and the *Evangelium Gaspar*.

Tucking the map into his jacket pocket, Cædmon came to a halt in front of a massive four-storey building. 'I believe this is the joint, as you Yanks are wont to say.'

Edie's jaw slackened, 'the joint' being an impressive baroque block-style residence that boasted half a dozen Juliet balconies, ornamental frieze work and a stone balustrade around the roof. 'It's more like a grand *palacio* than a simple *casa*.'

'The upkeep of which may explain why the Marqués was forced to sell it off.'

'Still, nice digs.'

According to their Internet research, the Marqués de Bagá's fortunes had taken a nosedive twenty years ago, the result of bad investments and a sour global economy. Soon thereafter, he'd sold Casa de Pinós to a real estate developer who turned it into swanky upmarket apartments, the Marqués residing in one of the renovated flats.

Cædmon opened the imposing metal-studded wooden door. 'After you,' he said, motioning her into the public vestibule.

To Edie's surprise, the tunnel-like foyer led to an expansive, sun-filled courtyard, the focal point being a *petit* covered bridge that spanned two sections of Casa de Pinós. Arched, it had decorative leadlight windows and carved stone medallions. 'It's absolutely lovely,' she gushed, charmed by the unexpected architectural detail. 'It puts me in mind of the Bridge of Sighs in Oxford.'

'Mmmm . . .'

Hearing another of Cædmon's obligatory replies, Edie realized that his attention was focused, not on the connecting overpass, but on a large fountain in the middle of the courtyard, the stone base of which was shaped like a splayed Templar cross. In the centre was a gigantic bronze pine cone that copiously spewed water from an opening in the top, rivulets running down the tarnished scales.

'We obviously have the right address.' Then, her thoughts running along a more lurid path, she cocked her head to one side and said, 'Is it just me or is that a blatantly erotic pine cone?'

'It is,' Cædmon concurred. 'Since ancient times, the pine cone has been considered a phallic symbol.'

'Which is not something that I normally associate with the celibate Knights Templar. So, which flat are we looking for?' she asked, changing the subject.

'Number eight.'

'There she be.' Edie pointed to an elaborate doorway on the far side of the courtyard, the lintel embellished with a framed blue and white Delft tile rendering of yet another overly phallic pine cone.

'Right. Ready to storm the barricade?'

'Just a sec.' Reaching up, she smoothed a hand over a few flyaway locks of Cædmon's hair, patting the strands into place. Although neatly attired in a white polo shirt and grey linen suit, with his bruised cheekbone and bandaged left temple, he more closely resembled a backstreet ruffian than a respectable author.

Her last-minute ministrations induced a ghost of a smile. 'Wasted effort,' Cædmon said as he raised the knocker.

'Well, you can always tell the Marqués that you're a war correspondent who's just returned from the –'

The front door suddenly swung open.

'Sí?' a diminutive grey-haired woman enquired. The plainly tailored black dress and white apron tied around her waist indicated that she was the hired help.

Not wanting to give Don Luis Fidelis de Pinós, the Marqués de Bagá, an opportunity to deny their request for a meeting, Cædmon had decided to catch the nobleman unawares. Worried that the Marqués would refuse to divulge any information regarding the *Evangelium Gaspar*, they were posing as journalists from *The Times* who'd been sent to Madrid to write a sympathetic piece regarding the

Sovereign Order of the Temple's lawsuit against the Vatican. The perfect cover to ask questions without arousing undue suspicions.

A rapid-fire Spanish exchange took place between Cædmon and the housekeeper, the older woman annoyed by the fact that she'd not been informed of the interview with 'Don Luis'. Profusely apologizing, Cædmon explained that the interview had been arranged several weeks earlier, but that the office secretary obviously forgot to call ahead and confirm the appointment. Mollified somewhat, the housekeeper reluctantly motioned them inside.

So far, so good.

Finding herself in a formal reception area, Edie silently marvelled at the opulent surroundings. Paintings stacked all the way to the ceiling, twenty-foot-long velvet drapes, Greek sculptures, Chinese vases, and a polished suit of armour replete with shiny sword and battle shield emblazoned with an inlaid golden pine cone. Wherever the eye fell, there was some dazzling object to arrest one's gaze.

Raised in impoverished circumstances – her childhood bedroom decorated with ripped-out magazine pictures taped to the wall – Edie was torn between *oohing* and *aahing* and grabbing a pitchfork.

The housekeeper, noticeably limping, her legs encased in compression stockings, shepherded them up a flight of steps that was outfitted with a mechanical stairlift, a modern addition that Edie surmised was reserved for the master of the house and off-limits to the aged domestic.

At the top of the staircase, Edie paused in front of an impressive oil painting of a dark-haired, goateed man attired in a black velvet doublet with an elaborate white ruff.

'I think that's a Velázquez,' she murmured, the 'wow factor' having just gone up another notch. While the Marqués may have lost the family fortune, he'd obviously kept the family heirlooms.

The housekeeper, muttering under her breath in Spanish, led them down a wide corridor lined with an extensive collection of medieval armament – battleaxes, maces, war hammers – mounted on each wall. At the end of the corridor, she stopped in front of a closed door. Casting Cædmon a narrowed-eyed sideways glance – as though she suddenly doubted the veracity of his story – the elderly domestic rapped on the dark-stained entry. A few moments passed before a curt voice bid her to enter. Permission granted, the housekeeper opened the door and announced their arrival.

Unsure what to expect, Edie nervously straightened her skirt as she and Cædmon entered a study with forbidding baroque furnishings. The climb up the flight of stairs notwithstanding, she suddenly felt as though they'd descended into the bowels of hell, an impression culled from the fact that the walls were painted an ominous shade of oxblood. A massive fireplace, large enough to roast a skewered stag, was situated on the far side of the room. Adjacent to that was a line of Gothic-style gilded bookcases, jam-packed with leather-bound incunabula, proving that even the devil liked to read in his free time.

The housekeeper, submissively bowing her head, backed out of the room.

Seated at an ornately carved wooden desk was the wheelchair-bound white-haired Marqués de Bagá.

'*Qué descaro!*' the Marqués spat out, clearly angered by the intrusion. '*Esto es un ultraje!*' Eyes narrowed, he opened a desk drawer and, to Edie's horror, removed an antique flintlock pistol.

31

'While you may be outraged, Don Luis, he who is of noble birth must acquit himself nobly,' Cædmon said in a measured tone, uncertain which would kill him first, a lead musket ball or the Marqués de Bagá's deadly glare.

'I not only hail from a noble ancestry, but an illustrious one as well,' the old patrician rasped in a scathing tone of voice.

Although the retort grated – a not so subtle reminder that it was the Spanish who introduced the asinine notion that a nobleman's blood was blue not red – Cædmon was relieved that Don Luis Fidelis de Pinós spoke fluent English. In his experience, when conversing with the infernal serpent, it was always best to do so in one's native tongue. It minimized the risk of a fatal misunderstanding.

Biting back his annoyance at the other man's insufferable conceit, Cædmon contritely bowed his head. 'Please accept our apologies for the scheduling error,' he said with feigned deference. 'Miss Miller and I have travelled a long distance to speak to you regarding the Sovereign Order of the Temple.'

The glare still affixed to his face, the Marqués deposited the ancient flintlock into a desk drawer. Despite being a wheelchair-bound octogenarian, the Marqués de Bagá obviously fancied himself the daring musketeer. And quite the dandy as well, the man immaculately attired in a cream-coloured double-breasted suit, his bold striped tie and paisley pocket square studiously mismatched. A sartorial affectation that conveyed a sense of dégagé at odds with the nobleman's withering condescension.

'How do I know that you're not an agent provocateur sent by the Vatican to discourage me from proceeding with the lawsuit?' the nobleman hissed.

Detecting a steel core beneath the aristocratic veneer, Cædmon pondered how best to flake the gild.

Suddenly inspired, he approached and purposefully placed his right hand on the polished desktop. The midday sun streaming through the nearby floor-to-ceiling window glinted off his Templar signet ring.

'As you can plainly see, Don Luis, I am not your enemy.'

Eyes suspiciously narrowing, the Marqués glanced downwards. An instant later his facial muscles visibly relaxed as he waved a liver-spotted hand, gesturing to the two vacant chairs in front of his desk.

An audience having been granted, Cædmon pulled out one of the velvet-covered chairs for Edie.

'Actually, if you don't mind, I'd like to shoot some pictures for the article,' she demurred, removing a Nikon D3X camera from her leather satchel. 'If that's all right with you, Don Luis.' Camera in hand, she waited expectantly for the nobleman's permission to take his photograph.

Acting as though he'd only just noticed her presence, the Marqués gave Edie a cursory appraisal. Several moments passed before he nodded his consent. 'Yes, I think that's an excellent idea. I want the world to see the man who has the courage to confront the cassocked jackals inside the Vatican.'

'Thank you, Don Luis. And no need to pose. I think candid shots will work best. Just act natural and pretend as though I'm not here.'

'Seven hundred years may have come and gone, but do not think for one moment that the Church's crimes are not ongoing,' the Marqués intoned as Cædmon seated himself. 'In the past, our *cri de coeur* has gone unanswered. This time, however, the self-styled Princes of the Church will have to acknowledge that they wilfully and illegally stole a fortune from the Knights Templar.'

Cædmon wondered if that massive swindle was any different from the fortune that the Spanish Conquistadors stole from the Aztec Empire. *Thieving parasites, the lot of you.*

Determined to polish the gnarled piece of wood, Cædmon shoved his personal feelings to the wayside and said, 'Indeed, it's a story that appeals to those fascinated by medieval history. Particularly given that you claim to be a direct heir to the Templar legacy.'

'I do not claim to be a direct heir . . . I *am* a direct heir.' As he spoke, the Marqués grasped the arms of his motorized wheelchair. A monarch gripping his throne.

Thinking that the perfect segue, Cædmon removed a spiral reporter's notebook and pencil from his inside jacket pocket, two purchased accoutrements to add credence to the artifice. Out of the corner of his eye, he saw Edie go down on bended knee to snap a few close-up photographs.

'Enlighten me, please,' Cædmon invited. He had no qualms about the fraudulent obtrusion, willing to do or say whatever was necessary to glean actionable intelligence.

'From the very beginning, the De Pinós family was

closely involved with the Knights Templar, making generous donations of land, coinage and property. As did many other noble Spanish families.' The Marqués jutted his chin towards the bookcases filled with leather-bound volumes. 'No one familiar with medieval history can dispute the strong presence of the Knights Templar on the Iberian Peninsula. The warrior monks played a decisive role, not only in the Reconquista, but in protecting the pilgrim routes to Santiago de Compostela as well.'

Edie lowered the camera from her face. 'I apologize for not being up on my Spanish history, but what's a "reconquista"?'

'Soon after the Muslems conquered the southern half of the Iberian Peninsula in the year 711, the Christian kingdoms in the north began a series of military campaigns to vanquish the Moors from the peninsula. The Reconquista finally came to a close when the Christian forces under Isabella of Castile reclaimed the Kingdom of Granada, the last Moorish stronghold,' Cædmon said in response to Edie's question, galloping through eight centuries of Spanish history.

'While the Vatican authorized the creation of the Knights Templar because they needed a cadre of warriors who would swear fealty to the pope rather than a European monarch, the Templars' true agenda was one that the Church did not foresee and was at great pains to suppress. *That* is the real reason for the bloodthirsty *auto-da-fé* of 1307,' the Marqués was quick to emphasize.

'I gather that you're referring to the Templars relentless search for knowledge,' Cædmon said, the subject near and dear. 'Indeed, it has often been said that the

Knights Templar were the proprietors of dark secrets that those in power greatly feared.'

'Nonsense!' the Marqués rebuked, dismissively waving a richly veined hand. 'The darkness emanated, not from the Templars, but from the pontiffs in Rome; depraved men who not only abused their power, but turned their backs on the teachings of Christ. *Los clérigos venden a Dios y las indulgencias por dinero contante.*'

'The clerics sell God and their indulgences for hard cash,' Cædmon translated. A maxim that even a devout Catholic would be hard pressed to deny.

'During their tenure in the Holy Land, the Templars came into close contact with Jews, Muslims and heretical Christian sects. This spawned a radical shift in their religious beliefs, the Templars realizing that the key to everlasting peace in the Holy Land was to establish a transcendent, ecumenical belief system that would unite the three people of the Book.'

'You refer, of course, to the doctrine of *Prisca Theologia*, which alleges that there is one universal theological truth that can be found within every religion,' Cædmon remarked.

'The Templars' search for that unifying strand of common spirituality is what engendered their demise.' Propping his elbows on the wheelchair's armrests, the Marqués threaded his fingers together. 'Had they been successful, it would have spelled the Church's doom.'

Cædmon thoughtfully stared at his notebook and the scribbled notes he'd made. He wondered if the Templars' 'radical shift' had inspired an odyssey that eventually ended with Fortes de Pinós sailing to the Malabar Coast of India.

An intriguing hypothesis.

In the near distance, a church bell tolled the hour. A stentorian call to the faithful.

The time having come to sharpen the inquest, Cædmon shot Edie a quick, meaningful glance before his gaze darted purposefully to a framed portrait hanging on the wall behind her. Picking up on his silent directive, she slipped the camera into her leather bag and walked over to the painting. Arms crossed over her chest, she slowly tipped her head from side to side, giving every impression of being totally engrossed with the portrait of a seated man grasping a skull.

Just as Cædmon had hoped, the Marqués manoeuvred his wheelchair over to where Edie was standing.

'It's an impressive piece of artwork,' Edie murmured, intently staring at the painting. 'Is it a portrait of one of your ancestors?'

'Captured for posterity by Murillo, one of Spain's great baroque artists,' the Marqués off-handedly informed her.

Getting up from his chair, Cædmon joined the pair. 'I'm curious, Don Luis, about another of your ancestors: a Templar by the name of Fortes de Pinós.'

'Where did you hear this name?' the Marqués hissed, craning his neck to peer up at Cædmon.

'I happened upon it while doing some research in the Vatican Secret Archives.'

His cheeks stained with angry red splotches, the other man pointed an accusing finger. 'This is the *real* reason why you're here, isn't it?'

Since there was nothing to gain by denying the charge, Cædmon nodded. 'And given your livid reaction, I was correct in initially withholding the true purpose of our visit. However, now that the cat is bounding about the room, it's pointless to continue the deception.' He stuffed the notebook into his jacket pocket. 'Specifically, I am seeking information pertaining to an ancient gospel called the *Evangelium Gaspar* that Fortes de Pinós had in his possession.'

At the mention of the gospel, the Marqués's eyes opened wide, the man clearly startled.

'I've never heard of the *Evangelium Gaspar*,' he avowed a split second later, yanking the figurative shutters closed.

'Given that the Templars' Grand Master Jacques de Molay sent Fortes de Pinós to India to retrieve the *Evangelium Gaspar* from the Nazrani Christians, I find it hard to believe that you've *not* heard of the long-lost gospel.'

'How dare you insinuate that I am lying! Get out!'

'Not until you tell me everything that you know about Fortes de Pinós and the *Evangelium Gaspar*,' Cædmon replied, refusing to yield.

'I will not tolerate this insolence!' Grasping the joystick mounted on his armrest, the Marqués quickly pivoted the wheelchair and zoomed back to his desk. Jerking the top desk drawer open, he rifled through the drawer's contents.

'By any chance are you looking for this?' Edie enquired, brandishing the flintlock pistol.

32

Rione di Borgo, Rome

Peter could most definitely do with a few extra pennies, Cardinal Franco Fiorio ruminated, the Archives budget forecast for the next quarter dismal at best. Uncertain how he was going to pay Paul, he now regretted having brought the financial papers home with him.

Earlier in the day he'd feigned a migraine headache, escaping the Vatican to work on the reports in quieter surroundings, his flat in the Borgo providing the solitude and privacy that he needed. More importantly, he didn't want to deal with meddlesome interlopers should Father Santos contact him with an update.

Discouraged by the bleak projections, Franco shoved his reading glasses to the top of his head and rubbed his eyes. Balancing the budget was a tedious and thankless endeavour. In order to make ends meet, he would have to dismiss twenty employees, the Secret Archives still reeling from the disastrous licensing deals that his predecessor had naively entered into. Misappropriation and mismanagement of funds were two problems, among many, currently plaguing the Holy See.

'It's enough to make a grown man weep,' he muttered, the Vatican in dire fiscal straits. Having survived barbarian invasions, the Plague and the Protestant Reformation, it was now the bankers banging at the gate.

As Vatican observers knew, shaky finances were the reason behind many of the notorious scandals that had besieged the Holy See in the last few decades, desperate cardinals and bishops having resorted to illegal means to raise funds. Money laundering. Embezzlement. Bank collapses. Just a few of the charges levelled at the Vatican in recent years, the fallout of which had caused a spate of unsolved murders, mysterious suicides and, if the rumours were to be believed, the death of Pope John Paul I. That unsavoury bit of business occurred a mere thirty-three days into his pontificate, a high-ranking member of the Curia supposedly using deadly means to prevent the newly elected pope from exposing the massive corruption taking place within the Vatican Bank.

Over the centuries, as the Church had expanded, so too had the administrative duties of the Roman Curia. Until, in modern times, it had taken on the size and function of a multinational corporation. Vatican, Inc. *The dollar is down. The euro is up. Gold is trading higher.* Beset with annual budget crises, sordid corruption and a swollen bureaucracy, the unwieldy leviathan was in dire need of an overhaul.

Leaning back in his shabby, velvet-covered chair, Franco stared out of the French windows on the other side of the study and set his weary gaze on St Peter's. His flat boasted an unobstructed view of the gleaming dome, the iconic masterpiece soaring above the tiled rooftops. A simple man, unlike some in the Curia, his residence was far from opulent, with the apartment's sixteenth-century bones clearly visible, the windows framed with plain marble cornices and the ceilings braced with wooden beams. Two of the walls were lined with glass-encased bookcases with stacks of other books strategically placed throughout his study. The hallway that ran the length of the flat, as well as three of the walls in the dining room, were also lined with floor-to-ceiling bookcases. All-in-all, an austere residence more befitting an Aquinas-like theologian than a Prince of the Church.

Impatient for an update from Father Santos, Franco drummed his fingers on the wooden desktop. A few seconds later, he picked up his half-eaten *porchetta panino*. His housekeeper, Beatrice, had unobtrusively entered his study a short while ago, setting the luncheon plate on the edge of his desk.

There once was a time, during the high Renaissance, when powerful cardinals built magnificent palazzos where they held court supported by hundreds of retainers and sycophants. And though he could undoubtedly reside in more luxurious surroundings had he opted to live within the papal city, Franco had declined the Vatican apartment set aside for the Prefect of the Secret Archives. Under normal circumstances his decision to live 'off-campus' would have rippled the papal waters, but in this instance Pius XIII was only too happy to have a cardinal that he considered a dangerous enemy sequestered in the Borgo.

Little did Pius know that an enemy cannot be hidden away like some crazy uncle in the attic.

Finished with the pork sandwich, Franco shoved the plate aside and got up from his desk. Placing his hands on the small of his back, he stretched, causing several bones to loudly crack. As he walked towards the set of French windows he momentarily stopped in front of the framed photograph of the Fiorio family, circa 1960. The blissful years before the infamous 'Fall from Grace'. Before his mother's divine visitation changed the course of their lives.

Opening the French windows, Franco stepped out on to the rooftop terrace. As always, he tuned out the raucous sound of the traffic below; a constant in Rome. In addition to the small bistro table with two chairs, scattered around the base of the balustrade were pots of leafy shrubs and trailing vines, including several tomato plants brimming with ripened fruit. All tended to by Beatrice who, in addition to being a meticulous housekeeper and superb cook, was blessed with a green thumb. Deeply devoted to the Church, she was a consecrated virgin; and had been handpicked by his mother to manage his household when he was elevated to the cardinalate. The latter meant that Beatrice Vaccarelli's loyalties were, first and foremost, to Rosella Fiorio.

Although ninety-one years of age and wheelchair bound at a senior retirement community in Baltimore, his mother was determined to keep tabs on Franco, with the housekeeper acting as her eyes and ears. After the shameful debacle involving his brother Angelo, she wasn't about to let her younger son veer off course. She'd learned her lesson. In hard, painful fashion.

After Rosella's second visitation from the Blessed Virgin Mary, there was no doubt in her mind that Our Lady intended for her eldest son Angelo to join the priesthood and consecrate his life to Christ's ministry. While Angelo, then fifteen years old, wasn't nearly as certain, he did revel in the sudden attention that he received from family, parish priests and the nuns at Fourteen Holy Martyrs Catholic School. Despite the fact that money was always tight in the household coffers, funds none the less became available for Angelo to go on weekend retreats and various other activities sponsored by the archdiocese. The bill for those events was footed by parish benefactors who were certain that the Blessed Virgin had chosen Angelo for great things.

The prodding worked, Angelo finally relenting and entering the seminary; breaking his girlfriend's heart in the process. In the winter of 1968, he was ordained at the Basilica of the National Shrine of the Assumption of the Blessed Virgin Mary. The day was one of joyful celebration for family and parishioners alike, one of their own about to begin a most holy undertaking.

Left on the sidelines, Franco was free to decide his own future, having won an academic scholarship to Georgetown University, that great Jesuit institution of higher education. Since the family didn't have the money to send him to college, he'd had to work his ass off to get there. Unlike Angelo's divinely dictated aspirations, his were motivated by the fear of getting drafted into the military and shipped to Vietnam. It was one of the reasons why he'd decided on a philosophy major. Granted, he'd always been something of an argumentative bastard, but he could also drag that particular major out to years of graduate work, deferring the draft indefinitely.

Everything was running smoothly for Franco when, suddenly, 'the Great Fall' befell the Fiorio family.

It was early spring, midway into his junior year, when

Franco received a frantic phone call from his mother, ordering him to straight away drive home to Baltimore. Worried that Rosella may have fallen ill, he jumped into his beaten-up Volkswagen Beetle and made the forty-mile trip in record time. Leaping over the front gate, he ran inside the house, momentarily stopped in his tracks by the thick smell of Three Kings incense and the heat thrown off from the twenty or more lit votive candles set up on the altar in front of the Virgin's statue.

But that was nothing compared to the welcoming committee that waited for him in the living room. In addition to his teary-eyed mother, the parish priest, Father McCarty, and Monsignor Hellerman were present. Wondering what incited the heavy artillery, Franco eased himself into the chair that had been placed in front of the sofa, inexplicably feeling like a prisoner in the dock.

Because his mother was too distraught to speak, it was Father McCarty who got stuck with the unpleasant task of informing Franco that his brother Angelo had left the priesthood under sordid circumstances; the announcement of which caused his mother to start sobbing anew. Clearly uncomfortable, the old parish priest, in a lowered voice, went on to say that Angelo had got involved with a woman whom he intended to marry. And to ensure that his mother never recovered from the shock, the woman in question was a Carmelite nun.

Franco didn't know whether to laugh or cry.

Or to beat a hasty retreat. Because *suddenly* the room had gone very quiet, all three of them – his mother, the priest and the monsignor – staring at him expectantly.

When, a few seconds later, his mother got up from the sofa and fell to her knees in front of his chair, flinging her arms around his waist as she begged his forgiveness, Franco was thrown into a state of complete confusion.

'Forgiveness for what, Mom?'

'I had the wrong son, Franco. All these years, I've been blind to the fact that Our Lady chose *you* to be Her Son's emissary here on earth.'

Hearing that, Franco tried to break free of his mother's embrace. But she only tightened her hold on him.

Not only did he love college, but he'd just started dating a cute girl in his Ethics class. *He didn't want to become a priest!* He wanted to live a normal life. Raise a little hell. Then settle down. Get married. Have two point five kids. He did not want to pass out communion wafers at Sunday Mass.

Sensing that he was about to punt the ball, Monsignor Hellerman got up, walked over to the chair and put a staying hand on Franco's shoulder.

'You've been selected, Franco, by the Queen of Heaven, to continue Her Son's work. There can be no greater joy for a man. To turn your back on Our Lady would constitute a grave sin.'

Terrified, the life he'd not yet lived passing before his eyes, Franco found himself wordlessly nodding his head. The fear of hell had been ground into him from an early age, the nuns at Fourteen Holy Martyrs having done a bang-up job. Since his father Sal had died two years earlier, he had no one in his corner. No one to argue his case. There was nothing he could do but capitulate.

In that instant, Franco felt as though he'd been shang-haied.

As the years passed and the fallout from the Second Vatican Council became more obvious, Franco belatedly realized that he'd been the victim of the lax morals that had infiltrated the Roman Catholic Church in the after-math of those despised 'reforms'. Angelo Fiorio wasn't the only priest to leave the Church during that tumultuous period. By the late sixties and early seventies, they were leaving in droves. All jumping ship. Swimming ashore. And getting drunk as sailors.

Leaving the real men, like Franco, to clean up the mess.

In promoting their watered-down faith, the liberals had sullied the purity of the Church. Seducing the clergy and laity alike, liberals were no different from Lucifer in the Garden. Forcing Roman Catholics to gorge on the false fruit of Vatican II.

Although it didn't happen on that long-ago after-noon when he was pressured into joining the priesthood, in time Franco had his epiphany. When it did come, it was just as powerful, just as furious, as Paul's instant-aneous conversion on the road to Damascus. In one shattering, life-altering moment, he was made to realize that he *was* the chosen one. The one who'd been selected by the Queen of Heaven to purify Her Son's Church.

Hearing his mobile phone ring, Franco stepped back into his study and snatched the phone off his desk. Pleased that the call was from Gracián Santos, he hit the 'talk' button.

'I'm listening. Go ahead,' he said gruffly.

'Forgive me if I've called at an inconvenient time, Your Eminence. However, there's been an unusual development that I thought you should be apprised of. The Englishman has gone to see a nobleman in Madrid.'

The skin on the back of Franco's neck instantly prickled. 'Do you know the nobleman's name?'

'According to my men, it is the Marqués de Bagá.'

Hearing that, Franco gasped aloud. *No! No! No!*

The Marqués de Bagá had been very vocal about his intentions – he wanted to crush the Vatican. Revenge for the *auto-da-fé* that destroyed the Knights Templar.

'I need a moment,' he grated, yanking the mobile away from his ear.

Horrified by the latest turn of events, Franco grasped his pectoral cross. So hard that the gold edges cut into the palm of his hand.

Why did Cædmon Aisquith seek out the Marqués? Was the Englishman hoping to strike an alliance with the old aristocrat? Or was he simply seeking information pertaining to the Marqués's ancestor, Fortes de Pinós?

Franco didn't know on which side of the great divide the answer fell. While he had faith that the Englishman would relinquish the *Evangelium Gaspar* to save his daughter's life, he couldn't take the chance that a known enemy of the Church would be privy to the gospel's explosive contents. Should that happen, there was no doubt in his mind that the Marqués de Bagá would use the ancient gospel like a weapon. One capable of obliterating the Roman Catholic Church.

I must stop the enemy in his tracks!

His mind made up, Franco put the phone back to his

ear. 'The Marqués de Bagá poses an imminent threat,' he hissed. 'Under no circumstance can we allow the Spaniard to obtain the *Evangelium Gaspar*.'

'But, Your Eminence . . . perhaps Cædmon Aisquith simply went to Madrid to gain information pertaining to the gospel's whereabouts,' Father Santos argued nervously.

'No doubt he did. Which is why I want your men to wait until the Englishman takes his leave before dealing with the Marqués. And while they're at it, I want them to sweep the premises clean and destroy any documents pertaining to the Sovereign Order of the Temple.'

'Wh-what does that mean?' the priest stammered.

'Do I have to spell it out for you?'

The question was met with silence.

Damn the man! He has balls the size of raisins, Franco fumed silently.

Well aware that Gracián Santos was a coward at heart, Franco knew that he had to press the only leverage he had with the priest – his fear of losing Sanguis Christi to foreclosure. Without the fellowship, Santos would emotionally implode for Sanguis Christi was his child. His family. His *raison d'être*.

Needing Santos to stiffen his backbone, Franco said quietly, 'I should have the funds to pay off your mortgage later this evening. As soon as your men secure the *Evangelium Gaspar*, I'll be able to wire you the money.'

'Your Eminence, I . . . I can't thank you enough!' the priest gushed, his relief all too evident. 'Tell me what must be done and . . . and I will see that your orders are carried out.'

Franco smiled, the priest having quit the field without so much as raising his sword. 'The Marqués de Bagá is an enemy of the Church and must be shown no mercy.'

None whatsoever.

To safeguard Christ's Church, crusades had been launched, inquisitions ordered and bloody wars fought. And just as Franco was prepared to give of his own blood to protect the one true faith, he had no qualms about shedding the blood of an unrepentant heretic.

33

'Well played, Miss Miller,' Cædmon complimented.

Edie, flintlock pistol in hand, walked over and ceded him custody of the weapon.

The nobleman glared at both of them. 'I protest! This is an outrage!'

'Don Luis, I refuse to believe that a man who's devoted so much time and effort into researching his Templar lineage is unaware of Fortes de Pinós's voyage to the Malabar Coast in 1307 to retrieve the *Evangelium Gaspar*. This makes me think that you've been economical with the truth.' Cædmon aimed the pistol at the older man's chest. 'I suggest that you reconsider your position and spill some valuable beans.'

'I can't tell you what I don't know.'

Cædmon kept his gaze on the nobleman, searching for telltale signs – pupil dilation, averted gaze, indrawn breath – to determine if the wily bastard was being disingenuous. 'It will be to your benefit to be forthcoming, Don Luis.'

'Is this where, in a sinister tone of voice, you inform me that if I don't comply, you'll put a bullet through my heart?'

'Ah! You know the drill.' Cædmon smiled humourlessly. 'That simplifies matters immensely. I'm all for efficiency.' Glancing over at Edie, he said, 'Would you kindly pull up the Chinon riddle on your iPad?'

Approaching the desk, computer in hand, Edie shot Cædmon a chastising glare, clearly unhappy with his bully-boy tactics.

A bit too late for that, Cædmon thought sourly. She had, after all, commandeered the weapon.

'When your ancestor Fortes de Pinós was questioned by the Dominican inquisitor regarding the whereabouts of the *Evangelium Gaspar*, this is the reply that he gave.' Cædmon gestured to the iPad that Edie had placed on the desk in front of the Marqués. 'Does this mean anything to you?'

The Marqués made a big to-do of peering at the tablet computer. A moment later, shaking his head, he said, 'It's nonsensical gibberish.'

Undeterred, Cædmon slowly recited the riddle. '"To see the house where Lucas dwelled, the faithful pilgrim sought the brother's way. Setting forth from the lion's castle, he dropped the French iron in a Spanish harbour." Does any part of that strike a chord?'

'Your instrument is badly tuned. As I said, it's complete rubbish. Nothing more than the ramblings of a man subjected to excruciating torture.'

Cædmon might have agreed with the Marqués's dismissive assessment had the rest of the transcript not been so lucid, each one of Fortes de Pinós's replies pitch perfect. 'As I'm running short on time and patience, I want you to –'

'Hold the phone!' Edie exclaimed suddenly. Standing near the fireplace, she excitedly gestured to a medieval jousting shield mounted above the mantelpiece. 'The "lion's castle" is right here on this shield!'

'Bloody hell! Are you serious?' Still keeping the pistol

trained on the nobleman, Cædmon strode over to the mantelpiece and examined the shield painted in bold shades of black, red and gold.

His jaw nearly came unhinged, a key piece of the puzzle having been in blatant view all along. 'This jousting shield bears the coat-of-arms for the medieval Kingdom of Castile and Léon. Or "the lion's castle" as Fortes de Pinós referred to it in his riddle.'

Hand tightening around the wooden pistol grip, Cædmon stalked back to the desk. Under no circumstance could the Marqués have *not* known the significance of 'the lion's castle'. Originally two separate kingdoms, Castile and Léon were united in 1301. As the old man knew full well.

'An oversight on my part,' the nobleman said blithely, having correctly deduced Cædmon's thoughts. 'Like most men, I don't think clearly when I'm staring down the barrel of a loaded gun.'

Hearing that, Cædmon's pulse pounded furiously in both temples, inducing a nauseating burst of pain.

He took a deep breath. Then another. Until just a few

moments ago, he'd not considered that Fortes de Pinós might have travelled to the Iberian Peninsula before he was arrested in France and taken to Chinon Castle.

If that were the case, Fortes may have hidden the Evangelium Gaspar *somewhere in the Kingdom of Castile and Léon.*

And he reckoned the Marqués de Bagá knew where precisely that might be.

'Don't trifle with me, old man.' He pressed the barrel against a pulsing blue vein in the Marqués's left temple, severely tempted to thumb the hammer into the firing position.

'I refuse to cooperate with a disreputable English treasure hunter.' The Marqués obstinately folded his arms over his chest; a Spanish Grandee standing his ground.

'Allow me to correct an oversight; I don't seek the *Evangelium Gaspar* for fortune or fame.' Lowering the half-cocked pistol, Cædmon retook his seat on the other side of the desk. 'A week ago, a group of men working under the auspices of the Church kidnapped my daughter from her home in Fort Cochin, India,' he said matter-of-factly, opting for honesty. 'They have demanded the *Evangelium Gaspar* as ransom for her safe return.'

Clearly surprised, the Marqués de Bagá's eyes opened wide. In that instant, Cædmon saw a flicker of compassion.

'Is this true?' The Marqués put the question to Edie.

She nodded. 'In fact, we had a run-in with one of her captors yesterday in Kottayam, India,' she replied as she walked over and sat down in a vacant chair.

The Marqués swung his head back in Cædmon's direction. 'How do you know that the kidnappers are Church operatives?'

'Not only do they take their marching orders from a Catholic priest, but all of the kidnappers have a Chi-Rho cross branded on the palm of the right hand.'

'*In hoc signo vinces*,' the Marqués murmured, clearly aware of the cross's significance. An instant later, he pushed out a deep breath; a show of surrender. 'To answer your earlier question, yes, I have heard of the *Evangelium Gaspar*. However, I don't have it in my possession. To the best of my knowledge, the gospel is still cached where Fortes de Pinós hid it in December of 1307.'

'Did he hide it in the Kingdom of Castile and Léon?' Edie asked, taking the question right out of Cædmon's mouth.

'I believe that he did.' The Marqués opened a desk drawer and removed a thick folder. 'These are the evidentiary documents that I've compiled for my court case against the Vatican,' he said as he removed a single sheet of parchment sheathed in a Mylar sleeve from the folder. 'This is a letter written on December the eighth, 1307, by a Knight Templar named Rodrigo Yañez. He was the provincial Grand Master in the Kingdom of Castile and Léon. According to his missive, Fortes de Pinós asked for and was granted safe sanctuary at a Templar-owned estate.'

'Does the provincial Grand Master mention where the estate is located?'

'He does not.' The Marqués handed Cædmon the letter for inspection. 'He merely stipulates that it is located in the Kingdom of Castile and Léon.'

Cædmon hurriedly scanned the Latin-scribed parchment. Just as the Marqués claimed, Rodrigo Yañez didn't reveal the specific location of De Pinós's safe sanctuary.

'This letter proves that Fortes was on the Iberian Peninsula in late 1307,' Cædmon said, handing the document back to the Marqués. 'Yet, soon thereafter, he travelled to France. Whereupon, he was arrested by the king's men and sent to Chinon Castle. In March of 1308, he died while held in captivity there.' He drummed his fingertips on the desktop, trying to fit the pieces together. 'According to the Chinon transcript, Fortes de Pinós attempted to use the *Evangelium Gaspar* to bribe King Philippe le Bel into releasing the Knights Templar.'

'Knowing that the French monarch had arrested so many of the Knights Templar, Fortes had reason to be leery,' Edie remarked. 'I'm guessing that he stashed the gospel in the Kingdom of Castile and Léon, knowing that he could later retrieve it if the king agreed to the swap.'

Cædmon nodded, her premise having merit. Turning his attention back to the Marqués, he said, 'Because of the nature of your lawsuit against the Vatican, I presume that you've researched the known Templar holdings in Castile-Léon.'

Thumbing through the open folder, the Marqués extracted a second document, a crisp photocopied sheet of paper. 'This is a map of the medieval kingdom with all of the Templar-owned churches, castles, farms and fortresses marked.'

Interested to see the list, Cædmon took the proffered sheet of paper.

'As you can see, the list of known Templar properties in the Kingdom of Castile and Léon is extensive.'

'Good God!' Cædmon exclaimed, stunned. 'There's at least sixty properties indicated on this map. I had no idea that the Knights Templar had owned so much real estate in the one kingdom.' It would take weeks, if not months, to search each and every holding. 'Is there any way to narrow the list?'

The Marqués made no reply. A silence that spoke volumes.

Cædmon raised the flintlock, the old man trying to fob him off with a lie of omission. 'Tell me what I want to know and you'll live to fight another day.'

The ploy worked, the Marqués acquiescing with a terse nod. 'While the Spanish Templars weren't arrested en masse, the pope did send an apostolic inquisitor to the Iberian Peninsula to investigate the Order. Fearing the worst, Rodrigo Yañez asked a Castilian prince to take possession of four Templar fortresses in Castile-Léon.'

'And what reason did the Grand Master have for doing this?'

'Yañez wanted to safeguard the four fortresses from the covetous papal emissaries.'

'I guess you know what the next question is going to be.' Edie leaned forward in her chair. 'Which four properties made the cut?'

'Alcañicies, San Pedro de Latarce, Ponferrada and Faro,' the nobleman replied, tapping his fingertip on four different locations on the medieval map.

'Why these four?' Cædmon enquired, certain now that Fortes de Pinós had hidden the *Evangelium Gaspar* at one of the four fortresses.

The Marqués shrugged. 'I presume it was because a piece of the *Lignum Crucis* was safeguarded at each fortress.'

Edie glanced over at Cædmon. 'Since you're my Latin go-to guy, I'll ask you: what's a *lignum crucis*?'

'It's Latin for "the True Cross",' Cædmon replied. 'Pieces of which were brought to Spain from the Holy Land.'

'"*Lignum cruces arbor scientiae*",' the Marqués recited solemnly. 'The wood of the cross is the tree of knowledge.' Pronouncement made, he grasped the joystick and navigated the motorized wheelchair to the sideboard on the other side of the room.

Cædmon let the older man pass without comment; he'd gleaned all that he could from the nobleman. Now that he had actionable intelligence, he and Edie needed to be on their way.

Anxious to depart, he set the half-cocked flintlock on top of the desk.

The Marqués pulled the stopper on a cut-crystal decanter. 'Full-bodied and potent, the 1994 Vega Sicilia Unico is a sentimental favourite. Not only was it an exceptional year for a venerable wine, but a memorable year as well. June of 1994 was the last time that I could make love to my wife, my mistress and the upstairs maid in the course of a single day.'

Purposefully ignoring the older man's braggadocio, Cædmon held the map aloft. 'Don Luis, may I have this photocopied map of the Kingdom of Castile and Léon?'

The Marqués waved a hand, indicating that he was free to take the map. 'If you're successful in finding the *Evangelium Gaspar*, I ask only that you send me a copy of it. I would be very interested to know the secret that my ancestor took to his grave.'

'By all means,' Cædmon replied. He folded the map and slipped it into his jacket pocket. Getting to his feet, he offered Edie a helping hand.

'Be forewarned, Señor Aisquith, the Church very badly wants what you seek.' Raising his wine glass, the Marqués de Bagá smiled caustically. 'Go with God.'

Cædmon inclined his head in the nobleman's direction. 'Good day, Don Luis.'

'So all we have to do is figure out at which of the four fortresses Fortes de Pinós hid the gospel,' Edie said a few moments later as they descended the grand staircase.

At the bottom of the steps, Cædmon took hold of Edie's elbow and ushered her across the reception hall. 'Given the clues embedded within the Chinon riddle, I have reason to believe that – Good God!'

Cædmon stopped in his tracks at seeing the elderly housekeeper slumped over in a velvet-covered armchair. She was drenched in blood and skewered to the chair with a gleaming broadsword.

Horrified, he rushed over to her.

Too late!

Her throat slashed, the poor woman had already given up the ghost.

34

Hurled into the depths of a hellish maelstrom, Edie opened her mouth to scream.

In that same instant, pivoting in her direction, Cædmon slapped a hand over her mouth, stifling what would undoubtedly have been a piercing screech.

Horrified by the gory scene, she stared, her stomach roiling at the sight of the murdered housekeeper. *Somewhere inside Casa de Pinós a psychopath was on the loose!*

'We mustn't let the killer know that we're here,' Cædmon warned in a low voice as he turned her away from the ghastly sight. 'Focus on your breathing. Can you do that?'

Incapable of speech, Edie gulped a serrated breath; a mouthful of air that got stuck midway between her mouth and her lungs.

Only a monster would kill a defenceless grey-haired woman.

'We have to warn the Marqués,' Cædmon whispered in her ear. 'Are you composed enough to accompany me upstairs?'

Not about to remain alone in the reception hall, Edie nodded, still too petrified to speak.

Taking hold of her hand, Cædmon hurriedly led her to the staircase. Ready to battle the monster, he had a fierce expression stamped on his face. Head throbbing, heart pounding, Edie could barely battle her fear let alone a deranged killer.

As they climbed the white marble staircase, she saw glossy drops of blood. Blood that she'd not noticed when they had descended the stairs a few moments ago.

At the top of the steps, Cædmon put a staying arm across her torso as he peered down the corridor. Edie tugged on his arm and pointed to the trail of blood drops that ran down the deserted hallway. Nodding, he gestured for her to stay put.

Thinking that a *very* bad idea, she moved her index and middle fingers in an ambulating motion. *I'm coming with you!* she silently mouthed.

Grim-faced, Cædmon gave his assent.

Side-by-side, they wended their way down the corridor. When they came abreast of the mounted display of medieval armaments, Cædmon pulled her aside. Perusing the display, he yanked a four-foot-long battleaxe off the wall. With its sharpened blade, the weapon had once been capable of piercing the heaviest of helms. Edie knew that Cædmon, who did not suffer from weak-kneed principles, would use it to slay the monster.

Suddenly noticing a curved ghostly imprint, she pointed to the empty wall space.

'He's got a falchion sword,' Cædmon whispered.

Hearing that, Edie unthinkingly reached up and snatched a small jewelled dagger, arming herself.

Just then a single shot loudly reverberated. A deafening boom caused by a spark hitting a wad of gunpowder. *Someone just fired the flintlock pistol!* Which meant that the killer was inside the study with the Marqués.

An instant later, Edie heard a muffled scream; one that was almost immediately silenced.

She froze, terror and shock coalescing on impact. The dagger slipped through her fingers, clattering on to the floor. From chest to head and back again, her pulse fiercely pounded.

The battleaxe grasped in his right hand, Cædmon yanked her away from the wall display.

'Follow my lead!' he ordered.

Relieved that they were charging back to the staircase, Edie was bewildered when Cædmon suddenly veered towards a closed door. Yanking it open, he pulled her across the threshold and hurriedly locked the heavy wooden door behind them. Disorientated, she wondered what they were doing on the 'Bridge of Sighs', the narrow passage illuminated with sunshine that streamed through mottled leadlight windows.

'Wh-why the d-detour?' she stammered as they rushed across the bridge to the closed door on the other side of the overpass.

'Because we don't know how many accomplices the killer has with him. If we exit on the other side of the quad-rangle, we can hopefully escape without detection,' Cædmon informed her as he reached for the handle on the wooden door. 'Damn! It's locked.'

Muttering a few choice expletives, he banged on it with his left fist.

To no avail.

'Did you bring your lock-picking kit?'

Cædmon shook his head. 'It's inside my duffel bag in the boot of the hire car.'

Gesturing to the old-fashioned lock assembly, she said, 'Maybe you can break the lock with the battle—' Hearing a loud crashing sound, she stopped in mid-sentence. In stupefied horror, she watched as the Marqués, seated in his motorized wheelchair, crashed through the study window. Landing in the courtyard below, he lay sprawled on the cobblestones. Unmoving. His body surrounded by a glistening sea of broken glass.

Hit with a burst of primal fear, Edie screamed.

'H-he d-d-doesn't have a –'

Head! The killer had decapitated him.

Edie's heart pounded in her ears. A thundering din. Suddenly dizzy, she swayed.

Afraid she would collapse on to the floor, Edie clutched hold of the stone window frame to keep herself upright, her legs quivering unsteadily.

'Damn bloodthirsty bastard!' Cædmon rasped as he pushed open one of the Gothic-style windows. Propping the battleaxe against the stone wall, he leaned his upper body out of the opening.

'Wh-what are doing?'

'We need to escape this death trap. Particularly since nobody seems to be on the premises other than the two of us and a cold-blooded killer. There's a cast-iron drainpipe attached to the exterior wall. It appears sturdy enough.'

'To do *what*?!' she screeched.

'I would think that's obvious.' Cædmon put a steadying hand on her shoulder. 'The drain pipe will support each of us as we descend to the courtyard. It's no more than fifteen feet to the bottom. Do you wish to go first or shall I?'

Edie peered out of the open window. Fifteen feet never looked like such a vast distance. 'You go first. That way you can catch me if I fall,' she told him, her legs still wobbly.

'Right.' Cædmon picked up the battleaxe and, leaning out the window, let it drop on to the cobbles. That done, he swung a leg over the window sill and, ducking his head, went through the window.

Sucking in a mouthful of air, Edie held her breath as she watched him grab hold of the sturdy cast-iron pipe. A moment later, he slid to the ground. No sooner did he make landfall than Edie heard a clanging noise on the far side of the bridge.

Someone was trying to break the lock!

She hastily clambered over the window sill. Mimicking Cædmon, she balanced herself on the stone ledge adjacent to the pipe. Clinging to the sill, she rested her cheek on the sandstone, afraid to look down. Frozen in place.

'Edie, stop puttering about!'

'I c-c-can't m-m-move!'

Panic-stricken – her dread fear of heights kicking in – she whimpered.

'Come on, love. You can do this,' Cædmon prodded, his tone noticeably softened.

A gentle breeze lifted her skirt hem. As though she'd just been hit with a gale force wind, her fear escalated tenfold. Paralyzed, she clung to the stone. 'I can't do this, Cædmon. You're going to have to –'

The door at the other end of the bridge suddenly swung open.

The killer! He's coming for me!

Edie let go of the sill and reached for the cast-iron pipe, her fear of death greater than her fear of heights.

Again imitating Cædmon, she clutched the cylinder between her hands. Pressing her thighs against the surprisingly warm metal, she slithered safely to the cobbles.

She spared a quick upwards glance. Framed in the open window, snarling malevolently, was a rabid animal in the guise of a man.

'Come! There's no time to waste!'

Together they charged across the courtyard and rushed through the corridor that led to the street exit. When they reached the metal-studded door, Cædmon flung it wide open.

'What the bloody hell is *that* doing on the pavement?'

Directly in front of them, blocking the exit, was a white service van. Holding the battleaxe in his right hand, Cædmon banged on the van with his left.

Within seconds, the vehicle's back door slid open with the jangling grate of metal on metal. Standing in the opening, a semi-automatic weapon gripped in his right hand, was Hector Calzada.

'*Buenos dias, amigos.*' Smiling savagely at Cædmon, he aimed the gun directly at Edie's head. 'One false move, *cabrón*, and the pretty lady will go *adiós.*'

35

'What the hand dare seize the fire?'

One emblazoned with a Chi-Rho cross, Cædmon thought dispiritedly, forced to watch as Hector Calzada proceeded to put to the flame a folder confiscated from the Marqués de Bagá's study that contained all of the evidentiary documents that the Marqués had compiled for his court case against the Vatican. Many of the records were centuries-old documents and pertained to the Knights Templar. Heartsick, he stared at the smouldering pile; parchment, vellum and paper, all consigned to the fire. Lost for ever.

With the evidence destroyed, the Sovereign Order of the Temple would likely be forced to drop their lawsuit.

Displaying a pyromaniac's intemperate glee, Calzada ripped a last sheet of vellum out of its Mylar sleeve. Brows drawn together, he held it at arm's length and scrutinized it. Then, chortling, he dropped it on to the small make-shift bonfire that he'd lit on the cobbles in the alleyway.

A barbarian of the first order.

After being subjected to a humiliating body search, he and Edie had been whisked into the back of the van and driven to the alleyway. Although he had no idea where precisely they were currently parked, the Moorish style architecture of the nearby buildings suggested that they were still in Madrid's Latin district.

Finished with his task, Calzada grabbed a long-necked

green bottle from his cohort, the homicidal maniac who'd slain the Marqués and his elderly housekeeper. The sword-wielding executioner, who had yet to utter a single word, used a primitive sign language to communicate with Calzada. Cædmon deduced that the man was incapable of speech. He also assumed that the mute was the third 'bandito' who'd been in India, Roberto Diaz. With his wispy goatee and shaved head, the bloodthirsty thug bore little resemblance to the passport photograph that he'd examined in Fort Cochin. A fact which had presumably enabled Diaz to shadow them to Madrid. For all he knew, the bastard had been on the same flight.

Seating himself in the van's open doorway, Calzada belched, the pair having toasted their murder spree with a bottle of Dom Pérignon that they'd nicked from Casa de Pinós.

Cædmon, huddled next to Edie in the van's cargo hold, could only fantasize about taking his revenge. If he went full tilt, Calzada would draw the Beretta semi-automatic that was shoved into his waistband and reward his ill-considered heroics with a nine millimetre bullet to the brain. Or, even more horrific than that, his swordsman would behead him. A falchion, with its blocky, curved blade, required little finesse, having been a favourite with crusading foot soldiers.

As though he'd suddenly read Cædmon's mind, the mute raised the falchion in a threatening fashion. Growling like a rabid animal, he forcefully thumped on his chest with his balled left fist.

The macho theatrics set Edie to trembling.

'Look away,' he urged in a low voice, the sight of that well-honed blade unsettling to an extreme.

Averting her gaze, Edie, instead, peered over at him, her eyes brimming. Cædmon could see that she was holding on to her emotions by a very fragile thread, a tear breaking free from its mooring and rolling down her face.

'Hey, *bella*, I also shed tears,' Calzada said, pointing to a blue teardrop that was tattooed in the corner of his right eye. 'But do not hold it against Roberto that he takes pleasure in a job well done.'

Sadistic pleasure at that, Cædmon silently appended.

'There were three of you in India. Evidently, Cerberus has lost one of its snarling heads,' he remarked, trying to steer the bastard's attention away from Edie.

'*Que?!*' Calzada stared at him, uncomprehending.

'I refer, of course, to your companion, Javier Aveles.'

'He stayed behind to keep an eye on the Indian bitch.' Closing his eyes, Calzada smiled wistfully. 'That one makes my prick twitch. Same goes for the daughter.' Opening his eyes, he looked over at Edie. 'You, too, *bella*. I could fuck all three of you.'

Cædmon glared at the moustachioed Bête Noire, rage hardening his belly. He very badly wanted to smash his fist in the other man's face.

'What's the matter, English? You look constipated. Did I say something to upset you?' Calzada raised the champagne bottle and took a noisy slurp. Wiping his mouth with his shirtsleeve, he looked over at his cohort. 'Hey, homie, toss me that bag.'

In the process of cleaning the blood off the falchion blade with a dirty rag, the mute stopped what he was doing and passed Edie's leather satchel over to Calzada.

Setting the bottle down, the Bête Noire unzipped the

bag and unceremoniously dumped its contents on to the floor of the van. With a cavalier air, he rifled through Edie's personal effects. *Passport. Purse. Lipstick. Hairpins. Nail file. iPad. Sunglasses.* Wearing a fool's grin, he plucked a cellophane-wrapped peppermint from the messy pile and ripped it open with his teeth. 'Umm. *Menta*, my favourite. *Gracias, bella.*'

'My pleasure,' Edie muttered.

A few moments later, as he removed the Nikon D_3X from a separate camera bag, Calzada whistled appreciatively. 'Somebody likes to take pictures. How much this set you back?'

'It's for my job. I'm a photographer,' Edie informed him in a quavering voice, clearly upset that he was handling her camera.

'That's not what I asked, *bella.*'

Bending her head, Edie stared at the ribbed floor of the van. 'It cost five thousand dollars,' she murmured dejectedly, no doubt fearing it would soon become a sunken cost.

'I always wanted a good camera. You can't take a picture worth shit with a cell phone.' Leaning against the van's open doorway, Calzada bent a knee. Languidly swinging his other leg, he proceeded to review the photographs stored in memory. 'The old dude had a high opinion of himself, didn't he? You can see it in his face. That fucker got what was coming to him. Isn't that right, homie?'

Diaz grinned, showing off a gold-plated tooth.

'Hey, I got a good idea –' he handed the camera to Diaz – 'I want you to take my picture with *bella.*'

The comment elicited a terrified whimper from Edie.

Patting the spot next to him, Calzada said, 'Slide your ass over here so Roberto can shoot the photo.'

When Edie balked, refusing to budge, Cædmon gently nudged her with his elbow. 'Do as he says,' he urged, worried that her truculence might antagonize the pair. Calzada and his 'homie' had violent predilections, killing for the sheer joy of it. The wise course of action was appeasement. As distasteful as that was.

Evidently coming to the same conclusion, Edie awkwardly crawled over to the other side of the van. Lips quivering, her face drained of animating colour, she seated herself beside Calzada.

'Make sure that you use the flash,' Calzada instructed as he smoothed a hand over his hair. 'I want a good picture.'

Cædmon watched as the bastard roughly grabbed hold of Edie's chin and, pursing his lips with clownish exaggeration, kissed her cheek. The spectacle incited a burst of impotent rage. Powerless to intervene, he had to bide his time. Wait until he could attack from a position of strength.

A few seconds later, the flash went off.

When, in the next instant, Edie made a move to return to Cædmon's side, Calzada cuffed a hand around her upper arm. 'Stay where you are, *bella*. Don't you want to see our portrait?' His lips curved in a maniacal leer as he reviewed the photo on the Nikon. 'We make a cute couple, huh? And now I have a memento to remember you by.'

'A m-m-memento?' Edie stammered, a confused look on her face. 'Wh-what are you talking about?'

Calzada licked the end of his index finger before jabbing it in the middle of Edie's forehead. 'Just because you give me a hard-on doesn't mean that I'm not going to put one right between your eyes.'

'She's done nothing to warrant your enmity,' Cædmon was quick to point out, the conversation having suddenly veered on to *very* dangerous ground.

'The bitch is dead freight. Eye candy, that's all she is.'

'Not true. As a researcher, Miss Miller is integral to finding the *Evangelium Gaspar.*' A bead of perspiration trickled down the side of Cædmon's face, his fury laced with a heart-pounding terror. 'I implore you to reconsider.'

Lip curled disdainfully Calzada shook his head, the plea for clemency falling on deaf ears.

Panic-stricken, her eyes glistening with unshed tears, Edie clasped her hands together. Silently begging for her life.

Stay strong, love. Chin up.

Since it was impossible to negotiate with a savage, Calzada and Diaz no better than the beasts in the field, Cædmon cleared his throat and said, 'I demand that you immediately call G-Dog.'

'You don't give me orders, English,' Calzada snarled. Grasping the stippled grip on the Beretta, he yanked it out of his waistband. He then straightened his arm and twisted his wrist forty-five degrees, holding the gun at an angle. A cock-eyed way to hold a firearm; one made popular by American gang members.

Cædmon held his ground, staring the bastard directly in the eyes. In those telling moments, he could see that the man had no soul, Hector Calzada a human in name only. He lowered his gaze, refocusing his attention on the stainless-steel gun barrel that slightly moved with each indrawn breath.

It would take little incentive for Calzada to pull the trigger.

'Are you afraid of me, English?'

'I'm wary of any man who wields a gun with such jaunty exuberance,' Cædmon replied.

'Do you know what will happen if I pull the trigger?' When no answer was forthcoming, the question perversely rhetorical, Calzada smirked. 'Your brain will be blown out the back of your head, splattering bloody chunks all over the van.'

'Leaving you to find the *Evangelium Gaspar* all by yourself. Are you up to that challenge?' Cædmon deliberately waited two beats before returning the smirk. 'I didn't think so. Call G-Dog. *Now!*'

Calzada's heavy-lidded eyes narrowed, reptilian-like, into brown slits. An instant later, proving himself a true psychopath, he chuckled. 'I like you, English. You got steel ping-pongs.' Shoving the Beretta back into his waistband, he snatched Edie's iPad from the floor and proceeded to access the Skype application.

As he waited for the call to go through, Cædmon knew that he had to play to his strength as a medieval historian who, along with his research assistant, was uniquely qualified to find the *Evangelium Gaspar*. Whatever was contained in the ancient gospel, the Church had been very keen in 1308 to retrieve it. The fact that G-Dog was a Roman Catholic priest was proof positive that they were still intent on finding it.

Truth be told, he was incensed that the Church was involved in this murderous plot. Given that the pontiff had recently died, Cædmon could scratch him off the suspects' list. But the fact that Anala was kidnapped soon after Gita contacted the Vatican Secret Archives in regards to Fortes de Pinós made him wonder if perhaps a cardinal or bishop had orchestrated the abduction. His gut feeling was that the priest, G-Dog, was merely a lackey. If true, it begged the question . . . *who was his master?*

After updating the priest about the events at Casa de Pinós – 'We took care of the old dude'; an outrageous understatement if ever there was – Calzada passed the iPad to Cædmon.

'You consulted with the enemy,' the priest promptly accused.

'How was I to know that the Marqués de Bagá was your enemy?' Cædmon shot back. Then, going on the offensive, he said, 'I will consult with *anyone* who can help me find your damned gospel. I told you that I'll find it and I shall.'

'Who's the woman sitting beside Hector?' the priest demanded to know.

'Miss Miller is my research assistant.'

'I can pop her, G-Dog, no problem,' Calzada said in a loud voice from the other side of the van. 'Take care of her like we did the old *patrón*.'

The remark made the priest visibly nervous, his demeanour putting Cædmon in mind of a terrified rodent. It was clear that playing the warlord did not come naturally to the man. Unlike his two underlings, who were rabid with bloodlust.

'Based on the information obtained from the Marqués de Bagá, I now know where the *Evangelium Gaspar* is hidden,' Cædmon announced, dropping his bombshell in a clipped, expressionless tone of voice. 'But I won't be able to find it without Miss Miller's assistance.'

'I'm . . . I'm not sure . . . I will call you back in a few minutes with my decision,' the priest stammered before abruptly disconnecting the call.

Cædmon stared silently at the iPad screen. G-Dog obviously had to consult a higher authority. And he'd wager that it wasn't God Almighty.

Someone at the Vatican, more than likely.

36

'*That* was too close a call,' Edie said with a shuddering sigh. 'Now I know how death-row prisoners feel when the warden issues a stay of execution.' Readjusting her seatbelt, she glanced in the hire car's rear-view mirror. As though it were a billowing white sail cresting the horizon, the service van tucked in directly behind them, Hector Calzada at the wheel. 'I don't understand how anyone can revel in bloodshed.'

Cædmon also peered into the rear-view mirror as he navigated the Volkswagen Passat in and out of the heavy northbound A-6 traffic. 'Be grateful that you can't comprehend the heart of darkness,' he said quietly. 'Therein is the quick path to madness.'

Distressed by that thought, Edie opened the glove compartment and removed a packet of chocolate biscuits that she'd purchased at the airport.

The flight from Mumbai to Madrid had been gruelling. The only available seats had been in economy; her tailbone had yet to recover from the thinly padded seat cushion. And with three infants onboard, sleep had been out of the question. Added to that was the emotional duress of knowing what would transpire if they didn't find the *Evangelium Gaspar*. They now had less than three full days to meet the ransom deadline, the clock ticking with a funerary persistence.

In all honesty, she didn't know how Cædmon was holding it together. Her thread was seriously frayed.

As they left the city behind, the scenery changed dramatically, the billboards giving way to the rolling foothills of the Sierra de Guadarrama. Nestled in the bucolic landscape were picture-perfect villages bordered by undulating swathes of green grassland, herds of grazing cattle and fields filled with red poppies. It was here, sequestered from the Vatican's watchful eye, that eight hundred years ago the Knights Templar enjoyed the privileges that came with being the favoured sons of the Iberian kings. Showered with land grants, castles, farms and fortresses, they were a force to be reckoned with.

Although they never reckoned on the unrestrained malice of a French king whose long arm extended to even this remote part of the world.

Package opened, Edie offered Cædmon a chocolate biscuit. When he refused with a silent shake of the head, she plucked one free and chomped down on it, in dire need of a sugar fix.

'Are you *absolutely* certain that you know where the *Evangelium Gaspar* is hidden?' she enquired anxiously.

Cædmon spared her a quick glance. 'The clue couldn't have been clearer had it been sung by a choir of heavenly angels. It's right there on the Marqués's map of Castile–Léon.'

Picking up the photocopied sheet of paper, Edie studied the beautifully executed map, medieval cartography a lost art form. 'To see the house where Lucas dwelled, the faithful pilgrim sought the brother's way. Setting forth from the lion's castle, he put the French iron in a Spanish harbour,' she recited from memory. Shaking her head, admittedly befuddled, she said, 'Okay, which harbour am I supposed to be looking at?'

'There is no harbour. At least, not a literal one,' Cædmon clarified. 'Although harbour is an essential piece of the word puzzle. And it doesn't matter whether one deciphers the riddle in the original Latin or in modern English, the clues lead to the same place.' As he spoke, Cædmon reached for his water bottle and, holding the steering wheel with his wrists, twisted the cap. 'Like you, I originally thought that Fortes had hidden the *Evangelium Gaspar* at a Templar naval port.'

'A logical conclusion since the Templars once had the largest standing navy in Europe.'

'But to solve the riddle, you have to dig all the way down to the root.' Cædmon took a quick swig of water before he elaborated and said, 'By that, I mean Fortes de Pinós was a Spaniard who served as grand commander at the Templar preceptory in Paris. In addition to Latin, he would have been fluent in both French and Spanish. To decipher the last fragment of the riddle, both of those languages must be employed.'

Needing a more potent pick-me-up, Edie snatched the Starbucks coffee cup out of the plastic holder. The cappuccino was hours old, having been purchased at the airport. 'You're referring to the "he put the French iron in a Spanish harbour" piece of the puzzle, right?'

Cædmon nodded as he flipped the indicator and manoeuvred the sedan into the left lane. 'The Spanish word for "put" is *pon* and the French word for "iron" is *fer*. Lastly, the Spanish word *rada* refers to a protected area for ships.'

'Aka, a harbour.' Grimacing, Edie took a sip of the cappuccino.

'String it all together and you end up with *Ponferrada*.'

Her eyes opened wide, the name ringing a bell. 'Wasn't that one of the four Templar fortresses that the provincial Grand Master tried to safeguard from the Church?'

Cædmon confirmed with a nod. 'Moreover, if you examine the map, you'll notice that Ponferrada is the only one of the four fortresses that's situated on the Camino de Santiago.'

Locating Ponferrada Castle on the map, Edie looked over at him. 'That's the famous pilgrim route that leads to the cathedral of St James at Compostela, right?'

'It is. And, as you know, the Templars were sworn to protect Christian pilgrims, both in Iberia and the Holy Land.'

'The faithful pilgrim sought the brother's way.' Suddenly, Fortes's riddle made perfect sense. 'While I'm not as fluent in Spanish as you are, I do know that *camino* is the Spanish word for "way". So, clearly, Fortes is referring to the Camino de Santiago. The way of St James.'

'A bit of clever legerdemain on Fortes's part, I might add, given that Fortes was a brother monk and James was the brother of Jesus.'

In a celebratory mood, Edie reached for another biscuit. 'You're right, very clever. But what about the first part of the riddle, "To see the house where Lucas dwelled"? What the heck does that mean?'

'I have no bloody idea,' Cædmon confessed with a shrug. 'While I haven't completely deciphered the riddle, as soon as I realized that Fortes de Pinós hid the *Evangelium Gaspar* at Ponferrada Castle, I couldn't have jumped higher.'

'Or driven the Volkswagen faster.' Edie pointedly glanced at the speedometer. 'Maybe you should slow down a bit. This is, after all, an unfamiliar road.'

'We have another two hundred kilometres to traverse,' Cædmon informed her. 'In case you've forgotten, the deadline looms. I have no choice but to sail close to the wind.'

Properly chastened, Edie looked away from the speedometer. She knew that the haunting image of Anala Patel, bound and gagged, was never far from Cædmon's mind.

'*We* have no choice,' she stressed, reminding him that he wasn't alone. They were a team. *Like Isabella and Ferdinand. Or Holmes and Watson.* 'Luckily, the castle stays open late during the summer months.' Before leaving Madrid, they had done a quick Google search. Not only was Ponferrada Castle open to the public, but the castle was remarkably well-preserved. 'According to the website, they don't pull up the drawbridge until eight thirty.'

Dropping his hand to the clutch, Cædmon changed down a gear, revving the engine as he took a tight curve. 'I estimate that we'll arrive at six o'clock or thereabouts. That'll give us at least two hours to scour the premises.'

Edie peered over her shoulder; the van was keeping pace with them.

Smiling lewdly at her, Hector Calzada made a very crude hand gesture.

Disgusted, she quickly looked away.

'I really, *really*, hope that time wounds all heels,' she muttered. 'Were you aware of the fact that the teardrop Calzada has tattooed in the corner of his eye is a Latino gang symbol?'

Cædmon glanced over at her, clearly surprised. 'I did think it rather odd.'

'It signifies that the tattooed individual had a friend or family member who was killed while serving time in prison.'

'A twist on wearing one's heart on one's sleeve.' Cædmon accelerated, passing a slow-moving lorry. 'The Bête Noire also has the Virgin of Guadalupe tattooed on his back.'

'Believe it or not, that's another popular gang tattoo.'

'Bloody hell! Is there nothing that these animals hold sacred?'

'That's the weird irony; the Virgin Mary *is* revered by Latino gang-bangers.' Living in a Latino neighbourhood in Washington, Edie had more than a passing familiarity with the culture. 'When someone has the Virgin of Guadalupe tattooed on his person, it symbolizes that the man is both sinner and saint. Kinda like a medieval warrior monk.'

'How so?'

'Think about it: the Knights Templar professed their love of God by slaughtering infidels in the Holy Land. Making them sinner *and* saint. And just like the medieval warrior monks, Latino gangs live by a very strict code that emphasizes God, honour and brotherhood.'

'Honour as gangsters define it,' Cædmon was quick to point out. 'The Knights Templar did not force their members to commit murder as an initiation rite. What I witnessed earlier today undoubtedly made the angels weep and Jesus Christ prostrate with grief.'

'I'm not defending these murderous fiends. I just think that you should know who you're dealing with. "Knowledge is power" and all that. If they're not active members of a Latino gang, Calzada and Diaz were affiliated with gang-bangers at some point in time.' Ravenous, Edie finagled another cookie out of the cellophane package. 'What I can't figure out is how they became involved with a Catholic priest.'

'Twice now I've spoken to this G-Dog via Skype and my sense of it is that he's merely the expediter.'

'In other words, someone else is conducting the orchestra.'

'Precisely. And I suspect that it's someone within the Vatican. As you'll recall, the initial ransom email was sent by an individual called Irenaeus. An alias, obviously. Whoever he is, Irenaeus has positioned himself far enough away from the bloodshed that he can't be held accountable.'

'Unlike the priest. Which certainly explains his Nervous Nellie demeanour.' Edie sighed, exasperated by the fact that they were being manipulated by an unseen puppet master.

'There's one other thing.'

'What's that?'

Cædmon reached up and adjusted the rear-view mirror. Staring at the trailing van, he said, 'I have reason to believe that as soon as Calzada and Diaz get their hands on the *Evangelium Gaspar*, they'll take us to a remote location where, to use the vernacular, they will then "pop" us.'

37

Standing in the middle of the castle bailey, Edie turned full circle. 'By my calculation, if we "leave no stone unturned", it shouldn't take more than a year to conduct a thorough search of the castle.'

Cædmon peered at the looming stone edifice.

They'd arrived at Ponferrada Castle forty minutes ago. After rushing through the quotidian preliminaries – parking and purchasing tickets – they'd piggybacked on to the last tour of the day. Their guide had studiously, and with no small amount of pride, pointed out all of the standard features that one expects to see in an 800-year-old castle: curtain walls, barracks, armoury, chapel, kitchen, barbicans, great hall and posterns. And though he'd carefully scrutinized everything that they'd been shown, Cædmon had not spotted anything that could be construed as a signpost.

Only an interminable store of mortared stone.

'At least a year,' he muttered.

Damn Euripides and his infernal proverb.

Bleary-eyed, Edie put a hand to her mouth, unsuccessfully masking a yawn. She then shook her head brusquely, the way people do when they're trying to clear the cobwebs. Revived somewhat, she gazed at the nearest watchtower and said, 'With all of these crenellated walls, the Templars' castle has a decidedly gloomy aspect. In a no-frills, bare-bones sort of way.'

The observation was bang on. All that remained of Ponferrada Castle were the stones. And they, in turn, lent the gravitas of the grave. Silent and lifeless.

Despite the bustling town nestled on the other side of the curtain wall, *el castillo Templario de Ponferrada* was a place steeped in mystery, the heavy weight of history embedded in each arched entryway, each soaring tower. Set on a hillock overlooking the River Sil, it was the perfect medieval construct. Magnificent and forbidding in the same breath. Not even the honey-toned Spanish sun could temper its stern visage.

Had this massive stone edifice been designed to protect a secret? *One that the order feared the Church might not approve of?*

'Hey, English! How much longer are you going to stare at these rocks? You think they're gonna tell you something?' Calzada taunted with uncanny accuracy.

Having shadowed him and Edie into the castle – ordered to do so by their master, G-Dog – the two Latino cut-throats were now loafing on a bench, their backs propped against a stone foundation wall. Diaz, eyes closed, mouth wide open, appeared to be fast asleep, exhausted from his day's labour. Calzada lounged beside him, awake, but heavy-lidded. Evidently even monsters suffered from jet lag.

Ignoring them, Cædmon focused his attention on the curtain wall that bordered the castle.

The bloody gospel could be hidden anywhere in these towering battlements, the complex boasting numerous chambers and a total of twelve towers.

A thought that induced a fearful dread, the knot tightening in his lower belly.

Cædmon glanced at his watch; the castle would be closing in an hour. *Damn.* Most of the tourists had already quit the premises and he worried that a zealous guide would soon be shooing them on their way.

'I suspect that the opening fragment of the riddle – "To see the house where Lucas dwelled" – may be some sort of a signpost.'

'Makes sense since that's the only piece of the riddle that we haven't solved,' Edie said, peering up at the circular tower that soared above them.

Hit with a stray thought, Cædmon contemplatively tapped his chin. 'Since Lucas is the Latinized name for Luke, the signpost might well pertain to the Evangelist Luke, the author of one of the four canonical gospels.'

Edie shoved her sunglasses to the top of her head. 'We're looking at nearly sixteen thousand square metres of stone. Even if we make the connection between Luke and Ponferrada, I put our odds at one in a thousand.'

'Like you, I'm not wildly optimistic,' he muttered in a dispirited tone of voice. 'Nevertheless, we must soldier on.'

'I'm too frazzled to charge into battle. Every time I blink, I wipe out the memory of what I just said.' Shoulders slumping, his usually plucky partner sat down on the grassy lawn. Her cheeks pale and her eyes rimmed with dark circles, Edie appeared to be on the verge of total collapse. 'Sorry, but my brain stopped working about an hour ago.'

'Why don't you walk into town and get us a hotel room?' he suggested. 'You can take a quick nap while I –'

'I'll sleep when you sleep.' Gracing him with a weary

247

smile, Edie unfolded the tourist pamphlet that they'd been issued at the ticket counter. The supply having been picked over, the only available brochure had been the French-language version.

'While I appreciate your steadfast commitment to –'

'*Oh . . . my . . . God!*' Edie suddenly exclaimed. 'I think Ponferrada's twelve towers have something to do with the zodiac.'

'I beg your pardon?' Cædmon wondered if he'd heard correctly. 'Did you say "the zodiac"?'

'Here. See for yourself.' Edie handed him the tourist brochure. 'Your French is a whole lot better than mine. Read the sentence beneath the aerial shot of the castle complex.'

Cædmon quickly scanned the line of text. '*Les douze tours de la forteresse imitent schématiquement les douze constellations ou signes du zodiaque.*'

'The twelve towers of the fortress schematically mimic the twelve constellations or signs of the zodiac,' he translated aloud. Elated, he glanced at his partner, his lips curving in an appreciative smile. 'Brilliant *and* beautiful.' He extended a hand in Edie's direction. 'Come. Let's investigate whether the audacious claim is true or not.'

'Where the hell are you two going?' Calzada abruptly demanded to know, eyeing them suspiciously.

'No need to sound the alarm,' Cædmon assured him. 'We're simply going up to the parapets so we can better scan the compound.'

The explanation sufficed, Calzada waving them on their way. His lack of concern undoubtedly stemmed from the fact that there was only one exit from the castle interior via the gatehouse. In order to escape, he and Edie would have to first steal past the gun-toting Bête Noire, who would not hesitate to draw his weapon.

Green light given, Cædmon set off for the nearest set of stairs, Edie in tow.

Both of them breathless, they reached the top of the staircase and rushed down the walkway adjacent to the curtain wall. Finding a good vantage point to view the castle complex, Cædmon stopped at a crenellated parapet.

Perfect. Bird's eye.

In the near distance, the slow-moving River Sil snaked past the adjacent town where tourists traipsed along cobbled lanes in groups and pairs, roving from hotels to tapas bars in a boisterous meander. In the far distance, the Aquilianos Mountains rose up out of the shadowed landscape in a sober montage of beige, brown and amber. More Rembrandt than Renoir.

Cædmon took a deep breath, the late-day sun coaxing from the landscape a heady mixture of scents: citron, thyme and a hint of saffron.

Gazing at the stone-laden compound, he could see that the castle conformed to a rectangular plan, the focal point being the drawbridge and gatehouse flanked by twinned towers. There was one other set of identically matched circular towers to the rear of the gatehouse; the other eight towers, positioned around the twenty-foot-high curtain wall, were irregular in design, six of them being square-shaped, the remaining two spherical. A dry moat bounded two sides of the castle.

Cædmon carefully scrutinized each of the towers, able to detect where, over the centuries, repairs had been made, mismatched mortar the giveaway. While medieval towers inevitably delighted modern observers, during the Middle Ages they served a strictly military purpose. But the towers of Ponferrada also contained a hidden esoteric meaning.

If only these stones could speak.

Moving her index finger in the air, Edie silently counted. 'Okay, I've verified that there are indeed twelve towers.'

'A numeral that harkens to a surfeit of associations: months of the year, the apostles of Christ, fruits of the Cosmic Tree. The list is endless.'

'And let's not forget, the signs of the zodiac. Incidentally, didn't our tour guide mention that Ponferrada is the *only* Templar fortress constructed with twelve towers?' When he nodded, Edie continued and said, 'Okay, so we've established that twelve is a number chock-full of significance. But it's a mystery to me how these twelve towers relate to the known constellations. I thought the word "zodiac" meant "circle of animals".'

Again, Cædmon nodded. 'The word is taken from the Greek *zodiakos*, from which is derived the abbreviated "zoo".'

Edie fingered a line of dry mortar on the parapet, the work of a skilled craftsman long since dead and buried in his grave. 'But all of these towers are set around a square design.'

'They are at that.'

She raised a quizzical brow. 'So, then, there's no *zodiakos*.'

'Ah, but there is.' Cædmon unsnapped his rucksack and removed pen and paper. Using the top of the parapet as a makeshift desk, he quickly drew what he believed to be the Ponferrada zodiac.

'As you just mentioned, the signs of the zodiac are based on twelve constellations or star groups, each designated by a different animal; an ancient mnemonic device originated by the Babylonian astrologers.' Finished with the drawing, he handed Edie the sheet of paper.

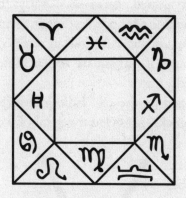

'While the circular zodiac is the more familiar design, during the Middle Ages a square zodiac containing the twelve houses was occasionally used. The triangular shape is symbolic of the fact that each house of the zodiac governs mind, body and spirit and does so throughout the course of one's life from birth through adulthood until death.'

Smiling, Edie lightly slapped her forehead with the base of her palm. 'Of course! Lucas's "house" refers to one of the twelve houses of the zodiac. Begging the question: which house? Other than the Star of Bethlehem, there's no mention of a celestial event in Luke's gospel.'

Cædmon gestured to her shoulder bag. 'Would you mind

booting up the iPad and accessing the Gospel of Luke so that – Belay that!' he blurted suddenly. Having just figured out the clue, he excitedly pointed to the square zodiac and said, 'The Apostle Luke *is* the bloody key to the cipher!'

'How do you know that?'

'Because in the Middle Ages, the four evangelists – Matthew, Mark, Luke and John – were each symbolized by a different animal. Luke was always depicted as a winged ox.' Cædmon tapped his finger against one of the triangles on the zodiac. 'And *that*, in turn, corresponds to the second house of our square zodiac, Taurus, which, as you undoubtedly know –'

'Is symbolized by the ox,' Edie interjected. Snatching the pen, she quickly scrawled the symbol for Taurus.

'And I might add that Taurus also symbolizes hidden treasure.'

'Brilliant *and* beautiful!' Edie exclaimed, leaning over and kissing him soundly on his unshaven cheek.

'I couldn't have figured it out without your attentive eye.' Indeed, he'd been too quick to discount the tourist pamphlet when they'd first arrived.

'So all we need to do is figure out which of the twelve towers represents Taurus.'

'Since Taurus is the second house of the zodiac –' he again tapped the triangle inscribed with the symbol for Taurus before pointing to the two twinned towers at the entry – 'I believe the correct tower is one of the matched set that flanks the gatehouse.'

'Because those are the first two towers that a person encounters when they enter the castle,' Edie correctly deduced.

'And I would further posit that, as one stands on the drawbridge and faces the castle, the tower on the left-hand side is Aries, the first house of the zodiac, the constellations traditionally configured anti-clockwise.'

'Making its twin on the right, Taurus. Second tower, second house. Makes perfect sense,' Edie concurred.

For several long moments Cædmon stared at the second tower, contemplating his next move. 'Fortes de Pinós could have very easily cached the three copper plates in an arrow slit or recessed window. The opening would then have been sealed over with stone and mortar. A simple but effective means to hide something of great value from prying Church eyes.'

Edie hitched a hip on to the edge of the parapet. 'And I'm guessing that our brother knight would have then marked the new stones in some way to distinguish them from the thousands upon thousands of stones at Ponferrada.'

'Our thoughts run a similar course.' Folding the sheet of paper, Cædmon placed it inside his rucksack. 'Fortes de Pinós lived in dangerous times and clearly did not intend to take the secret of the *Evangelium Gaspar* to the grave. That's why he devised the Chinon Riddle. Even at the end, when he knew that he wouldn't survive his ordeal, he still clung to the hope that a brother knight, perhaps Jacques de Molay or another high-ranking Templar, would be acquitted and released from custody.'

'Little did Fortes know that Jacques de Molay would be burned at the stake in front of Notre-Dame cathedral.'

Cædmon hefted the rucksack on to his shoulder. 'In the time remaining we need to search the circular stairwell inside the second tower for a *signum*, a mark or sign, to indicate where Fortes may have hidden the gospel. And we mustn't rule out the possibility that the *signum* was placed on the tower's exterior.'

Hearing that, Edie's eyes opened wide. 'But that would mean you'd have to scale the outside of the tower. Surely, you wouldn't attempt that without climbing gear?'

'I'm not as reckless as all that,' he assured her. 'If we hurry, we should be able to locate a shop in town where I can purchase the necessary equipment. At the very least, I'll need a torch, chisel and hammer, and a length of rope.'

She shot him a sceptical glance. 'And then what?'

'We'll then return to the castle and burrow inside a shadowy passageway until everyone has cleared the premises. Luckily, there aren't any security cameras on site. Once the castle closes for the night, we'll have the run of the place.'

While he didn't relish the idea of scaling the tower's exterior, he accepted that it might come to that.

'Cædmon, it would dangerous enough to climb that

tower in broad daylight and downright foolhardy to attempt to do so at night,' Edie said, brows drawn together in a worried frown. 'The darned thing is at least four storeys high. If you fall, you could break your neck.'

'I daresay you're right.'

But needs must.

38

Enough foot dragging. Just do it!

Worried that she might not get another chance, Anala slowly swung her right leg over the edge of the bed, her foot dangling a few inches above the floor. Holding her breath, she glanced at the guard, verifying that he was still asleep in his chair.

He was, his hands limply grasping a video game console.

Moving at an agonizingly slow speed – to prevent the bed frame from creaking in her wake – she adjusted her hips, next moving her left leg off the mattress.

For almost two days now she'd been staring at the overlooked piece of glass glittering benignly on the floor, obsessively fixating on how she might retrieve it. More importantly, she'd been scheming about what she would do once she had it in her possession. After yesterday's little Q & A session, she had a very real fear that if she didn't escape, she'd suffer a calamitous fate. *As in 'worse than'.*

She had a valid reason for her fear: during her interrogation, the oddly named G-Dog had informed her that she was being held for ransom. Not a monetary pay-off, mind you. No, instead, the ransom was an ancient gospel that had once been in the possession of a fourteenth-century Knight Templar. The likelihood of her mother meeting the kidnapper's demand was bugger-all. Even if her biological father *was* a Templar scholar. It was a thought that generated an ambivalent surge of emotion, Anala still grappling with the disturbing bombshell.

Why the big secret? Why hadn't her mother revealed the truth about her father? Didn't she care that her dark secret might –

Don't go there! Anala mentally chastised herself as she eased her hips off the bed. *Stay focused on the task at hand.*

Double-checking, she shot another glance at the guard, relieved to see that his blubbery mouth now hung wide open. God only knew what would happen if he suddenly awakened from his slack-jawed reveries. *Her* jaw still ached from the roundhouse punch he'd given her four days ago when he'd discovered her trying to escape through the window.

Refusing to contemplate the worst-case scenario – why dwell on the negative? – Anala placed a bare foot on the linoleum floor.

So far, so good.

Ever so carefully, she lifted her bum off the bed and stood upright.

Swaying slightly, she drew breath, pulling musty air through her nostrils to her lungs. Unfortunately, she wasn't functioning at a hundred per cent physically. Given the lack of exercise and dreadful fare – a nauseating rotation of spaghetti hoops and cheese sandwiches – she was operating at about sixty per cent.

Hopefully, that would provide enough steam to get the job done.

Again, she longingly eyed the thick piece of glass. It was only eight feet away. Eight paltry steps. Sixteen in total from start to finish.

I can do this.

Determined to retrieve the object of her obsession, Anala took the first step – toe to heel – gently easing her weight as she shifted her hips. In that same instant, she heard the wooden chair squeak. Pulse racing, she immediately tensed up. Bracing for disaster, she peered at the guard.

Still sleeping like a baby.

She relaxed a bit and took the next step. And another. Then, just wanting to get the nerve-wracking escapade over and done with, she took the last five steps in quick succession.

Bending at the waist, she plucked the thimble-sized piece of glass off the floor and carefully palmed it. She wasted no time making the return journey back to her lumpy bed.

Three steps from the finish line, she heard a loud crash.

Whipping her head round, Anala was horrified to see the fully roused guard jumping to his feet, awakened by the sound of his game console falling to the floor.

'What the hell are you doing?' he rasped.

Blindsided with fear, she immediately crouched over, grasping her lower belly. 'I think . . . I'm going to . . . be sick . . . I – I didn't want to – to vomit on the mattress.'

Moving surprisingly fast for a man who'd been sound asleep a few seconds ago, the guard snatched a plastic bag and held it under her chin. 'Puke into this!' he ordered. 'I don't want to have to mop the floor.'

'Thank you for –' Heaving violently, Anala retched on cue, the spaghetti hoops finally getting the better of her.

39

'Three bloody well better be the charm,' Cædmon muttered as he released the rope on the rappel device and slowly slid down the side of the tower.

Literally on the brink, this was his third descent down the exterior wall of the four-storey tower. Unable to find a *signum* inside the Taurus tower, he was now in the process of examining the exterior; a laborious undertaking made all the more difficult by virtue of the fact that night had fallen and the only illumination was the golden fan of light from his headlamp.

Luckily, he and Edie had found a sporting goods shop in town with a mountaineering section where he'd purchased fifty metres of rope, a rappelling harness, headlamp and leather gloves. Two doors down, at the hardware store, he'd bought some basic tools. Purchases made, they'd hurried back to Ponferrada Castle, managing to find a secluded *garderobe* where they'd hidden until the staff had departed the premises. Calzada and Diaz had stationed themselves outside the castle, taking up a position near the public entryway. Neither of them wanted to be caught inside the castle lest the alarm was sounded.

Edie, who had very succinctly informed him that clambering down the tower in the dead of night was akin to madness, waited for him at the bottom. Bated breath a given. And while he was unable to entirely banish his own queasy doubts about the risky endeavour, he did manage to shove them to the far corners, refusing to dwell on the fact that the rope was secured to an 800-year-old merlon, the high part of the squared saw-tooth that rimmed the top of the tower.

If, indeed, Fortes de Pinós had left a telltale *signum* on the tower's exterior, he too would have had to rappel down a length of rope.

Those damned Knights Templar.

While the warrior monks had always fascinated him, quite frankly he had never understood what would have compelled a man to join. Although the Templars were glamorized in modern movies and novels, monastic life was one of endless privation. Once initiated into the order, a warrior monk led an austere and grim existence. Meals were taken in silence; the monks were forbidden personal possessions; and to make even their slumber a torturous affair, they were forced to sleep with the lights on. During their waking hours, when they weren't busy with rigorous martial training, a Templar monk strictly adhered to the Liturgical schedule of prayers, Mass and biblical readings. All-in-all, a cheerless and loveless life. The latter would have been particularly hard to bear. Unless a man had joined as a widower, he would never have known the joy of hearth and home.

At the midpoint of the descent, Cædmon glanced down at Edie, the stolen glimpse causing him to momentarily loose his footing.

'Fine time to be a stumble-bum,' he rasped, exhaustion beginning to set in.

'Cædmon! Be careful!' Edie called up to him, her voice fraught with worry.

'No need to be concerned. I simply –'

Fuck me! There it was. The *signum* that he'd been searching for. An unmistakable symbol carved into a smooth stone – the Tau – from whence derived the astrological sign of Taurus, the bull.

The nineteenth letter of the Greek alphabet, it was a symbol steeped in sacred meaning. A visual depiction of the spiritual precinct where the earth meets the heavens, it harkened to the *Templum Hierosolyma*, the Temple of Jerusalem from which the Templars took their name.

The Tau.

A key to treasure – *clavis ad thesaurum* – the symbol had been used since ancient times to mark the place where riches had been hidden.

The Tau.

The age-old sign of redemption.

'Oh, how I do hope,' Cædmon whispered. Relief washing over him in waves, he rested his cheek against the cool stone, waiting for his heart to beat at a less dizzying rate.

'Cædmon, are you all right?'

'Yes, I . . . I've found the *signum*,' he yelled down to

Edie as he wrapped the rope around the brake rack on his harness.

'Are you sure about that?'

Cædmon smiled. 'Quite.'

Securely locked into place, he removed the chisel and mallet from the gear loops on his harness and began to chip away at the mortar around the stone. Raising his arm, he bit back a groan, his joints stiff, his body having been pushed to the limit over the last few days. Despite the pain in his shoulders and neck, he experienced an exuberant burst of hope as small chips of lime mortar pelted his cheeks.

This had *to be where Fortes de Pinós cached the* Evangelium Gaspar.

Since their demise in 1307, rumours had long swirled that the Knights Templar had devised a secret code known only to twelve high-ranking knights: the Grand Master Jacques de Molay and eleven of his closest associates. In case of a Doomsday scenario, any surviving member of the twelve-man cabal could use the code to retrieve the Templars' most sacred relics. *But from where?* That had always been the big mystery, many Templar scholars claiming the hidden stash was safeguarded in faraway Scotland.

Cædmon was beginning to suspect that the Templars' treasure had been squirreled in Spain rather than the Highlands.

I shall soon find out.

Finished chipping out the mortar, he shoved the chisel and mallet into their respective gear loops and reached for a flat-edged screwdriver. Prying the slender tool under the loosened stone, he slowly eased it forward. A southerly breeze lifted strands of damp hair off his brow, his face beaded with perspiration. He finagled the stone a few inches, just enough to enable him to get a firm, two-handed grip.

Time to raise the curtain.

Slipping the screwdriver into a loop on his harness, he grasped hold of the block and slid it free.

'Stand back,' he instructed Edie. 'I'm going to drop a stone to the ground.'

He glanced down, verifying that she'd moved out of range before he let go of the liberated block.

Releasing a tightly held breath, he peered into the cavity.

Seeing the tarnished copper plates cached in the hollowed-out space, he experienced a giddy burst. Heart pounding wildly, he reached inside the stone niche and removed the copper plates, which were approximately ten inches by twelve inches and –

Christ, no!

There were only two plates! *Where the bloody hell was the third plate?*

The blood fast drained from his face, his hope of securing the full ransom obliterated.

Would two plates suffice?

Somehow, he didn't think so.

'Did you find them?' Edie called up to him.

'Yes . . . no. Er, not entirely,' he sputtered.

'What do you mean "not entirely"?'

'I'll tell you when I get down.' Panic-stricken, his thoughts jumbled, Cædmon stuffed the two plates inside his rucksack. It was Thursday night; the deadline for delivering the ransom was noon on Sunday. That left him precious little time to find the third plate.

The sodding Tau.

Symbolic of the Temple and the Templars and *tempos.* Father Time. Ticking, ticking, ticking.

Maybe there was another Tau carved on to a different stone. Or perhaps there'd only been two plates to begin with.

No, he self-corrected. According to the Chinon Transcript, there were three copper plates. *So, why would Fortes de Pinós have only put two plates in the –*

Without warning, the rope suddenly jerked. Plunging a full twelve inches, his knees pounded into the stone façade with a bruising impact. Immediately he checked the rope twined around the brake rack and verified that it was tightly wound. Wondering what could have caused the sudden drop, he peered up towards the saw-toothed merlon at the top of the tower. Even in the shadowy light, he could see that it was askew.

Christ.

Unlike the ancient Romans, who added aluminium oxide and silicon dioxide to make a dense mortar, the stonemasons of the Middle Ages used lime. Full of impurities, cured lime mortar was known to deteriorate under long-term exposure to wind and rain. Ponferrada Castle had been exposed to the elements for eight full centuries.

Cædmon stared at the cockeyed merlon, transfixed, afraid to move, afraid the merlon would give way at any moment. Body curved, he dangled like a displaced quarter moon.

The rope jerked another few inches. While he knew it was an illusion, the stars in the night sky seemed to jerk in unison.

Disorientated, he heard Edie shouting at him from below. He glanced down and saw that she was frantically waving her arms. A dancing shadow.

He made a quick calculation. It was a long drop. A good twenty-five feet. One that could very well prove fatal. People had been known to break their bloody necks from as little as a five-foot fall.

The thought made him feel very much like a dead man on shore leave.

His pulse pounded in his ears.

But it wasn't his death that he feared. He was terrified of what would happen to Edie, and to Anala, should he plunge to his death. Before she even had time to mourn, the bloodthirsty Calzada would undoubtedly execute Edie. Pull the trigger, 'pop' her, and be done with it.

He stilled his breathing, afraid that even the slightest motion would send him hurtling through the air, base over apex.

In the next instant, just as he'd feared, the merlon gave way, chunks of stone flying through the air.

Bracing himself, Cædmon fell to earth.

40

'Ding-dong.'

Hearing Anala's overture, the guard glanced up from his video game, an annoyed frown stamped on his face.

'I'm not feeling well,' she told him, wincing in pain. Having carefully written the script, Anala raised her manacled hands, showing him a blood-smeared palm. She then gnawed worriedly on her bottom lip, trying to appear as mortified as humanly possible. 'As you can see, I've just started to menstruate.'

The guard's eyes opened wide, genuinely horrified by the disclosure. *So far, so good.* She was banking on the fact that, like most men, he'd have an unnatural fear of anything related to the female reproductive system.

'Wh-what does that have to do with me?' he stammered, staring at her as though she'd just sprouted horns, hoofs and a tail.

You sodding moron, what do you think? I need to use the toilet!

'Can you please take me to the loo? Since I tend to be a heavy bleeder, this is something of an emergency.' Bringing her knees together, Anala tried very hard to convey the image of a woman holding back the dam.

The indelicate postscript worked, the guard nodding brusquely. 'Hurry up. Let's go.' Getting up from his chair, he motioned for her to get off the bed. As he saw the dark red bloodstain on the cot mattress, he visibly blanched.

Head bent at a submissive angle – not wanting to arouse his suspicions – Anala obediently followed him down the hallway to the toilet.

'Thank you for being so kind,' she said just before she closed the door.

In a hurry to execute the plan, Anala flipped on the light and stepped over to the disgustingly filthy sink. Finagling a hand into the pocket of her cargo trousers, she retrieved a wadded paper napkin. Inside the napkin was the piece of glass that she'd earlier used to puncture her fingertip so that she could stain the cot.

She pinched the thick piece of glass between her thumb and index finger and, turning her manacled wrist, began to saw through the plastic band.

Hurry, hurry, hurry!

When the band finally snapped apart, her shoulders sagged with relief.

Worried about what the future held, certain that her mother would never be able to meet the outrageous ransom demand, she'd devised an escape plan. And while the thought of having to hurt, maim or even kill someone turned her stomach, the fear of being summarily executed was even more gut-wrenching.

Rewrapping the piece of glass in the napkin, she shoved it back into her pocket. Ready to implement Phase Two, she removed the heavy porcelain lid from the back of the toilet, taking care not to make any undue noise. Tightly grasping the lid, she stepped behind the door and raised the lid above her head.

'H-help me!' she croaked in a weakened tone of voice. 'I can't get up!'

Hearing a heavy footfall, she held her breath, her heart beating so fast she feared it might jump the tracks.

A split second later, the door flew open. As soon as the guard charged into the room, Anala struck him on the back of the head. Caught by surprise, he staggered several feet before toppling forward, collapsing on the floor in an ungainly heap. Knocked out cold.

Still holding the lid, she quickly put it back on the toilet.

'Excuse me. Have to dash,' she said, stepping over the sprawled body.

Rushing out of the loo, she sped towards the wooden staircase at the end of the hallway, taking the stairs two at a time. The treads creaked and groaned under her weight. At the top of the stairs, she came to a sudden stop, taken aback at finding herself in an empty assembly hall. She turned full-circle, searching for an exit. Spotting a set of double doors at the other end of the hall, she sprinted in that direction.

Fear giving way to euphoria, she flung the doors open and ran outside, gulping in mouthfuls of crisp air. For days now, she'd been forced to breathe the most foul, mildew-laden air imaginable.

Amazed that the plan had gone off without a hitch, she peered at the hilly countryside, the towering trees casting ominous shadows. For some inexplicable reason, she was actually comforted by the fact that there was no sign of human habitation. Until she figured out where she was, she didn't know who, if anyone, she could trust.

Craning her head, she glanced at the building she'd just escaped from.

Blimey!

Her mouth fell open, astonished that it was a small-scale replica of the Greek Parthenon.

'I am *definitely* not in Athens.'

So where the bleep am I?

41

Death, be not proud.

Or, at the very least, don't be quite so brutal, Cædmon silently pleaded, the journey to the great beyond turning into a gruelling ordeal. His head hurt, his ribs ached and his right hip felt as though it'd been ripped from his body. Punishment for a life of sin and cynicism. If he'd known beforehand, he would have parked his arse in the pew with greater frequency.

Too late now.

'Cædmon! Wake up!'

Somewhere, in the far distance, a woman called to him through a dimly lit tunnel. A muffled voice filtered through a dense cirrostratus cloud. A preposterous juxtaposition. *Why was there a cloud inside a tunnel?*

Annoyingly persistent, the woman again called his name. More strident this time, the summons was accompanied by a sharp slap to the cheek.

Bloody hell! That's a fine way to treat a dead man.

He blinked, the light inside the tunnel growing brighter with each passing second. First white, then yellow, and then a luminous shade of Persian blue. *St Elmo's Fire.* An incandescent ball of plasma that left him awestruck.

A beautiful will-o'-the-wisp.

He raised a hand to touch the glowing orb, struggling to keep his eyes open. A frustratingly impossible endeavour.

'Whatever you do, don't close your eyes,' the woman in the tunnel ordered.

Thinking his Angel of Death a stern mistress, he managed to keep his lids from draping over his pupils. 'He was one of the Fourteen Holy Helpers.'

'Who was?'

Belatedly realizing that she was shining a torch directly into his eyes, he shoved it aside. 'St Elmo, of course.'

Slowly coming out of his stupor, Cædmon became aware of the fact that he was sprawled on the ground, the Taurus tower looming above him. A voracious stone vulture. Unnerved by the sight, he struggled to sit up, groaning as he did so.

Edie put an arm around his shoulders, helping him to raise his back off the ground. The effort cost him, every muscle in his body shrieking in protest. While no bones were broken, he most assuredly had suffered several cracked or bruised ribs, making each indrawn breath an agonizing affair.

'How many fingers am I holding up?'

'That's an asinine question,' he snapped. Even as he said it, Cædmon obliged and glanced at Edie's raised hand. 'Two.'

'Do you have any broken bones?' she next enquired.

'I don't think so.' A miracle given that it'd been a bleeding long drop. He sucked in a deep breath, biting back a painful moan.

'Just to be on the safe side, I'm going to call an ambulance.' Edie opened her messenger bag and removed a mobile phone.

Cædmon immediately snatched hold of her wrist. 'I don't want Calzada to know that I'm injured.'

'But you could be suffering from a concussion.'

'If I am, being jostled about in an ambulance isn't going to cure me,' he countered, rest being the only remedy for that particular malady. 'The copper plates are inside my rucksack.'

Her worried expression instantly morphed into animated expectancy. 'So you *did* find the *Evangelium Gaspar*?'

'Yes, but there were only two copper plates inside the cavity.'

Her brow crinkled again. 'According to the Chinon Transcript, there are supposed to be three plates.'

'Leaving me somewhat in the lurch.' Unsnapping his rucksack, he removed the plates and set them on the ground, grateful that they'd not been damaged in the fall. 'For whatever reason, Fortes de Pinós only placed two plates inside the niche.'

His headlamp lost in the fall, Cædmon snatched Edie's torch, aiming it at the ground. Although badly tarnished, the incised lettering was still clearly visible. Written in Aramaic, the language spoken by Jesus and his apostles, both sides of each plate were engraved. A precursor to modern-day Hebrew, Aramaic was one of those dead languages that he'd never taken an interest in. *Alas.*

Crouched beside him, Edie stared intently at the plates as she ran her fingers over the incised surface. An instant later, she jerked her hand away as though she'd just been singed. She didn't say a word. She didn't have to. She knew that the *Evangelium Gaspar* had spelled Fortes de Pinós's doom.

God only knows what was scribed on the two plates.

'Do you think that Anala's captors will accept two plates as full ransom?'

Cædmon took a swig of water from Edie's bottle, rinsing the metallic taste from his mouth. 'I intend to call G-Dog and find out. But first, I want you to make rubbings of each plate as we discussed earlier.'

In addition to the climbing gear, they'd also purchased white butcher's paper and wax crayons during their shopping foray, worried that if he did find the *Evangelium Gaspar*, Edie wouldn't be able to take clear enough photographs of the 2000-year-old gospel with the iPad. Hector Calzada, a thieving bastard as well as a murderous thug, had confiscated her Nikon.

While Edie efficiently went about her task, Cædmon unhooked the climbing harness from around his waist and thighs, ignoring the painful shots across the bow. Clenching his jaw, he rummaged through Edie's bag and removed the iPad. As soon as she was finished with the rubbings, he would Skype G-Dog and email him photos of the *Evangelium Gaspar*.

If the two plates didn't satisfy the ransom demand, he had a back-up plan.

Assuming that his old group leader at MI5 would be able to get a trace on G-Dog's phone number and pinpoint the priest's exact location, he still had three days to put a rescue mission into play. That, of course, presumed that Anala was being held at the same location as the priest. Success furthermore depended upon his being able to elude Calzada and Diaz who, like *Ruti*, the twinned Egyptian lions that guarded the underworld, were waiting outside the castle gate, loaded Beretta and deadly falchion at the ready.

Too fatigued to think straight, Cædmon leaned back, his elbow jutting against the Tau stone that he'd earlier tossed to the ground. Wincing, he pushed the block to one side.

Which is when he noticed the strange carving on the square chunk of limestone.

'Would you mind passing me the torch?' he asked Edie as he pulled the stone closer to him.

Bent over a paper-covered copper plate, Edie stopped what she was doing and handed him the flashlight. Cædmon aimed it at the stone, illuminating several rows of encoded 'text' that was comprised of lines and dots.

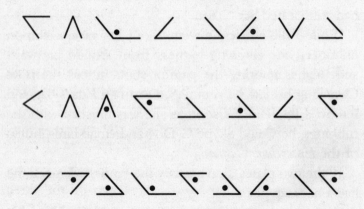

'Bloody hell,' he murmured. 'We have our divining rod.'

'What are you talking about?'

Relieved, and horrified to think that he'd very nearly *not* seen the code, Cædmon said, 'Fortes de Pinós carved an encrypted message on the backside of the Tau stone.'

'Oh my gosh!' Brown eyes glimmered. 'I'm guessing that our wily Templar knight didn't want to put all his eggs into the one castle basket. So he stashed the third plate in a different location. And then left a cryptogram with directions.'

Faced with a new challenge, Cædmon shoved out a deep breath. 'Of course, this means that we now have to crack the blasted code.'

'But at least Fortes left us a road map.'

Still amazed by his chance discovery, Cædmon palmed the stone. 'Let us hope that is indeed what this is.'

'As soon I finish with the copper plates, I'll make a rubbing of the stone.'

'Thank you, love.' He smiled wearily, grateful to have Edie at his side.

A few minutes later, rubbings finished and neatly rolled up for safekeeping, Cædmon accessed Skype on the iPad. He then put on his 'game face' as the Americans called it.

'I have news to report,' he said without preamble when G-Dog answered the call. 'I've managed to locate two-thirds of the *Evangelium Gaspar*.'

'Two-thirds? I . . . I don't understand,' the other man sputtered.

Thinking the priest a dim-witted bloke indeed, Cædmon elaborated and said, 'I've uncovered two of the three copper plates. Stand by for the digital images which I am now emailing to you.'

'Where's the third plate?' G-Dog asked a few moments later, confusion replaced with suspicion.

Opting for the truth, Cædmon shrugged. 'I have no idea.'

'You *must* give me all three of the copper plates.'

'One rarely hits the bullseye with the first arrow. It pains me to say,' he added sarcastically, his body wracked with it. 'However, Fortes de Pinós left an encrypted code that I am confident will reveal the location of the third plate. The Knights Templar were talented code writers, the Order having devised a number of clever encryption systems.'

'Why would the Templar do that?'

'You mean conceal the third plate in a different location?' On the verge of informing the priest that he wasn't a bloody mind reader, Cædmon, instead said, 'Fortes de Pinós knew that the Templars who'd been arrested in France were having a jolly time of it at Chinon Castle, what with having their nuts roasted over an open fire. He had hoped to use the *Evangelium Gaspar* to secure their freedom. And while I can only speculate as to his rationale, it seems that he wanted to have a reserve cache in case he was betrayed by the French king.' *A prudent manoeuvre as one should never trust a monster*, he thought, but didn't say aloud.

'Will you be able to decipher the code?'

'I have some experience with codebreaking,' Cædmon told him, not about to reveal that he'd gained that experience during his tenure at MI5. Then, needing to quell the other man's doubts, he said with a full measure of confidence, 'I *will* find the third plate. This is a mere hiccup. Nothing more.'

42

Sanguis Christi Fellowship, Dutchess County, New York

'Why do the righteous suffer?' Gracián Santos murmured, deeply concerned about what would happen if the English-man failed to find the third plate.

As he entered the Sanguis Christi Chapel, he felt akin to Job, a righteous man made to suffer an unwarranted trial at the hands of Satan.

Emotionally frayed, Gracián flipped the light switch, turning on the low-wattage lamps that hung from the heavily carved walnut panelling that lined each side of the chapel. Dipping his fingers into the stoup, he blessed himself with a few drops of holy water.

'In the name of the Father, and of the Son, and of the Holy Spirit.'

Although a small chapel, it was elaborately ornate with stained-glassed windows depicting the Four Evangelists. A place of spiritual renewal, he encouraged the students to visit the chapel often so that they could ponder the meaning of the four Gospels in their lives.

But now a fifth, heretofore unknown gospel, had become the focus of Gracián's life in recent days.

When Cardinal Fiorio first approached Gracián about

finding the *Evangelium Gaspar*, he had expressed reservations about retrieving the ancient text. *What does a simple priest know of these things?* But the cardinal had been quick to remind Gracián that throughout the Church's 2000-year history, it had often utilized a cadre of men, like the Knights of St John, who were willing to battle the Evildoers in the Lord's name.

Tonight, Gracián feared that the Devil might be winning the bout.

'Money is indeed the root of all evil,' he whispered in a hoarse voice, knowing that he'd earlier permitted a heinous act to occur because he was desperate to repay the $2.2-million bank loan.

When he made the crucial phone call giving Hector Calzada the execution order, Gracián had become a merchant of death. *A Diablo.* And though his hands might not be stained with the Marqués de Bagá's blood, his soul most assuredly was.

While Cardinal Fiorio considered the murder of the Spanish nobleman a righteous act, no different to a medieval crusader slaying an infidel, Gracián wasn't entirely convinced. Granted, history wasn't his strong suit, but he seemed to recall that Pope Urban II had issued a blanket indulgence to all Christian crusaders, absolving them of any sins incurred during those blood-thirsty engagements. No such indulgence had been issued to Gracián or the two Diablos who participated in the blood spree.

If the third plate isn't found, I will lose everything. The Sanguis Christi Fellowship. My ministry. And after this deadly day, perhaps even my mortal soul.

For the first time in twenty-seven years, Gracián's faith was on shaky ground. Over the course of those years, ever since he'd made the acquaintance of a Maryknoll nun named Sister Marita Daniel, he'd been firm in his religious convictions. Never questioning. Never doubting.

'O most merciful Jesus, with a contrite heart and penitent spirit, I bow down in profound humility before Thy divine majesty.'

That was the prayer that Sister Marita Daniel would recite at the beginning of her gospel workshops, the attendees of which were all hardened men; men who, for the most part, had stopped going to Mass years ago; men who'd committed grave sins and heinous acts. Hard-hearted, they were all inmates at the Sing Sing maximum security prison, each man having a different motive for attending the weekly workshop. Some, riddled with guilt, had embraced The Way of the Cross. Some were bored by the tedium of prison life and sought a diversion. And a few, like Gracián, craved the sound of a female voice. Even if that voice belonged to a stout middle-aged Catholic nun.

While he enjoyed the melodic, sweet sound of Sister Marita Daniel's voice, he paid scant attention to her gospel lessons. *What was the point?* Having killed a man in cold blood, he didn't hold out much hope, if any, that he would receive a warm welcome in heaven. Not when the Devil would be waiting for him with open arms. Gracián was, after all, a Diablo. The Devil's own.

Then, one day, the dulcet-toned nun began to speak of something that Gracián had never heard of before: the Blood Atonement. According to Sister Marita Daniel, sin bars a man from Heaven's gate, a precept that he readily accepted, having condemned himself to Hell the instant he plunged a serrated knife into another man's neck. '*But because He loves us unconditionally, the sinless Jesus willingly died upon the Cross for our sins, sacrificing Himself in our stead so that all sinners may enter the Kingdom of God.*'

All sinners?!

When he'd heard that, Gracián had suddenly became *very* attentive to Sister Marita Daniel's lesson, wanting to know if it was really true, if Jesus' crucifixion meant that even a murderous Diablo could enter into Heaven? Sister Marita Daniel assured him that's exactly what the Blood Atonement meant, provided that he made a true and heartfelt penance. '*You are not a Diablo. You, Gracián Santos, are a* Beatus Vir, *a blessed man of God. The Blood Atonement is the balm that heals all wounds.*'

The waves of relief that Gracián had felt could not be described. The nightmares that he'd suffered since that blood-drenched night when he'd beheaded a rival gang-banger suddenly ceased, his dreams now filled with heavenly light and future promise.

From that moment on, Gracián was a man reborn. Not only did Sister Marita Daniel give him spiritual guidance, but she tutored him so that he could earn his GED, General Equivalency Diploma. After that, he took advantage of the higher educational opportunities provided by the prison. When he left Sing Sing at the age of twenty-one, he had a college degree in hand. More importantly, over the course of his five years of incarceration, he'd developed a deep connection to the dying

Christ, devouring every religious text that the dulcet-toned nun advised him to read.

Revelling in the fact that he *was* a blessed man of God, Gracián, now at a crossroads, decided that he could gain no greater joy than to consecrate his life, not to *Los Diablos de Santa Muerte*, but to the Roman Catholic Church.

The momentous decision made, Gracián entered seminary school, his expenses paid for by Catholic charities.

When, at the age of twenty-eight, he was ordained into the priesthood, Sister Marita Daniel was the first one to give him a 'welcome to the family' hug.

From the onset, there had never been any question as to how Gracián could best serve the Lord. By reaching out to gang-bangers and at-risk youth, he would help tormented young people break the cycle of violence. To that end, he founded the Sanguis Christi – Blood of Christ – Fellowship. Aided by the Archbishop of New York, Franco Fiorio, Gracián was able to secure some *very* large foundation grants, the seed money that enabled the Fellowship to purchase the Porter Women's College at public auction.

Without a doubt, Gracián owed Cardinal Franco Fiorio a very big debt of gratitude.

But do I owe him this *much? Do I owe the cardinal my very soul?*

Deeply troubled, adrift in a sea of doubt, Gracián approached the altar.

'O most merciful Jesus,' he whispered fervently. 'With a contrite heart and penitent spirit, I bow down in –'

'G-Dog! We've a big problem! The girl's escaped!'

Hearing Jacko Maciel's unexpected exclamation, Gracián turned away from the altar and grabbed a nearby pew.

Suddenly lightheaded, the chapel spinning off-kilter, his voice came out in a hoarse whisper: 'We must find her!'

43

The alarm had been sounded.

Hearing the roar of an engine, Anala dodged behind a tree. Breathless, she put a hand to her aching side and glanced behind her. About three hundred metres from her present position, a black pickup truck zoomed and criss-crossed the bucolic landscape, the hunters on the prowl.

She estimated that she'd been running for nearly an hour through the gloomy thickets and shadowy wood-land. In her bare feet no less. It was utterly insane to think she could blaze a trail through the forest.

Worried that she may have been running in circles, she frantically surveyed the surrounding copse. Everywhere she looked there were forbidding shadows. The wind rus-tling through the splayed boughs spiked her dread fear.

I have no bleeding idea where I'm at.

'Just an unforeseen glitch,' she murmured, fighting back the tears. 'Soon enough, I'll find my way out of this eerie glen and –'

I still won't have a clue as to my whereabouts.

All along she'd been labouring under the delusion that she could easily make her way to safety. That clean clothes, a warm meal and a freshly brewed cup of tea were waiting for her around the bend. *Silly girl.* She had no idea where 'the bend' was even located. Didn't know what continent, let alone what country, she was in.

Panic clawed at her as she crept forward. She'd gone no more than a few feet when she tripped on a gnarled root and stumbled.

'Mind the step,' she muttered under her breath as she fell to her knees.

Panting softly, she remained on all fours. Incapable of getting up. Incapable of coherent thought. Hit with a dizzy onslaught, she swayed slightly.

I need to keep moving. I need to get a weapon. I need to find a knight in shining armour. I need . . . some sleep.

Yes, sleep.

Thinking that the best alternative of the lot, Anala crawled towards a big leafy bush. She'd not slept in the last twenty-four hours, too revved up about her escape plan. But the wax had melted from her wings and she'd just crashed to earth.

Convinced her fortunes would improve once she could think more clearly, she tucked herself under the sheltering briar bush. Closing her eyes, she inhaled the scent of pine needles and decayed vegetation. Fecund smells that made her think dreamily that she was nestled in the Earth's womb.

As she drifted into a deep slumber, Anala heard the rustling of a small animal burrowing in the underbrush. Surprisingly, the sound comforted her.

I'm not alone.

44

Pontifical North American College, Rome

In a celebratory mood, Cardinal Franco Fiorio raised his glass and took a measured sip of the Sciacchetrà dessert wine.

Today, he'd rid the Church of a dangerous enemy.

But others still lurked, he conceded, his gaze falling upon Thomas Moran, the Cardinal Secretary of State. A *pro tempore* title, the cardinal's term of office had officially ended upon the death of Pope Pius XIII. After the upcoming conclave, the newly elected pontiff would appoint the cardinal of his choice to fill the vacant position.

And somehow I don't think that it's going to be Thomas Moran.

Seated at a circular banquet table with eleven other dinner guests, Franco surveyed the refectory where the fundraising gala for the Pontifical College was being held. Nearly four hundred well-heeled attendees were packed inside the hall, the black-tie event boasting a stellar guest list that included prominent members of the Roman Curia, the American ambassador to the Holy See, a famous television news anchor, the US Senator from New York and a retired four-star Army general. The American contingent of the Roman Catholic family had come together to raise money for the college located atop Janiculum Hill, the seminary where bishops from the

United States shipped their most promising candidates for the priesthood. A number of whom were serving as waiters for the event. A second group, who were waiting in the wings, would soon be presenting the evening's entertainment, a medley of Broadway show tunes.

One of the 'waiters', attired in a black clerical suit and Roman collar, offered Franco a second slice of the *torta di ricotta*. Smiling politely, he waved off the very tempting piece of cheesecake. He was getting flabby around the middle, the years of Italian cuisine combined with the sedentary lifestyle having added thirty pounds to his once wiry frame.

Not a big Rodgers and Hammerstein fan, Franco excused himself from the table and made a hasty beeline for the exit, hoping to escape before the seminarians who'd already gathered in front of the microphones broke into a rousing rendition of 'Oklahoma'. En route, he again caught sight of the Cardinal Secretary, seated at one of the front tables. Smiling broadly, the 'camera-ready cardinal' was engaged in a convivial conversation with the ambassador's helmet-haired wife.

A Prince of the Church holding court.

And a man who, at nine-to-four odds, the bookies at least were certain would be the next Vicar of Christ. So, too, a majority of the Catholic glitterati attending this evening's festivities, the Cardinal Secretary designated as *papabile*. An Italian term used by Vatican insiders, it literally meant 'popeable' or 'one who could become pope'.

Someone's going to be in for a very rude surprise once the conclave begins.

Those same insiders had another expression, one that

was entirely apropos: 'He who enters the conclave as Pope, leaves it as a cardinal.' Meaning that all the expectations in the world couldn't get a man elected pontiff if he was unable to secure a two-thirds majority of the College of Cardinals.

For the time being, however, the Cardinal Secretary had caught the attention of the media and sycophants alike, the man basking in the adoration. But the papacy wasn't a beauty contest where the most telegenic cardinal won the prize. The very soul of the faithful was at stake, Franco convinced that liberals constituted the most dangerous threat the Church had faced in its 2000-year history.

One need only review a sampling of some of Moran's more outrageous statements to know that the man was a clear and present danger, the Cardinal Secretary having expressed some truly despicable opinions. Such as his belief that it was permissible for a married couple to use condoms if one of them had AIDS. He was also on the record as having publicly stated that homosexuals should be allowed into the priesthood provided they kept to their chastity vow. And Moran had even gone so far as to claim that it was better to masturbate than to cheat on one's spouse. None of which was acceptable in Franco's book.

And this was the man that Vatican insiders wanted to be the next apostolic successor to Peter!

As he passed the rector's table where the Cardinal Secretary held his admirers in thrall, Franco pursed his lips in disapproval. He knew that many of the guests seated there considered the Prefect of the Secret Archives a reactionary. A conservative throwback to an earlier era when Catholics ate fish on Fridays, went to confession once a week and attended early-morning weekday Mass. Traditions and practices that the liberals were only too happy to consign to the rubbish heap.

His earlier good cheer having suddenly dissipated, Franco left the refectory hall and made his way past study halls and empty classrooms. Leaving the building, he headed towards the cloister in the centre of the college where there was a small group of tables. His belly full, he eased himself into a metal chair. In dire need of an after-dinner smoke, he reached into his cassock pocket and removed a box of cigarillos along with his mobile phone. A few seconds later, he blew a puff of smoke into the night air, the fusion of Madagascar vanilla and Cuban tobacco having a calming effect.

In the tumultuous years following the Second Vatican Council, a rampant sexual decay had infiltrated the Church. Strong-armed into the priesthood by his mother, Franco, at the age of thirty, had a crisis of faith. Overcome with anarchic thoughts that threatened to emotionally unravel him, he'd decided to leave the priesthood, unable to navigate his way in the new liberal-minded Church.

His mind made up, Franco had written a resignation letter to the bishop. Having placed the sealed envelope on his desk, he'd left the rectory to visit a sick parishioner in the hospital; for what he assumed would be his last pastoral duty. When he returned a few hours later, to his utter astonishment there was a single red rose petal on top of the addressed envelope.

In that awestruck instant he had his epiphany.

The rose petal was a sign from heaven. A clarion call

announcing that he *was* the chosen one. He *was* the Fiorio son who'd been selected by the Queen of Heaven to safeguard the Church against all those who would do Her harm. *The liberals. The naysayers. The atheists. The Jews. The Protestants.* The fault line that had been opened in the aftermath of the Second Vatican Council was actually a battle line. Drawn, not in the sand, but on the spiritual plane.

'*My Son and your son.*'

Certain that he'd been singled out for great things, Franco journeyed to Rome, a fire in his belly. At the Pontifical Gregorian University, he earned advanced degrees in theology and ecclesiastical history. In the years that followed, he wrote books; the most notable, *Anno Domini*, was an in-depth treatise on the sacred mysteries of the Church; he served as secretary of the Apostolic Nunciature; and was appointed Dean of Students at Catholic University. Receiving his episcopal consecration, he was named the Archbishop of New York.

During those same years, plagued by scandals and losing the faithful at an alarmingly fast rate, the Roman Catholic Church staggered into the new millennium.

'Your Eminence, I hope that I'm not disturbing you,' a voice said, a man suddenly stepping out of the shadows. 'I received your earlier message.'

Lost in thought, Franco jerked his head, startled.

Belatedly recognizing the dapper man in the dark suit, he hastily stubbed out his cigarillo, pleased that Len Garvey, a wealthy media mogul and vocal conservative Catholic, had followed him out of the banquet hall.

Going down on his left knee, Garvey chastely kissed

the ornate gold ring that adorned Franco's right ring finger.

After verifying that no one lurked in the cloisters, Franco motioned for the mogul to sit down in the vacant chair beside him. Despite the surge in liberalism within the Church, there were still influential Roman Catholics who ardently believed that the ground so foolishly surrendered in the 1960s must be regained. Len Garvey happened to be one of those men.

Never one to play coy, Franco got right to it. 'What if I told you that I have the means to place an ultra-conservative cardinal on Peter's chair?'

If he was shocked by the bold assertion, Garvey gave no indication. Pokerfaced, he said, 'Meaning what exactly?'

'Meaning the repeal of Vatican II, the end of ecumenical outreach and strict enforcement of the more heinous lapses.'

An experienced negotiator, Garvey immediately counter-offered. 'Only if those lapses include birth control, divorce, stem-cell research, homosexual marriage and – the worst lapse of them all – abortion.'

Franco smiled. 'Consider it done.' He paused a moment, the next proposition a bit stickier. 'Since you're a businessman, you'll understand that there's a cost attached –'

'How much?' Garvey interjected.

'Two point two million.'

'Euros or dollars?'

'Dollars,' Franco told him, bracing for an objection, the price steep. Even for someone with deep pockets.

To his surprise, Garvey chuckled softly. 'At eleven thousand a head, there are plenty of Catholics who would consider that a bargain basement price.'

Leave it to a hard-nosed businessman to have calculated the cost per cardinal.

'I'll drop off the cheque tomorrow.'

Still marvelling at how easily he'd secured Gracián Santos's 'blood' money, Franco said, 'Aren't you the least bit interested in the details?'

'Probably best that I not know,' Garvey replied. 'Between you and me, I just want to revert to the old ways. To worship God like we did when I was an altar boy at All Saints' Church.' Dropping to his left knee, the mogul again paid homage.

Franco gave a commiserating nod. 'To return the sacred *mysterion* to the Mass.'

'We're reading from the same page, Your Eminence.' Len Garvey stood upright. 'I'll call around nine o'clock.'

'I look forward to the visit.'

A few moments later, about to relight his cigarillo, Franco instead picked up his phone which had begun to vibrate, skittering a few inches across the tabletop. He checked the display; it was an incoming text message from Father Santos.

> Aisquith has found 2 plates.
> Will immediately send plates
> to Rome w/ Diaz.

Breathless with excitement, Franco stared at the display, his hand shaking. Providence was clearly at work this night, having blessed him yet again.

Soon the years of tedious work, of hiding in the shadows, would come to fruition.

Ever since Pius XIII had 'demoted' him to Prefect of

the Secret Archives, Franco had been planning for the next conclave. That was the reason why he'd spent hours scouring through the long-forgotten files pertaining to the Knights Templar, searching for a secret weapon that he could use to blackmail the College of Cardinals when the time finally arrived.

But in order to achieve his aims, Franco's threat had to have real bite. That meant he *had* to have all three copper plates in hand before the conclave convened. To twist the knife even deeper, he would threaten to include the *Evangelium Gaspar* in the upcoming Secret Archives exhibition where it would be on public display and seen by the entire world. Because the exhibition was being held in Rome's Capitoline Museum rather than the Vatican, the College of Cardinals wouldn't be able to stop him. Their power ended quite literally at the Sant'Angelo Gate.

Franco estimated that it'd take all of about forty-five seconds for the news of the heretical gospel to go viral on the Internet. Sounding the death knell for the Holy See.

Such a simple plan.

Yet it was one which the College of Cardinals would be defenceless against, leaving them with no choice but to capitulate to his demands.

One demand, actually.

The College of Cardinals must elect Franco Fiorio as the next pope, giving him Peter's keys to the Church. *'That whatsoever you should bind on earth might be bound in heaven.'*

A bloodless coup, there would be no messy cover-up. No digging of mass graves to hide the bodies. And because of the strict secrecy of the conclave, the famous Code of Silence, no one outside of the locked conclave door would ever be the wiser. *Maledictus*. Cursed be the offender.

Such a simple but momentous plan.

45

Hotel Los Templarios, Ponferrada, Spain

Lightning flashed on the achromatic horizon, Zeus hurling a mighty bolt.

Assuming you believed that sort of thing, Edie thought as she stood at the hotel window and peered at the gloomy night sky. Four storeys below, the golden glow of street lamps created a lambent contrast to the stone structures that flanked the deserted street, the town of Ponferrada putting her in mind of a medieval theme park.

Located on the last leg of the Camino de Santiago, the four-star Templar Hotel catered to more affluent pilgrims. Those in dire need of an elegant suite, a gourmet meal and that most desired of all amenities, Wi-Fi. Although the on-site pharmacy ranked a close second, where Edie was able to purchase a bottle of aspirin, a roll of bandages and a tube of antibiotic ointment to patch-up Cædmon's various abrasions. The walking wounded, he refused to let her call a doctor, insisting that his ribs were bruised not broken and that his head 'never felt better'. At times, and this was one of them, his stiff-upper-lip stoicism could be infuriating.

'People die every day from undiagnosed head injuries,' she'd insisted. To which he'd drolly replied, 'Pray that doesn't happen.'

Unbeknownst to Cædmon, that's exactly what she'd been doing, her prayer list including everyone from Anala Patel to the Marqués de Bagá. Earlier, when they'd checked into the hotel, she and Cædmon had been horrified by the news story that they'd seen broadcast on the flat-screen television mounted in the lobby. Hector Calzada, who'd stood beside them at the front desk, had grinned at the grainy footage of ambulance personnel removing 'butchered' bodies from Casa de Pinós in Madrid. '*Dia de muertos*,' he'd cackled heartlessly.

Day of the dead.

Shivering at the recollection, Edie glanced over her shoulder at the locked door on the other side of their hotel room. The fact that the monster had the adjoining chamber would undoubtedly mean a fitful night's sleep. His sword-wielding compadre, the mute Diaz, had been dispatched to some unknown destination – presumably G-Dog's lair – taking the two copper plates with him. Leaving Calzada in charge of the store. Prayer might be a powerful weapon, but somehow she didn't think it'd stop Calzada from slaughtering the shop customers.

'Any luck?' she enquired, breaking the dull silence. Still standing at the window, she looked expectantly over at the writing desk on the other side of the room.

Cædmon glanced up from the pile of paper scattered in front of him, shook his head and muttered, 'Bloody Knights Templar.'

'I'll take that as a "no",' she said when he bent his head and resumed his deciphering, attempting to crack Fortes de Pinós's code of slashes and dots.

For the last two hours, he'd been going nonstop.

Soon after checking into their room, he'd emailed digital photographs of the copper rubbings that she'd made at Ponferrada Castle to a scholar at Oxford who was an expert in ancient languages. That done, he'd phoned Gita with an update, the relief in her voice heart-breaking. Even Cædmon had been rendered misty-eyed, his stiff upper lip quivering ever so slightly.

'Would you mind grabbing the journal out of my ruck-sack?' he asked. 'I'm going to need more blank paper.'

Happy to oblige, Edie walked over to the king-sized bed. Dramatically canopied with a length of luxurious fabric in deep crimson shot through with gold threads, the bed was a magnificent lodestone. Juxtaposed with the stone walls and beamed ceiling, it was fairy-tale perfect. Under any other circumstance she'd find the medieval ambiance wildly romantic. A scene right out of *Camelot*. But not this night.

As she removed the journal from Cædmon's rucksack, a photograph slipped free, having been stuffed between the pages. To Edie's surprise, it was a picture of Anala and Gita standing side-by-side in front of a college at Oxford. On the verge of asking about the photo, she glanced at Cædmon. For days now, he'd been pushing himself to the physical limits. All to save the life of the daughter he'd never met.

Without saying a word, she tucked the photo into the journal. Obviously he cared more than he let on.

Although he'd not broached the subject, she wondered if Cædmon regretted not having been involved in Anala's life. Coming into the story mid-book, he'd missed all of the watershed moments that define fatherhood. While she could only imagine the turmoil that he suffered, Edie had no difficulty empathizing with Anala Patel. Orphaned at a young age, she too had endured the emotional havoc of growing up without a father, having to make the tumultuous passage from adolescence to adulthood on her own.

'How about a cup of coffee?' Edie glanced at the tray that room service had earlier delivered.

As Cædmon took the journal from her, his lips curved ever so slightly. 'One sugar, please.'

A few moments later, two cups of fresh-brewed coffee in hand, Edie sat down at the writing desk. The oversized baroque chair nearly swallowed her whole. She noticed that Cædmon had removed his wristwatch and set it on the desktop, in plain sight, the second hand inexorably pulsing around the dial. A visual reminder that the deadline loomed.

Cædmon drummed his fingers on the desktop as he stared at the encrypted message. 'It's a little-known fact that the Templars invented international banking as a means to protect defenceless Christians on pilgrimage.'

Wrapping her hands around her coffee cup, Edie wondered if she'd fallen asleep and missed something. 'Sorry, I'm not following. What does that have to do with Fortes de Pinós's code?'

'More than meets the eye,' he informed her. 'Before pilgrims set out on their months-long journey to the Holy Land, Rome or Santiago de Compostela, they would deposit the balance of gold and silver that they'd need for the upcoming trip at a Templar preceptory. The pilgrim would then be issued a paper cheque that indicated the amount of the deposit.'

'Okay, I see where this is headed. When the pilgrim then needed cash to pay for food and lodging, he'd stop at the nearest Templar preceptory, traveller's cheque in hand, and make a withdrawal.' Detecting a glaring flaw in the system, Edie said, 'What was to stop someone from pulling a fast one and forging a cheque?'

'The Templars had devised an ingenious system of codes that was foolproof. If history is to be believed, there were no cheque frauds committed on the Templars' watch.' Gaze narrowed, Cædmon stared at the series of slashes and dots. 'I've studied many of those codes. However, this doesn't fit any of the known patterns.'

'But you told G-Dog that you could crack the code.'

'And I *will* crack it,' Cædmon said as he carefully drew a blank grid on to a clean sheet of paper. With his jaw clenched tight, Edie could see that he was determined to do the impossible and pull a fast one on the Knights Templar.

'Obviously, there's something here that we're not seeing.' As she spoke, Edie raised a hand, beating him to the punchline. 'And, please, no droll asides about my *extraordinary* powers of deductive reasoning. I'm just flipping to a fresh page.'

'You're very good at thinking outside the box,' Cædmon said quietly, having the good grace to look chagrined. 'And I appreciate any help that you can –' He stopped in mid-sentence and picked up his vibrating mobile phone. 'Excellent. I've just received an email from Trent Saunders, my old group leader at MI5.'

Edie mentally crossed her fingers, hope renewed. 'Please tell me that the spooks at Five have sent glad tidings.'

He glanced up from the mobile. 'They've traced G-Dog's phone number to a listing in Dutchess County, New York. The number belongs to an organization called Sanguis Christi Fellowship.' Glancing back at the email, his brow furrowed. 'I've seen that name recently, but damned if I can remember where.'

'I'm guessing that "Sanguis Christi" is a Latin phrase.'

'It means "Blood of Christ".' Recognition dawning, he slapped his palm against the desktop. 'Sanguis Christi was engraved on to the cover of Javier Aveles's bible. I came across it in his hotel room when I paid an unexpected visit.'

'Javier Aveles is the third bandito, right?'

Cædmon nodded. 'Now that we have a lead, let's see where it takes us.'

Reaching for her iPad, Edie typed 'Sanguis Christi Fellowship Dutchess County New York' into the search engine. 'We're in luck. There's quite a few entries on the Internet,' she said, pulling up a *New York Times* article from 2006. She held the computer pad so that they could both read the article at the same time.

NEW YORK CITY
JUNE 15, 2006

Father Gracián Santos, the founder and current director of the Sanguis Christi Fellowship, is the latest recipient of a $100,000 Opus award given in recognition for his faith-based gang intervention program.

The Sanguis Christi Fellowship, which assists former gang members in the New York City area, is instrumental in reshaping lives and giving hope to inner-city youths through an outreach program that includes education and vocational training.

Attending last evening's award ceremony, Fr. Santos profusely thanked his mentor, Archbishop Franco Fiorio, who played an instrumental role in establishing the Catholic fellowship in the mid-1990s.

Santos has pledged to use the monetary windfall to renovate an abandoned nineteenth-century college situated on 300 acres in Dutchess County, New York. 'With the new facility, we will be able to provide at-risk youths with multi-level solutions that go beyond vocational training to include a charter high school, as well as gainful employment in several industries which we hope to develop with local business leaders.'

Past Opus recipients have included –

Edie stopped reading once the article veered off-topic. 'The photograph of the awards ceremony seals the deal: G-Dog and Father Gracián Santos are definitely one and the same.'

'The good padre forgot to mention that his "multi-level solutions" include murder, abduction and extortion,' Cædmon snapped, his cut-crystal accent more clipped than usual. 'Making Sanguis Christi a crime syndicate rather than a Catholic fellowship.'

'I'm not so sure that Father Santos is the godfather that you're making him out to be,' Edie countered, struck by the glaring disconnect between the admirable do-gooder in the article and Cædmon's criminal mastermind. 'Don't get me wrong – Santos is up to his eyeballs in this mess. But you gotta admit that the guy's a Nervous Nellie. It almost makes me think that the timorous Father Santos is acting against his will. Perhaps he's being pressured by someone.'

Her defence of the priest didn't go over well, the conversation instantly nose-diving into a brooding silence.

Scowling, Cædmon reread the article. A few moments later, he sighed resignedly. 'It pains me to say that you may have a point. And, of course, we still haven't accounted for the individual who sent the original ransom email to Gita, the self-styled Irenaeus.'

'The newspaper article mentioned that Santos has a mentor who aided him with the fellowship, an archbishop.' Inspired, Edie typed 'Archbishop Franco Fiorio' into the computer search engine.

'Did you find anything?'

'*Oh . . . my . . . God*,' she murmured, stunned. 'The archbishop is now *Cardinal* Franco Fiorio, the prefect and head librarian at the Vatican Secret Archives. What do you wanna bet that he's –'

'Irenaeus,' Cædmon interjected, beating her to the punch. Grabbing the iPad out of her hands, he examined Cardinal Fiorio's official Vatican photograph. '*Let us detest all priestcraft*,' he grated between clenched teeth, his scowl deepening.

46

Cædmon stared at the photograph of the red-caped bastard. At that moment the rallying cry of the English Enlightenment seemed as bang-on relevant as it had 400 years ago.

Although he had no proof, his gut instinct was that Cardinal Franco Fiorio was the mastermind behind Anala's abduction, Father Gracián Santos his reluctant minion.

'They're not all bad apples,' Edie remarked, quick to come to the Church's defence. 'There are plenty of good priests on the tree.'

'While that is undoubtedly true, the problem is, and always has been, that it's impossible to regulate an entity that holds the keys to heaven. They have the congregation right where they want them and they know it.' Still holding the iPad, Cædmon committed Cardinal Franco Fiorio's thickly jowled, balding features to memory. 'Pudgy little porker,' he scoffed uncharitably.

The impolite slur caused a frown to instantly materialize on Edie's face. 'Do you think that they're holding Anala in Dutchess County at the Sanguis Christi Fellowship?' she asked, abruptly changing the subject.

'They're certainly not holding her at the Vatican. A remote 300-acre complex in upstate New York seems a likely location.' *To commit a whole host of crimes*, he thought but didn't dare utter. If he couldn't find the third plate, there was no doubt in his mind that 'Irenaeus' would carry out his deadly threat against Anala.

Of course, Cardinal Fiorio won't be the one pulling the trigger.

The clergy never do. They had a despicable habit of hiring mercenaries to do their 'wet work'. It was how they absolved themselves of their more heinous crimes. *Ecclesia non novit sanguinem* – 'The Church never sheds blood' – was a doctrine that dated to the fourth century when Priscillian, the bishop of Ávila, was beheaded, the first Christian heretic put to death by fellow Christians. The Catholic synod of bishops had condemned Priscillian to death, but let Emperor Magnus Maximus carry out the execution order. It was a barbarous tradition that reached its zenith during the Inquisition and surely the most atrocious hypocrisy ever perpetrated by a religious entity that supposedly embraced the teachings of the Prince of Peace.

'We can compile background dossiers on the principals and download satellite imagery of the Sanguis Christi compound later. Right now, we need to decipher this blasted code.'

'In that case, another cup of coffee is in order,' Edie said. Scooting her chair back, she walked over to the service tray.

Picking up the sheet of paper on which he'd drawn a grid cipher, Cædmon refocused his attention on the series of slashes and dots. Although he knew that it was his imagination, the lines seemed to bleed, one into the other.

Fuck the Knights Templar! And the horse they both rode in on.

He bit back the profane utterance. Scrunching up the sheet of paper, he tossed it across the room, the 'ball' landing in the rubbish bin next to the bedside table.

Hag-ridden, he lurched to his feet. His ribs ached with a brutal intensity; the four aspirin that he'd earlier ingested had merely put a dent in the pain. And a small one at that.

Needing to clear his mind, he strode to the window and unlatched the metal lock. Then, very slowly, his bruised body protesting each and every movement, he slid the window open and inhaled deeply. The smell of rain was thick in the air. *The scent of the gods.* Or so the ancients believed, unaware that the unique odour emanated from plant oils released during a rain shower.

He stared at the moody landscape, the rain falling with a monotonous patter.

Just then, a fork of lightning broke free from the charcoal-coloured clouds and pierced the night sky. The atmospheric pyrotechnics briefly illuminated the monumental bronze equestrian statue set in the middle of a nearby roundabout. In that burst of bright light, he could see that the bloke on the horse was a medieval Knights Templar. The Keeper of the Secret riding off into the rain-drenched night. Willing to risk life and limb to safeguard the *Evangelium Gaspar.*

Edie approached and, smiling wearily, handed him a cup of coffee. Long moments passed as they stood, silent, at the window. Two etiolated sprigs clinging to a wilted vine.

'When I was a graduate student at Oxford, I arrogantly believed that I had unravelled the mystery of the Knights Templar,' he said, breaking the silence, his gaze still set on the bronze horse and rider. 'It turned out to be a very foolish profession of faith.'

'The guys in white had you fooled, huh?'

'And damn them for doing so. I rue the day I ever heard of the Knights Templar.' Realizing how petulant that sounded, he snorted derisively. 'I'm sulking. Forgive me.'

'Given everything that you've been through these last couple of days, you're entitled to a little self-pity.' Edie sidled closer and leaned her head on his shoulder. Her physical presence comforted him, proving that misery does indeed love company.

The rain began to fall harder, the hypnotic sound inducing a somnolent wave.

Cædmon took a sip of his coffee, fighting the surge.

'It's as though I'm banging my head against history's stone wall; and receiving nothing for my efforts but a blistering headache. I could have the Wisdom of Solomon and still not be able to crack Fortes de Pinós's blasted –' He stopped abruptly, hit with a latent memory. 'Wasn't there something in Fortes de Pinós's inquisition transcript about King Solomon?'

'I honestly can't recall. Let me pull up the transcript on the iPad.' Stepping over to the desk, Edie retrieved her computer. A few seconds later, she began to read aloud the pertinent passage from the Chinon transcript: 'When asked why he had carved the Seal of Solomon on to the wall of his cell, Brother Fortes claimed that he had been contemplating the wisdom of that great king which he believed to be a precursor to the wisdom that our Lord Jesus Christ imparted to his twelve disciples.' Edie glanced up from the iPad. 'Would you like me to continue reading?'

'No, that won't be necessary. Medieval historians have long been intrigued by the fact that many of the incarcerated Templar knights carved glyphs and symbols on to the dungeon walls at Chinon Castle.' Seized with a germinal hope, Cædmon dashed over to the desk, coffee sloshing en route.

'So, they were – *what?* – secretly communicating with one another from inside their cells?' Edie asked, joining him at the desk.

'Undoubtedly. And, as you just read, Fortes carved a Seal of Solomon on to the wall, a symbol better known as the Star of David.'

'That's the six-pointed star that's on the Israeli flag, right?'

'It is.' Snatching a pencil, Cædmon drew the Seal of Solomon – a six-pointed star – on to a blank sheet of paper. Then, because Fortes had specifically mentioned the twelve disciples, he inserted twelve dots on to the star.

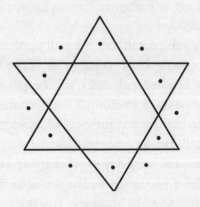

'The Templars were particularly fond of substitution ciphers in which each letter of the alphabet was replaced with a symbol, dots being a favourite encryption device. Now, bearing in mind that the letters "j" and "u" weren't in use during the early-fourteenth century, we should be able to add the twenty-four letters of the Medieval Latin alphabet on to the star,' he told Edie as he placed the first letter – 'a' – in the twelve o'clock position.

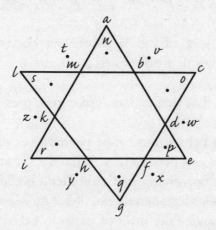

'Yes, that's it,' he whispered a few moments later, his pulse racing. 'All of the slashes and dots that Fortes de Pinós carved on to the Tau stone are contained on the Seal of Solomon.'

Edie's eyes glimmered brightly. 'So, let's hurry up and decipher the code!'

'Right.' Placing the sheet of paper with the rubbing from the Tau stone next to the Seal of Solomon, Cædmon used the star to decipher the encoded message.

Anticipation building, his heart thumped annoyingly

l a v i e r g e

d a n s e p i s

c o p v s p r e s

against his sore ribs as he wrote out Fortes's message, adding slashes to divide words.

La/vierge/dans/episcopvs/pres

Standing behind him, Edie peered over his shoulder. 'I'm on pins and needles here. What does it say?'

'*La vierge dans episcopvs pres.*' Admittedly baffled, Cædmon pondered the deciphered text. *What the bloody hell does it mean?* He handed the sheet of paper to Edie. 'The phrase is a combination of Latin and French. Translated into English, it reads, "the virgin in the bishop's meadow".'

'Yes! Thank you, baby Jesus!' Edie exclaimed with a joyful whoop. 'I am officially riding a little happy high.'

'I wouldn't shout from the rooftops just yet. I have no bleeding idea what it means,' Cædmon informed her.

Edie's jaw slackened, bubble instantly burst. Crestfallen, she eased herself into a vacant chair. 'You're kidding, right?'

Thunder boomed in the near distance.

'Would that I was,' he murmured, his blitz-battered mind struggling to make sense of the new riddle. *Christ!*

He didn't have time to meander through another medieval conundrum. There were only three days left.

Damn you, Fortes de Pinós.

'The virgin in the bishop's meadow,' Edie repeated as she planted an elbow on the desktop. Sighing deeply, she rested her chin on top of her balled hand. 'I know that what I'm about to say is probably due to sleep deprivation, but it reminds me of that board game; the one with Colonel Mustard in the library.'

'With the infamous candlestick. Were it only as simple as a game of Cluedo.' He stared at the deciphered message.

Think, man, think!

'The "virgin" undoubtedly refers to the Virgin Mary,' he said at last, sloshing into the breakers. 'With the word "bishop" being the key that unlocks the riddle.'

Hearing that, Edie set down her coffee cup and reached for the colourful brochures stacked on the edge of the desk. 'If so, the copper plate might be hidden somewhere in or around the cathedral at Compostela.'

'Good God! I hope not,' he retorted. 'It's a stone colossus. What makes you say that?'

'I read something about a bishop in the tourist brochure that I picked up in the hotel lobby.'

He gave the pamphlets a disinterested glance.

Undeterred by his lack of enthusiasm, Edie unfolded a brochure emblazoned with a photograph of Santiago de Compostela. 'Listen to this: "In the year 814, Theodomir, the bishop of Iria Flavia, discovered the bodily remains of Saint James the Great. After official validation by the pope as a sacred relic, a pilgrimage settlement was founded by Bishop Diego Gelmirez."' She glanced up from the brochure, verifying that she had his full attention. 'Right there, we've got, not one, but *two* bishops mentioned.' She emphasized the last point by raising two fingers. 'And here's another interesting tidbit: "Legend has it that Theodomir was guided to the site by a star in the night sky. Thus giving to the settlement the name Compostela, a corruption of the Latin phrase *Campus Stellae*, meaning –"'

'Field of stars,' Cædmon interjected. 'A field and a meadow, one and the same.'

'*And* Fortes de Pinós encoded his message on to a star.' A determined look in her eyes, Edie tapped a finger against the Seal of Solomon that he'd drawn.

'Does your guide book mention that Santiago de Compostela is one of the largest cathedrals in the world?' he countered in a crabby tone of voice. 'I wouldn't hazard to guess how many statues, paintings and holy objects involve the Virgin Mary. It also bears mentioning that while the Knights Templar owned numerous holdings along the Camino de Santiago and were commissioned by the kings of Iberia to protect the pilgrim routes, I don't believe that they had any direct affiliation with the cathedral.'

'Which explains why Fortes de Pinós might hide the third plate at Santiago de Compostela. He figured it'd be the last place the inquisitors would look.' Remarkably steadfast, Edie continued to argue her case. 'Here's one last point to ponder: if Fortes was worried about being apprehended, he could very easily have shaved his long Templar beard, chucked the snowy white mantle, picked up a walking stick and disguised himself as a pilgrim.

The Camino de Santiago went right past Ponferrada Castle. All he had to do was hop on the love train and walk to the cathedral. A very easy way to get out of Dodge.'

'Mmmm.' Cædmon mulled it over, Edie's argument a persuasive one. Moreover, had he been in Fortes's leather-clad boots, that's precisely how he would have evaded arrest. *Except . . .*

He shook his head, annoyed by a niggling detail. 'According to the deciphered message, Fortes intended to take the third plate to the bishop's field. Not the "field of stars". If he planned to cache the plate at the cathedral at Compostela, why didn't he simply encode the Tau stone with –'

The bishop's meadow!

'Of course,' he murmured, peeved that the solution hadn't come to him sooner. 'Your theory is absolutely correct except for one small detail. When Fortes left Ponferrada disguised as a pilgrim, he did travel to a church. But it wasn't Santiago de Compostela.' Cædmon glanced at his watch. 0143 hours. 'We must quickly devise a plan to elude Calzada. If the Bête Noire gets his hands on the third plate, we'll have no leverage.'

'As in "pop" goes the weasel.' Grim-faced, Edie looked at the bolted door that separated the two adjoining rooms. 'Making you and me a pair of defenceless weasels.'

'We're not as defenceless as you seem to think. Clearly you're unaware of the fact that "weasel" derives from the old Anglo-Saxon word *weatsop*.'

'Okay, I'll bite. What does that mean?'

Smiling humourlessly, Cædmon said, 'Roughly translated, *weatsop* means "a vicious, bloodthirsty animal". The sweet-faced weasel's secret weapon.'

And one that he intended to use to devastating effect.

47

Santiago de Compostela, Spain

Friday

Tourist brochures in hand, Cædmon and Edie made their way across the Plaza del Obradoiro, the grand square that fronted the western façade of Santiago de Compostela. Craning his head, Cædmon peered over his shoulder. *Excellent.* Hector Calzada still trailed in their wake.

It was a clear August morning and camera-wielding visitors and the devout faithful thronged the open expanse. An exuberant press of humanity. While many, if not most, had disembarked from a tour bus, there were hardy pilgrims in the swarm who'd made the journey on foot, having departed from such faraway locales as Paris and Lisbon. No different to the pilgrims who first paid homage to the Apostle more than a millennium ago, twenty-first-century visitors were anxious to fulfil the age-old rite of passage – to tour the cathedral and see the Apostle's tomb.

Feigning an interest in the flamboyant cathedral, Cædmon slowed his step, enabling Calzada to catch up to them. 'Few people are aware of the fact that, during the Middle Ages, the famous apostle was known as Santiago Matamoros, St James the Moor Slayer,' he remarked, having assumed the role of tour guide.

Shoving her sunglasses on to the top of her head, Edie glanced over at him. 'And just how did St James earn the name Santiago Matamoros?'

'Interesting story that. In the year 844, the Apostle James supposedly resurrected himself from his tomb and led the Christian army to victory at the Battle of Clavijo,' he nattered on blithely, if for no other reason than to lull the Bête Noire into a false sense of security. 'Cervantes himself declared St James one of the most valiant knights the world has ever seen.'

'When Jesus commissioned his disciples to go out into the world and spread the Good News, I'm not exactly sure that's what he had in mind.' Although outwardly calm, the muscles in Edie's neck were visibly taut, betraying her anxiety. Like Cædmon, she was aware that, hidden under his shirt tails, Hector Calzada had a Beretta semi-automatic pistol shoved into the waistband of his trousers.

'I suspect you're right. Invoking a saint's intercession to aid in the slaughter of one's enemies is not something likely to have been condoned by the Prince of Peace.'

Cædmon again glanced about, ostensibly taking in the sights. Just as he'd hoped, Calzada appeared awestruck by the huge baroque construct that dominated the plaza. Slack-jawed, his reaction was no different to that of a medieval wayfarer who'd trekked across the whole of Europe to see the cathedral and view the holy relics.

Designed to evoke that very response, the opulent façade, which was added to the original Romanesque cathedral in the eighteenth century, cut an impressive silhouette against the cloudless blue sky. Flanked by matching pagoda-like bell towers, the cathedral was decorated with highly ornate columns and pilasters, along with a dizzying array of stone statuary. The more attentive pilgrims were quick to notice that there were multiple statues of St James, the saint looking surprisingly dapper in his wide-brimmed hat and flowing cape.

Continuing to make their way towards the cathedral, they passed through an elaborate wrought-iron gate. As they ascended the zigzagging granite staircase, Cædmon placed a solicitous hand on the small of Edie's back. The movement incited a fierce twinge of pain in his ribs. He ignored it as best he could. If the situation turned dicey, and no doubt it would, he hoped the adrenalin surge would mask the pain. At least long enough for him to set the trap. Too much was at stake for him to let his injuries dictate his actions.

At the top of the steps, Cædmon came to a standstill. With the serpent's smooth guile, he motioned Calzada into the cathedral.

Unaware of the fate that awaited him, the Bête Noire stepped across the threshold.

Although he and Edie had had only a narrow window to formulate a plan of action, in the pre-dawn hours they'd managed to make airline reservations, download maps and floor plans, and devise a scheme to give Hector Calzada the artful dodge. The plan now officially in play, they were on a tight timetable, their flight scheduled to depart Santiago de Compostela Airport in two hours' time.

Since the international airport was located on the out-skirts of Compostela, they'd both agreed that the cathedral, a monumental structure inundated with statuary, ancillary chapels and holy relics, would be the perfect lure. They had only to entrap Calzada who, thus far, seemed oblivious to the skulduggery. To further cement the treachery, before leaving Ponferrada Cædmon had spoken with G-Dog, informing the priest that there was no doubt in his mind that Fortes de Pinós had cached the third copper plate at Santiago de Compostela. In fact, he'd made his case using the very same argument that Edie had put forth the previous evening. Pleased with the progress report, Father Santos ordered Calzada to follow them to the cathedral. Because they had no idea how the Bête Noire would react once they arrived at Compostela, during the two-hour drive from Ponferrada they'd carefully plotted three different 'take-down' scenarios.

Once they gave Calzada the slip, the plan was to retrieve the third plate and use it to negotiate Anala's safe release. After yesterday's carnage at Casa de Pinós, Cædmon had good reason to suspect that if he turned the last plate over to Calzada – as the duplicitous priest had instructed – he and Edie would meet the same fate as the Marqués de Bagá. Since he was fairly certain that Anala was being held somewhere on the 300-acre Sanguis Christi compound in upstate New York, he would demand that the exchange take place in the near vicinity.

Entering the cathedral, they moved from the baroque splendour of the exterior façade and approached an enclosed Romanesque porch. The difference between architectural styles was striking, the older structure exuding a curvilinear grace of form that fused the best of ancient Rome and Byzantium.

Following the centuries-old custom, they paused at the

magnificently carved *Pórtico de la Gloria*, the original twelfth-century entrance into the cathedral. A tour de force of Romanesque architecture, the stone statuary on the triple-arched doorway depicted the heavenly Jerusalem as described in the Book of Revelation.

'This must have been an overwhelming sight for a medieval pilgrim from the backwaters of France or Spain,' Edie sagely observed, craning her neck to peer at the Twenty-Four Elders of the Apocalypse who, strangely enough, were all playing musical instruments.

'It's why they came: to be beguiled and bedazzled. In fact, as soon as word leaked that the mortal remains of St James had been unearthed in Compostela, Christians set out in droves to venerate the Apostle, the far-flung shrine soon becoming one of the most popular pilgrimages in all Christendom.' Cædmon peered at the crush of twenty-first-century pilgrims who'd formed a queue a few feet away; each waiting to take a turn at kneeling in front of a statue of the Apostle. 'Cutting a colourful swathe across medieval Europe, sinners, saints, kings and peasants made their way along the Camino de Santiago. A raucous ramble straight out of Chaucer.'

'What were they expecting to happen once they arrived?' Edie enquired, playing the ingenuous accomplice to perfection.

'The reasons for making the perilous journey varied: many wished to atone for their sins; some hoped to cure a physical malady; and others simply wanted to embark on a grand adventure. Regardless of the individual reason, those intrepid pilgrims knew something that modern man has long since forgotten.' Cædmon paused a moment, ensuring that he had Hector Calzada's undivided attention. 'And that is that holy relics have a transformative and magical power.'

'*Si*, the old ones were very wise,' the Bête Noire solemnly intoned, nodding his head as he spoke.

Delighted with Calzada's naive observation, he gestured to the stone portal. 'Let's get to it, shall we? We have a gospel to find.'

A few moments later, as they trooped down the centre aisle, Cædmon scanned the vast interior. A typical Romanesque layout, the cathedral was comprised of a long nave with three aisles and a north-to-south transept, the whole of which formed a Latin cross. As with all Catholic cathedrals, the focal point was the high altar.

'While I'm no expert on Catholic cathedrals, the "wow factor" is off the charts,' Edie remarked, her gaze focused on the monumental altar and gilded baldachin situated at the other end of the nave.

Heavily laden with gold and silver ornamentation, the altar soared six storeys into the air, the baldachin held aloft by gigantic, scantily clad angels, who had presumably descended from the heavens for that very purpose. At the top of the altarpiece, there was an equestrian statue of Santiago Matamoros astride a white steed. Closer to the base was a more sedentary, seated statue of the saint. Excessively gaudy – and visually at odds with the Romanesque elegance of the nave – the baroque altar brilliantly gleamed in the soft light cast by enormous cut-crystal chandeliers.

'*Dios mío*,' Calzada whispered, enthralled by the lavish splendour. '*Que es magnífico!*'

'I hadn't planned to tour the cathedral,' Cædmon said offhandedly. 'We're only here to retrieve the copper plate from an ancillary chapel.'

'No!' the other man exclaimed angrily. 'We are here! We must see the altar!'

Cædmon glanced at his wristwatch. 'Time really doesn't permit –'

'Don't fucking mess with me!' Calzada hissed in a lowered voice. 'I must pay my respects to Santiago.'

'As you wish,' he acquiesced with a nod. 'Far be it for me to come between a man and his religious convictions.'

Trap set, neither he nor Edie said a word as they made their way towards the main altar. There was no need to speak; the architects who created the cathedral had crafted the perfect lure. They had only to go with the flow, their job made all the easier by the scent of incense that hung heavy in the air, the pungent aroma slightly intoxicating. Evidently, a high Mass had recently been celebrated. More than likely a memorial service for the lately deceased Pope Pius XIII, the Roman Catholic Church in the midst of a nine-day mourning period.

A jaded sceptic, Cædmon had always considered the medieval Church's use of fragrance, candlelight, Gregorian chant and stained glass a not-so-subtle attempt to numb the intellect. To overwhelm the faithful with sight, scent and sound and, in so doing, create an enchanted world of mystery which only the priests could decipher. It worked a thousand years ago. And, given Calzada's wide-eyed look of awe, it still worked today.

Stopping near the front of the altar, Calzada genuflected and made the sign of the cross.

'The blessed Santiago looks so real,' he whispered in a reverential tone, mesmerized by the seated statue of St James.

Not about to inform Calzada that the lifelike effect was created by enamel paint applied to the stone statuary, Cædmon said, 'It's customary for pilgrims to climb the steps behind St James's statue and embrace the saint from the backside. Furthermore, it's my understanding that if you kiss the saint's mantle, you'll be granted plenary indulgence.' Again, the Catholic Church had made the entrapment all too easy; 'kissing the Apostle' was a centuries-old tradition at Santiago de Compostela.

Calzada raised a questioning brow. 'What does this mean, a plenary indulgence?'

'A plenary indulgence is the remission of God's punishment for the sins that you've committed heretofore.'

The other man's eyes opened wide. The significance of that bit of Catholic catechism had grave import to a sinner with blood on his hands. 'Meaning that when I die, I won't go to hell, *sí*?'

'Exactly so.'

'Then I *must* kiss Santiago's mantle!' Calzada didn't just nibble the bait; he gobbled it whole.

'The stairway that leads behind the altar is right over here.' Smiling blandly, Cædmon led the beguiled Calzada towards the side aisle, steering him away from the crowd of tourists clustered around the altar.

Completely ensnared, glad-hearted that his slate of sins would soon be wiped clean, Calzada accompanied him into an empty alcove fronted by graceful Romanesque arches. As they entered the dimly lit snuggery, Cædmon shot Edie a surreptitious glance. Trailing a few feet behind, she subtly jutted her chin. *Good.* They were both pulling their oars in the same direction.

About to teach Hector Calzada a harsh lesson about blind faith, Cædmon gestured to a closed door situated in a dark corner of the alcove. 'This is the entryway that leads to the *camarín* behind the altar.'

Just as Calzada reached for the doorknob, Cædmon advanced. Thrusting his left hand under the other man's loose shirt tails, he made a quick grab for the Beretta semi-automatic.

48

'Look out, Cædmon! He's making a move!' Edie shrieked when Calzada abruptly shoved his right hand behind his back to grab the gun at the exact same instant that Cædmon reached for the weapon.

To prevent Calzada from drawing first, Cædmon captured the other man's right wrist, violently jerking his arm at a bent angle behind his back. He then cinched his left arm around Calzada's neck, pinning him firmly against his chest in a chokehold. Grunting, like an animal caught in a hunter's trap, Calzada twisted and turned, repeatedly ramming his left elbow backwards, trying to hit Cædmon in the ribs.

Heart in her throat, Edie helplessly watched the violent flurry.

Afraid that one of the elbow punches would connect, she frantically searched the small antechamber for something – *anything* – that she could use as a weapon. On the far side of the alcove there was a plain marble altar. Behind the altar, set in a niche, was a silver crucifix approximately eighteen inches tall. She charged across the room and snatched the cross by the base, intending to use it to bludgeon Calzada over the head. Hopefully, knock him unconscious. Or, at the very least, incapacitate him so that Cædmon could grab the gun still shoved into Calzada's waistband.

Seized with a fierce sense of urgency, Edie pivoted towards the two struggling men. Just in time to see Calzada slam his boot heel against Cædmon's shinbone.

'Christ!'

Gasping in pain, Cædmon stumbled backwards, enabling Calzada to wheel out of the chokehold and jerk his right wrist free.

In a blurred whirl, Calzada drew his weapon. A split second later, Edie heard the attention-grabbing grind of metal on metal as he yanked the slide on the semi-automatic.

Grimacing, Cædmon gathered himself to his full height.

Thank God he could *stand*, Edie thought, relieved. For a horrified moment, she'd thought that his leg had been broken. Immobilized with fear, she stood several feet away, the cross clutched to her chest. She had every reason to believe that retribution would be swiftly administered.

'You tried to deceive me with your fucking bullshit!' Lip curled, Calzada aimed the gun directly at Cædmon's head. 'Do you know what will happen, English, if I pull the trigger?'

'I believe the correct reply is a failure to thrive,' Cædmon rasped. 'But if you do that, you'll never find the third plate. Unless you think that Santiago Matamoros will answer your prayers and lead you to the hiding place.' Challenge issued, he returned Calzada's sneer.

Edie held her breath. Caught on the end of a very sharp tenterhook, she prayed that the criterion for pulling the trigger was as unassailable as Cædmon seemed to think.

To her surprise, Calzada yanked his head in her direction. 'Put down the *crucifijo*. Then take off your sweater.'

'*What?!*' She shook her head, mystified by the request.

'You heard me, bitch!'

Edie flinched at the vicious epithet, unsure why the brute's attention had suddenly focused on her.

Cædmon held her gaze. 'Do as he says, Edie.'

Bending at the waist, she carefully set the silver crucifix on the floor. That done, she shrugged out of the garment and passed it to the gun-toting brute, hoping that the lightweight silk sweater was the only piece of clothing that Calzada wanted.

'*Gracias*,' the monster said with a lurid grin, licking his lips as he eyed her bare arms, now exposed in the sleeveless summer dress. Still holding the Beretta in his right hand, he pulled it close to his belly before draping the Kelly green sweater over his forearm, completely obscuring the gun. 'No more fucking around, *cabrón*. You find that plate. *Comprende?*'

'Perfectly,' Cædmon replied, his face an impassive mask.

Edie stared at him, confused, uncertain why Cædmon was still continuing the subterfuge. *Did he have an escape plan? Would he launch another assault? Or was he going to come clean and tell the truth about the third plate?*

'Let's go.' Calzada jutted his chin at the aisle on the other side of the antechamber. 'And if either of you pulls any shit, I'll shoot to kill. House of God be damned.'

Edie wordlessly stepped next to Cædmon, wondering how they were going to pull off the impossible and find a copper plate that wasn't hidden at Santiago de Compostela. The ruse had not only been thwarted, but now she feared that they'd navigated themselves into a dangerously precarious spot, their prospects of eluding Calzada dim. As in total blackout. Dark side of the moon. *How long could they continue the deception before Calzada caught on to the fact that the cathedral had been a red herring?*

'Steady on,' Cædmon whispered as they made their way back to the nave.

She cast him a quick glance, unable to decipher the intention behind his glittering blue eyes.

Having just passed through the side aisle, the three of them were forced to stop in order to allow two robed men carrying a massive *botafumeiro* that dangled from a wooden pole supported on their shoulders to pass in front of them. The highly ornate censer – which resembled a gigantic silver lamp – emitted plumes of smoke, filling the air with the fused scents of frankincense, myrrh and Damask rose. A heady mixture that caused Edie's eyes to instantly water.

Calzada, standing directly behind them, began to hack, the thick smoke irritating his lungs.

I think he's allergic to smoke.

That was Edie's last cogent thought before she saw Cædmon forcefully ram his elbow backwards into Calzada's chin, catching the other man unawares in mid-cough.

Blood instantly spewed through the air, Calzada having bit his lip.

Which, in turn, caused him to pull the trigger on the gun hidden beneath the Kelly green sweater.

The deafening shot went wild, striking the *botafumeiro*. Hollering in Spanish, the censer bearers dropped their smouldering load, the silver vessel hitting the stone floor with a loud clamour.

Screams of terror immediately reverberated inside the cathedral, the gunshot inciting an uproar. As smoke and ash clouded the air, pilgrims and tourists ran pell-mell. Edie stood transfixed, stunned by the disharmonic din of yelling, coughing and mournful wails. A torrential onslaught of sound and smell.

Seizing his chance, Cædmon whipped round and pounced on Calzada, grabbing hold of his right wrist with one hand and the barrel of the gun with the other. His movements quick and efficient, Cædmon shoved the stippled handle against Calzada's thumb – the weakest part of the hand – enabling him to rip the gun out of the other man's grasp. In a smooth, viciously precise motion, he then used the gun to swipe Calzada on the side of the head, the force of the blow hurling him against the upended *botafumeiro*. Yanking his shirt tails free of his trousers, Cædmon shoved the gun under the wrinkled fabric. Out of sight.

Before Edie could grasp what was happening, Cædmon grabbed her by the hand and charged down the aisle. Her heart thundered in her ears, muffling the cacophony, but also disorientating her, everything whirling past in a dizzying blur. Rib-vaulted bays. Soaring arches. Panic-stricken pilgrims.

By the time they reached the end of the transept, Edie was panting loudly, struggling to draw enough oxygen into her lungs. A group of dishevelled pilgrims, most of them burdened with heavy packs, dashed past, running headlong in the opposite direction. Towards the mayhem at the altar.

Without warning, Cædmon came to a skidding halt, the one still figure in the rushing throng.

'What now?' she asked anxiously, swaying from her exertions. In the distance, she could hear the blare of sirens. *The alarm had been sounded.*

Cædmon pointed to a set of heavily carved wooden doors. 'This way.' Still holding her hand, he pulled her towards the crowd who'd bottlenecked near the exit.

Moments later, having shouldered their way through the swarm, they exited the cathedral. Cædmon hurriedly ushered her down a long flight of stone steps that led to a small square enclosed on two sides: a monastery to the right of them and an imposing clock tower to the left. Although sirens wailed in the near distance, clusters of tourists leisurely roamed, apparently unaware of the pandemonium inside the cathedral.

Halfway down the flight of steps, Edie stumbled, pitching forward. Without missing a beat, Cædmon swung his right arm out to the side, catching her before she fell on her face.

'Keep moving,' he said gruffly. 'You can rest later. Right now, we need to get free and clear of the square before Calzada shows up.' Although his tone was brusque, Cædmon reassuringly squeezed her arm.

'Do you think that he –'

'I'm certain,' he interjected, peering back at the doorway. 'He was merely stunned. He'll be back on his feet in no time.'

When they reached the bottom of the stairs, Cædmon clamped a hand around Edie's elbow and pulled her over to a large fountain in the centre of the square. Crystal-clear water arched through the air, expelled from four stone horses placed around the base. Cool droplets misted her face. Without thinking, Edie scooped up a handful of water and splashed it on her flushed cheeks.

Suddenly hearing a *plunk*, she glanced down, surprised to see the gun nestled at the bottom of the water basin.

'Why did you toss the gun in the fountain?' she asked, confused. 'I would think that you'd *want* a weapon.'

'If I keep custody of the Beretta, not only will the airline officials not permit us to board our plane, I'll be arrested on the spot.' He snatched hold of her hand. 'Come on! If we're to catch our flight, we need to get to the hire car.'

Free and clear of the square, they raced through the labyrinth of narrow streets that surrounded the cathedral.

By the time they reached the car, Edie was on the verge of total collapse. Grateful to have safely reached the Volkswagen Passat, she hurriedly opened the passenger door and climbed inside. They'd purposefully left the doors unlocked to enable a quick getaway.

'We did it!' she exclaimed, slamming the door shut. 'We successfully eluded the bad guy.'

'Think again, pretty lady.'

Hearing the unfamiliar, slightly accented voice, Edie swung her head towards the back seat, horrified at finding herself face-to-face with a dark-haired, moon-faced man. Who, she presumed, had been hiding in the rear footwell. Seeing the gun grasped in his hand, she instantly recoiled, clutching the dashboard to steady herself.

'Where the bloody hell did you come from?' Cædmon snarled. 'You're supposed to be in India.'

Wielding the gun with confident ease, the other man snickered and said, 'Hands where I can see them.'

Cursing under his breath, Cædmon placed his hands on the steering wheel while Edie obligingly put hers into the air. The age-old act of surrender, of yielding oneself to a deadly foe.

The devil take the hindmost.

49

Anala opened one eye, then the other.

Peering through the branches of her leafy bower, she could see that dawn had arrived with a tangerine glow. She sucked in a deep breath. The early-morning air had a chill brace that was strangely medicinal. A tonic for the fear and anxiety of the night just passed. Straining her ears, she listened attentively, relieved that the only sound she could detect was trilling birdsong. The cacophony put a smile on her lips. The first in days.

The nightmare had ended.

Ready to set sail, she cautiously crawled out from under the briar bush, scraping her arms and face in the process. Not that she cared. She was free. And rested. Ready now to tackle the problem of finding a safe harbour. Not insurmountable by any stretch. She simply had to find a kind stranger with a mobile phone who would notify the authorities about the kidnapping ring. Once that was done, she would immediately call her mother who was undoubtedly out of her mind with worry.

A very good plan.

Slowly rising to her feet, Anala brushed off the leafy debris from her clothes as she gazed at the verdant landscape. Last night's gloom had morphed into a bucolic splendour teeming with trees and rolling hills and vast green expanses. Not a soul in sight.

'I've got my work cut out for me.'

Up to the challenge, she set off, filled with a breathless expectancy. Bobbing awkwardly, lightheaded from hunger, she stumbled on a stone. She glanced down, noticing that her bare feet were filthy dirty.

Oh, for a hot bath. And an artery-hardening, high-calorific fry-up served with a steaming pot of breakfast tea.

About ten minutes into the ramble, she came upon a low-lying stone wall that separated the fields and woodland from a paved lane. Thrilled, certain that she'd soon happen upon a village or hamlet, she scurried over the stone partition. She scanned the horizon in both directions, seeing what appeared to be a building of some sort situated atop a knoll. Tacking in that direction, she picked up the pace, anxious to put the whole traumatic episode behind her.

Trudging along, Anala glanced up, just in time to see a flock of birds in flight, all in perfect triangular formation, flapping across the blush-hued sky.

'I'm jealous. They obviously know where they're going,' she muttered good-naturedly. 'Not like some of –'

Hearing a car engine, she stopped in her tracks. *My prince has come!* Bursting with excitement, Anala stepped out into the middle of the lane and waved her arms madly.

'Help me! Help me!' she hollered as the vehicle approached.

The white SUV swerved to one side to avoid hitting her, the driver slamming on the brakes. Anala ran towards the SUV, noting with great surprise that there were New York State plates affixed to the back of the vehicle. *Blimey!*

It had never occurred to her that she'd been spirited to the United States.

The driver's side window slid down. A handsome middle-aged man with salt-and-pepper grey hair gaped at her in wide-eyed astonishment.

Anala leaned towards the open car window. 'Can you please help me, sir? I . . . I've been kidnapped . . . and against all odds, I . . . I've managed to escape my captors,' she blurted haltingly, not wanting to unduly alarm him. 'If you could take me to the authorities, I'd be ever so grateful.'

Clearly shell-shocked, the man nodded jerkily, leaning over to unlock the passenger side door.

Kind stranger, indeed!

Anala scrambled into the passenger seat, somewhat taken aback that the man behind the wheel was dressed in black clerical garb.

Having yet to find his vocal cords, he handed her a bottle of water.

'Bless you.' No sooner did she utter those words than Anala giggled, succumbing to a bout of giddiness. 'That's what you're supposed to say to me, isn't it?'

As he turned into a tree-lined driveway, the clergyman smiled wordlessly at her.

Peering anxiously through the windshield, Anala sighted a majestic stone mansion on the knoll. An estate right out of America's gilded age, it boasted numerous turrets, gables and arched walkways.

The clergyman pulled the SUV up in front of a six-bay coach house. Like the nearby mansion, it was constructed of stone. No sooner did he turn off the ignition than

Anala heard the patter of shoe leather crunching on gravel. Within seconds her car door was yanked open and she was forcibly dragged from the vehicle.

'Hey! What are you doing?'

The boom crashed to the deck so quickly, Anala could barely process the fact that it was one of her guards who now held her in a vice-like grip, her arms pinned behind her back.

'Take Miss Patel to the old root cellar at the caretaker's cottage,' the driver instructed.

Anala immediately recognized the clergyman's voice. *It was G-Dog!*

Hammered with a burst of fear, she bucked and writhed, trying, without success, to break free. In mid-struggle, she felt a stab of pain in her bicep. Turning her head, Anala saw a hypodermic needle protruding from her arm.

'Please forgive me,' G-Dog murmured before he turned his back and headed towards the stone mansion.

'You heartless bastard! I hope you rot in –'

In the next instant, the ship went down, quickly sinking into a cold, dark sea.

50

Sanguis Christi Fellowship, Dutchess County, New York

'Keep her alive until the third plate has been recovered.'

'I'm not questioning your wisdom in this matter, Your Eminence, but . . . is it really necessary to –'

'Yes, it is absolutely necessary,' Cardinal Fiorio interjected with a testy edge to his voice. 'Grácian, surely you know that you are doing God's work? More importantly, it's your sacred duty to protect our Holy Mother Church from the heretics bent on destroying her. And you have my word, you *will* be amply rewarded. Keep me informed of any further developments.'

Hearing a dull click on the other end of the line, Gracián Santos replaced the telephone receiver in its cradle.

If I am truly doing God's work, why does it feel like I'm the Devil's right-hand man?

The cardinal had even gone as far as to suggest that since Anala Patel was a Hindu pagan, her abduction – and Gracián assumed her subsequent death – would not be considered a mortal sin. When Cardinal Fiorio first broached the subject of retrieving the gospel, there'd been no mention of killing anyone. But now that Anala Patel had escaped and knew about the Sanguis Christi Fellowship, she had to be executed. And the Englishman as well.

Gracián had no idea what was contained in the ancient gospel. *But whatever it was, did it justify all of this bloodshed and brutality?*

Deeply troubled by the situation, Gracián got up from his desk and walked over to the diamond-patterned window, his gait sluggish as though each foot was weighted with a guilt-laden brick.

Standing sentry, he watched as the Fellowship SUV pulled up to the stone archway, the porte cochère, Jacko Maciel jumping out of the back seat and rushing into Mercy Hall. Gracián had ordered Jacko and the other two Diablos who'd been guarding the Patel woman to drive to the Catskills and join the others at the Catholic retreat. He didn't want their souls to be stained crimson red.

'Yo, G-Dog, wassup?' Jacko warmly greeted him as he stepped into the office. 'I thought I'd drop off the mail before we hit the road.'

Gracián took the small bundle of envelopes. 'Thank you, Jacko.' Thinking it better *not* to mention 'what was up', he forced his lips into a semblance of a smile and said, 'Drive safely and have a good trip. May the Lord bless and keep you.'

'You too, Father G,' the young man replied, clearly excited about the road trip.

Sending Jacko on his way with a pat on the shoulder, Gracián walked back to his desk, the bundled mail clutched in his hand. The envelope on top was from the First New York Loan and Trust Bank. Over the last two years, he'd received so many demands for payment from the bank that he was now immune to the shock.

Dispirited, Gracián tossed the bundle into his in-basket and left the office, making his way down a lavishly appointed corridor that displayed all the exuberance of the late-Victorian period. Originally a women's college, Mercy Hall had catered to daughters of the wealthy elite, the building certainly worthy of their privileged progeny.

Stepping into the main lobby, an expansive area with dark-stained wall panels, richly carved columns and a massive oak staircase with an oriental stair runner, Gracián was unnerved by the silence. Somehow it made the flamboyant lobby seem strangely forlorn.

That was when it occurred to him that, for the first time in years, he was completely alone. Even in prison, he'd always had a cellmate.

Hoping that some fresh air would clear his turbulent thoughts and give him some much needed clarity, he exited the lobby. He then hurried across the crushed stone driveway to the porte cochère where his golf cart was parked. A few moments later, he was navigating the electric golf cart across the undulating fields behind Mercy Hall, careful to steer clear of the occasional rock outcropping. The terrain on the western end of the property was particularly wild and overgrown.

Cresting a small hillock, he braked to a stop. For several moments, he admired the lovely view. This was the Promised Land. A bucolic paradise where scarred youths received the necessary education and job skills to live productive lives. Unlike other priests who would never know the happiness of being a father, Gracián had one hundred and fifty teens in his care. Not only did he love and cherish them unconditionally, but he would do anything to protect them from the violence that lurked beyond this safe sanctuary.

He had just never dared to imagine that 'anything' would include murder and mayhem.

I thought I'd left that life behind me.

Awash with guilt, he stared at the abandoned caretaker's cottage that was nestled in a small grove of oak and maple. In a derelict state, the two-storey abode was covered in bindweed with many broken window panes. Approximately twenty metres from the ramshackle cottage, there was an underground root cellar that had once been used to store vegetables and salted meat. The underground storage cellar was entered through a trapdoor which had earlier been secured with a new padlock.

This time there will be no escape.

Ever since Anala Patel had arrived at the Fellowship, he'd repeatedly reminded himself that he mustn't feel any compassion for her. She was a Hindu who'd wilfully chosen to worship a false god – *no, a hundred gods!* – the Hindu religion inundated with devas, deities and avatars. Because of her chosen religion, Anala Patel was hellbound.

Extra ecclesiam nulla salus.

There is no salvation outside of the Church.

Gracián stared at the root cellar, the padlock on the trap door glimmering in the summer sun.

'*Keep her alive until the third plate has been recovered.*'

'How can I kill her?' he whispered, overcome with a dread fear.

Turning his head, Gracián gazed at Mercy Hall – his

City upon a Hill – the massive building dominating the skyline on the eastern knoll. One hundred and fifty young people *completely* depended on him to take care of them. And he could only do that if he repaid the bank loan.

His gaze returned to the root cellar.

How can I not kill her?

51

Compostela, Spain

Javier Aveles toggled his semi-automatic pistol. 'Don't either of you fuck with me!'

'The field is yours,' Cædmon grated harshly, not about to test the other man's resolve. Although he could hear police sirens blaring in the distance, he suspected that wouldn't stop Aveles from pulling the trigger.

Edie, her earlier shock at being waylaid by Aveles having morphed into weary dejection, sagged against the car seat.

Christ! The entire time that they were at the cathedral, Cædmon had arrogantly presumed that he was pulling the wool over Hector Calzada's eyes when he and Edie were the ones being duped. Perhaps it was due to mental exhaustion, but he'd never considered the possibility that the third bandito would arrive in Spain; a replacement for Diaz. And because he'd not taken that possibility into account, they'd been caught with their knickers down.

Demoralized, an abject sense of failure now clung to him. Despite the fact that he was seated in a parked car, he felt as though he were falling. Into a deep, inky-black pit patrolled by feral, phantasmagoric creatures. The sort of snarling beasts that inhabited a Schongauer print.

He glanced at his watch. *Shite!* They'd squandered

too many hours. With absolutely nothing to show for it.

'We have airline reservations,' he said abruptly, meeting Aveles's gaze in the rear-view mirror. 'If you want the third plate, you must allow us to catch our –'

Just then Aveles's mobile phone rang, the ringtone a ridiculously jaunty mariachi tune. Keeping the semi-automatic trained on them, he removed the phone from his breast pocket and flipped it open.

'It's for you,' he said a few seconds later, handing Cædmon the mobile.

Assuming it was G-Dog, Cædmon got right to it. 'This delay is intolerable,' he said. 'I'm booked on the next flight out of Compostela. If you want me to find the third plate, I need to be on that plane.'

'You have an impolite manner, Mr Aisquith. Whatever happened to English civility?'

Hearing an unfamiliar voice, Cædmon frowned. Although he couldn't be completely certain, he assumed that he was speaking to Cardinal Franco Fiorio, the self-styled 'Irenaeus' and the prefect of the Vatican Secret Archives.

'Forgive me, Father, for I have sinned,' Cædmon retorted. 'Is that more to your liking, Irenaeus?'

'Such a droll sense of humour.'

'I'm not here to amuse you; I'm here to find your bloody gospel. Assuming that we're to be released from armed custody.'

'Given that you purposefully misled my associates, I can only conclude that you have designs on the third plate,' Irenaeus was quick to accuse.

You red-caped bastard! Do you think I'd actually sacrifice my own daughter for a blasted copper plate?

Tamping down his anger, Cædmon said, 'I have absolutely no intention of keeping the third plate.'

'Your avowal pleases me no end. So where is it?' the other man demanded to know.

'"The virgin in the bishop's meadow" was the encrypted clue that was carved on to the Tau stone. From that, I have deduced that the third plate is located in Paris in "the bishop's meadow",' Cædmon readily confessed, there being no advantage in telling a lie.

'I've been to Paris and so I happen to know that there are precious few meadows.'

'Seven centuries ago there were fields aplenty,' Cædmon clarified. 'The meadow in question was located at an abbey named for a sixth-century bishop of Paris who, upon his death, was canonized as a saint.'

'Ah! Of course! The abbey at Saint-Germain-des-Prés!' Irenaeus exclaimed as though he'd just single-handedly deciphered the Tau stone. 'It's French for Saint-Germain-of-the-Meadow. But how can you be so certain that the Templar actually took the third plate to Paris?'

'Fortes de Pinós knew that in order to secure the Templars' release, it would be insufficient to claim that he had the *Evangelium Gaspar*. He had to *prove* that the claim was true. The third plate was the Templar's *carte de visite*. His carrot. His bargaining chip. Call it what you will.' Belatedly realizing that he'd allowed a noticeable ire to creep into his voice, Cædmon reined himself in. He was dealing with a man possessed of immense ego. *A Prince of the Church*. He needed to stroke, not pound. 'Because the Knights Templar had always maintained a collegial relationship with the Benedictines who ran the abbey, Fortes knew that he could safely stow the plate at Saint-Germain-des-Prés until he had need of it.'

Several moments passed before Irenaeus finally said, 'Well done. You've proved your case. Aveles will accompany you to Paris.'

'While I will do all in my power to meet the Sunday deadline,' Cædmon said, 'if you would be so kind as to extend the deadline by a few extra days, it would –'

'No! I must have the third plate no later than Sunday at twelve noon!' Irenaeus heatedly interjected. 'There will be no extensions, no exceptions and no extenuating circumstances! Am I making myself clear?'

'Crystal,' Cædmon muttered, wondering at the reason for the cardinal's vehemence.

The Catholic Church has waited seven hundred years to get their hands on the Evangelium Gaspar. *What difference could a few extra days possibly make?*

'Then I won't keep you any longer, Mr Aisquith. You have a flight to catch. Godspeed.'

52

Saint-Germain-des-Prés, Paris, France

Edie removed her sunglasses and peered at the oldest church tower in Paris.

According to Cædmon, the Abbey of Saint-Germain-des-Prés had been founded in the sixth century by Childebert, a Merovingian king. Plainly constructed, the stone bell tower had a brawny, utilitarian appearance, sturdy enough to withstand periodic flooding from the Seine. Once encompassing a huge swathe of land, the abbey had originally included church, cloister, chapter house, library and dormitories. A long-forgotten memory, all but the church had yielded to the ravages of time.

She next cast a furtive glance at Javier Aveles who'd been discreetly trailing them since they left Compostela, having accompanied them on the nonstop flight to Paris. While he wasn't as menacing as Hector Calzada, Javier cut a mean figure none the less. With his narrowed eyes and curled sneer, he put her in mind of a rabid junkyard dog. Ready to maul anyone who crossed its path. On the plus side, however – and it was a *huge* plus at that – he was no longer armed, forced to dispose of his weapon before they entered the airport at Compostela. His sidekick Calzada was still missing in action but given the slew of phone calls that

Aveles had recently received, Edie deduced that the Bête Noire was en route.

As they entered the vestibule, Cædmon scanned the glut of pamphlets, brochures, prayer books and loose-leaf sheets of paper scattered about, the day's tourists having pillaged the place.

'I don't know about you, but I am all churched out,' Edie muttered in a lowered voice. 'So, now that we're here, how do we go about finding "the virgin in the bishop's meadow"?'

Cædmon plucked a guide sheet out of a plastic holder. Squinting studiously, he examined the floorplan. 'The Chapel of the Virgin is located behind the altar,' he said, jabbing a finger against the dog-eared sheet of paper. Spinning on his heel, he strode towards the aisle that ran down the left side of the church, a general leading his war-weary troops.

Following in his wake, Edie had only taken a few steps when Javier Aveles cinched a hand around her upper arm.

'You try to escape me, and it'll be the devil's kiss . . . for the both of you,' he snarled.

'No need to worry. We're just going to the Virgin's Chapel,' she informed him, yanking her arm out of his grasp. 'Feel free to tag along.'

Savage beast soothed, Edie rushed down the aisle. Scurrying to catch up to Cædmon, her rubber-soled espa-drilles squeaked rudely on the stone floor. Not that the obtrusive sound much mattered; that late in the day, there was only a handful of visitors to be annoyed. As she hurried down the aisle, she glimpsed a blur of ecclesiastical artwork in the ancillary chapels and sundry niches . . . *Saint*

Frances Xavier . . . Saint Rita . . . Saint Joseph . . . Saints Peter and Paul.

'Is it just me? Or do they burn *way* too much incense in these places?' she grumbled as they entered a semi-circular candlelit chapel. 'There must be some rule that –' She stopped in midstream, belatedly realizing that they'd just entered the Chapel of the Virgin. Slack-jawed, she stared at the marble statue of the Virgin Mary holding the baby Jesus.

Crappola.

Edie didn't need a tour guide to know that she was gazing at a nineteenth-century statue ensconced in a neoclassical-style chapel replete with Greek-style pediments, Corinthian columns and a very realistically painted frieze. As near she could tell, there wasn't a medieval fixture in sight.

'For fuck's sake,' Cædmon rasped, irreverently dropping an F-bomb, plainly stunned at seeing the nineteenth-century statue in a medieval church. Lean-cheeked and haggard with bloodshot eyes and unshaven face, he looked like a homeless bum who'd wandered into the sanctuary in search of a quiet corner to take an afternoon nap.

'Since this statue is obviously a much later addition to the church,' Edie said, 'it's unlikely that this is where Fortes de Pinós hid the third plate.'

'Yes, thank you, Edie. I'm well aware of that fact.'

Ignoring Cædmon's sour-milk tone of voice, she peered around the candlelit chapel. 'Maybe there's another sanctuary dedicated to the Virgin. We passed a whole slew of chapels as we came down the aisle.'

'According to the guide sheet, this is the only one dedicated to the Virgin.'

She could see that Cædmon was marooned between relief at locating the right church and despair that they wouldn't be able to find the third plate now that they were here.

Or was it the right church?

'Maybe we misread the clue,' she said, wondering if they needed to cast a wider net.

Cædmon scotched the notion with a terse shake of the head. 'I'm *certain* that Fortes de Pinós brought the third plate to the abbey at Saint-Germain.'

Having run out of ideas, Edie fell into a dejected silence, fatigue causing her thoughts to jumble together. While they'd both managed to nap on the two-hour flight, it wasn't enough. Depleted of body and mind, she figured her spirit would next fly the coop.

Clenching his fists, Cædmon glared at the nineteenth-century marble statue of the Virgin and Child, the candlelight turning his eyes a piercing shade of Delft blue. 'Where in God's name is the third plate?' he muttered, peering heavenwards.

Edie knew the root cause of his foul mood; it was a gut-wrenching fear of what would happen to Anala if he didn't locate Fortes de Pinós's cache. To combat that fear, he was going at the problem with a feral tenacity.

Craning her neck, Edie glanced at Javier Aveles who was lounging against a wooden statue of Saint-Germain. Impudently returning her stare, he scratched negligently at his testicles, oblivious to the fact that they'd just hit a major snag.

'Why don't we head back to the vestibule and rifle through the printed material?' she suggested. 'There was a lot of information scattered about pertaining to the history of the abbey.'

Cædmon wearily nodded his assent. 'We'll need to compile a list of every single painting, statue and holy relic that relates to the Virgin Mary.'

As they trudged back down the aisle, Edie swivelled her head from side to side, hoping that something would miraculously resonate, every nook, every cranny, every shadowed niche rife with possibility.

Spotting an older priest headed in their direction, Cædmon waved his hand to waylay the black-robed cleric. He showed the priest the guide sheet and explained that they were searching for statuary or sacred artwork related to the Virgin Mary that had been commissioned or crafted prior to the year 1308.

If the priest was surprised by the unusual request, he hid it well. 'I think that you are looking for the medieval Chapelle de la Vierge,' he replied in English. 'It was built during the reign of Saint Louis in the thirteenth century.'

'Yes! The medieval Chapel of the Virgin.' Cædmon's relief was plain to see, his lips actually curving in a smile. 'If you would be kind enough to take us there, we'd be grateful.'

The priest gestured towards a nearby doorway. '*Avec plaisir.*'

Cædmon's euphoria was contagious, Edie almost giddy with excitement as they followed the cassocked priest. They'd travelled a long, winding road and were now at journey's end. *The virgin in the bishop's meadow.* It could only refer to the thirteenth-century Chapel of the Virgin.

The priest swung a wooden door wide open and

motioned them through. On the other side of the threshold was a small outdoor garden with park benches and chunks of stone artistically arranged on a circular patch of lawn. Attached to an exterior wall of the church, there was a delicate set of quadruple arches, each capped with a Gothic trefoil. Beside that was a sturdy column that appeared to have been blasted in two, the top half missing.

Cædmon frowned, no doubt thinking, as Edie was, that there'd been a miscommunication.

'There's nothing here,' he said, pointing out the obvious.

Clearly befuddled, the priest shook his head. 'I thought that you wanted to see the site of the original Chapel of the Virgin.'

'Yes, that's precisely what we'd like to see. So where the bloody hell is it?' Cædmon growled, making no attempt to hide his annoyance, exhaustion getting the better of him.

'But you are looking at it, monsieur. In the year 1794, during the Revolution, the church was used as a warehouse for gunpowder. A calamitous accident occurred, one which caused more than fifteen tons of gunpowder to ignite. The original Chapelle de la Vierge was destroyed in the explosion.' The priest pointed towards the Gothic arches. 'Alas, this is all that remains.'

53

The chapel was demolished two centuries ago!

As the realization hit, the ballast in Cædmon's hold turned over. Gasping for air, he swayed unsteadily, on the verge of fainting.

Rage . . . Pain . . . Desperation.

It all swirled and eddied. A hideous flotsam flung on to the beach. *How does one even begin to recover the wreckage?* Let alone swim to shore.

Over the crashing waves, he heard Edie thank the priest in a solemn tone of voice. Then she took hold of his arm. She may have spoken to him as well. He couldn't be sure, certain of only one thing: the third plate of the *Evangelium Gaspar* no longer existed. It had been obliterated. Blown to smithereens.

Edie led him to a nearby park bench; a kindly nurse leading a confused sanatorium patient. Dizzy, he tumbled on to the bench, grateful for her assistance.

'Put your head between your knees.' The order was accompanied with a firm hand to the back of his skull.

Cædmon complied, bending at the waist as his head and arms gracelessly flopped downwards. Gripping his head in his hands, he was seized with a disorientating panic. *How am I going to rescue Anala?*

Long moments passed before he was able to sit up.

'Are you okay?' Edie asked anxiously, once he'd righted himself.

'Yes, I'm –' He caught himself about tell a patent lie. He wasn't fine, or all right, or even okay. He'd damned near swooned, devastated by the horrifying news.

The chapel was gone.

His heart in his throat, he stared at the four delicate arches with their elongated columns and elegant trefoils; all that remained of the Chapelle de la Vierge. A hauntingly lovely bit of debris.

'How could this have happened?' he rasped, fighting to keep his composure.

'It looks as though they used the rubble from the explosion to fill in the holes,' Edie remarked, shading her eyes with her hand as she peered at the façade of the church.

From where they sat in the small garden square, the ravages that the abbey had suffered from the gunpowder blast were discernible, the exterior wall a patchwork of mismatched stone and mortar; pieces, indeed, entire chunks of stone were still missing two hundred years after the fact. In those places where 'restoration' work had been done, it appeared as though odd scraps had been used to patch the gaps. A bruised and battered lady if ever there was.

Just then the church door swung open. Javier Aveles, a sneer plastered on his face, strode over to the bench where they were sitting.

'What are you doing lazing about?' he snarled. 'You said that the plate was hidden inside the church.'

'And it is,' Edie was quick to assure the brute. 'But it's not as if the location is posted on the church floor plan with a big X. We need time to search the interior. Several hours at least. However, this late in the day, the light inside the church is too dim to conduct a thorough investigation,' she said, having crafted an ingenious excuse on the fly.

'I'm only going to say this one time, you ass-licking gringos –' eyes glittering with suspicion, Aveles jabbed a finger in the air – 'don't pull a disappearing act.'

The unspoken addendum being '*on pain of death*'.

'That guy needs to be slapped in the face with a moral absolute,' Edie muttered as Aveles, taking up a position on the far side of the square, leaned against the garden fence.

A heavy silence descended, Cædmon unable to summon the will, let along the strength, to rise to his feet.

Wordlessly, he and Edie watched as a woman with two small children in tow, twin girls in matching yellow sundresses, entered the garden square. Squealing with childish delight, the rosy-cheeked pair chased after a ball.

Edie sighed heavily. 'It's hard to believe that five days ago we were strolling arm-in-arm along Boulevard Saint-Germain, just a stone's throw from where we're now sitting.'

'On our way to have an aperitif at Café de Flore.' And then Gita showed up, waylaying him with a revelation he was still grappling to come to terms with. 'It would seem that we have travelled full circle,' he ruminated, also struck by the bitter irony.

'So, now what?'

'We'll have to manufacture a forgery,' he informed Edie, that being the only viable solution. 'Luckily we have digital photographs of the first two copper plates. The damned thing merely has to pass muster long enough for the exchange to take place.'

Edie's head bobbed. 'A fake plate could actually work. I mean, look at how many people were fooled by that stone ossuary in Israel.'

'That's because the eye often sees what it wants to see.'

'There is one other option . . .' Edie paused and gnawed a moment on her lower lip before saying, 'We could always come clean and tell Irenaeus that the Chapel of the Virgin was destroyed during the French Revolution. How can he expect you to deliver a ransom that no longer exists?'

'We're dealing with monsters,' Cædmon countered, having already discounted that particular option. 'Such creatures are, by their very nature, difficult to reason with.'

'Even a monster has to understand that . . . Never mind.' Edie's voice drifted into silence, the proposal failing to reach locomotive force. Opening her canvas tote, she retrieved a plastic shopping bag. From that, she removed a packet of chocolate biscuits. 'Food of the damned. Care for one?'

Cædmon shook his head. He needed something a bit stronger than sugar to assuage the pain. 'Once we get back to my flat, I'll contact Gita. She may be able to assist in fashioning a fake –'

'Hold that thought,' Edie interrupted as a breeze suddenly blew the plastic shopping bag off her lap. Lurching to her feet, she chased after the airborne bag, which pirouetted on an updraught. As she tried to retrieve it, the bag fluttered out of reach.

Cædmon shifted his gaze away from Edie and the dancing plastic bag, his thoughts turning inwards. For several days now, they'd been swinging the figurative machete, hacking away at a hidden trail; never once considering that what they sought might have been lost to history several centuries ago. But Irenaeus was also unaware of that fact. Which is why they might possibly be able to fob him off with a counterfeit plate.

'Cædmon, there's something that you need to see.'

'Hmm?' Shaking his head, he glanced at Edie who, slightly breathless, retook her seat, plastic bag in hand.

Leaning close to him, she said in a lowered voice, 'Don't get excited.'

'Not a prayer,' he grunted.

'No, I mean don't let Aveles see you get excited . . . It might sound off the wall, but I think the third plate is *on* the wall.'

He cocked his head to one side, wondering at her game. 'Either I'm dreaming or this is a very cruel joke.'

'One that I would never play. Not with Anala's life at stake,' she added. 'Now, without being obvious about it, I want you to stroll over to the wall behind the Gothic arches. To the left of the last arch, about three feet above the ground, you'll see a rectangular outline of a patch that's been adhered to the exterior wall and plastered over. Some of the plaster has flaked off one corner, revealing a pistachio green piece of metal.'

His eyes opened wide, his head quite literally spinning. *Oxidized copper!*

Immediately rallying, Cædmon stood up and, placing his hands in the small of his back, slowly stretched. He then paced a bit, head bent, giving every appearance of being a man lost in contemplation.

Serendipity intervened, one of the twins kicking the rubber ball towards the Gothic arches.

Smiling indulgently, Cædmon stepped over to retrieve it for the child. As he crouched to pick up the ball, he examined the plastered-over piece of metal.

'*Voilà, c'est ça!*' he exclaimed hoarsely a few seconds later.

That's it!

54

Paris

1930h

Lost in thought, Cædmon stood at his study window and gazed at the courtyard three storeys below. Planning. Strategizing. Plotting how best to scale the dreadful, slippery slope.

The third plate survived the eighteenth-century gunpowder explosion! Even more amazing, someone had salvaged the sheet of copper from the rubble and used it as scrap metal to patch the damage caused by the fateful blast; oblivious to the plate's content. Or to the fact that, five hundred years earlier, a Knights Templar had hidden the ancient gospel inside the chapel.

A bloody miracle.

One that he and Edie were very keen to keep under wraps. To that end, he'd informed G-Dog that the search for the third plate had been temporarily halted due to insufficient lighting inside Saint-Germain-des-Prés. '*But, rest assured, we shall return on the morrow when the church interior will be flooded with morning sunlight.*'

The lie passed muster, giving them a provisional reprieve. With the time purchased, he had to devise a plan to elude G-Dog's henchmen.

As he mulled over various options, Cædmon stared contemplatively at the enclosed courtyard. The summer sun lingered on the western horizon, bathing the rough-hewn cobbles in soft shades of blush and vermilion. Hector Calzada, attired in baggy denims and an oversized black T-shirt, looked out of place amidst the pots of cheerful red geraniums as he stood sentry a few feet away from the building entrance. He'd arrived on the scene a short time ago. Evidently, Rosencrantz and Guildenstern had divvied their duties, one sleeping while the other skulked.

Returning Cædmon's stare, Calzada puffed out his chest as he insolently grabbed his crotch.

Oh, for the love of God.

Cædmon stood motionless, refusing to react to the macho theatrics. *And how exactly was one supposed to respond? With a similar bit of scrofulous machismo? Really.* The other man's behaviour would be laughable if not for the fact that Hector Calzada was a bloodthirsty psychopath.

He raised his highball glass in mock salute. 'Cheers, mate.'

Turning away from the window, Cædmon gulped down the gin-less tonic, the citrus-laced quinine water warming his stomach. There had been a time in his life when he'd dematerialized into the haze of near-constant inebriation. Curiously enough, it had been the Knights Templar and their infernal secrets that brought him out of his alcoholic fog and gave him a new purpose in life, the result being his first book, *Isis Revealed.*

Exhausted, his body wracked with pain, Cædmon grasped the edge of his desk and gingerly lowered himself into the swivel chair. Rubbing a hand over his unshaven cheek, he gazed at the cluttered smorgasbord of file folders, stacked reference books, a small bronze bust of Winston Churchill, several dated editions of *Le Monde* newspaper and a ridiculously ornate Victorian lamp that he kept meaning to toss into the rubbish bin. *Chaos and old Night.* His kingdom. Or, as so aptly expressed by the great English jurist, Sir Edward Coke, 'The house of every one is to him as his castle.'

While he might not be the most fastidious monarch, Cædmon knew where every file was located, knew where every book was shelved in the floor-to-ceiling cases and, other than occasionally fluttering the feather duster, didn't see the point in tidying up. Since he was in the midst of writing his second book, an in-depth study of religion, science and magic in the ancient world, he found it counterproductive to clear his desk at the end of each day as it forced him to lose valuable time the next day searching for the very items he'd recently put away.

Nerves stretched thin, he slumped inelegantly, resting his elbows on top of the desk. He knew that he should get some sleep, a nap at the very least, the jet lag grinding away at him. *But first I need to devise an escape plan.* Unfortunately, Calzada and Aveles had the upper hand in that there was only the one exit out of the apartment building. Eluding them would be no mean feat.

'How's the war plan coming along?' Edie enquired, strolling into his study. She'd just taken a shower, damp ringlets framing her face. Attired in a ribbed vest top with a colourful sarong tied around her waist, she was a brilliant-hued splash against the dark-stained bookcases and leather-bound volumes.

'I'm mulling over two different plans of attack,' he replied, not yet ready to divulge any details. At least not until they'd had a chance to discuss the potential dangers and risks.

Edie padded over to the window. For several moments she gazed at the shimmering point in the distance where the heliotrope haze melded into the urban landscape. She then tilted her head and peered at the courtyard below.

Shuddering slightly, she walked over to Cædmon's desk. 'You know, I'm still having a difficult time connecting the monstrous three banditos with the feel-good story about Father Gracián Santos and his work with inner-city youths.'

'I think it's obvious that, somewhere along the line, Gracián Santos suffered a misstep,' Cædmon remarked. 'Moreover, I suspect that his fall from grace involves Cardinal Franco Fiorio, the self-styled Irenaeus.'

'Speaking of whom: since the College of Cardinals will soon be going into conclave to elect a new pope, Cardinal Fiorio will officially be out of the picture, sequestered behind locked doors.' Pushing a stack of file folders aside, Edie hitched her hip on to the edge of his desk. 'From what I understand, once they go into conclave, the cardinals are incommunicado.'

Her passing remark caused the proverbial chill to scuttle up his spine.

Christ Almighty! The conclave!

Abruptly twisting in the swivel chair towards his laptop computer, Cædmon quickly accessed a search engine.

'I need to find out when the conclave is scheduled to convene.'

'Unless I'm mistaken, it's supposed to happen sometime early next week.'

'Try Monday morning,' he said, glancing up from the laptop. 'Which is why the ransom deadline has been set for Sunday at twelve noon. It also explains why each time I've asked for an extension, the request has been adamantly denied.' His jaw tightened, the abyss having just become deeper and darker.

'Do you think Cardinal Fiorio would actually use the *Evangelium Gaspar* to affect the outcome of the papal election?' Edie enquired, her brows knitted in a worried frown.

'It wouldn't be the first time that a papal election has been ruthlessly manipulated.'

'Yeah, back in the Middle Ages. But this is the twenty-first century,' she insisted, evidently believing that modern man was more honourable than his medieval predecessors.

'Because of the centuries-old procedures governing the conclave, no one knows what goes on once the cardinals enter the Sistine Chapel and the doors have been sealed shut,' Cædmon was quick to point out. 'While they take an oath to uphold the rules of the conclave, arm twisting and brokered deals still occur. So, too, the occasional Machiavellian plot. Rumours have long swirled that in 1958 the duly elected Cardinal Giuseppe Siri had the papacy yanked out from under him when the conservative block that elected him immediately came under dire threat. Two days after Siri's supposed election, an entirely different cardinal was proclaimed the new pope.'

Edie's eyes narrowed, the rose tint removed. 'All of which makes me think that Gaspar's gospel contains something incredibly explosive if Cardinal Fiorio is intending to use it to blackmail the conclave.'

Of like mind, Cædmon checked his email account. *Damn.* 'I've yet to receive a reply from Cedric Lloyd.'

'He's your Oxford go-to guy in Graeco-Roman Jewish history, right?'

Cædmon confirmed with a nod. 'Until we know the gospel's contents, all of this is mere speculation.' Leaning back in his chair, he crossed his arms over his chest as he pondered the unexpected twist. While he didn't have the evidentiary proof, he suspected that a dark conspiracy was at the heart of Anala's abduction. 'What we do know is that Cardinal Franco Fiorio has gone to extreme lengths to retrieve the *Evangelium Gaspar*. So extreme, one would think that he'd been born into the House of Borgia.'

'In other words, murder and mayhem are mother's milk to him.' Getting up from the desk, Edie paced in front of the tall library-style bookcases.

'The *plotting* of the murder and mayhem,' Cædmon corrected. 'Franco Fiorio is one of those puppet masters who keep to the shadows as they yank their marionettes to-and-fro.'

'And he's got a particularly nasty troupe of puppets at his command.' Edie glanced pointedly at the window that opened on to the courtyard.

'Which brings up a matter that I've been meaning to discuss with you.' Cædmon pushed his chair back from the desk and walked over to the bookcases, forcing Edie to stop in mid-pace. In the far distance, he heard the plaintive bleat of a police siren; in the near distance, the high-pitched *bleep-bleep* of an electronic car lock. Prosaic everyday sounds in a world gone mad.

He pulled Edie close, protectively wrapping his arms around her. Sighing, she rested her forearms on his chest as she sagged against him. Silent seconds stretched into a drawn-out moment, neither speaking. They were, at that moment, of like mind. Like heart.

The first to stir, Edie tipped her head back to meet his gaze. The last light of day cast a chiaroscuro glow on to her skin.

'Twilight becomes you,' he murmured.

'Stop beating around the bush and spit it out, Cædmon. You didn't get up from your desk and hobble over here to pay me a compliment, lovely though it was.'

'Very well.' Striving for a calm that he didn't feel, Cædmon said matter-of-factly, 'I don't want you to accompany me to Saint-Germain-des-Prés.'

'Did I miss the email where I got kicked off the team?'

'Getting out of the building undetected is going to be dicey as hell. I can't bear the thought of something unforeseen –'

She put a hand over his mouth, silencing him. 'Through thick and thin,' she informed him. Undaunted, there was a determined glint in her eyes.

At a loss for words, Cædmon stared into those luminous brown eyes, awed by her grace and riveted by her beauty. But he was also astonished by her strength, Edie Miller, a curly-haired tower of it. Without a doubt, she was a gift. One that he felt singularly unworthy of. A loner at heart, if it weren't for Edie he suspected that he might wall himself up completely. Retreat into his study and retire from the world.

'We're more than a team,' he assured her. 'You do know that, don't you?'

Rather than answer, Edie went up on tiptoes, her warm breath caressing his lips. Cædmon put a hand to her cheek, smoothing away a damp ringlet. Then, bending his head, he kissed her.

Pure magic.

Cradling Edie's head, Cædmon deepened the contact between their two mouths as his other hand slid to her breast. Feeling the pound of her heart against his palm, he shuddered. In that instant, he felt the clash between tender feelings and a fierce, more primal emotion, an intense heat spreading from his spine to his lower body.

With an agonized groan, Cædmon reluctantly broke off the kiss. 'I haven't shaved in days,' he muttered apologetically. 'If we keep going like this, you'll soon be covered in a red rash.'

Smiling, Edie caressed his unshaven jaw. 'I like it. It makes you look dangerous. And you don't actually expect me to wait around for you to shave, do you?'

Amused by her eagerness, he returned the smile. 'I wouldn't dream of making you wait.' Caught up in the moment, Cædmon bent to sweep his lady love into his arms. Only to reconsider the romantic impulse a split second later. 'I would carry you into the bedroom, but –'

'Your bruised ribs.' Taking him by the hand, Edie led him towards the door. 'Bit of a battered warrior, aren't you?'

Cædmon raised her hand to his lips. 'Fear not. I shall soldier on.'

'I should certainly hope so!' Edie retorted, a flirtatious twinkle in her eyes.

55

Paris

Saturday, 0100h

As he sat at the small bistro-style kitchen table waiting for the electric kettle to boil, Cædmon stared at the computer screen.

'The mind boggles,' he whispered, having just finished reading the translations from the *Evangelium Gaspar* that Dr Cedric Lloyd at Wolfson College had emailed to him. 'And I now know why the Knights Templar went to such extraordinary lengths to find the ancient gospel.'

Astounded, Cædmon reread the first translation.

The Birth of Yeshua bar Yosef

Truly the heavens declare the glory of the Eternal One for great was the sign in the night sky! The star shone, radiant and gleaming, and it foretold of the Anointed One who would be born with the Fishes. The Magi had long awaited the One who would bring the Light of redemption and become a mediator between the Father and his Children.

Having seen the sign, we set forth from the Kingdom of Parthia in a great caravan to that land that had been set aside for the Children of Moses. We travelled at night when the star was brightly visible to the town of Bethlehem where it had been foretold in the Book of Micah that the Anointed One would be born.

Guided by the Shekinah, we came upon a dwelling that was set inside a deep cavern. Bearing our gifts, we entered the room where the infant slept in his mother's arms, the father near at hand. The Nazorean Elders were also present and they welcomed us warmly for our arrival had been prophesied to them many years prior.

We then approached the family and presented our gifts to Yosef and his young wife Miriam. We offered frankincense to open the portal to God; gold to honour the Anointed One's elevated status; and myrrh to usher the Anointed One into the next life.

The Elders then led us outside where their leader, a man named Zerah, spoke of how the Angel Gabriel had appeared to their ancient forebears with specific instructions so that they could fulfil the Divine Plan for the birth of the Anointed One. For seven generations they had assiduously purified themselves in advent of the birth. When they knew that the time was near, they took great care in selecting the perfect vehicle of conception who would bring the Anointed One into the world. Zerah gave assurance that Yosef and Miriam were both descended from a line of pious Nazoreans. When I made enquiry as to the nature of the preparations, Zerah revealed that when Miriam was four years of age, her mother Anna had brought her to the monastery at Mount Carmel where she was ritually dedicated and underwent eight years of training and study. She was one of many maidens who were similarly consecrated in the hopes that they would be perfected in mind and body should one of them be chosen. During this time, the consecrated virgins drank no wine nor did they consume the flesh of animals.

When Miriam was twelve years of age, she and the other virgins were led to the altar at the monastery to burn incense for their morning *prayers. Suddenly there was a flash of lightning in the sky and a golden halo of light formed around the young virgin Miriam. The Elders who were present at the altar knew that it was the sign from the Eternal One that He had selected Miriam to be the vessel to bring the Anointed One into the world. Three years would pass before she wed Yosef who had been carefully chosen by the Elders because he was a man of pious and righteous character.*

Now that the Divine Plan had been fulfilled, the Nazorean Elders were gravely concerned about the barbarous king who ruled Judea. Fearful that this wicked monarch would learn of the child's birth, a plan was made to safeguard the family. Two of my brother Magi were to accompany Yosef, Miriam and the baby Yeshua to Egypt where the family would seek sanctuary with the Nazorean healers who lived on the banks of Lake Mareotis. Zerah and I then decided that I should return in twelve years' time.

And so I did.

No sooner had Cædmon finished rereading the text from the first plate than Edie padded barefoot into the kitchen. Attired in a white silk robe, she appeared rested, but pale.

'Heya, Big Red,' she said, smiling warmly as she sat down beside him. 'I don't know about you, but the three-hour nap did me a world of good.'

Cædmon gestured to the laptop computer. 'I received the translations of the two copper plates.'

She flicked a swatch of curly hair over her shoulder before pulling her robe more snugly across her bosom. 'And . . . ?'

'And I now have a much clearer understanding of the Templars and their beliefs concerning the historical Jesus.'

Curious to get her reaction, he spun the computer in her direction. 'This is the translation of the first plate.'

'It's subtitled "The Birth of Yeshua bar Yosef",' Edie remarked as she adjusted the computer screen, tilting it slightly.

'Yeshua bar Yosef is Aramaic for "Jesus son of Joseph". Yeshua is, in fact, Jesus' actual name and the one by which his family and, later, his disciples knew him,' he explained. 'Similarly, Miriam translates into the English name "Mary".'

'Well, then, let me have at it.'

Getting up from the table, Cædmon walked over to the counter and snatched the kettle from the electric plate. While Edie read the translated gospel, he poured the boiling water into the glass cafetière. As the grounds steeped, he removed two mugs from the cupboard. Knowing Edie's penchant for sweets, he rummaged through a drawer, managing to locate a tin of shortbread biscuits which he placed on the table along with a sugar bowl and a small carton of milk.

As he plunged the coffee, Edie looked up from the computer. Just as he expected, she had a flabbergasted expression on her face.

'Wow. I mean . . . wow,' she reiterated, slack-jawed. 'Do you think it's true? That Yosef and Miriam were hand-picked by the Nazorean priests to be the "vehicles of conception" for the prophesied Messiah?'

'What reason would Gaspar have to fabricate a lie?' he countered. 'That the Nazoreans planned so carefully is astounding. Clearly, the birth of the Anointed One was not a chance event.'

'If Gaspar's account is to be believed, it also wasn't a divine event either,' Edie said pointedly, addressing the biblical elephant in the room. 'Meaning that Jesus wasn't conceived by the Holy Spirit and born of a virgin.'

'Most Christians are unaware of the fact that in the first and second centuries, a divine saviour god born of a virgin was a popular pagan belief, Dionysus and Sol Invictus two of the more famous examples.' Pouring the fresh-brewed coffee into two mugs, Cædmon carried them to the table and retook his seat. 'Eager for converts, Paul's protégé, a Gentile physician named Luke, described the immaculate conception at some length in his gospel, inventing a divine event that would compete with the prevailing pagan traditions. The Jews, however, never had an expectation that the prophesied Messiah would be a divine being.'

'Okay, so Luke was fishing for Gentile converts,' Edie conceded as she poured a dollop of milk into her coffee. 'But how do you explain the fact that in the Old Testament, the prophet Isaiah stipulated that the Messiah would be born of a virgin? "Behold, the virgin shall conceive and bear a son, and they shall call his name Immanuel,"' she recited, levelling him with a challenging stare.

'And I'll have you know that Isaiah prophesied no such thing. Rather he prophesied that an *almah* would give birth. *Almah* is Hebrew for "girl" or "young woman".' Pausing, Cædmon took a sip of his coffee before continuing. The brew too bitter, he reached for the milk carton. 'When the Church Fathers decided to create a divine Messiah, they intentionally mistranslated the original Hebrew text, thus corrupting Isaiah's prophecy. While the Church wants us to believe that the lyrics of "Hark the Herald Angels Sing" ring true, Gaspar would have us singing about a not-so-immaculate conception.'

'It's easy for you to make a mockery of this, isn't it?' Edie retorted, clearly taking exception to his last comment. 'You don't attend church service. Or even subscribe to a particular religion.'

Surprised by her fervour, Cædmon carefully weighed his reply. 'Here's another possibility to consider: Miriam's conception was absolutely "immaculate" in that the planning and foresight were impeccable. According to Gaspar, the Nazorean elders did everything possible to ensure that two pure and righteous individuals would bring a special child of destiny into the world.' Opening the biscuit tin, he passed it to Edie.

'I'm almost afraid to ask what's contained in the second translation.'

'The second plate of the *Evangelium Gaspar* pertains to the "Lost Years".' Cædmon turned the computer in his direction and pulled up the next email attachment. 'Those eighteen years from the time that the twelve-year-old Jesus had discourse with the high priests in the Temple to when he began his ministry at the age of thirty.'

Edie's eyes popped wide open, her surprise plainly evident. 'Do you mean that the *Evangelium Gaspar* actually contains information about those missing years in Jesus' life?'

Cædmon spun the laptop back in her direction. 'Brace yourself.'

369

The Education of Yeshua bar Yosef

The First Lesson

When Yeshua bar Yosef was twelve years of age he was entrusted to me so that I could oversee his continued education. Before this time, he had lived at Mount Carmel where the Brothers taught Yeshua from their library of sacred texts and had trained him in the healing arts.

We set out on the great trade route with a group of silk merchants who were making the return trip to their homeland. One night, Yeshua asked what he would learn once we arrived in the East. I explained that he would learn how to prepare and purify his mind, his body and his spirit to receive the Father's greatest gift, that of enlightenment. Only in an awakened state could a man communicate with the Eternal One.

I then taught Yeshua the first of many lessons: how the great prophet Zoroaster preached that the Heavenly Law of the Father is averse to the sacrifice of animals and that anyone who commits such wickedness shall be severely judged and punished. For this is a cruel act that causes the perversion of the mind and the loss of morality. The man who lives this Truth is a blessed child of the Father.

Yeshua is Mistaken for an Avatar

In Yeshua's nineteenth year, we journeyed to the country of the Āryas and the land of many deities that is called Jagannath. His arrival was met with much acclaim for he had grown in wisdom and stature. The Brahmin priests taught Yeshua the celibate virtues and the yogic practices that would enable him to change the lower forms of energy into a creative fire. In this way Yeshua moved closer to the Eternal One.

The priests in the temples marvelled at Yeshua's righteousness and asked if he was an avatar, what they know to be an incarnation of the Supreme Being. And Yeshua said, 'I am the Son of Man.'

Yeshua lived in peace with all men and this caused a great disturbance amongst the Brahmin priests who believed that the Holy Scriptures could not be taught to those men of low caste. And when they forbade Yeshua from preaching to these lowly men, Yeshua refused to heed their command for he knew that the Father loved all of His Children.

The priests in the temple raged against Yeshua and they planned his murder. But Yeshua was warned of this evil plot and we fled in the middle of the night. We then sought refuge with the monks who lived in the eastern mountains.

Yeshua Becomes Enlightened

While studying with the holy men who adored the sublime Buddha, Yeshua spent many years reading the Sacred Rolls that contained the Wisdom of the Sutras. And he was drawn to that which spoke of the good we must do unto others as this is the sure path that leads to communion with the Eternal One. This was when he endeavoured to live his life free of all violence and to forgive those who had wronged him in the past.

The llama at the monastery taught Yeshua how to turn his gaze inwards so that he could see that there were other worlds to behold. It was then that Yeshua began to comprehend that which had eluded him.

One day, Yeshua walked into the mountain forest for he sought communion with the Father. He had come to realize that the Father's Kingdom was not to be found in the pages of a sacred text or in a beautiful temple. Nor did the Eternal One dwell in the Heavens above. He now knew that the Eternal One dwelled within each man.

Yeshua remained in deep meditation for many days and many nights; and he was tempted by the Evil One who appeared in the guise of lust. But Yeshua spurned this temptation. Then the Evil One tried to lure him with the fear of death, but Yeshua had no fear for he was finally one with the Father and safe in his Father's House. He now knew the inner peace that comes with enlightenment for Yeshua had become an awakened being.

And so his education was completed and, in his twenty-ninth year, Yeshua and I began the long westward journey back to the land of his birth.

56

Rione di Borgo, Rome

'Heretical horseshit!'

Disgusted, Cardinal Franco Fiorio glared at the translations that he'd been working on for the better part of the night. Essene elders selecting a 'vessel' was the very sort of sensationalism that would cause Catholics to doubt their faith. To question the validity of the canonical gospels. *Jesus, as the pre-existent Son of God, had been conceived through a divine fertilization of his mother Mary's virgin womb!* That doctrine was beyond reproach. Beyond questioning even. At the First Council of Nicaea in 325 AD, the Church Fathers definitively determined that Jesus had been 'Born of the Father before all ages.' *Et ex Patre natum ante ómnia sæcula.*

Deeply offended and angered by what he'd just read, Franco reached for the shot glass of grappa that his housekeeper Beatrice had placed beside his espresso cup. Since he was putting in a late night, she'd brought him a *caffè corretto*. Rather than pouring the pomace brandy into the espresso, to 'correct' the strong brew, he downed the glass of spirits in a single gulp.

An instant later, a fiery heat exploded in Franco's lower belly, causing him to grimace involuntarily.

During his tenure as the head of the Congregation for

the Doctrine of the Faith, he had overseen the excommunication of a Jesuit priest who'd postulated that the virgin birth was merely symbolic. At the time, he'd bitterly lamented that the Church no longer burned heretics at the stake.

As for the content of the second plate . . . as much as it pained him to concede the point, it wasn't out of the question. In the Gospel of John, there was a tantalizing hint that Jesus was something other than a carpenter's son.

'And there are also many other things which Jesus did, the which, if they should be written every one, I suppose that even the world itself could not contain the books that should be written.'

Even if it could be proved that Jesus spent his youth in India, the Church would simply deny that Christ patterned his ministry on Hindu gurus or Buddhist llamas. The notion that God sat atop the mountain and that there were numerous paths to ascend the divine summit, all equally valid in the eyes of God, was not only a false precept, it was a blasphemous doctrine that smacked of Freemasonry. Orthodoxy had always been crystal clear on that point: *Extra Ecclesiam nulla salus.* Outside the Church there is no salvation.

Hindus, Buddhists, Muslims, Jews, they were all damned. The Protestants, too.

While the content of both plates was shocking, to his frustrated ire neither plate contained the Great Heresy. The secret that could destroy the Church in one fell swoop. As Franco knew full well, the Great Heresy was the only weapon powerful enough to coerce the College of Cardinals into electing him the next apostolic successor to Peter.

I must have the third plate in hand before the conclave convenes!

Roman Catholics the world over clamoured for a pope, a saviour, who would reassert the authority of the one, true Church and deliver them from the soulless decrees of Vatican II. That was the reason for the spiritual malaise that now permeated the Faith. If the College of Cardinals elected another liberal pontiff, the Roman Catholic Church would eventually lose all relevance.

'And I'm not about to let *that* happen,' Franco muttered as he got up from his desk.

Needing to take a break, bleary-eyed from the strain of having spent hours translating the two copper plates, he stepped over to the bookcase where there was a CD player wedged between the stacked volumes. He flipped through several plastic CD cases, selecting one of his favourites, *The Very Best of Maria Callas*.

Years ago, he'd taken his mother to hear Callas sing in Washington at the DAR Constitution Hall during the soprano's 1973 farewell tour. Although he'd never been a big opera fan, Rosella loved it and Maria Callas had always been her favourite. Franco, who'd been given the tickets by a parishioner, didn't know what to expect on that chilly November night when he and his mother were ushered to their orchestra seats. He certainly didn't expect that when the lights dimmed and the statuesque dark-haired woman stepped on to the stage, he would become transfixed.

Some critics claim that Callas had a flawed voice. But, oh, what a flawed beauty she was. Utterly ravishing. *La Divina*. As though it had happened yesterday, Franco could still vividly recall sitting in that dark concert hall, in his plain, black clerical suit, mesmerized, unable to take his eyes off the Greek beauty in the long flowing gown.

'*Bravissimo! Bravissimo!*'

His only regret that night was that he hadn't had the foresight to purchase a bouquet of red roses to toss at her feet.

A sucker for romantic arias, Franco popped the CD into the player and adjusted the volume. Loud enough that he'd be able to hear it on the terrace, but not so loud that it would awaken Beatrice.

On hearing the opening strains of the hauntingly beautiful '*O Mio Babbino Caro*', he stepped outside. In the near distance, the illuminated dome of St Peter's stood in stark contrast to the night sky. A beacon. A constant reminder of the great work that lay before him.

When he became the next pontiff, Franco's first priority would be to repeal Vatican II and clean house, disinfecting the Church of the liberal rot. *Toss the hippy-freak Catholics and their hootenanny guitars to the kerb.* Along with any sexually deviant priests. If he had his way, the cassocked perverts would all be strung up by their testicles in the middle of St Peter's Square.

Disgusting homosexuals, the lot of them!

Franco was living proof that a heterosexual man *could* overcome sexual lust and devote his life to the Church. And that Church would be pure, purged of liberals, feminists and sodomites. Bigger was not better, the Big Tent church an utter failure. The Holy See needed to cull the herd of all the undesirables. For too long now the Church had carried the sinners and heretics on its back. Coddling them as though they were naughty children. Unwilling to take a hard stance.

Over the course of human history, when did appeasement ever work?

In a word, never. A man cannot bargain with purveyors of vice and lust and deviant behaviour. The end result of sin was eternal damnation. Full stop. The end.

Those sinners and liberals who were unwilling to repent *would* be excommunicated. Dragged from the pews kicking and screaming if need be. And to ensure that happened, the CDF would be given greatly expanded powers to fast-track the excommunication process, a necessary measure to protect the flock from heresies and to keep the laity firm in their beliefs.

One Church, one Faith. Heresy would not be tolerated.

Those who clamoured for a 'kinder, gentler' Church had no true comprehension of the dynamic of faith. The Faith of the Church Fathers was not meant to be easy or convenient. No drive-through church-on-the-go for the men who forged a religion at Nicaea in 325.

Leaner and meaner. That's how it was done in those days.

His second priority would be to get the Vatican's financial affairs in order. Years ago, when Pope John XXIII was asked how many people worked at the Vatican, he famously quipped, 'About half.' When Franco became pontiff, the other half would get the axe. The Church could no longer afford to keep an army of 'do nothings' on the payroll. Also, by immediately eliminating all ecumenical outreach programmes, the Vatican would save untold millions.

Becoming the Vicar of Christ wasn't a vainglorious desire rooted in the ego. In truth, it would require that he make a tremendous sacrifice. But he was willing to make that sacrifice to save the Faith. The Church was his family. And had been ever since he received his Holy Orders.

Like any man, Franco would do whatever was necessary to protect his family from the evils of the world.

Yes, there would be the inevitable hue and cry. The protests. The backlash. The hippy-freaks and their infernal marches. But those who braved the storm would soon bask in the Church's love. More importantly, they would deepen their bond with the heavenly host through the sacred mysteries. Through the old rituals and rites, their souls would be burnished, their faith renewed.

Franco stared at the illuminated dome dramatically outlined against the horizon. Michelangelo's masterpiece. To his surprise, he realized that there were tears streaming down his face.

Mi struggo e mi tormento! I am anguished and I am tormented!

His heavenly benefactors had brought him so very far. They would not – *could not* – abandon him now. They *wanted* him to refurbish the Church. To make it whole. And pure. As it had once been.

They *wanted* him to purge the Church of all heretics. All liberals. All of those who, through sin and vice and heresy, followed the Wicked One.

They *wanted* him to declare open warfare on the enemies of the Church. To battle those who refused to follow the dictates of the one true Church.

Commissioned by the Queen of Heaven Herself, Franco had pledged to do just that.

And I will take no prisoners.

57

Paris

0215h

'I believe that it was Napoleon who said "history is the lie commonly agreed upon",' Cædmon remarked as he handed Edie a wine glass half-filled with amber Muscat.

'That's one way of putting it,' she murmured, everything that she thought she knew about Jesus having been turned on its head.

Glass in hand, she sat down in a leather club chair. A short while ago, they'd adjourned to Cædmon's study to discuss the second plate of the *Evangelium Gaspar*.

'How are we doing on time?'

Cædmon glanced at his watch. 'We have two hours and thirty minutes before we make our escape.'

Already anxious, Edie peered at the closed window. 'Is Calzada still –'

'Yes, unfortunately, he's still on the prowl,' Cædmon interjected as he sat down in the club chair opposite hers. 'Vigilant bastard.'

Hearing his muttered addendum, Edie tore her gaze away from the window. Like Cædmon, she was worried that Calzada's vigilance would prove a dangerous monkey wrench.

Cædmon jutted his chin at her untouched glass. 'Well, drink up. It's Falstaff's favourite sack, so do it justice.'

'Smells a little bit like raisins.' She took a measured sip, well aware that the 'sack' was Cædmon's not-so-subtle attempt to calm her nerves before they flew the coop.

'What's so bloody astounding is that the *Evangelium Gaspar* explains the mystery of the eighteen "Lost Years" on which the canonical gospels are strangely silent,' Cædmon remarked, returning to their original conversation. 'Only one of the gospels, Luke's, mentions in passing that during those years "Jesus increased in wisdom and in stature and in favour with God and man." A mere fourteen words to describe more than half of a man's life.'

'Yeah, well, I gotta tell ya, it's an astonishing explanation as to how he gained his wisdom and stature.' Edie paused, the images swirling through her head in cinematic fashion. 'We're talking about Jesus meditating and practising yoga. Like everybody else, I thought he was in the carpentry shop making tables and chairs with –' She stopped in mid-sentence, suddenly noticing that Cædmon appeared remarkably blasé. 'Aren't you the least bit surprised to find out that Jesus spent eighteen years cosying up to Magi, Hindu gurus and Buddhist sages?'

'Actually, it explains a longstanding mystery,' he informed her. 'In the *Hadith*, which is the collected sayings of the prophet Muhammad, Jesus is referred to as the "Prince of Travellers". Anyone who's ever seen a map of the Holy Land knows that the journey between Galilee and Jerusalem hardly warrants such a noteworthy title.'

'So why isn't Jesus called the "Prince of Travellers" in the New Testament?'

One side of Cædmon's mouth twisted in a caustic sneer. 'Because in the third and fourth centuries, the Church Fathers carefully cultivated the image that they wanted us to have of Jesus.'

Edie shook her head, angered by the centuries-old deception. 'What do you wanna bet that it was the Church Fathers who concocted the myth about Jesus building furniture with Joseph in the carpentry shop?'

'Oddly enough, it's a myth grounded in the truth. Just a moment . . . I need to retrieve my Aramaic dictionary.' Gripping the arms of his chair, Cædmon pushed himself to his feet and walked over to one of the floor-to-ceiling bookcases on the other side of the study. Hands on hips, he perused several rows before pulling the wheeled ladder to the centre case.

A few moments later, he walked back to the club chair, a leather-bound volume tucked under his arm. 'Keeping in mind that Aramaic was the language spoken by Jesus and his disciples, the Aramaic word *naggar*, which was used to describe Jesus, has two distinctly different definitions.' Retaking his seat, Cædmon balanced the heavy dictionary on top of his legs and flipped through the yellowed pages. 'Ah! Here it is. The first definition is a carpenter or woodworker. However, the second meaning of the word *naggar* is a learned man. Given that Jesus studied with religious teachers from the age of six to twenty-nine, he was a scholar by anyone's definition.' Point made, he closed the dictionary and set it on a side table. 'The Church does not want the Faithful to know that Jesus was influenced by the ancient Eastern religions.'

Putting her wine glass down, Edie drew her knees up to

her chest. 'I actually think that the *Evangelium Gaspar* can bring the world religions closer together by uniting the East and the West,' she ventured tentatively.

'Interestingly, the Knights Templar believed the very same thing.' Straightening his spine, Cædmon reached for his coffee mug. He took a few sips before saying, 'Two days ago when we were at Casa de Pinós, the Marqués de Bagá mentioned a doctrine known as the *Prisca Theologia*. Do you happen to recall the conversation?'

'Not really.' She shrugged. 'Sorry. Everything that happened two days ago is a mashed-up jumble.'

Cædmon gave a commiserating nod. 'A *Prisca Theologia*, or pristine theology, is a religious concept that presumes there is one pure and fundamental belief that originated from the pre-eminent Divinity. That belief was then woven into all of the world's religions. A common thread, as it were.'

'In other words, a universal path to God,' Edie murmured, intrigued.

'To derive the *Prisca Theologia*, the Templars knew that the layers of ritual, dogma and orthodoxy that had been heaped upon Jesus' original teachings by the Church Fathers had to be stripped away.' Leaning forward in his chair, Cædmon rested his elbows on top of his thighs, his hands steepled together. 'I can only presume that the Knights Templar sought the *Evangelium Gaspar* because they'd hoped it contained the *Prisca Theologia*. Alas, they paid a heavy price for their beliefs,' he added solemnly.

'It's as though the Church doesn't want us to be one big, happy, harmonious family.'

Cædmon snorted derisively. 'I rather doubt that they

do. Particularly since Jesus' teachings were hijacked by ambitious fourth-century bishops hell-bent on creating "a religion", an institution by which and through which they could maintain and exert power over the congregants. And they have zealously held on to that power ever since. Even in our own day and age, one doesn't have to look far to see what a callous lot they can be.'

Edie could hear the fury building, Cædmon having quickly gone from blasé to slow simmer to rip-roaring boil.

'Through heavy-handed editing, forgery, repressive censorship and purposefully omitting eighteen years of Jesus' life from the gospel accounts, the Church Fathers cobbled together the divine Son of God, the Gentile Jesus of Nazareth,' he continued. 'They then set themselves up as the intermediaries through whom one must pass in order to have communion with this divine saviour.'

'Giving them all of the power.' Like so many people, Edie took comfort in reading the New Testament. But she now wondered which passages were factual and which were some bishop's flight of fancy. 'So, in other words, we're talking about a major religious conspiracy and subsequent cover-up.'

'That is *precisely* what occurred.' Cædmon paused, his chest heaving with the force of his emotions. 'Yeshua's mission was to enlighten the world with a doctrine centred on love, compassion and tolerance. Too often, the Vatican pays lip service to that spiritual triune while acting in an overtly aggressive manner. Theirs is a long and ruthless history of eradicating anyone who didn't practise the Catholic faith. Europe, India, the New World, the list is endless.'

'But the *Evangelium Gaspar* contains vitally important information about the most important man in history,' Edie insisted, certain that Buddhists, Hindus and open-minded Christians, once they all got past their initial shock, would be excited by the gospel's contents.

Cædmon rose to his feet and carried the Aramaic dictionary back to the bookcase. 'Since Cardinal Franco Fiorio undoubtedly intends to use the *Evangelium Gaspar* to blackmail the upcoming conclave, the gospel will probably never see the light of day.'

'Then we have to stop him!' she exclaimed.

Abruptly spinning round, Cædmon shot her a silencing stare. 'To do so would endanger Anala's life,' he rasped through clenched teeth. 'Cardinal Fiorio can drag the Church down in flames for all I care. A fitting end, I might add. God knows that they tossed enough innocents on to the bonfire.' Scowling, he checked his wristwatch. 'Enough said on the topic. I need to call Gita and give her an update before we leave.'

58

Fort Cochin, India

'– and I uncovered documentary evidence that proves that Jesus did visit India when he was a young man,' Gita informed Cædmon and Edie, having just called them back via Skype. 'Corroborating what Gaspar wrote in his gospel account.'

After she'd examined the translated text of the first two plates that Cædmon emailed to her, Gita had done a quick fact check. Surprised by what she'd discovered, she'd immediately phoned to apprise him of the startling find.

Seated beside Cædmon, Edie scooted a few inches closer to the computer monitor. 'What kind of evidence are we talking about?' she asked, wide-eyed.

'There's a lengthy mention of Jesus in the ancient Hindu scripture known as the Bhavishyat Maha Purana.'

Cædmon thoughtfully tapped an index finger against his chin. 'Correct me if I'm wrong, but the Puranas describe the history and mythology of the Hindu pantheon, don't they?'

'That's correct. In this particular Purana, written around the year 115 AD, verses seventeen to thirty-two describe an encounter between Jesus and an Aryan king called Salivahana.'

'Fascinating,' Cædmon murmured as he scribbled the details on to a sheet of paper.

'So, what happened during this encounter?'

Having anticipated Edie's query, Gita reached across her desk for the text from which she'd mined the astonishing revelation. 'Since the passage is rather lengthy, I'm only going to translate the pertinent details.' Bleary-eyed from lack of sleep, she slipped on a pair of glasses before reading aloud: '"The king asked the teacher, 'Who are you?' To which the young man replied, 'I am the teacher of the true religion. Because our souls are torn between good and evil, a man can only attain a state of purity by speaking the truth, worshiping the immovable Lord, and living in harmony with all of life. I preach these principles and thus I am known as Isha-Masiha.'"'

Finished reading, Gita closed the text and removed her glasses.

'Of course, you know the follow-up question,' Cædmon said on cue. 'What does "Isha-Masiha" mean?'

Gita paused a moment before replying, 'It means "Jesus the Messiah".'

'Wow,' Edie murmured, her eyes having got a tad rounder. 'Why don't Christians know about this?'

'I presume for the very same reason that the Church doesn't want anyone to know about the *Evangelium Gaspar*.' Wrapping her hands around the cup of chai that she'd brewed, Gita stared at the untouched beverage.

When the archaeology team had first excavated the Maharaja Plate from the silt at the ancient port of Muziris, the curatorial staff at the Cultural Museum had been ecstatic. Other than Marco Polo's epic journey, there was little evidence of European travel to India during the Middle Ages.

Certain that the discovery, and subsequent publication of the find, would mean career advancement, Gita had insisted on conducting the historical research herself rather than delegating the laborious task to a junior curator. Riding high on accolades not yet earned, she'd contacted the Vatican Secret Archives to request information pertaining to Fortes de Pinós, the knight mentioned by name on the Maharaja Plate. Little did she know that her communiqué would incite a religious firestorm, someone on the receiving end wrongly believing that she knew the whereabouts of the long-lost *Evangelium Gaspar*.

And because of that damning email, Gita had unwittingly placed her daughter in great peril.

Anala's abduction is my fault entirely. If I'd not been so ambitious and —

Feeling the sting of bitter tears, Gita self-consciously turned away from her laptop.

'Gita, I need you to look at me,' Cædmon urged in a quiet tone of voice.

Embarrassed by her loss of composure, Gita hastily raised a fold of her linen sari, dabbing at the telltale tears. Braving the monitor, she saw that Edie Miller was no longer in the camera frame. 'Forgive me,' she whispered. 'It's just that the ransom is due tomorrow at twelve noon and I'm terrified that —'

'Very shortly, I shall have the third plate,' Cædmon said over her. 'Rest assured that this nightmare will soon be over.'

Comforted by his assurance, she unthinkingly blurted

out, 'You must believe me, Cædmon, when I say that years ago I wish that I had – Call me as soon as you can,' she said abruptly, some things better left unsaid.

'I will.'

An instant later, Cædmon's image blipped off the screen. Shoulders slumping, Gita closed her laptop.

Stay strong, daughter! Your father is on the way.

59

Anala Patel flipped off the torch to conserve the battery, instantly plunging the subterranean prison into an ebony darkness.

'Welcome to Bleak House,' she muttered. Having hit the depths of despair, her emotional control was fragile at best.

Waking up from her drugged sleep, she'd been terrified to find herself locked in a small cellar. Approximately three metres by five metres, the underground burrow had a hard-packed dirt floor and stone walls that were lined with empty shelves. Once upon a time it had been used for storage, but given the surfeit of dust and old cobwebs, she assumed that had been aeons ago. There were no windows or electric lights, the lack of which was depressing beyond words. A condemned woman, she had nothing to warm the cockles of her heart save for a scratchy wool blanket, a plastic jug of water, a can of raw almonds and several packets of dried fruit. No bed. And no toilet.

Heartless monsters!

In Hinduism, every living thing – every creature, tree, stone and blade of grass – was imbued with divinity. *But where was the divinity in* this? *This was hell on earth.* A death sentence.

'To be or not to be,' she muttered, wondering why her captors even bothered to supply her with food and water.

Perhaps it'd been done to alleviate the priest's guilt. And how absolutely bizarre was *that*? A priest master-minding her abduction in order to obtain some ancient gospel? That her mother was involved in the plot was *beyond* surreal.

Confined to the murky dungeon, her sense of time had slipped away. The fact that her hands and feet weren't manacled indicated that her captors were confident she couldn't escape. And they were right. She'd spent an excruciating amount of time crawling on her hands and knees with the torchlight, examining every square inch of the bunker. The only point of egress was through a trap-door that she surmised had been secured on the other side with a heavy chain. There wasn't a tincture of hope that she'd be able to escape her new prison.

Huddled on the dirt floor, Anala propped her back against the stone wall. Pulling her arms and legs against her chest, she rested her cheek on top of her knees. She struggled mightily to hold back the flood of tears as her thoughts drifted into decidedly morbid territory, going through a mental checklist of what would happen once she died. Somewhat crazily, she imagined the backlog of emails that would never be answered.

Ping, ping, ping. You have mail.

Silly thought. *Or was it?* Since she'd never written down her passwords, no one would be able to access her email accounts. And while her friends and acquaintances would eventually be apprised of her death, spam and junk mail would be piling up, unopened and –

Oh, sod it.

Utterly forlorn, she suffered from an existential dread.

And who wouldn't? She had enough food and water to last for only a few days. Once her meagre supplies were depleted, this miserable hole in the ground would become her final resting place. Buried alive in a dark womb room.

How ironic, since her hopeless predicament had something to do with her mother and the father she'd never met. A man named Cædmon Aisquith.

Bloody bastard, she railed silently, thinking him as good a person as any to blame.

When she was younger, she'd missed having a father in her life. But now she didn't know what she'd do with one, quite frankly. At her age, 'dear old dad' seemed rather superfluous. However, it did explain why her mother never spoke of the past, as though the family history was a crate of eggs that she was terrified of smashing. Because of that, Anala had never been able to knit her life together in a tidy narrative. There were gaping holes in the story. Still were. Just not as many as before.

Thinking of her mother, Anala envisioned her dressed in a cotton sari, carrying a plateful of flowers – jasmine, hibiscus and pavizhamalli, her favourite night flower. When she was a young child, her mother had explained to her that plants and flowers had a special energy that could express the contents of one's heart.

Such a lovely memory.

Overcome with emotion, Anala sniffled loudly, causing those bits and bobs of memory to scatter like frightened tadpoles.

There are so many things that I need to ask my mother. So many things that I should have said but didn't.

Since she had no flowers to give to her mother to

convey what was in her heart, Anala pulled her hands close together, moving her thumbs over an imaginary keypad. Knowing how Gita loathed emoticons and anything that smacked of an abbreviation or acronym, she 'typed' out the message in its entirety. Even going so far as to include proper punctuation. While the digital device was a figment of her imagination, the sentiment of the message had never been so keenly felt.

'*I love you, Amma.*'

Tears puddling at the corners of her eyes, Anala hit the 'send' button.

60

Paris

0445h

Cædmon raised the ceiling hatch. 'Tread gently,' he cautioned. 'We don't want to awaken the occupants below.'

Who would undoubtedly freak out if they thought there were two fingersmiths prowling on the apartment rooftop, Edie mused. A case of mistaken identity to be sure. But try telling that to the Paris Metropolitan police.

While they weren't looters with sacks full of plunder, she and Cædmon were trying to make a getaway, the roof the only point of egress where they could exit the apartment building undetected. Hector Calzada and his sullen-faced sidekick had been keeping a vigilant eye on the building entrance since they'd returned from Saint-Germain-des-Prés, taking turns manning the courtyard below.

Edie held on to the steel service ladder anchored into the wall of the upper-storey hallway as she popped her head through the hatch opening. Above her, the stars in the night sky twinkled in the firmament. Almost immediately the celestial lights induced an onslaught of vertigo, the stars appearing to spin like tops on steroids.

Buck up! It's just an illusion.

'All in my mind,' Edie murmured to herself, repeating the 'buck up' mantra a few more times to stiffen her resolve.

Mentally shoving her anxiety aside, she scrambled through the opening. Too much was at stake for her to suffer a panic attack. She'd trekked in the Himalayas, scaled climbing walls and even hiked to Machu Picchu without incident. However, there was something about being on top of a building that always gave her the heebie-jeebies. Why rooftops should prompt such extreme anxiety, she had no idea. Rooftop entertaining was popular in Washington DC and she'd had to give a stammering excuse to more than one hostess when she'd been forced to make an abrupt party exit, having succumbed to severe vertigo.

Other than bulky vents and one or two skylights, there was nothing of interest on the rooftop. Farther afield, the lights of Paris gleamed. A million plus glow-worms illuminating the urban landscape. Although Edie knew that it wasn't physically possible, it *felt* like every hair follicle on her body was standing on end. She swayed slightly, her heart racing.

'Are you all right, love?' Knowing that she suffered from vertigo, Cædmon solicitously grasped her by the elbow.

'I'm fine.' Edie shot him a shaky smile . . . even as she envisioned herself plunging off the side of the apartment building. She was, as the saying went, whistling in the graveyard. Trying desperately to keep the ghosts at bay.

Cædmon's brows drew together, the man seeing right through her false bravado. 'Don't look down.'

'Or up,' she murmured, both inducing a spinning sensation. Looking straight ahead, she concentrated on her breathing. The only thing she had even a remote chance of controlling.

Several moments passed, her heartbeat finally slowing to a more normal rate.

Okay. I can do this. Piece of cake.

Resolve bolstered, Edie shifted the strap on the black rucksack a bit higher on her shoulder; it contained her iPad, mobile phone, passport, wallet, a change of clothes and some basic toiletries. From Saint-Germain-des-Prés, they were going straight to Charles de Gaulle airport, having booked two seats on the first nonstop flight to New York City.

Wordlessly, Cædmon gestured to the Romanesque spire visible in the distance – the Saint-Germain-des-Prés bell tower – indicating that it was time to depart.

Sidestepping the skylights, they made their way to the far side of the roof where there was a metal scaffold, approximately seven feet long and three feet wide, parked against the exterior wall of the building. Cædmon had spotted the mechanical platform earlier in the day when they'd returned from the church. The work crew that had been contracted to install new wrought-iron balconies was using the scaffold to transport men, equipment and materials up and down the six-storey building.

'Mind your step,' Cædmon warned as he swung a leg over the side of the steel carriage. There was no need to add the obvious – that a misstep could have fatal consequences.

Edie took hold of his outstretched hand, allowing him

to assist her from roof to carriage. 'Kinda daring, don't you think?'

'No more daring than scaling the tower at Ponferrada Castle.'

'Yeah, and as I recall, you took quite a tumble. Scared me witless.'

'An unforeseen accident,' Cædmon muttered as he crouched in front of a locked metal box. Prying a screwdriver under the cover, he popped it open, exposing a simple control panel.

'Ready to set sail?'

Edie nodded, not bothering to point out that ships were safer when anchored in the port. But that, of course, wasn't why they were built.

'Let's hope the bark floats,' Cædmon said as he pressed the 'on' switch.

The platform jerked violently.

Edie clutched the steel safety bar. 'Or at least doesn't sink too swiftly,' she murmured.

Hit with another wave of dizziness, she closed her eyes, forcing herself to think about something – *anything* – other than the fact that the moonlit rooftops had started to careen wildly. Instead, she thought about the *Evangelium Gaspar* and a teenage Yeshua bar Yosef setting out to see the world on what would prove to be an eighteen-year spiritual odyssey. *To boldly go where no one had gone before.*

Although she'd been initially stunned by the gospel, now that she'd had time to reflect, the idea, somehow, seemed *right*. Jesus was, after all, a mortal human being, endowed with a curiosity about the world. Would such a gifted individual have been content to spend his youth in the backwaters of Galilee? Because he travelled to foreign lands during those eighteen 'Lost Years' to study other religions, she believed that it made him the wise and compassionate man that he came to be when, at the age of thirty, he began his ministry. Obviously, he was secure enough in his own faith to respectfully study other spiritual beliefs. Jesus, the mortal man, was a seeker of the truth who knew that God dwelled in every corner of the universe.

Opening her eyes, Edie glanced at Cædmon who stood, legs braced wide apart, in front of the control panel, ready to hit the 'off' button before the slow-moving platform reached the ground level.

'I trust the vertigo has dissipated,' Cædmon said as the steel carriage came to a shuddering stop several inches above the pavement.

Relieved to be on *terra firma*, Edie gave a thumbs-up. 'I'm made of sterner stuff,' she informed him with a self-deprecating chuckle.

'You are at that.' Taking her by the arm, he helped her to scramble over the safety bars.

For several moments they stood side-by-side, two shadowy figures on the narrow cobbled lane.

Cædmon glanced over at her, blue eyes glittering. 'Ready?'

Bolstered by the knowledge that the hard part was done, Edie nodded gamely. 'All set.'

'Right, then. We're off to the crusades.'

61

'Where the hell have you been?' Javier Aveles hissed, shooting Hector an accusing glare as he entered the courtyard.

'Who are you, my old lady? I took a pussy break. Try it some time, amigo.' Peering up at Aisquith's flat, Hector saw a faint golden light shining in the window. 'Any movement?'

Javier shook his head. 'Not recently. They were up and moving for a while, but –' his lips turned down at the corners as he shrugged expressively – 'I'm thinking they hit the sack.'

'So, why didn't they turn off the light?' Hector wondered aloud, suddenly suspicious. As he'd painfully and humiliatingly discovered, Cædmon Aisquith was a crafty fucker.

The skin on the back of Hector's neck prickled as he remembered what had happened at Santiago de Compostela.

I've got a bad feeling about this.

Suddenly suspicious, he strode into the apartment building. A few moments later, he exited the creaky elevator, stormed down the corridor and kicked in the door of Aisquith's flat.

It took only a few seconds to verify that the Englishman and his bitch had escaped the premises.

Fuck! I leave Javier alone for two hours and this is what happens!

Enraged, Hector fought a very strong urge to set Aisquith's flat on fire. Light up one of the thousands of books and torch the place to the ground. Like blood, fire was a cleansing balm.

But first I have to track down the English cabrón.

According to Javier, earlier in the day Aisquith and his bitch had spent a lengthy amount of time at a nearby church.

What do you wanna bet that's where they're at?

Unfortunately, he didn't have a gun on him. But he had a very sharp blade. Sharp enough to cut through the silver thread that tethered the English fucker to the earth. Hector's homeboys back in Spanish Harlem used to always say that he was like a pitbull bred for the ring. A beast that kept fighting until it drew its last breath.

As you, English, will soon find out.

62

Cædmon and Edie quickly wended their way along the cobblestone alleys and narrow lanes that were tucked behind looming seventeenth-century buildings. A hidden section of the Saint-Germain-des-Prés neighbourhood, it was a slice of old Paris, the district inundated with antique shops, art galleries and intimate bistros. All were closed, the windows shuttered, daybreak still an hour away. A few minutes ago, they'd passed a fruit vendor unloading crates of fresh produce from a lorry. Other than the lone pedlar, the streets were deserted.

As they emerged from a covered alleyway, the street lamps shed a soft light that shrouded the enclave, dividing it into areas of hazy illumination and inky pools of dark shadow. He and Edie hugged the latter. Should they encounter an inquisitive passer-by, he didn't want anyone to be able to later identify them. They were, after all, en route to pinch a 2000-year-old gospel from the oldest church in Paris. Stealing antiquities was a criminal offence, one that would unquestionably be punished to the full extent of French law should they be caught. A lengthy prison term was a given.

On their guard, they approached the small courtyard that was adjacent to the church. The garden was illuminated by a twenty-foot-high street lamp that bathed the entire area in incriminating light – including the Gothic arches of the destroyed chapel.

Damn.

'I didn't anticipate the street lamp,' Cædmon muttered as he opened the courtyard gate, the hinges squealing harshly. Swivelling his head from side to side, he surveyed the area, checking to make sure that no vagrants lurked. Satisfied, he gave the all-clear. '*No hay Moros en la costa.*'

Edie shot him a quizzical glance. '*Que?*'

'There are no Moors on the coast,' he translated. 'It's the Spanish version of "the coast is clear".'

Peering upwards, Edie gnawed on her lower lip. 'The lamp could be a problem. Particularly if someone walks past the courtyard while we're removing the plate,' she whispered, glaring at the street lamp as though it were an intruding Cyclops, a circle-eyed member of that ancient race of primordial giants.

'I agree.' Annoyed by the unforeseen hitch, Cædmon bent at the waist and retrieved a good-sized stone from the ground. Jack-knifing into an upright stance, he bit back a grunt, his bruised ribs protesting the motion. Stone in hand, he took aim and sent the rock hurling through the air.

The ornate glass shade shattered, instantly plunging the courtyard into a desolate gloom. The noise caused several birds roosting in the nearby eaves to take flight in a squawking flurry of flapping wings.

'Bullseye!'

Cædmon made no reply as he hurriedly shed his rucksack, keeping his movements as streamlined as possible. Efficiency the name of the game during any illicit undertaking, he removed several tools and two pieces of soft foam which he handed to Edie for safekeeping. 'I want you to keep a close watch while I pry the plate off the exterior wall.'

'What do we do if someone enters the churchyard?' She peered furtively over her shoulder at the shadows cast by stone and tree and things unseen.

'We snatch the plate and run like bloody hell.'

Game plan iterated, Cædmon went down on bent knee in front of the Gothic arches, the plastered-over plate at eye level. He placed the slanted edge of a small chisel on the stucco, near to the plate, but not on it.

Very carefully, he began to tap the end of the chisel with a hammer, bits of stucco arcing through the air. Unfortunately there was nothing he could do to muffle the sound, the repetitive *taptaptap* echoing off the exterior wall of the church, breaking the somnolent silence. A laborious exercise, each tap caused a corresponding bolt of pain to radiate along his ribcage. Grimacing, he kept at it, mining for a treasure that would undoubtedly be used to further the ambitions of a ruthless Roman Catholic cleric. So be it.

I will do whatever is necessary to save Anala's life.

Edie stood behind his left shoulder, a lone night watchman. 'Cue the spooky music,' he heard her mumble. 'I'm thinking "Ave Satani" from that movie *The Omen*.'

'Or perhaps "Dies Irae" from Mozart's Requiem.' He glanced at his wristwatch, verifying that they were on schedule, the Paris subway due to open in twenty minutes.

It took nearly ten minutes of chipping away at the plaster before he was able to *very slowly* slide a four-inch flat putty knife behind the plate, taking great care not to cause any damage. With a slight tug of the wrist, he pried the plate from the exterior wall.

'Yes! We've got it!' Edie handed him the two pieces of soft foam.

'We'll clean it once we get to the airport,' he said, sandwiching the plate between the foam to keep it safe in transit. He'd packed several solvents that they could use to remove the stucco which had mercifully protected the blasted thing from the elements. Once cleaned, they could make a copper rubbing that he would then email to Cedric Lloyd at Oxford. He also intended to contact Father Gracián Santos as soon as they boarded their early-morning flight to inform him that he had secured the plate and was en route.

In a hurry to abscond with their ill-gotten gains, Cædmon stuffed his tools and the makeshift packing case inside his rucksack.

'Looks like we're in for a downpour,' Edie remarked anxiously.

He glanced heavenwards, noticing that the stars were now obscured by ragged-edged storm clouds. A savage sight that portended a rip-roaring storm. 'We should be able to make it to the underground before the –' He stopped in mid-sentence, detecting a worrisome sound.

'What is it?' Edie asked.

Holding up a hand, Cædmon strained his ears. In the far distance, he heard a car door slam. Much closer, perhaps half a block away, he heard the steady pound of an insistent footfall. Bearing in their direction.

Damn.

It could be nothing. An early-morning jogger taking advantage of the empty pavements. Or it could be the warden searching for his two fugitive prisoners.

Unwilling to take a chance with so much at stake, Cædmon hastily removed the hammer from his rucksack before handing the pack to Edie. 'Can you manage both of them?'

'Yours and mine? Yes, but –'

'Someone's approaching. I want you to go to the far end of the churchyard and climb over the chain-link fence. Be sure to stay in the shadows,' he instructed. 'We'll rendezvous in ten minutes at the agreed-upon coordinates. If I don't arrive, you are to proceed to the airport without me.'

Edie vehemently shook her head. 'I'm not going to let you be a sacrificial lamb.'

'I prefer the charging bull metaphor.' Grasping the hammer in his right hand, Cædmon held it aloft. 'As you can see, I'm well armed. Now, hurry.'

'Cædmon, *please*, be careful.'

I may not have a choice in the matter, he owned, mentally battening the hatches as he watched Edie run to the other end of the courtyard. Should calamity strike, he had complete faith that she would take the third plate to New York and arrange for Anala's release. They'd already discussed how that could be accomplished in a way that would ensure no one got killed.

Scanning the courtyard, Cædmon decided to take a position behind a five-foot-high stone pedestal. On top of the plinth there was a massive bronze bust of a woman's head. The unexpected piece of artwork – a Picasso unless he was mistaken – was large enough to conceal him.

He gave the bust a passing glance, noticing that it was dedicated to Guillaume Apollinaire. It seemed an odd inclusion in a churchyard, but there was no time to ponder the incongruity of a Picasso sculpture dedicated to a Surrealist poet whose best-known work involved a woman who undergoes a sex change, her breasts floating into the stratosphere like a pair of helium-filled balloons. He could only assume that the priests at Saint-Germain-des-Prés had never read *The Breasts of Tiresias*.

A few moments into the wait, a lone man appeared on the other side of the chain-link fence. Cædmon immediately recognized the stocky fellow with the swaggering saunter.

Sensing that the real storm was about to break, he watched as Hector Calzada warily traipsed through the open garden gate that led to the courtyard, the gravelled pavement crunching with each deliberate footstep. There was a ferocious look etched on the man's face.

Cædmon slowed his breath. *Waiting. Watching.* Monitoring Calzada's every move.

His right hand tightened on the hammer, ready to swing with all the strength that he could muster. Crack the bastard's head wide open. As long as the Bête Noire was conscious, he was a threat.

Calzada ambled past the stone plinth.

Ready to channel his adrenalin rush into a violent onslaught, Cædmon launched from his position . . . just as a car turned on to Rue de l'Abbaye.

Startled by the flash of halogen headlamps, Calzada whipped his head round. Catching sight of Cædmon, briefly limned in the passing glow of light, he dodged reflexively to the right.

In the next instant Cædmon heard an ominous *click*.

Damn! He has a flick knife!

Growling, Calzada came at him. Cædmon swerved, managing to parry the deadly swipe with the raised hammer. Before he could cock his arm to retaliate, Calzada rushed him again. Chest heaving, Cædmon again recoiled, the blade coming within a hairbreadth of his throat.

Incapacitated by his bruised ribs, his reflexes were sluggish. So sluggish, he feared that it might prove a deadly rout.

Calzada toggled the knife from hand to hand, taunting him. 'Death frees the soul from the prison of the body,' he said, smiling ghoulishly.

'What are you saying? That I should *thank* you for slashing my throat?'

'Give me the third plate, English, and I won't lay a hand on you.'

'Very well. I surrender. The plate is located in the church tower,' he said, tossing the hammer aside.

'Lead the way, English. But one false move and I'll skewer you on the end of my blade.' Calzada touched the serrated knife with his index finger. '*Sí*, it's *very* sharp.'

Biting back a sarcastic retort, Cædmon resignedly nodded his head, hoping that he appeared sufficiently defeated. As they headed towards the chain-link fence, he knew that he had one chance – and only the one – to take down the beast.

As ordered, he led the way through the open gate, his adversary a few feet behind him.

Suddenly, without warning, Cædmon dived to one side. Snatching hold of the wrought-iron gate, he slammed it into the Bête Noire's belly.

Windmilling backwards, Calzada howled in animal rage as he was knocked on to his arse in an ungainly heap.

Cædmon seized his chance and ran down Rue de l'Abbaye. At the corner, he veered into an alley jam-packed with parked cars, motorcycles and scooters. He raced to the end of the passageway, which dead-ended in a seven-foot-high stone wall.

Hearing a pounding footfall – Calzada having quickly recovered – Cædmon leaped on to the boot of a parked sedan. The action triggered a screeching blare, the car alarm activated. He scrambled on to the roof and hoisted himself over the stone wall. Bracing for what he knew would be a jarring impact, he dropped anchor, landing on all fours.

Grunting, he righted himself and kept running.

A few moments later, winded, each breath an agony, he saw two green LED headlamps just before the outline of two sturdy bicycles – Vélib' rentals – materializing in the charcoal gloom. The rental bikes and their green head-lamps were a familiar sight on the city streets. Edie, dependable as always, had secured the rentals for their use. Worried that Calzada and Aveles might canvas the area and discover that they'd boarded a subway train bound for the airport, he intended to outwit the bastards by biking to a station in the next *arrondissement*.

'Thank God!' Edie exclaimed as he came to a shudder-ing stop.

Bent over, gasping for air, he grabbed the handlebars and swung a leg over the seat. 'We have to leave! Now! Calzada is right behind –'

That was all Edie needed to hear. 'I'll meet you at the

Metro station!' Handing him the second rucksack, she pushed off, pedalling madly.

Hearing a resounding *clop!clop!clop!* echoing behind him, Cædmon quickly shoved his arms through the pack's nylon straps and, like Edie, made haste to depart.

Adiós, Hector. Hasta la vista. And, lest I forget, sod you!

63

Piazza San Pietro, Rome

0602h

Rosy-hued dawn was still thirty minutes beyond the horizon, St Peter's Square shrouded in dark shadows.

Making his way on foot, Cardinal Franco Fiorio entered the keyhole opening in the magnificent colonnade. Seeing a brace of wobbly pigeons foraging for crumbs, he frowned, instantly put in mind of the pigeon-hearted cardinals and bishops who'd been too afraid to stand up to the liberal apostates in their midst.

Franco had never been afraid.

But he was now desperate, his despair so great that he couldn't help but wonder if the particulars of his life had been part of a cosmic scheme designed to taunt him. *The Blessed Virgin Mary. The red rose petals.*

'The saint has yet been born who, in their darkest hour, did not hate God,' he murmured, trying to hold on to his love of the Heavenly Host even though he feared that he'd been cruelly abandoned.

Uncertain what the new day would bring, Franco scurried across the deserted piazza. A short while ago he'd received a phone call from Gracián Santos, the hysterical priest informing him that the Englishman not only had the third plate, but he'd managed to elude the two sentries.

Why did Aisquith escape with the plate? Did he intend to sell it on the black market? If he did, the ancient gospel would undoubtedly command a *very* high price. One that would cost Franco dearly. Without the third plate in his possession, he would be unable to affect the outcome of the conclave.

Cardinal Thomas Moran, the first papabile, will be elected the next pontiff.

When that happened, Moran and his liberal allies within the Curia would lead Christ's sheep right over the cliffs of heresy. Assuming that the Church didn't first implode. Which would undoubtedly occur should Aisquith, instead of selling the third plate, go public with it.

God help us all if he does.

The ensuing chaos would destroy the Christian Faith. Leaving nothing but rubble and ash.

In the early centuries of the Church, the bishops had gone to extreme lengths to suppress the dark secret surrounding the life and death of Jesus the Nazorean. Every heretical gospel that contained the secret had been destroyed, whole libraries burned to the ground. Because the record of that great purge was safeguarded in the Vatican Secret Archives, Franco wasn't the only prelate in the Holy See who knew the particulars of the dark secret. Many cardinals knew that the Jesus of the canonical gospels was a fiction. But since there was no longer any documentary proof, all of them slept soundly at night secure in the knowledge that the Faithful would never be privy to what had come to be known as the Great Heresy.

May God damn Cædmon Aisquith for all eternity!

Distraught, Franco gazed at the western horizon. Rising above the rooftops of Rome, the dome of St Peter's dominated the charcoal grey sky.

Like a child seeking the much-needed comfort of a loving parent, he made his way to the basilica. Designed and constructed by some of the great baroque masters – Bernini, Maderno, Bramante, Michelangelo – it rose up from the piazza in breathtaking splendour.

In ancient Rome, the area adjacent to the piazza had been the site of Nero's infamous Circus where Christians had been slaughtered wholesale because of their beliefs. Jeered and taunted, the Apostle Peter was crucified upside down during one of Nero's more gruesome spectacles. His body had then been removed and buried in a nearby cemetery. More than two centuries would pass before the newly converted Emperor Constantine would revoke the ban on the Christian religion, an act that finally put an end to the bloodthirsty persecutions. Inspired by his new-found faith, that great and good emperor had built a basilica over the burial ground where St Peter had been laid to rest. For more than a millennium, Constantine's basilica served pilgrim and pope alike until it was razed to the ground in the sixteenth century to make way for a far more magnificent structure.

Franco gazed at the familiar façade. *Statues. Balustrade. Columns. Vestibules. Niches.* It was so staggering that it was akin to a sky with two suns. The geographical centre of the Roman Catholic faith, St Peter's was the last bastion in a world gone mad. A world overrun with heretics and atheists, and those who despised all things Catholic.

Exhausted from his night's labour, Franco trudged up the steps that led to the portico. When he reached the dimly lit atrium, a uniformed Swiss Guard shot him a questioning glance, clearly surprised to see him, the basilica closed. Tight-lipped, Franco brusquely gestured to a massive bronze door, indicating that he wished to enter. He was a Prince of the Church; he didn't have to explain his actions.

As the guard hurried to open the door, Franco dismissively glanced at the large plaque set into the marble pavement that bore the coat-of-arms of Pope John XXIII. The plaque commemorated the pontiff who, in 1962, had convened the Second Vatican Council.

Heresy was no different than trash blowing hither and yon, Franco silently condemned as he entered the nave. It *had* to be cleaned up or it would litter the Holy See beyond recognition.

Well aware that his unplanned visit was an act of desperation, he rushed down the centre of the nave. The marble-laden aisles that flanked either side brimmed with monuments, side altars and statues of martyrs, saints and angels that at times seemed to defy gravity itself. Consumed with fear, Franco barely took notice, his attention focused straight ahead on the papal altar.

Who is Cædmon Aisquith? The question kept reverberating, gong-like.

Although he'd received a dossier from the Vatican secret service, there had been no mention in it of the Englishman's relationship to Anala Patel or her mother Gita. More worrisome, according to the Patel girl's official documents, her father was one Dev Malik. In light of

Aisquith's spotty dossier – twelve years unaccounted for – Franco should have questioned whether he was truly the girl's father. Particularly since Gracián Santos claimed that the girl had never heard of Cædmon Aisquith, a fact that Franco had conveniently ignored, driven – *no* – blinded by ambition.

Now, a man who was a known conspiracy theorist had in his possession the greatest conspiracy in all of human history.

Breathless, Franco came to a halt in the middle of the transept. Above him, the great dome soared above the 95-foot-high baldacchino, the famous bronze canopy that surmounted the papal altar.

Tilting his head, Franco stared at the giant letters on the gold background that were scribed around the rim of the dome's base. Those letters spelled out a phrase that perfectly articulated the basilica's sacred purpose: *Hic una fides mundo refulgent.* 'From here a single faith shines throughout the world.'

His gaze next moved to the gigantic block of Greek marble. *The Altar of the Confessio.* It was here that the most sacred mystery of the Mass took place; when bread became the Body of Christ and wine was transformed into His Blood. The rogue Protestants had always rejected that most sacred of mysteries, the Transubstantiation. Yet *that* was the sole reason for celebrating the Mass, the heretics unable to grasp that the mystical rite was performed, not for the salvation of the few, but for the salvation of the entire world.

While there were many who accused conservative Catholics of being slaves to ancient rituals and medieval ceremonies, Franco knew that the rituals imparted a sense of history that assured each member of the Faithful that they belonged to something greater than themselves. Something that began on the eve of the Crucifixion when Christ and his disciples gathered to partake of that last meal together.

But ever since Vatican II, the sacred *mysterion* had lost its power to spiritually move the laity. Because the liberals could not know the mind of God, they rationalized the Faith. In their materialistic worldview, there was no room for miracles, angels or demons. Or even hell, for that matter.

Tears pooling in his eyes, Franco stared at the altar that covered the grave site of St Peter the Apostle. The Rock upon which Christ built His Church.

Petrus est hic.

'Peter is here,' he whispered softly. Enshrined in the spot that was the beating heart of the basilica.

Overcome with emotion, Franco bent at the knees, slowly lowering himself on to the marble floor. Spreading his arms wide, he prostrated himself before the holy altar.

Forgive me, Father, for I have sinned.

By merely paying lip service to his role as Defender of the Faith, Franco had allowed this latest calamity to unfold. Not wanting to bloody himself, he'd refused to jump into the fray. Instead, he'd remained in the safe shadows, letting the unreliable Gracián Santos act as his surrogate.

Give me another chance, Heavenly Father, and I will do all in my power to ensure that Your Will —

Franco stopped in mid-plea, startled by his mobile

phone vibrating against his waist. Propping himself on his elbows, he unclipped the phone and flipped it open.

It was a text message from Gracián Santos:

Aisquith will deliver ransom
tomorrow morning.

His breath caught in his throat. So great was his joy, Franco could almost feel the red rose petals raining down upon him.

Determined to follow the path set before him, he shoved himself to his feet. The years of steadfast devotion had brought him to this momentous crossroads. No longer would he be the lone voice crying out in the wilderness. Soon the entire world would hang on his every word.

For I AM the man who will become the next pope!

PART IV

'The bravest are surely those who have the clearest vision of what is before them, glory and danger alike, and yet notwithstanding, go out to meet it.'

Thucydides

64

New York State, USA

Saturday, 1515h

Cædmon awoke with a jolt, the drone of the engine having lulled him to sleep.

Disorientated, he glanced about; most of the train passengers were either reading or tapping away on a laptop computer. Nothing the least bit eyebrow raising.

'*Carpe dormio,*' he muttered. *Give him forty winks, and he'll turn up as fresh as clean sawdust and as respectable as a new bible.*

If only, he thought, glancing at his watch. Since they were scheduled to arrive at their stop within the hour, just the ten winks would have to suffice. The deadline for delivering the ransom was in its waning hours. He couldn't afford to indulge in a lengthy nap.

Covering a yawn with a balled fist, he drew back the navy blue curtains from the picture window.

'I say,' he murmured, the scenery first-rate. Spectacular, in fact, with the midday sun glinting off the Hudson River in a diaphanous shimmer. Just beyond the flowing waters, there was an impressive ridge of craggy mountains. Upholstered with plush foliage and towering trees, the vista evoked the majesty of another age, harkening to that shoal of time when the English explorer Henry Hudson embarked on his failed venture to find the Northeast Passage to China.

As he caught sight of several colourful kayaks loping past, his arcadian vision instantly vanished.

Pulling his gaze away from the window, Cædmon glanced over at Edie's empty seat and retrieved the folded sheet of paper that she'd left in plain view. The scrawled note read, 'Gone to the snack bar. Will be back soon with a luncheon feast.'

One can only hope that the fare is more appetizing on the train than the plane.

To be sure, he regretted eating the rubbery sausage and egg sarnie on the transatlantic flight, the slapdash repast having stayed with him for an uncomfortably long time. The only available airline seats had been in slum class, as Edie called it, where the meals were often a begrudging afterthought.

Luckily, they'd been able to secure comfortable business-class seats for the train ride to Rhinecliff, New York. According to the online map, the Sanguis Christi Fellowship was located forty-five miles from the train station. He'd already booked a hire car. As soon as they arrived at the fellowship grounds, he would contact Father Gracián Santos and negotiate the exchange.

Picking up Edie's iPad from where she'd left it on the drop-down tray, Cædmon checked his email. Pleased that Cedric Lloyd had already translated the third plate, he opened the attachment. Tablet in hand, he stretched his legs, made himself more comfortable and commenced to reading the last section of Gaspar's gospel entitled 'The Ministry of Yeshua bar Yosef'.

Halfway through, his hands began to shake. He took several deep, calming breaths. Not that it did any good – by the time he'd finished the text, he could barely draw breath.

Fuck me. 'I never saw that coming,' he whispered, stunned by Gaspar's eye-opening disclosure.

He reached towards the pull-down tray for his G&T, only to realize that he didn't have a drink.

'I need one.' *Jesus.*

While the contents of the first two plates had been astounding, the revelations contained in the third plate were absolutely explosive. The sort of thing that could ignite a religious conflagration. On a big, bloody global scale. One which would make the wars of religion fought in the wake of the Protestant Reformation seem little more than a trifling affair.

It certainly explained why Cardinal Fiorio had gone to such extreme lengths to procure the *Evangelium Gaspar.* Particularly in light of the upcoming conclave. With the ancient gospel in his possession, the red-robed bastard could strong-arm the College of Cardinals into doing his bidding.

And I'll warrant that none would dare contest the tyranny. Too terrified of what would happen if the gospel ever saw the light of day.

Still trying to get his bearings, the intellectual wind knocked out of him, Cædmon stared out of the train window, too lost in thought to notice the flying landscape that passed in a green and blue blur.

A few moments into his depressing fugue, Edie appeared, her arms laden with foodstuffs. A cheery smile on her face, she announced, 'I've got chilli con carne, cheese sandwiches, two questionably fresh garden salads and hot coffee. Pick your poison.'

Cædmon held the iPad aloft. 'After you read Cedric Lloyd's email, you may opt for a stiff drink instead.'

65

The Ministry of Yeshua bar Yosef

The Baptism at the Jordan River

During Yeshua's thirtieth year, we arrived in his homeland. Great changes had taken place in those eighteen years since we had left Mount Carmel. The Children of Israel cried out in torment for they had lost faith in all things.

It came to pass that Yeshua's cousin, a great holy man who had once lived with the Nazorean brotherhood at Qumran, preached that the Kingdom of Heaven is at hand. He bade his followers to confess their sins and be made pure in the waters of the Jordan River.

Yeshua and I travelled to Galilee for he desired to see his cousin. The sun was at its zenith when Yeshua waded into the cool water. Yuhanna, who was baptizing, halted when he caught sight of Yeshua. The two cousins spoke briefly before Yuhanna immersed him into the water. When he re-emerged, arrows of piercing light enveloped Yeshua and the water that dripped from his face and chest seemed to have changed colours. The light of the sun then turned a blinding white which dazzled the eyes of all who stood near. There arose a great clamouring from those gathered on the riverbank who had witnessed the marvellous sight and many wondered what had transpired. Although they had seen with their eyes, their minds could not comprehend that Yeshua had become one with the Logos; and that he had twined his spirit with that divinity of creation through which all things are made possible.

And so it came to be that the Logos filled Yeshua so that he would know the mind of the Father. It was for this reason that Yeshua had come into the world.

The crowd of followers marvelled at the transformation for they saw that Yeshua's eyes were brightly lit with an inner fire. Several cried out in fear, but his cousin Yuhanna stepped forward and told them that Yeshua was the Anointed One who had been baptized in the ineffable water of purity and had become the Christ. 'Follow him!' Yuhanna extolled the crowd. 'For he will lead you to the Father.'

And Darkness Fell Upon the Land

During the next three years a multitude followed the Master wherever he went and never left him. Alarmed by these reports, Pilate sent his soldiers to arrest Yeshua.

And they cast Yeshua into a dungeon where he was made to suffer much physical pain in the hopes that he would confess to his crimes. His agonies were great but the Logos was with him and did not suffer him to die. The soldiers conducted Yeshua to the hill known as the place of the skull. It was there that he was nailed to a wooden cross. The family and disciples of Yeshua wept copious tears as they watched his agony upon the cross. So great were his torments that the Logos became detached from his body and returned to the realm of the spirit.

Yeshua cried to the heavens, 'My God, My God, why have you forsaken me?'

And darkness fell upon the land as a strong wind swept across the hillside. There was much wailing as lightning flashed and thunder rolled. A Roman soldier jabbed a spear into Yeshua's side, but the Master did not move.

In the violence of the storm, the spectators scattered and only Yeshua's mother and brother remained. Yosef of Arimathea arrived with an order from Pilate to remove Yeshua's body. This was all according to plan for none on the hillside knew that Yeshua did not die upon the cross.

One of the trusted disciples, a man named Nicodemus, aided Yosef and me as we removed the body to a nearby tomb that had been prepared with lengths of linen and healing herbs and a salve made from myrrh. There were two white-garbed Nazorean healers who were already there awaiting our arrival. We spent several hours tending to the Master before we smoked the grotto with aloe and rolled a large stone in front of the tomb opening. As we left the tomb, there was a blood moon in the night sky, a sign in the heavens that would be scribed for all eternity.

The Shepherd and His Sheep

Forty days would pass from that dreadful time when the wicked ones tried to kill the Master.

When Yeshua was finally recovered from his ordeal, he gave to us his last sermon in which he prophesied that two thousand years would pass before an Age of Light would illuminate mankind. And it would be then that the true meaning of his teachings would be revealed. Until that time, there would be great darkness and many would be oppressed in the name of the Father.

Yeshua told his disciples that he must leave them and there was much sadness amongst them. To each he gave a commission to ensure that his teachings would not wither on the vine but would thrive.

And Simon asked if they should establish a new religion in his name.

Yeshua said, 'The teachings were not given so that you would glorify or make a king of me. I came to teach that the Kingdom of God is within. Rituals and sacrificial lambs lead men away from the path. A temple can never be my Father's House.'

Several of his disciples informed Yeshua that there were many claiming that he was the Son of God.

This angered him greatly and he said, 'Do not make a god of me. For the Father is greater than I and we are all His Children.'

Then Yeshua took me aside and revealed that he was going to search for the lost tribes of Israel so that he could preach to them.

And a mist arose as Yeshua bar Yosef departed in the direction of the rising sun.

66

Still shell-shocked, Edie lifted the plastic lid on her coffee.

Cædmon was right . . . I need something more potent than caffeine to mitigate the shock.

'The crazy thing is that I now have this strong desire to learn as much as possible about Yeshua and his life.' She glanced at Cædmon's rucksack where the third plate was stowed, carefully wrapped in foam. 'There must be other ancient gospels out there, waiting to be discovered.'

'There are. Although I daresay any first-century texts that survived the fourth-century purge are well hidden.'

Hearing that, Edie frowned, convinced that there were many open-minded Christians, like herself, who would be interested, passionate even, in uncovering the truth. And who would also be mad as hell to find out that the truth about Jesus had been purposefully hidden or destroyed.

'There's no way to put this delicately except to say the *Evangelium Gaspar* turns two thousand years of religious belief on its head. It delivers a coup de grâce to the canonical gospels,' she added before taking a swig of the acrid-smelling coffee.

Cædmon peered out of the plate-glass window, the midday light glazing his hair a deep shade of auburn. 'Ascertaining the truth is often a painful process, no exorcism without its torments,' he intoned solemnly.

'I don't know how Roman Catholics will react, but I'm

fairly certain that if the *Evangelium Gaspar* ever goes public, the backlash from evangelical Christians will be fierce.' Edie spoke in a measured tone, careful to keep her voice lowered so as not to be overheard by any of their co-passengers. 'In recent years, news stories have been popping up in the American press about Christian zealots, armed with guns, walking into churches during the Sunday sermon and killing congregants because they weren't deemed "Christian enough".'

'No different to what occurred during the bloodthirsty Inquisition,' Cædmon remarked as he unwrapped a sandwich. 'The Dominicans, and the Jesuits after them, fervently believed that orthodoxy must be adhered to at all costs. Without it, the Church loses its power.'

'It's disheartening to think the Catholic Church did *exactly* what Jesus declared that he didn't want . . . they created a religion in his name. Just so they could control the masses.' Realizing what she had just said, Edie winced. 'Do me a favour and overlook that truly bad pun.'

'I'll add to it. To further muddy the holy water, the Church created a cult that revolves around a god-man who rose from the dead and ascended bodily into heaven.' Cædmon lifted the slice of bread, giving the limp layer of yellow cheese a dubious glance. Passing on the sandwich, he said, 'The truth of the matter is that an incredibly enlightened man, who I do believe was a pure vessel for the Logos, preached that the Kingdom of God is not *up there* —' raising his hand, Cædmon pointed skywards – 'but is, instead, housed within each of us.'

'Yeah, how often do you hear *that* in the Sunday sermon?' More adventurous, Edie snatched his uneaten sandwich. 'Although I think we both know that's not what'll rile people. The fact that Yeshua survived the crucifixion is what will incite the outrage.'

'Indeed, it is a radical departure from the conventional tale. Take away the Blood Atonement – that uniquely Christian belief that Jesus came to earth so that he could sacrifice himself upon the cross to remove the stain of Original Sin – and you take away the foundation upon which the Christian church was built.'

'While I can accept that Jesus travelled to India and studied with Hindu and Buddhist holy men, it's going to take a bit longer for me to come to terms with the fact that he survived the crucifixion.' Conflicted, Edie stared at the seat in front of her as she corralled her tumultuous thoughts. 'And yet . . . what if he did survive?' she said after a lengthy pause. 'It doesn't change the content of his message one iota. Jesus preached about love and tolerance and forgiveness. None of which has anything to do with the crucifixion or the Blood Atonement.'

'It bears mentioning that in the Koran it's clearly stated that Jesus, or *Isa* as he's known in Arabic, did not die on the cross.' Grabbing the iPad, Cædmon typed in a search query. 'Ah! Here it is: "they did not kill him, nor did they crucify him, but he was made to appear as one crucified to them".' He obligingly passed Edie the computer tablet so that she could examine the verse in the Koran for herself.

Edie stared at the iPad, agog.

'The techniques used in Roman crucifixion are well-documented.' Having rejected the sandwich, Cædmon removed a garden salad and a packet of Italian dressing from the brown bag. 'If one examines the historic data, it becomes glaringly clear that Jesus' execution did not follow the standard procedures as dictated by Roman protocol. One could even say that what took place on that long-ago Friday afternoon atop Golgotha hill was highly abnormal.'

Edie wiped the corner of her mouth with a napkin. 'Abnormal in what way?'

'As you undoubtedly know, Jesus was on the cross for a mere three hours. I say "mere" because the Romans preferred to keep their victims dangling in pain for two or more days. And they were quite efficient in dragging out the agony,' Cædmon said succinctly, obviously thinking it an important point. 'When it was finally decided to end the poor bloke's misery, the *crurifragium* was performed.'

Edie shoved her half-eaten sandwich aside, having lost her appetite. 'That was when a Roman soldier would break the crucified man's legs so that he couldn't support himself on the footrest that was attached to the vertical beam of the cross.'

Cædmon nodded. 'The victim then died from heart failure or asphyxiation, whichever came first. But Jesus was only on the cross for three hours. During which time he succumbed without having his legs broken. To determine if he was indeed dead, a soldier jabbed him in the right side with a spear.'

'"And at once there came out blood and water",' Edie said, reciting from the Gospel of John.

'A very telling detail from a forensics perspective in that the presence of blood and water indicates Jesus was still alive.'

'Yet he was pronounced dead and removed from the cross.'

'So he was.' Abandoning the salad after just a few bites, Cædmon resumed drinking his coffee. 'However, I suspect that Jesus was in some sort of cataleptic trance. Having spent all those years studying with Hindu gurus, he had undoubtedly learned how to induce that type of deep mental state.'

'Which fooled the Romans into thinking that he was dead.' Cædmon's explanation made perfect sense, with Edie suddenly able to envision how the hoax was engineered.

'Curiously enough, this business regarding the "blood and water" raises an interesting tangent that pertains to the Knights Templar and the Shroud of Turin. The fabled shroud is, of course, the original burial cloth that was used to wrap Jesus' body when he was taken down from the cross.' Cædmon paused a moment, ensuring that he had her full attention before saying, 'There are marks on the shroud that clearly show blood seepage.'

'Makes perfect sense if Jesus was still alive when he was wrapped in it. But what does that have to do with the Knights Templar?' she asked, unable to make the connection.

'Before it became "the Shroud of Turin", the burial linen was known as "the Edessa Cloth". Legend has it that Thaddeus Jude, one of Jesus' disciples, took the cloth to the ancient city of Edessa which was located in northern Mesopotamia. The cloth remained there until the tenth century at which point in time it was moved to Constantinople.' Cædmon crossed his legs as he angled himself in her direction, wincing as he did so. Although he tried to man-up and hide it, his battered ribs were still causing him an enormous amount of pain. 'Now jettison to the year 1204 when the Knights Templar confiscated the Edessa Cloth after the Christian crusaders sacked Constantinople. For the next hundred years, the Templars safeguarded the shroud until their demise in the early fourteenth century.'

Never having heard the story before, Edie said, 'I'm guessing that's when the shroud ended up in Turin.'

Cædmon confirmed with a nod. 'According to the Templars' trial records, they were accused of secretly venerating the shroud.'

'Kinda odd since the inquisitors also accused them of spitting on the cross. And, brace yourself for another bad pun, those two accusations are at cross purposes.'

'Not if the Templars knew that Jesus survived the crucifixion.' Setting his empty coffee cup on the pull-down tray, Cædmon folded his arms over his chest. He took a moment to collect his thoughts before explaining his baffling remark. 'Mind you, this is mere speculation on my part, but I suspect that the Templars venerated the shroud because it was a symbol of the *living* Jesus. And they may have spat on the cross because it represented what they'd come to realize was the foundational lie of Christianity. The Knights Templar weren't repudiating Jesus. They were repudiating the false symbol associated with Jesus.'

'To be honest, this is all incredibly hard for me to fathom,' Edie confessed, still grappling with Gaspar's mind-blowing revelations. 'Take away Jesus' divinity and –'

'One is still left with a divinely inspired message,'

432

Cædmon interjected. 'Jesus himself said, "I am my Father's son. But I am not Elohim." Be that as it may, during the Council of Nicaea, the bishops, true champions of democracy, put the issue to a vote whereupon it was decided that Jesus was a god rather than a mortal man. Personally, I'm inclined to believe Jesus on the matter rather than a cabal of fourth-century bishops.' Cædmon locked eyes with her, holding her gaze. 'Make no mistake: the Church will go to any length to hide their dirty little secret that Jesus survived the crucifixion. It's a whitewash. History is full of them.'

'Which begs the question . . . What *is* the truth? We look back two thousand years and it's like gazing through a kaleidoscope full of shifting images.' Her shoulders sagging, Edie sighed dejectedly. 'There's a part of me that wants to cling to what I was taught to believe as a kid and leave it at that.'

'Perfectly understandable,' Cædmon commiserated. 'While I, too, am deeply affected by the notion that the Christ of my childhood is not the historic Jesus, I'm rather drawn to this chap who travelled the world in search of spiritual knowledge.'

Just then, a blaring voice came through the audio system, announcing the next stop.

'That's us,' Edie said, quickly packing up their leftovers. Glancing over at Cædmon, she could see that his expression had suddenly turned grim. Putting the bag down, she reached over and took hold of his hand. 'I know you're worried, but we're going to get Anala back, safe and sound.'

'We're dealing with brutes and monsters who have

rejected the teachings of the Prince of Peace. Leaving me with no choice but to act in kind.'

'You mean to meet fire with fire?'

With a determined glint in his blue eyes, Cædmon said, 'Deadly fire, if need be.'

67

Dutchess County, New York

1832h

'It's like watching a scrolling nineteenth-century diorama,' Edie remarked, her gaze drawn to yet another hay-laden pasture bounded by a stone retaining wall. 'And my back aches just thinking about the fact that some long-dead farmer plucked each and every stone from a rocky field so that he could sow his seed.'

'Mmmm,' Cædmon murmured distractedly. His eyes were set on the roadway and he didn't spare the passing field an acknowledging glance. Understandably, his thoughts were focused elsewhere.

For the last forty-five minutes, they'd been driving along a serpentine single-lane road that twisted and turned through the rural countryside of upstate New York. The area was sparsely populated. Beyond the low womanly hills, Edie glimpsed only the occasional farmhouse; simple two-storey abodes that harkened to another era. A time before cars and planes. Or the Industrial Age for that matter.

'I think that's it up ahead,' she announced, pointing to a stately driveway that was visually off-key in the bucolic surroundings.

Cædmon slowed the Ford sedan, braking to a full stop at the shaded entrance. Massive stone pillars bracketed either side of the paved driveway; the pillar on the right-hand side had a large metal plaque mounted on it that read: SANGUIS CHRISTI FELLOWSHIP. Beneath that was a Chi-Rho cross.

His features set in an inscrutable expression, Cædmon cut the ignition.

Craning her neck, Edie peered down the winding, tree-lined driveway. From where they were parked, she was unable to see the school's main building, Mercy Hall. According to their Internet research, it had originally been an elite women's college before it was purchased by the Fellowship.

The fine hairs on her arms stood on end. All of the frenzied travel and the dangerous forays of the last week had come down to this moment – negotiating Anala's safe return and delivering the ransom. In a short while it would be over; celebratory champagne bash most definitely in order.

And yet she had the uneasy feeling that no one would be toasting the successful outcome any time soon. Cædmon also wasn't wildly optimistic, worried that Gracián Santos and his thugs would try to double-cross them. Ergo, the loaded shotgun sitting in plain view on the back seat.

After they'd picked up their rental car at Rhinecliff, the first order of business had been to drive to the nearest gun shop and purchase a Mossberg 500, popularly known as a 'Persuader'. Unlike handguns that required a permit, anyone with a valid driver's licence could legally purchase a shotgun with no waiting period. Once the transaction was completed, said person could blithely stroll out of the gun shop locked, loaded and ready to fire at will.

Needing some fresh air, Edie wound down her window. Somewhere nearby a bird cawed, a raucous *cheeter!cheeter!* To her ears, it sounded like a dire warning.

'Now what?' she asked, unnerved by the rural desolation. It had been at least fifteen minutes since they'd last seen a passing motorist.

'If you hand me your iPad, I'll ring the doorbell and see if Father Santos is at home.'

She passed him the computer tablet, sitting silent while he opened Skype.

As the call went through, Edie's gut churned. Apprehensive, she wished they'd had more time to prepare. *The transatlantic flight. The train. The rental car. The gun shop.* It all felt so whirlwind. Even the plan – to demand that the exchange take place at an abandoned farmhouse that they'd scouted a few miles away – seemed inchoate. Yes, it was neutral ground, but she'd feel better if weren't so remotely located. Yet Cædmon was adamant – even though he'd previously informed Gracián Santos by email that he'd make contact tomorrow morning, he didn't want Anala to remain in captivity another night.

It will be to our advantage to catch the cassocked bastard off guard.

'Good evening, Father Santos,' Cædmon said when the priest's visage appeared on the computer screen. 'As I mentioned in my earlier email, I have the third plate and I'm ready to negotiate the exchange. And just so you know, I'm now in Dutchess County, very close to your location. I thought it would be easier to facilitate the trade if I came to you. Wouldn't want to inconvenience you in the least,' he added in a mocking tone.

Gracián Santos appeared genuinely surprised. 'I was expecting you tomorrow morning, not – Never mind. Yes, of course . . . the, um, exchange.' The priest nervously licked his lips. 'Before we discuss the details, I demand some proof that you actually have the third plate in your possession.'

'Having assumed as much, I've already prepared the email attachments. Stand by while I send you digital photos, front and back, of the copper plate. Additionally, I'm sending you the translated text which I thought you might be interested in perusing. Unless, of course, you read Aramaic, in which case you may disregard the English translation. I'll give you several minutes to examine the file.' Pulling up the email program, Cædmon hit the 'send' button. 'Read it and weep.'

Her anxiety escalating, Edie stared at the now-blank computer screen.

Cædmon glanced over at her. 'So far, so good.'

68

What did he mean by 'Read it and weep'?

Curious as to the meaning of the Englishman's addendum, Gracián Santos opened the first email attachment. He gave the two digital photographs of the copper plate a cursory examination. Satisfied that the plate was genuine, he closed the attachment.

Despite the fact that he'd made contact a day early, Aisquith's sudden arrival was an unexpected boon. At that moment, Gracián was alone at Mercy Hall, Roberto having driven to New York City to meet the transatlantic flights from Paris and Rome. Cardinal Fiorio, who had contacts within the Vatican secret service, had discovered that Aisquith had booked two seats on a nonstop flight to JFK Airport. *'Clearly, the footloose Englishman is headed your way.'* To Gracián's surprise, the cardinal then announced that he intended to travel to New York to personally take possession of the third plate.

'I need to get the ghastly deed over and done with,' Gracián murmured resignedly. Since the student body and staff were gone, there would be no witnesses lurking.

Other than God Almighty.

But Gracián need not worry on that count, Cardinal Fiorio having assured him that everything he did to secure the ancient gospel would be forgiven, absolution always given to Defenders of the Faith. No matter how horrific their crimes. Even though it would weigh heavy on his conscience, it *must* be done to protect the Church and save the Sanguis Christi Fellowship. To that end, the old Parthenon folly would be the perfect location to set the trap. Afterwards, the Diablos could use a water hose to wash away any blood evidence.

Lost in thought, Gracián drummed his fingers on the desk.

The cardinal had been adamant that the *Evangelium Gaspar* was the Great Heresy that could destroy the Church. For that reason, there must be no witnesses left alive who knew of its existence. As for Anala Patel, because Gracián couldn't bring himself to kill her, he intended to leave her locked in the root cellar and let nature take its course.

Curious as to what was contained in the heretical gospel, Gracián opened the second attachment and began to read the translated text.

'*Ay Dios mio!*' he gasped when he reached the last line, shock squeezing the air out of his lungs. *Surely, this was someone's idea of a sick joke!* The gospel – if one could call it that – was an utter abomination. A heresy of the first magnitude, the *Evangelium Gaspar* couldn't possibly be a true account of –

But what if it were true? What if our Lord actually survived the crucifixion? Would he still be the Saviour of mankind?

Gracián swallowed a gastric bubble, the acid burning the back of his throat.

'No!' he exclaimed, banging the flat of his hand against the desktop. The *Evangelium Gaspar* was a hoax. A despicable parody. A few shreds of truth cleverly woven into a blatantly false script. Nothing more than that. And

Cardinal Fiorio was absolutely right to have gone to such lengths to retrieve the blasphemous gospel.

The Apostles' Creed clearly states that Jesus was 'crucified, died and was buried . . . On the third day he rose again.'

The beating heart of the New Testament had always been mankind's redemption from sin. Jesus Christ, our sweet Lord and Saviour, *willingly* sacrificed himself to atone for that hideous stain upon our souls. A stain that had prevented humankind, even the most devout of believers, from entering into Heaven. *Everyone knew this!* The Blood Atonement was not in contention. Even the Protestants wholeheartedly believed it.

Gracián glared at the translation, infuriated, certain that it was a perverted hoax.

'I shudder to think what sort of blasphemy was contained in the first two plates,' he muttered.

His blood boiling, Gracián turned on Skype and returned Cædmon Aisquith's phone call.

'How dare you!' he exclaimed when the Englishman's face popped on to the computer screen.

69

'Is this translation some sort of sick joke?' Father Gracián Santos demanded to know. Cheeks unnaturally flushed, eyes narrowed, the Catholic priest was in high dudgeon.

Grasping the iPad between his hands, Cædmon bit back a satisfied smirk. The other man appeared not so much rattled as shaken to his Catholic core. 'No joke, I can assure you. The translation that you've just read was made by a biblical scholar at Oxford University. Not only is it an accurate transcription of an authentic early-first-century gospel, unlike the four canonical gospels, I might add, but as you've undoubtedly realized, it's an eye-opening text.'

He paused a moment, letting the specifics sink in. Convinced now that Father Santos had heretofore been unaware of the gospel's explosive contents, Cædmon intended to shove the biblical blade as deep as possible. He wanted to weaken the other man's resolve before he delivered the ransom. Unless he was greatly mistaken, the priest had been purposefully kept in the dark by his master in Rome. If he shed enough light, it might be possible to turn Santos against the maniacal cardinal. Which would lessen the danger immeasurably.

Forcefully plunging the blade, Cædmon said, 'I have good reason to believe that Cardinal Franco Fiorio intends to use the *Evangelium Gaspar* to affect the outcome of the upcoming Vatican conclave.'

'No!' Santos clutched his heart with his right hand. 'First the Resurrection . . . now *this*! It's . . . it's more than I can bear,' the priest rasped, his eyes glimmering with unshed tears.

'Surely, as a priest, you know that the crucifixion story in the canonical gospels was crafted by the early Church Fathers in an editorial process similar to Jewish Midrash.'

Santos shook his head, uncomprehending. 'Wh-what are you talking about?'

'Midrash is a method of pasting and editing Bible verses together in order to elucidate certain theological tenets,' Cædmon explained, taking a savage pleasure in the other man's emotional turmoil. 'Which means that the end result bears no relation to the truth. As is the case with the crucifixion and the subsequent, albeit erroneous, resurrection.'

The priest's bottom lip began to quiver. 'B-but if there's n-no Resurrection, h-how can Jesus be the Son of G-God?'

Cædmon's own lip turned down at the corner as he shrugged and said, 'Afraid that you're asking the wrong chap. I'm an historian not a theologian.' Noticing the beads of perspiration that began to form at Santos's hairline, he intuited that the other man was teetering on the edge. Backpedalling a bit, he softened his voice. 'Grácian, all will be forgiven if you make restitution and release my daughter.'

A glossy tear rolled down Santos's cheek. 'The things

that I have done will never be forgiven. Not on earth, nor in heaven.'

Needing to extract a commitment from the other man, Cædmon tried a different tack. 'Turn my daughter over to me and you have my solemn word that I'll not go to the authorities.' *In other words, everything that has transpired this past week shall forever remain our deadly little secret.*

Hearing that, the priest readily nodded his assent. 'Yes . . . your daughter . . . she must be released. Come to my office at Mercy Hall and I'll –'

The iPad screen suddenly blipped before going blank.

'Granted, I'm no shrink, but Father Santos seemed to be in the throes of an emotional meltdown,' Edie remarked, brows drawn anxiously. 'I mean, he didn't say a word about taking custody of the copper plate.'

Cædmon stared contemplatively at the iPad. 'I, too, found that odd. While I'd hoped to unhinge Father Santos so that he would reconsider his loyalty to Cardinal Fiorio, I never expected him to forego the prize.'

'So, do we accept his invitation or do we stick to the original plan?'

'We need to lure Santos away from his stronghold. In my experience, it's always best to meet the devil on neutral ground.' That's why he'd purposefully selected an abandoned farmhouse where he could safely deliver the ransom and collect his daughter.

Annoyed by the unexpected twist, Cædmon quickly redialled.

'Damn! We lost the connection,' he muttered a few seconds later.

Clearly unnerved, Edie peered at the tree-lined driveway. 'Guess that means that we're accepting the invite, huh?'

Left with no other option, Cædmon turned the key in the ignition. 'Put on your happy face. It's time to properly introduce ourselves to the devil.'

70

'I was wrong . . . the *Evangelium Gaspar* is no hoax,' Gracián Santos murmured as he stared at the damning translation.

Did the Englishman know that he'd just delivered the death blow?

Unable to breathe evenly or to think clearly, all he could do was *feel*.

'*O my God, I cry out by day, but you do not answer.*'

Hands shaking, Gracián was seized with a hideous fear. His Catholic faith, which had always been so carefully proscribed, now had a gaping hole.

'I became a priest because I *believed* in the Blood Atonement.'

Believed in its purity. And virtue. And sanctity. Jesus, as the Son of God, was without blemish. Incorruptible. Therefore, His blood was incorruptible. *That* was the reason why His blood, and not anyone else's, could save mankind. And when He rose from the dead on the third day, the sacrifice was spiritually complete. The Blood Atonement was the *central* message of the Gospels. The rest was mere window dressing.

If Jesus didn't die on the Cross to save mankind from sin, how was anyone supposed to get into heaven?

Nothing else could save man's blighted soul. Holy water, rosaries, the altar rituals: they were only accoutrements to faith, but had no power to *redeem* mankind. Without the

Blood Atonement, without the Resurrection . . . *there was nothing.*

I am nothing.

No, he was a Judas. A man willing to forsake what few shreds of morality he still possessed for thirty pieces of silver. Cardinal Fiorio never intended to destroy the *Evangelium Gaspar* as he'd repeatedly maintained. All along, he'd planned to use it to manipulate the conclave. Which now explained why he'd been so adamant that the ransom had to be delivered no later than Sunday at twelve noon, the conclave scheduled to convene the following Monday morning.

Gracián had given his life to the Church, sacrificing his very manhood for what might well be a carefully crafted lie. *A Midrash.*

Was it really possible that the Christ he'd been taught to worship never existed? That, instead, a different Jesus walked the earth in the first century?

And if that was the case, what happens to the last two thousand years of the Christian faith?

Buddhism could easily survive without Siddhartha. Islam could even survive without Mohammed. But Christianity could not make it to the next sunrise without Jesus and the crucifixion.

Yes, admittedly, he'd always thought it odd that after the Resurrection a divine being would require food like any mortal man. But like so many strange anomalies in the gospels, it was one of those things that a Catholic must never question.

Clutching his head between his hands, Gracián stared out of the window, unable to stop the stream of horrific flashbacks. *Beating a defenceless man because he stole money from the Diablos. Extorting protection 'taxes' from frightened old shopkeepers. Dealing drugs to innocent children. And, of course, the worst crime of them all, beheading a rival gang member.*

'*Don't worry, homie. It's no different than cutting the head off a dead chicken.*'

A more illicit statement had never been uttered. Beheading a man was *nothing* like butchering a chicken. A plucked, lifeless bird didn't splatter your face with warm blood. Or make a horrible squishy *crunch!* as you hacked through bone and sinew.

Without the Blood Atonement, his sinner's slate could never be wiped clean.

And Cardinal Fiorio had known that all along. Moreover, the ruthless cardinal had felt no compunction in recruiting Gracián to do his bidding.

He actually wants me to kill an innocent young woman. After which, he will reward the heinous deed by wiring $2.2 million into the Sanguis Christi bank account.

Which made Gracián little more than a gun for hire. *A paid Vatican assassin.*

Fearing the dark night of the soul, he hastily opened his desk drawer and grabbed a yellow sticky pad. Mind made up, he scrawled a message and slapped it on to his computer monitor where it would be readily seen.

'I am damned,' Gracián murmured as he rushed from the office.

For all eternity.

Seeing the colossal stone mansion perched atop the knoll, Edie's mouth gaped.

'It looks like something straight out of a spooky Gothic novel,' she remarked, shivering slightly. 'Not only do the photos on the Internet *not* do this place justice, I now understand why they brought Anala here.' Given its vast size, she could be imprisoned in any one of a hundred different rooms.

Cædmon made no comment as he pulled the Ford sedan into an open-ended porte cochère.

Nerves stretched taut, Edie peered over her shoulder.

'Perhaps you should wait in the car with the doors locked and hold down the proverbial fort,' Cædmon suggested.

'And let you face the dragon all alone? Nothing doing,' she retorted in what she hoped was a strident tone of voice. A far cry from how she was actually feeling. 'Besides, I've already donned my chain mail. That said, let's hurry up and find Father Santos before the God Squad shows up.'

'Right.' Getting out of the car, Cædmon opened the back passenger door and reached for his newly purchased waist pack. It was specifically designed for hunters, with special compartments to hold shotgun shells, knives, et cetera. Given that it was a mossy shade of camouflage, it wasn't something that you'd ever take on a holiday. Not unless you were into hunter chic.

He snapped it around his waist, blue eyes glittering, hard as coloured glass. He then snatched the Mossberg shotgun and his rucksack from off the backseat.

'Stay close to me,' he instructed, meeting her gaze across the top of the sedan. 'Step softly. Speak softly.'

Edie nodded wordlessly. Even if she'd wanted to raise her voice, she doubted that it would be possible, her vocal cords constricted with fear.

As they made their way towards the entrance of Mercy Hall, loose scree crunched underfoot. Again, she turned her head and glanced over her shoulder. 'Sorry. Bad case of the jitters,' she whispered when Cædmon shot her a questioning glance.

'Perfectly understandable. We're treading on dangerous ground.'

'No kidding. It's like everyone vaporized into thin air,' she remarked, the thought inciting yet another visceral surge.

While she should have been relieved that no one was present, that they'd not been greeted by armed guards, she couldn't shake the feeling that something had gone terribly awry at Mercy Hall. The eerie silence was so unnerving that it was like a palpable, disembodied presence following in their wake.

As they ascended a wide stone staircase that led to a grand Victorian porch, an ozone-laden breeze rustled the nearby trees. To Edie's surprise, Cædmon walked over to one of the oversized concrete urns that anchored the stair railing and, slipping his rucksack off his shoulder, stuffed it into the opening. She had no idea why he did it – particularly since the third copper plate was inside the rucksack – but knew better than to question his actions. Not when they were standing, quite literally, at the castle gate.

With the shotgun braced against his torso, Cædmon opened the front door. Edie winced at the loud squeal made by the rusty hinges. Unsure what to expect, she followed him into an expansive hallway visually weighed down with a vast amount of dark-stained woodwork. *The walls. The staircase. The ceiling.* In a word, the hall took dreary to new decorative heights, the heavily carved wood everywhere. Overhead a crystal chandelier tinkled softly from the breeze that wafted in through the open front door.

Nudging Cædmon in the ribs, Edie drew his attention to a truly odd bit of Victorian whimsy: a built-in organ under the stair landing. 'If that thing starts playing Bach's Toccata and Fugue in D Minor, I'm outta here.'

'If that happens, I think I'll join you,' Cædmon whispered, the first indication that he, too, was unnerved that there wasn't a soul in sight.

Come out, come out, wherever you are.

On high alert, they cautiously traipsed down the corridor, following the posted signs for the 'Office'. The carpeted passage was illuminated by a row of Victorian-style wall sconces. She was no expert, but they looked like original fixtures; although 120 years ago the soft glow would probably have come from flickering gaslights rather than electric bulbs.

Cædmon stopped abruptly, Edie accidentally ploughing into his backside.

'I believe this is the office,' he said, jutting his chin at an opened doorway.

Looking around his shoulder, she saw what appeared to be an old-fashioned study with an ornate fireplace, again, more dark-stained panelling, and an entire wall of built-in bookcases.

'Where's Father Santos?' she asked. The office, like every other room they'd passed en route, was completely deserted.

'Haven't the vaguest.' Raising the Mossberg shotgun into shooting position, Cædmon tucked the butt against his shoulder. 'Stay put,' he silently mouthed to her.

The fear factor spiking off the charts, Edie anxiously watched as he slowly made his way into the room, his head swivelling from side to side. Stepping over to a large desk strewn with folders and messy piles of paper, he examined a yellow slip of paper that was stuck on to the computer monitor.

'Just what kind of game is this bloody bastard playing?'

72

'*Your daughter is in the root cellar at the caretaker's cottage that's located due west of Mercy Hall*,' Edie read aloud from the piece of yellow note paper. Like him, she was clearly perplexed by the scrawled message left on the monitor by the absentee priest. 'Do you think this is some kind of ruse to ambush us?'

'I'm uncertain what to make of it,' Cædmon confessed. Something was gravely amiss at the Sanguis Christi Fellowship, of *that* he was certain. 'Before we head to the caretaker's cottage, I need to see the satellite maps that we downloaded on to the iPad.'

Edie unzipped her messenger bag and retrieved the computer, silently passing it to him.

Tablet in hand, he examined the satellite photo. Moderately relieved, he nodded his head and said, 'There does seem to be a structure several hundred metres to the west.'

A determined look in her eyes, Edie stuffed the iPad back into her bag. 'Okay. Let's hit it. This place is giving me the creeps.'

And me, as well. Although if the firing squad was waiting at the caretaker's cottage, the brutes would be made to wish that they'd never left the egregiously named Mercy Hall. He would need little incentive to pull the trigger on his newly purchased weapon.

Leading with the shotgun, Cædmon took the point

position as they wended their way back to the hallway. With each footfall, his eyes blinked rapidly. Akin to a camera shutter clicking off each individual surveillance photo, he committed to memory doorways, corridors, staircases. Information he would need should they suddenly come under enemy fire. Like Edie, he worried that the priest was dropping enticing breadcrumbs that would ultimately lead them into a deadly trap.

Seeing a recessed emergency fire cabinet, he came to a sudden halt. Peering into the glass-fronted case, he inventoried its contents: in addition to the standard red extinguisher, it also contained other fire-fighting paraphernalia.

'Stand back,' he ordered just before he forcefully slammed the butt of his shotgun into the locked case, smashing the glass on contact.

Edie stared, button-eyed. 'What the heck are you doing?'

'A man can't have too many weapons,' he informed her, plucking a rubber-handled fire axe out of the cabinet. Twelve inches long and weighing approximately two pounds, the short-handled axe could puncture, slice or pry. *A very handy weapon, indeed*, he thought, tucking it into the nylon band on his waist pack.

'How about me? Don't I rate a weapon?' Edie griped under her breath as they continued down the hallway. Obviously, she was still peeved that he'd put his foot down at the gun shop, refusing to let her purchase a second shotgun.

'*One deadly weapon in the family is quite enough*,' Cædmon had said.

A few moments later, they emerged from Mercy Hall. In the short time that they'd been inside, fast-moving storm clouds had squeezed the last bit of sunshine from the sky, casting plum-coloured shadows on to the mansion and surrounding landscape. In the far distance, thunder rumbled.

'Looks like a killer storm is brewing,' Edie said worriedly as they descended the porch steps.

More concerned with the danger closer at hand, Cædmon raised the Persuader, pressing the butt snugly against his shoulder. His finger hovered over the trigger. Should they have a run-in with anyone whom he deemed a threat, he would unload a blast of double-aught buckshot. The 'shoot first, ask questions second' rule had gone into effect the moment they'd entered the Sanguis Christi grounds. This was enemy territory. The fact that the priest had disappeared was worrisome and he now wondered if some nefarious plot was about to unfold.

As they hurriedly made their way across the manicured gardens that bordered the mansion, his gaze darted from side to side, searching the shadows for any sign of movement. Off to one side, he saw a stone chapel. In the opposite direction he sighted a large six-bay carriage house.

They'd gone approximately one hundred metres when the neatly trimmed lawn gave way to an overgrown grassy meadow. A wide swathe had recently been mowed, creating a path capacious enough for a vehicle. The path led down the hillside, disappearing into a wooded glen. Given the deeply incised tyre treads in the mashed earth, a heavy vehicle had recently passed that way.

More breadcrumbs? he wondered as he scanned the surrounding area.

'I want you to stay here while I go find the caretaker's cottage,' he told Edie.

'But you might need me to –'

'I do need you, Edie,' he interjected. 'I need you to stand sentry.' He pointed to a thick-waisted maple. 'Right over there behind that tree where you can maintain a visual on both the mansion and the mowed swathe. Should you see anyone, you're to immediately call me on the mobile.'

Wearing a crestfallen expression, Edie nodded her head, realizing that it was the most prudent course of action. Cædmon wrapped his free arm around her shoulders and pulled her close, soundly kissing her on the lips.

'Call me the moment that you find Anala. And *please* be careful, Cædmon.'

'"Excuse me, then. You know my heart."'

Not feeling nearly as jaunty as his farewell suggested, he set off down the mowed swathe, shotgun at the ready.

At the bottom of the hill, he entered a dark glen. Towering trees ominously swayed under the force of a powerful wind gust. It was a dark, unruly landscape that reiterated what he already knew.

Every Eden had its snake.

73

'Good thing I'm not superstitious,' Edie muttered as she caught sight of a lone raven circling overhead. 'Because *that* is not the best of omens.'

She dragged her gaze away from the moody grey sky, the frail sun half-hidden by combative storm clouds, and resumed her surveillance of the Sanguis Christi grounds. As she stared at Mercy Hall, a breeze rustled the trees, causing goosebumps to instantly pop out on her bare arms. Attired in a black vest top and a pair of khakis, she wished she'd worn a summer sweater, the day having turned cool.

A building that size, you'd expect to see a few people hanging around, she thought for the umpteenth time. But there wasn't a soul in sight.

Unnerved, Edie glanced at her wristwatch, a chunky digital sports edition with a lime-green band. Equipped with more functions than she required – as if she'd ever need to know the altitude – the only thing her snazzy timepiece couldn't do was tell her if Cædmon was safe. Or if he'd found Anala alive and well.

Please, God, please.

'I don't think he could bear it if –'

She clamped her mouth shut, unwilling to think let alone articulate that dire scenario. It was one of those dark thoughts that you didn't want to casually toss out into the universe for fear someone might actually be listening. Earlier, during the drive from Rhinecliff, she'd asked Cædmon about Anala. Studiously avoiding her gaze, he'd mumbled something indecipherable. The way in which he'd sullenly turned inwards had put Edie in mind of a great wounded bear lumbering off to its den.

And yet he was willing to risk life and limb to save the daughter he'd never met.

Never good at hand-wringing, she folded her arms over her chest. A few seconds later, a blurred flash of motion snagged on the edge of her peripheral vision. Turning her head, Edie saw a black-clad priest scurrying across the expansive yard.

Father Gracián Santos!

She gasped in surprise, pressing herself closer to the giant maple as she surreptitiously observed the dastardly dog disappear into Mercy Hall. Her fingers dug into the tree bark. *He's plotting a deadly ambush.* What other reason could there be for the priest having earlier vanished into thin air?

Shuddering, Edie shot a quick glance at the dense foliage at the bottom of the hillside.

Come on, Cædmon! You need to hurry up and find –

Suddenly hearing a car engine, she peered around the gnarled bole. In stunned disbelief, she watched as a white SUV roared down the driveway, the driver stopping in front of Mercy Hall's massive stone porch. Disbelief immediately mutated into dread shock when the three banditos – Hector Calzada, Javier Aveles and Roberto Diaz – jumped out of the parked vehicle. Broadly smiling, Calzada then assisted a short, balding man garbed in a black cassock from the back passenger seat.

'It's Cardinal Franco Fiorio!' Edie croaked on a serrated breath. Unclipping her mobile phone, she hit the speed dial to warn Cædmon.

Getting nothing but dead air, she hurriedly redialled.

No! No! No!

Seized with an explosive burst of fear, she stared at the phone in utter disbelief.

There's no mobile phone service!

74

The devil at his back, Cædmon ran through the tall sweep of grass towards the dilapidated stone cottage. To one side of the abandoned house there was a low-lying field-stone enclosure that was overgrown with weeds and the odd sapling. On the opposite end, a forlorn, rusted-out lorry was parked under a metal lean-to, the structure completely covered in a tatter of tangled vines. By all appearances, the ramshackle cottage had been tenantless for a number of years.

He pulled up short, panting heavily as he swiped the back of his hand across his beaded brow, each ragged breath drawn from a heavy curtain of ozone-infused air. A violent tempest was on the way, grey clouds storm-trooping across the horizon.

So where's the sodding root cellar? Was it inside the cottage or was it a separate –

'There it is!' he rasped, espying a trapdoor half hidden in a sward of field grass and wild bramble, approximately twenty metres from the cottage.

Still huffing madly, his muscles burning with pain, he charged forward.

Seeing the sturdy padlock on the top of the trapdoor, Cædmon set down the shotgun and snatched the fire axe that dangled from his waist pack; grateful now that he'd had the foresight to pinch it. Going down on bent knee, he put his mouth close to the narrow crack that separated the two sides of the trapdoor.

'Anala! Are you in there?'

The query met with a weighty silence.

Fear instantly ballooned, on the verge of bursting with a deafening *pop!* He didn't want to consider the worst-case scenario. But given that there'd been no reply, what else was he to think?

Seized with a fierce urgency, Cædmon began to chop at the weathered planks of wood, chunks and chips arcing through the air. His bruised ribs protested each and every swing as he hacked and clawed with a feral resolve. Although he was on the verge of full-blown panic – *Why didn't she answer me!?* – he stayed focused. If he lost his concentration for even a split second, it could prove disastrous. It was a *very* sharp blade.

The relentless chopping paid off, Cædmon soon able to rip away enough wooden slats to create a large opening. From his side of the breach, he could see that there were four crudely carved stone steps that led into a dark and dank cellar.

Silent as the grave.

Anguish ripped at Cædmon's throat, before sinking its talons into the sinews of his heart.

Fumbling with his waist pack, he removed a small torch. He quickly flipped it on and shone it into the dark depths. Unable to see anything other than cobwebbed shelving, he took a deep breath . . . braced for the worst . . . and stepped into the subterranean pit.

In the far corner of the cellar his torch beam landed on a mound; a body curled in the fetal position, back turned to him.

Gasping, Cædmon rushed forward and knelt beside the unmoving body. His hand shook as he rolled Anala towards him. Despite the fact that her clothing was filthy and there were brambles in her hair and dirty smudges on her cheeks, he instantly recognized her from the photograph that Gita had given to him.

Just as he was about to check for a pulse, she opened her eyes.

She's alive!

A giddy tsunami of relief crashed over him.

'Piss off, you prick!' she rasped in a weakened voice; down but by no means out.

Taken aback by the rude welcome, Cædmon's jaw slackened, Anala Patel having succinctly delivered a defiant jab. For some inexplicable reason, her spirited reply pleased him immensely.

Still glaring at him, she muttered, 'Can't a body die in peace?'

The sullen addendum caused Cædmon's heart muscle to painfully constrict.

'There's no need for alarm,' he hastened to assure Anala, his voice sounding unnaturally gruff. 'My name's Cædmon Aisquith. Your mother, Gita, sent me to find you.' He purposefully mentioned Gita's name, hoping it would convince Anala of his honourable intentions.

Moaning softly, she levered her torso off the ground so that she could better see his face. 'The priest told me that you're . . . is it true?' Blue eyes, identical in colour to his own, stared, unblinking, as she waited for his reply.

Cædmon assumed that she was asking, albeit in a rather butchered fashion, if he was her biological parent.

He nodded. 'Yes, Anala. I'm your father.' Those three simple words – *'I'm your father'* – incited an emotional insurgence. One that he was wholly unprepared for.

As their gazes locked, he fought to keep his emotions in check.

The dishevelled young woman mewled softly. *She's as lost in the swirl of emotion as I am*, Cædmon realized belatedly. As though to prove the point, a translucent tear meandered down Anala's grimy cheeks. She looked like a street urchin who'd just wandered out of a Dickens novel. His larynx instantly tightened.

Is this what's meant by having one's heart in one's throat?

Having been so focused on finding her, he'd given no thought to what he would do or say once they finally came face-to-face.

Bloody hell.

The battle lost, Cædmon said nothing as he gently pulled Anala to his chest and wrapped his arms around her. She briefly resisted before collapsing against him, sobbing noisily. He suspected the opened floodgate had more to do with the realization that she'd survived her horrendous abduction than the fact that she'd just met a heretofore unknown parent.

Long seconds passed before Anala pulled free of the embrace. Frowning slightly, she said, 'I wouldn't have thought a redhead was my mother's type. God blind me!' she exclaimed on the next breath. 'Did I really just say that? A knight in shining armour, that's what you are.'

Clearly embarrassed, she extended her right hand. 'It's very nice to meet you.'

Cædmon took the proffered hand and gave it a business-like shake. 'Likewise.' Later, when they were clear and free of the Sanguis Christi Fellowship, they could sort out the emotional jumble. Now was not the time.

'Right. Time to beat a hasty retreat.' He gestured to the gaping hole in the trapdoor. 'Shall we?'

'I must end this,' Gracián Santos murmured as he stumbled over to his desk.

A desperate man, he'd gone to the chapel to beg for Divine guidance. His plea, however, had fallen on deaf ears. Resigned to his fate, he knew that he must now make restitution for having abducted the Indian woman. Yes, he'd been lied to and manipulated by an ambitious cardinal. But had he been more firm in his faith, more steadfast in his convictions, he would have seen through the duplicity.

Needing to turn himself over to the authorities, and publicly expose Cardinal Fiorio's wicked plot, Gracián picked up the telephone receiver and began to dial the three-digit emergency telephone number: *9, 1* –

'Hey, G-Dog! I'm back!' Hector Calzada announced as he stepped into the office.

Startled, Gracián dropped the telephone receiver on to the floor, the handset clattering against the wood parquet.

'You seem oddly perturbed, Gracián,' Cardinal Franco Fiorio remarked as he stepped across the threshold.

At a loss for words, Gracián stared at the two men standing across from him: one dressed in urban street garb and the other attired in a red-trimmed black cassock.

'Your Eminence, I . . . I didn't think that you . . . would arrive so soon.'

'Traffic from JFK airport was surprisingly light,' the cardinal remarked conversationally as he approached the desk. 'I trust that everything is going according to plan?'

'Er, yes . . . yes, the plan,' Gracián stammered, too emotionally distraught to concoct a lie.

The cardinal arched a quizzical brow . . . just before his gaze narrowed suspiciously. Stepping behind the desk, he bent over and retrieved the fallen phone receiver. He studied it for several seconds.

Gracián went stock-still, fervently praying that the cardinal didn't glance at the display screen, the numerals '9' and '1' still clearly visible.

Reaching across the desk, the cardinal was about to set the receiver in the cradle when he suddenly gasped. An instant later, he physically recoiled as though he'd just been struck by an unseen hand.

'You betrayed me!' Cardinal Fiorio rasped. Still holding the phone receiver, he accusingly pointed it in Gracián's direction.

'I have no idea what you're talking about, Your Eminence.'

'Don't play me for a fool!' the cardinal snarled. His face contorted with rage, he slammed the telephone handset on to the desk. 'You were about to dial 9-1-1.'

'Are you fucking kidding me?' Hector exclaimed, rushing over to where they stood. After verifying for himself that the incriminating numerals were on the display screen, he hurled the telephone console across the room, the heavy frame smashing into the fireplace mantelpiece. He then whipped a Glock semi-automatic pistol from his waistband.

Hearing the deadly grind of metal on metal as Hector yanked on the slide to chamber a bullet, Gracián swayed unsteadily on his feet.

'I don't have to tell you how the Diablos deal with traitors.'

Gracián wordlessly shook his head. No explanation was necessary. *Blood in, blood out.*

'Stand down!' the cardinal ordered gruffly, using the authority of his position to stop Hector from pulling the trigger. Noticing the piece of yellow paper that was adhered to the computer monitor, he peeled it off the screen. '*Your daughter is in the root cellar at the caretaker's cottage that's located due west of Mercy Hall,*' he read aloud before angrily balling the slip of paper. 'I assume this means the Englishman has already arrived at Sanguis Christi? Is he still here?'

'I have no idea,' Gracián answered truthfully. 'We spoke on the telephone, but I . . .' His voice faded into silence.

'Why, Gracián? Why did you betray us?'

'Because you told me that if I retrieved the *Evangelium Gaspar* and killed the girl that, as a Defender of the Faith, I would receive an indulgence that would absolve me of any mortal sin committed.'

Not even attempting to hide his disdain, the cardinal snorted. 'I lied.'

Hearing the cardinal's callous admission, tears welled in Gracián's eyes. '*I* am the one who has been betrayed. In truth, you're no different than Mephistopheles; a demon in the guise of a grey friar who tempts men to sell their souls to the Devil. You claim to be a Prince of the Church, but you are really an evil man.'

'Need I remind you that the much-maligned Mephistopheles never sought men whom he could corrupt. Rather, he chose only those pathetic characters who were already damned because of their sinful actions. *You*, Gracián Santos, are such a man. You sold your soul long before I ever made your acquaintance.'

'It is true. If I had been a stronger, *better* man, I would have spurned your advances instead of becoming that most despicable of creatures . . . a collaborator in a malevolent plot,' he murmured, heartbroken.

'Where's the third plate?' the cardinal brusquely demanded to know.

Gracián shrugged his shoulders. 'I have no idea, Your Eminence. Although, if there truly is a God, you'll never gain custody of the ancient gospel.'

Hearing that, the cardinal's face instantly flushed bright red, his fury plain to see. Livid, he turned to Hector and said, 'Kill the Englishman. He's a dangerous liability.'

Hector shook his head, baffled. 'But we don't have the third plate.'

'And now that Aisquith has his daughter, I very much doubt that he'll give it to us,' the cardinal retorted. 'But I want you to keep his partner, Edie Miller, alive. There's a reason why women are called the weaker sex. Trust me, she'll turn over the copper plate to save her life.' Orders issued, Cardinal Fiorio waved a dismissive hand in Gracián's direction. 'I'm through with Father Santos. He's all yours.'

Eyes burning with a dark fire, Hector raised the Glock.

The end nigh, Gracián spread his arms out to the side of his body. A human cross.

'Forgive me, Father, for I have sinned,' he whispered . . . seconds before he felt an excruciating burst of pain.

76

Edie extended her right arm into the air, desperately trying to get a mobile connection. About to step away from the maple – wondering if the massive tree might be blocking the signal – she suddenly froze.

'Oh my God!' she rasped, certain that she'd just heard a single shot ring out.

Someone inside Mercy Hall fired a gun!

Wondering what was going on inside the mansion, she watched as Javier Aveles dashed out of the building and jumped into the parked SUV. Loose scree flew into the air as he drove at a breakneck speed, heading in her direction.

Terror-stricken, Edie pressed herself tightly against the tree trunk as the SUV sped past, disappearing at the bottom of the hill.

He's going after Cædmon!

Again, she tried to get a phone signal.

'Damn it!'

Time for Plan B.

Clipping her phone on to her waistband, Edie sprinted towards the carriage house, vigorously pumping her arms up and down in the desperate hope that it would make her legs move faster. Since Cædmon had the keys to the hire car, she intended to steal a vehicle out of the Fellowship garage and go to his rescue.

Almost there!

Breathless, panting from exertion, she reached the stable door on the gable end of the carriage house. All thumbs, she fumbled a bit with the latch before she was able to fling the door wide open.

Quickly, she scanned the six bays: there was a black Toyota pick-up truck; a passenger van; a large, serviceable tractor; and a golf cart. The last two bays were empty. She dashed over to the truck, hoping to find the key in the –

'Damn it!' There was no key in the ignition.

Her stomach in knots, she hurriedly trotted over to the van. Again, no keys.

Hearing voices, Edie peered over her shoulder – just in time to see Calzada and Diaz enter through the open door. She immediately ducked behind the tractor.

Oh, God! Not those guys!

She didn't know who scared her more: the crotch-grabbing Calzada or Diaz, the monster who'd gleefully relieved the Marqués de Bagá of his head. Holding her breath, she inched to one side, risking a glance around the side of the oversized rubber tyre. Her eyes widened fearfully – *Diaz had a sub-machine gun clutched in his hand!*

Just as the two men were about to get into the black pick-up truck, a discordant sound echoed in the distance.

Poppoppoppoppop!

Instantly recognizing the terrifying chatter of automatic weapon fire, Edie's heart skidded against her breastbone.

Someone's shooting at Cædmon!

She watched as Diaz, gesturing wildly, made harsh noises in the back of his throat, sounding more like a wild animal than a human being.

'Calm down, bro,' Calzada hissed, his stern tone instantly

calming the savage beast. 'It's just Javier taking care of business. We'll man the front gate. No way in hell is that English fucker gonna escape the premises alive.'

Seconds later, the automatic garage door opened, the pick-up truck speeding down the paved drive.

Hands trembling, Edie unclipped her phone and punched the numerals 9-1-1 on to the keypad.

Nothing. Dead air. The fast-approaching storm must have knocked out the phone service. That meant there would be no taking up a defensive position behind the male bastions. She was on her own.

Another staccato burst of gunfire echoed across the dale.

Poppoppoppoppop!

On wobbly legs, Edie rushed over to the parked golf cart, relieved to see a chrome key protruding from the ignition. She yanked the plug out of the electric socket and jumped behind the wheel. As she drove the golf cart out of the garage, another burst of gunfire rang out; the sound nearly indistinguishable from the thunder that boomed in the near distance.

Praying that she wasn't too late, she drove at breakneck speed – all of twenty miles per hour – across the lawn.

A wild bull charging a red cape.

77

Poppoppoppoppop!

As they came under a barrage of gunfire, Anala shrieked loudly. Cædmon, furious, damned near shrieked, a bullet whistling past his left ear.

A very close call!

No sooner had they exited the root cellar than they'd come under attack, the shots fired fast and furious. A deadly pummel that was near-deafening. One bullet right after another. Whoever was firing at them obviously had a sub-machine gun.

For fuck's sake!

Although Cædmon had the Mossberg shotgun, there was no time to return fire. His first priority was to get Anala to safe cover.

Cinching his left hand around her upper arm, Cædmon charged towards the metal lean-to, Anala in tow. As they ran past a limestone outcropping, bullets ricocheted off the stone, causing sparks to momentarily flash as severed chips flew into the air. They ducked behind the lorry just as a stream of bullets ripped through the rusted-out frame. Anala lurched, crying out in pain as she hit the ground.

'Afraid I left my land legs back in the cellar,' she huffed, quickly scrambling to her knees.

Cædmon spared her a quick glance. She was holding up remarkably well. *Thank God.*

Crouched side by side, they weathered the next deadly barrage, Anala again shrieking as the driver's side window was suddenly blown out in a shattering blast. A third round tore up the turf beside the lorry, clods of dirt plopping through the air.

'Time for a dose of nasty-tasting medicine,' Cædmon muttered.

He rose up on bended knee and raised the Persuader over the back-end of the lorry. Bracing the rubberized butt against his shoulder, he took aim and fired. Then, just to give the unseen bastard something to ponder, he yanked on the fore-end, quickly chambering another shell. Again, he pulled the trigger, blasting a second load of double-aught buckshot in the gunman's direction before he lowered the shotgun and safely tucked himself behind the lorry.

Although it was by no means a superior weapon, the shotgun was still lethal enough to give their gunman a moment's pause.

Hunkered against the side of the lorry, neither he nor Anala said a word. There was no point in stating the bloody obvious: that they were ensnared in a deadly trap.

Cædmon peered round the corner, scanning the terrain. They needed a sturdier bulwark. Something that could withstand sustained fire from a sub-machine gun.

'Do you think that you have enough energy to run to the back door of the cottage?' he asked Anala.

Still huffing from the earlier dash, she gamely nodded her head. 'On three?'

'Right. One, two –'

Three!

They took off in tandem, both of them crouched low

as they ran towards the cottage. Gunfire followed in their wake, each fleeting second hideously drawn-out.

Anala was the first one to reach the back door. 'It's locked!' she hollered.

Another burst of gunfire erupted.

'Stand back!' Raising his right leg, Cædmon kicked the wooden door at its weakest point – just below the knob – as hard as he could.

The weathered door flew open, swinging forcefully on its hinges just as another round of shots was fired.

Anala dashed inside a small vestibule, Cædmon right behind her. Seizing a shovel that was hanging on the wall, he jammed it under the knob to keep the door closed. As he did, bullets pitted the exterior of the door, the impact rattling his spine.

Turning on his heel, he saw that the vestibule opened on to an old-fashioned kitchen. Dust-laden and cobweb strewn, the cupboards were all bare. The glass window over the kitchen sink suddenly shattered, a line of bullets ploughing into the far wall.

Bloody hell! The gunman had them in his sights!

Snatching hold of Anala's upper arm, he pulled her towards a row of cabinets. 'Get down!' he yelled as more shots were fired through the shattered window. 'We need to stay out of the gunman's line of fire!'

Anala obediently flung herself at the floor, wedging herself into the angle formed by two adjoining cabinets.

Sidling over to the sink, Cædmon popped into firing stance, aiming the Mossberg out of the shattered window. He wasted no time pulling the trigger, immediately yanking and shoving the fore-end, and firing a second shell. *Two blind shots*. While he didn't have a prayer of hitting the unseen gunman, he needed to draw enemy fire. It was the only way that he could determine the enemy's location.

The gambit worked, the load of expelled buckshot immediately answered with a *poppoppoppoppop!*

Catching sight of a muzzle flash, Cædmon ducked back to the floor.

'How many of them are out there?' Anala hissed in a low voice.

Not bothering to lower his voice – *what was the point?* – Cædmon said, 'I'm fairly certain that we're dealing with a lone gunman.' *At least for the time being,* he thought but didn't mention, not wanting to escalate her terror. He needed Anala to remain as calm as possible. No easy feat under the circumstances.

Unclipping his mobile phone, he handed it to her. 'Dial 9-1-1 and inform the emergency operator that we're at the Sanguis Christi Fellowship and to send a police car post-haste,' he instructed.

'A police car? I'm thinking an entire military battalion,' she muttered under her breath.

Cædmon risked a quick glance out of the window. 'Given the angle of the shots just fired, I'm fairly certain that our gunman has taken up a position on the outcrop of limestone that overlooks the cottage.'

'I can't get a signal,' Anala exclaimed angrily as she repeatedly jabbed her index finger against the mobile's keypad.

'I suspect the hilly terrain and stone cottage are the culprit,' he said, reclipping the useless mobile on to his waistband.

'Do you think we could make a run for it?'

'Out of the question. The gunman will mow us down before we reach the top of the hill.'

Anala pointedly glanced at the Mossberg. 'But you have a loaded shotgun.'

'Trust me. Not the best of weapons in a mad dash.'

Just then, another round of bullets was fired through the shattered window, shearing several chips of cabinetry.

Anala winced, clearly petrified.

'A rather pitiful knight in shining armour, aren't I?' he muttered.

'I didn't want to die inside that dark cellar. This . . . this is better.' One side of Anala's mouth curved in a rueful half-smile. 'At least now I won't die alone.'

Cædmon's gut twisted, horrified to think that her captors had intended for her to die all alone in that miserable little hole.

Extending his left arm, he put a steadying hand on her shoulder, needing her to emotionally hold it together. 'We *will* get out of this mess alive because I'm not inclined to die today.' He gently squeezed her shoulder before removing his hand. 'Here's the plan. I'm going to sneak out of the cottage and take down the gunman.'

'By that you mean kill him, right?' Anala didn't miss a beat. Or a euphemism.

'I have no choice,' he informed her, certain that in his daughter's eyes he'd just gone from white knight to dark demon. He considered telling her that he would derive no pleasure from the bloodthirsty act, but wasn't entirely certain that would prove true. 'The gunman knows that we're armed with a shotgun.'

'So, if he's a smart man, he's not going to enter the cottage.'

'Even a halfwit will avoid the deadly welcome that awaits him if he does. Since he knows that there are only two means of entering the house – through *this* door –' Cædmon jutted his chin at the nearby vestibule – 'or the front door located on the other side of the cottage, I suspect that he's taken up a position where he can safely monitor both points of egress.'

'But he won't be able to keep a watchful eye on all of the windows.'

Cædmon nodded. Even in a weakened condition, Anala had a nimble mind. 'Which is why I'll exit through one of the windows on the southern side of the house where, hopefully, I won't be observed.'

'Don't you mean that *we'll* exit?'

'Actually, it'll be safer if you remain inside the cottage. I'll leave you the shotgun.'

'But I think it would be better if –'

'The matter isn't open for discussion,' he interjected, tabling her objection.

She opened her mouth, presumably to lodge another protest; then just as quickly clamped her lips shut.

Cædmon passed her the Mossberg. 'Have you ever fired one of these?'

'No. So you'd better give me a quick primer before you leave.' Eyes narrowed, she peered over at him. 'While I never thought I'd ever feel this way, I'm rather hoping the bastard *does* walk through the kitchen door . . . I want to look him in the eye when I pull the trigger.'

78

The dead tread softly . . . And those stalking the living tread even more lightly.

A ghoulish thought that occurred to Cædmon as he slid open the dining-room window. Having already decided upon the one and only rule of engagement – that the last man standing at the end of the deadly bout would be declared the winner – he ducked his head and swung a leg over the sash, lowering himself to the ground.

Hugging the shadows, he stealthily moved away from the cottage, careful to stay out of the gunman's line of sight. It meant taking a more circuitous route; one that cost him precious minutes. But it was time he gladly relinquished in the hope that he could buttonhole the unsuspecting bastard.

Bent at the waist, he maintained a low profile as he snaked his way across the overgrown side garden. Happening upon a pile of metal posts – the kind of heavy-duty stakes that were used to pen farm animals – he pulled up short and plucked a five-foot-long pale out of the pile. It had good heft. More importantly for his purposes, it could be used as a deadly weapon. During the Middle Ages, before the advent of gunpowder, men marched into battle armed with far cruder weaponry.

Buoyed by his fortuitous find, Cædmon dashed across the overgrown front garden. Although he'd not yet seen the enemy, he'd pinpointed his position to a small limestone outcrop due north of the cottage. While that gave the gunman an obstructed view looking to the south, it also put the enemy at a distinct disadvantage: it left his aft unprotected. If Cædmon executed a wide flanking manoeuvre, he could creep up from behind and take the bastard by surprise.

A few minutes later, he crested the small rise that lay directly behind the gunman's position. A summer storm was almost upon them, dark clouds clashing and colliding as the tall grass violently wavered to-and-fro. Standing behind the cover of an ancient oak, he scanned the rolling fields, searching for his quarry. His gaze methodically moved from one clump of dried vegetation to the next. On a nearby hillock, he spotted a parked SUV. But no gunman.

Where the bloody hell are you?

About to move to another location, Cædmon suddenly saw a flash of motion in the field grass.

I've got you, you bastard!

The gunman didn't know it yet, but he was hiding in plain sight. If Cædmon had been armed with a firearm instead of a fence post, he could have easily bagged his quarry from where he stood. He trained his eyes on the jagged outcrop of limestone. The gunman was so cocksure of his defences that he'd actually set the sub-machine gun on top of the stone slab.

How bloody perfect is that?

Cædmon slipped the fire axe out of the loop on his waist pack, grasping it in his left hand. A man can't have too many weapons when charging into battle. The enemy's position pinpointed, he made his way across the overgrown meadow, steadily advancing on the slab of limestone.

Ten metres from his quarry, Cædmon was able to positively identify the man negligently leaning against the outcropping – it was Javier Aveles.

Well, well, well . . . what do you know?

Cædmon came to a halt; afraid that if he got any closer, Aveles would hear his approach. He eyed the sub-machine gun in plain sight on top of the stone slab. *A Mini-Uzi unless I'm greatly mistaken.* Prized for its compact design, it was highly coveted by Mexican drug lords.

Raising his right arm, Cædmon felt the muscles in his belly tighten. While he knew the element of surprise would be on his side, he also knew there would only be a few seconds to exploit the advantage. A few scant seconds to stun Aveles and seize the Uzi sub-machine gun.

He held the five-foot-metal stake like a spear as he cocked his arm back. His bicep bunched; a coiled spring. Gaze locked on the target, he hurled the stake through the air. Just as he'd hoped, the metal spike ploughed into the gunman's right dorsal – the soft, vulnerable patch of flesh protecting the kidney.

Howling in pain, Javier Aveles pitched to his left side. Away from the sub-machine gun.

Cædmon lunged forward. Panting breathlessly, he belligerently stood over his quarry, the well-honed axe in plain view. Cowering on the ground, Aveles stared up at him, wide-eyed, clearly aghast to see him.

Finish him off! a voice inside his head commanded. *This is no time for delicate sensibilities. This is war!*

With that thought in mind, Cædmon viciously swung the axe.

Only to swerve away from Aveles's neck at the last possible moment, the sharpened blade harmlessly *swooshing* through the air.

The will simply wasn't there to kill a defenceless man.

'I'm going to be pissing blood for the next week,' Aveles gasped with a pain-wracked shudder.

'Stop your griping, Javier. A dead man would envy you the ailment,' Cædmon snarled. Annoyed that he now had to contend with a prisoner, he jutted his head towards the parked SUV. 'Give me the keys.'

A nasty sneer affixed to his face, Aveles shoved his right hand into his jeans pocket and removed a key ring. Just as he was in the process of handing over the keys, Aveles suddenly tossed them into the nearby field. In the next instant, he jettisoned towards the limestone slab, making a desperate grab for the sub-machine gun.

No!

Cædmon reflexively swung the axe at that grasping hand, the sharpened blade cleaving the appendage at the wrist. A clean cut.

Aveles screamed in agony as a torrent of blood gushed from his amputated limb. A hideous, pulsating geyser. Still shrieking like a madman, Aveles suddenly rolled towards the Uzi, reaching for it with his left hand.

Christ!

Cædmon had no choice –

– He sliced the axe blade across Aveles's neck, severing his carotid artery.

More dead than alive, Javier Aveles glared at him in

those last few gossamer moments . . . just before he surrendered the ghost.

Still holding tight to the axe, Cædmon stared at the dead man: Aveles lay in an ungainly sprawl in the thick, overgrown grass. A butchered mess.

The vultures will dine well this evening.

The thought induced no pang of Christian guilt. Cædmon was mad as hell.

'You fucking stupid bastard!' he bellowed, infuriated that he'd been driven to kill. 'You didn't have to die.' *Why did you have to reach for your weapon? You had to have known that I'd counterattack?*

Enraged by how quickly he'd lost control of the situation, Cædmon snatched hold of the Mini-Uzi. The slight motion caused a tumult of pain. His ribs ached so intensely, it felt as though someone had maliciously taken a red-hot soldering iron to them.

Battered, physically and emotionally, Cædmon flung aside the blood-drenched axe and turned away from the carnage.

As he wearily made his way back to the stone cottage, he caught sight of a white golf cart on the far hillside.

What in God's name . . . ?

'. . . are you doing here!?'

'I came to warn you!' Edie shot back, receiving a less than enthusiastic welcome from Cædmon. Cheeks flushed from having run across the dale, he stood beside the parked golf cart, a sub-machine gun tucked under his arm. 'Javier is headed this way.'

'That particular threat has been neutralized. And I'm sorry to have roared.' Sighing wearily, Cædmon glanced down at his blood-splattered shirt. 'As you can see, we were embroiled in a rather precarious situation.'

'Please tell me that Anala is –'

'Unscathed.' Cædmon turned towards the small stone cottage. 'It's all right to come outside, Anala!' he summoned in a booming voice.

Within moments, the back door opened and Anala Patel, clutching a shotgun to her chest, tentatively emerged. Edie noticed that her finger was poised on the trigger – as though she wasn't completely convinced that the coast was clear.

Taking notice of Cædmon's blood-splattered shirt, Anala's brows worriedly drew together. 'Did you, um –'

'Yes, I did,' Cædmon interjected. 'He gave me no choice. Although our assailant left us a rather nice parting gift.' Grim-faced, he brandished the compact sub-machine gun.

'I was so terrified that he would hurt you,' the young woman said shyly.

'While I'm sure that he would have liked nothing better, the brute's plans were cut short.'

Anala peered at the golf cart.

'No need for alarm,' Cædmon assured her, noticing the direction of her gaze. 'This is my partner, Edie Miller.'

'Actually, the alarm is blaring,' Edie said on his coat-tails. 'Calzada and Diaz are on the prowl and, from what I overheard, they're gunning for you.'

'Christ!' Cædmon peered furtively at the hill that over-shadowed the ramshackle cottage. 'But that makes no sense,' he said a split second later. 'They don't have the third plate.'

Edie shrugged, at a loss. 'They didn't mention that they'd found it. And, by the way, Cardinal Fiorio has arrived at Mercy Hall.'

The announcement incited another irreverent expletive.

Again, Cædmon gazed at the towering hillside. 'In that case, we need to head in the opposite direction from Mercy Hall. It's imperative that we escape the Fellowship grounds.'

Within moments they were off, Anala riding up front with Edie, and Cædmon scrunched in the rear folding seat. Overhead, a brilliant pyrotechnic show flashed on the horizon, ominous silver streaks randomly materializing. As they made their way across the rolling hills, the skies opened up, treating them to a heavy rainfall. While the golf cart had a hard top, that didn't stop the rain from sluicing in from the sides.

'Did the priest ever show up?' Cædmon asked, raising his voice to be heard over the pounding rain.

'I saw him rush into Mercy Hall right before – Oh, no!' Edie exclaimed suddenly, catching sight of a vehicle in the distance. 'There's a pick-up truck headed our way!'

'We need to take cover!' Cædmon shouted. 'Quickly! To the Parthenon!'

Edie wondered if she'd heard correctly. '*Where?!*'

'He means the folly over on that hillock!' Anala said, gesturing wildly.

Surprised to see a miniature Greek temple, Edie yanked on the steering wheel, navigating in that direction. 'Hopefully, whoever's in the truck hasn't caught sight of –'

An ominous *ratatattat* of automatic weapon fire rent the air.

Terrified, Edie slammed her foot on the accelerator. But the golf cart refused to comply. They were stuck at a very sedate twenty miles per hour.

'Keep driving towards the folly!' Cædmon ordered. 'Don't stop!'

'Like I'd even consider it,' she muttered, flinching as Cædmon returned fire.

Edie glanced over at Anala, who was in the process of yanking on the fore-end of the shotgun. A split second later, she pulled the trigger, the recoil flinging her against the back of the seat.

Tightly gripping the steering wheel, Edie headed down a steep hill. Worried that they weren't going to make it to the folly before the truck overtook them, she whipped her head around and stole a quick glimpse at their assailants. Hector Calzada was behind the wheel and Diaz was leaning out of the passenger window, firing a sub-machine gun.

No sooner was that image imprinted on her ocular nerve than Diaz was hurled back into the truck, a cloud of red blood misting the windscreen.

Ohmygod!

'I think you killed –'

Just then the golf cart drove over a stony precipice that Edie hadn't seen in the tall grass. For a few seconds, all four wheels came off the ground before they landed with a shuddering impact that caused her to lose control of the cart.

The small vehicle jackknifed, first one way, then the other. Frantic, Edie slammed on the brakes. *A lost cause.* The grass was rain-slicked, the cart actually picking up speed as it hydroplaned down the hillside.

'We need to jump out! *Now!*' Cædmon ordered. 'Before this damned thing rolls over on us.'

Hearing that, Edie immediately leaned over and – flung herself free of the driver's seat.

For several seconds, she was airborne. *Soaring* . . .

Before gravity got the better of her.

Cædmon hit the ground with a spine-jarring thud.

Having no control over his limbs, he tumbled and bumbled – an ungainly free-for-all – before finally rolling to a stop. Stunned, he lay sprawled in the field grass, the rain pummelling his face.

Edie! Anala!

Gasping for air, he shoved himself up on to his hands and knees, nearly toppling over. Everything was off-kilter. Blurred around the edges. He blinked several times, desperately trying to bring the world back into focus. *No good.* It remained a topsy-turvy mess.

He shut his eyes, pressing his lids together as tightly as possible. He then quickly popped his lids wide open. The trick worked, his vision clearing. At a glance, he could see that the golf cart was lying on its side at the bottom of the hill.

Hearing a low moan from somewhere in the near vicinity, he called out, 'Edie! Anala!'

'Still in one piece,' he heard Edie gasp breathlessly. 'Just dented.'

Anala, her voice barely audible, assured him of the same. *Thank God.*

Biting back the pain, Cædmon turned his head in the other direction. He saw a parked pick-up truck and a hulking shape swiftly approaching on foot.

Hector Calzada!

The Uzi! Where in God's name is the Uzi?

His ribs screamed in protest as he hurriedly crawled through the tall grass on his hands and knees. Frantic, he swiped his hand back-and-forth across the tall blades of grass, fishing for the sub-machine gun which he'd tossed aside just before he'd jumped from the golf cart. *Afraid I'd blow my own head off.*

Just as his hand grazed across the blackened metal, a booted foot stomped down on the Uzi, preventing Cædmon from seizing it. He craned his neck and peered up at the looming brute who wielded a sub-machine gun in his right hand and the Mossberg shotgun in his left; he'd obviously plucked the latter out of the wet grass.

'Well done, Hector. Hats off to you,' Cædmon dead-panned.

Proving that he was impervious to irony, Calzada snarled, 'You're not going to be able to wear a fucking hat after I rip your head from your fucking neck, you fucking cocksucker!'

The foul-mouthed diatribe did not bode well, although Cædmon was reasonably certain that the brute wouldn't follow through on the vicious threat until *after* he had custody of the third copper plate. *My ace in the hole*, as the Americans were wont to say; the ace, of course, was the most propitious card in the deck. And one that he intended to keep securely stuffed up his sleeve.

None too gracefully, Cædmon, still on all fours, sat back on his haunches. 'Your language is appalling. Need I remind you that there are ladies present?'

The rebuke earned a swift reply, Calzada striking him in the side of the jaw with the butt of the shotgun.

Cædmon's head violently jerked to the right, blood spewing from a cut lip as his head exploded in an excruciating burst. As though he'd just been shot pointblank, a sickening bolt of pain radiated from his jaw to the back of his skull. He fought the urge to collapse in the tall grass, to give in to the siren's call, close his eyes and let his body be swallowed in soothing darkness.

Unmanned, tears pooled in his eyes, the pain agonizing.

In the next instant, Calzada aimed the sub-machine gun at Cædmon's chest. Ready to cut him to ribbons.

Gathering what stray bits of defiance he could summon, Cædmon flung his ace at the other man. 'Kill me and you'll never retrieve the last plate.'

'Your curly-haired bitch will be only too happy to turn it over to me.' Calzada spared a quick glance at Edie who, like Cædmon, was still on her hands and knees. 'Isn't that right, *bella*?'

'One small problem,' Cædmon countered on a painful hiss. 'She has no idea where I hid it. Ace up the sleeve, old boy. You didn't really think that I'd walk into the lion's den without taking a few precautions?' Tasting the coppery residue of blood, he pursed his lips and spat out a red ribbon.

'Where's Javier?' the bastard demanded to know, abruptly changing the subject.

'How the bloody hell should I know?'

'I'm not stupid, *cabrón*. That's his weapon.' Calzada jutted his chin at the Uzi still underfoot.

'Yes, that.' Cædmon gingerly rubbed his jaw, grateful

that it was still properly hinged. *A small blessing.* 'Javier handed the Uzi over to me. So to speak.'

'Get up! All of you!' Calzada ordered, sweeping the shotgun in a wide arc. As Edie and Anala both struggled to their feet, he returned his attention to Cædmon. Narrow-eyed, he snarled, 'One misstep, *cabrón*, and I *will* shoot pointblank into both of your fucking kneecaps.'

Cædmon returned the glare, his gaze focusing on the ludicrous teardrop tattooed in the corner of Calzada's eye. A teardrop that wrongly presumed Hector Calzada was capable of a tender emotion that could actually produce a tear.

Wincing, he shoved himself to his feet with a groan, having lost his dignity somewhere on the hillside. He swiped the back of his hand across his mouth, wiping a foamy smear of crimson saliva.

A few feet away, standing shoulder-to-shoulder, Edie and Anala both stood their ground. Bruised but not broken. Cædmon was unable to look either of them in the eye.

I'm a pathetic excuse for a knight. The Templars would have nothing to do with me.

Prodded forward by the well-armed brute, the three of them trudged across the meadow towards Mercy Hall. The smell of gun smoke still hung heavy in the air.

The smell of a battle lost.

81

Drenched to the skin, Edie shoved several hanks of wet hair away from her face. Walking beside her, Anala shivered. She resisted the urge to put a comforting arm around the young woman's shoulders, afraid that it would incite Hector Calzada's fury.

'Where is Father Santos?' Cædmon asked as Calzada ushered the three of them down a dimly lit hallway on the first floor of Mercy Hall. 'I had hoped to make his personal acquaintance.'

'G-Dog died a traitor's death,' the thug replied with a callous shrug. 'I was happy to pull the trigger.'

Edie gasped, horrified that anyone would actually brag about killing a Catholic priest. A heinous act, it not only qualified for a very long prison term, but a one-way ticket to hell.

'Go into the classroom.' Calzada gestured with his submachine gun towards an open room.

Like truant students who'd been dragged back to school, they trudged through the doorway. At a glance, Edie could see that it was a standard-issue classroom: several long rows of plastic-shell seats with attached tablet-armed desktops; oversized chalkboards on the front wall; and a teacher's desk with a lectern.

To her ire, the teacher's desk was piled high with her and Cædmon's personal belongings, someone having retrieved their tote bags from the hire car. Each and every one had been turned inside-out, the contents completely ransacked.

Somebody has obviously been searching for the Evangelium Gaspar.

Now, suddenly, it made perfect sense to her why Cædmon had shoved his rucksack into the cement urn. Never trust the enemy. Even if he wore a cassock and a cross. *Especially then*, some might say.

'Sit!' Calzada ordered, this time using his sub-machine gun to point to three desks at the front of the classroom.

Water dripping in their wake, each of them squeezed into a moulded plastic chair, with Cædmon taking the middle desk. Sighing wearily, Anala immediately slumped over, resting her head on her arms, a vision of utter defeat. Cædmon reached over and awkwardly patted her on the arm.

Several moments later, a short, balding man wearing a black cassock entered the classroom.

'I am Cardinal Franco Fiorio,' the cleric announced without preamble as he strode over to the teacher's lectern.

'Who, in addition to being an esteemed member of the Roman Curia, occasionally writes under the catchy pen name Irenaeus. It's my understanding that Father Santos is no longer among the living. I hope that you were considerate enough to have given him the Last Rites before pulling the trigger,' Cædmon said, cutting wit the only weapon in his arsenal.

The cardinal's expression turned decidedly frosty. 'Gracián Santos was a snivelling coward who refused to defend the Faith. He did not deserve to live.'

'To hear Christian compassion so poignantly expressed warms the cockles.'

Gripping the lectern, the cardinal glared at Cædmon. 'The battle is lost. You would be wise to show the victor proper obeisance.'

'And do what? Kiss your big golden ring?' Edie snapped irritably, jumping into the fray.

'*From battle and murder, and from sudden death, Good Lord deliver us.*' Cædmon paused, letting a full beat pass before he put a hand to his heart and mockingly bowed his head. 'Forgive the lapse. It's from the Great Litany in the Book of Common Prayer which is, undoubtedly, anathema to you. So, to the victor the spoils, eh?' He pointedly glanced at the messy heap of clothing, notebooks and toiletries.

'I'm on a very tight schedule. Where is it?'

'*It* presumably being the third copper plate.' Angling his hips, Cædmon leisurely crossed his legs. He then folded his arms over his chest and said, 'Before I divulge its whereabouts, we need to discuss the terms of the exchange.'

The cardinal graced him with a saccharine smile. 'What would you like?'

'I have but one demand: safe passage for the three of us.'

'Granted,' the cardinal readily agreed with an airy wave of his right hand, the overhead light catching on his ostentatious ring.

'Very well,' Cædmon said after a moment's considera-tion. 'You will find the copper plate cached inside the stone chapel. There's a concealed hole in the flooring under the pews. Second or third row,' he added with a befuddled shake of the head. 'I can't recall precisely. I was in a bit of a hurry.'

Edie kept her features carefully schooled, well aware that the third plate wasn't in the chapel. *He's stalling for time.* Which meant that Cædmon had a plan. At least, she *hoped* that's what it meant.

The cardinal turned to Calzada. 'Go find it. But before you leave –' Holding out his right hand, Franco Fiorio wiggled his pudgy fingers, silently asking for a semi-automatic firearm. Calzada obligingly yanked a chrome-plated gun from his waistband and passed it to the cardinal.

'Don't think because I wear a cassock that I won't pull the trigger to defend the Faith,' Cardinal Fiorio informed them as he expertly pulled back the slide on the semi-automatic, chambering a bullet.

Ignoring the gun pointed at his chest, Cædmon jutted his chin at the iPad on the edge of the teacher's desk. 'I take it that you've read the translation of the third plate that's saved on the computer tablet.'

'I did.' Cardinal Fiorio glanced at the iPad, his lips dismissively turned down at the corners. 'Tripe. From beginning to end. The *Evangelium Gaspar* should have been destroyed centuries ago. To suggest that our blessed Saviour is not the divine Son of God amounts to –'

'Spare me the moral outrage,' Cædmon said, speaking over the cardinal. 'We both know how Jesus' "divinity" came about. In the year 325 during the Council of Nicaea, the Roman Emperor Constantine gave the Christian bishops a mandate, ordering them to concoct a god to rival the solar deity Sol Invictus.'

Although Cardinal Fiorio remained silent, Edie could

see that he'd turned a fiery shade of red. Visible proof of his molten rage.

'I'm guessing that Constantine wasn't interested in a religion that focused on a mortal man who preached a message of peace, love and tolerance,' she remarked.

'Not interested in the least,' Cædmon concurred in a mocking tone of voice. 'But to give the bishops their due, they did an admirable job in decimating the historical Jesus. First rate, in fact. One would never guess that he'd ever been a mortal man. And to ensure that nobody questioned Jesus' newfound divinity, the Church Fathers methodically destroyed all evidence to the contrary.'

'Anyone who asserts that Jesus is anything less than the Son of God is a heretic,' the cardinal spat out, his self-control beginning to crack.

Cædmon smiled humourlessly. 'As I recall, it was that notorious sexual reprobate Pope Leo the Tenth who revealed the Church's grand stratagem when he boasted that "It has served us well, this myth of Christ."'

82

'Indeed, one has only to read the canonical gospels to know that Jesus repeatedly referred to himself as "the Son of Man",' Cædmon continued. 'A pesky detail that the bishops at Nicaea purposefully overlooked.'

'Like the despicable Catholic liberals, you're determined to remove all of the ancient *mysterion* from the Church.' Despite the fact that a muscle visibly twitched in Cardinal Fiorio's jaw, the man clearly enraged, the cleric still held the Beretta with a sure-gripped confidence.

Cædmon intended to rattle that confidence, in the hopes that the gun might shake loose.

And I need to swash the buckle before Hector Calzada returns from his fruitless scour inside the chapel.

'Furthermore, you wrongly believe that Gaspar's heretical gospel is a true and accurate account because it depicts a human Jesus who has no relationship to the Sacred Mysteries,' the cardinal hissed.

'On the contrary. There is a great and glorious mystery embedded within the third plate of the *Evangelium Gaspar*; one that is corroborated in the Gospel of John,' Cædmon informed the cardinal, unbowed. 'Since you've read the translation, you know that Gaspar is very clear: when Jesus was baptized by his cousin John at the River Jordan, the Logos entered into him.'

'Excuse me for not being up to biblical speed, but who or what is the Logos?' Anala enquired, wide-eyed.

'Ah! An excellent question and one that has divided theologians for centuries,' Cædmon replied. 'According to the eminent philosopher Philo of Alexandria, the Logos, also referred to in the Bible as "the Word", are divine beings who act as intermediaries.'

'By intermediary, you mean a heavenly go-between, right?' This from Edie.

Cædmon nodded. 'Interestingly enough, in ancient times, the Logos were considered God's first-born children.'

'The Logos is the Creator Spiritus, and as such is One *with* God the Father,' the cardinal heatedly asserted. '*In the beginning was the Word, and the Word was with God and the Word was God.*'

Although Cædmon considered Franco Fiorio a throwback to a very dark age, the cleric had just given him the opening that he'd been waiting for.

'Thank you, Your Eminence, for introducing the Evangelist John's famous first verse. May I have permission to approach the chalkboard?' The request was made in an innocuously polite tone of voice.

The cardinal hesitated a moment before nodding his consent; although he made a conspicuous to-do of training the Beretta on Cædmon as he approached the chalkboard at the front of the classroom.

Picking up a piece of chalk, Cædmon wondered how to best exploit their physical proximity – the cardinal now within pouncing distance – as he carefully wrote out a long line of Greek script.

εν αρχη ην ο λογος και ο λογος ην προς τον θεον και
θεος ην ο λογος

Finished, he set the chalk down on the rimmed edge of
the chalkboard. Unless the cardinal put the Beretta to his
head, he had no intention of retaking his seat.

Assuming a professorial air, Cædmon pointed to the
Greek inscription and said, 'This is a striking example of
the very sort of "creative editing" that the early Church
Fathers engaged in.'

Cardinal Fiorio cocked his head to one side, eyes narrowed. 'Writing the first verse from John's gospel in the
original Greek doesn't change a thing.'

'Therein you are wrong, Your Eminence. For, in fact, it
changes the whole of the Christian religion. As you just
noted, I have written John 1:1 in the original Greek. However, the correct translation is "In the beginning was the
Word, and the Word was with God and the Word was *a
god*."' The only benefit of physical pain was that it oftentimes had a bracing effect on a man's mental faculties.
Thoughts so crystal clear, they verged on shattering. This
was one of those thoughts.

'That's what I call a not-so-subtle difference that puts a
completely different spin on things,' Edie said astutely.

'Indeed. The cardinal's inaccurate translation equates
the Word, or the Logos, with God, the two being one and
the same. However, the correct translation makes it clear
that the Logos is a separate entity from God.' Cædmon
paused a moment, hit with a sudden urge to make a grab
for the Beretta while the bastard was stewing in his theological juices.

Mind made up, he inclined his torso towards the cardinal.

Only to reconsider a split second later. The risk was too great; the odds needed to improve before he attempted any derring-do.

Forced to bide his time, Cædmon continued with the Bible lesson. 'A few verses later, the Evangelist John makes the famous assertion that "the Word became flesh and dwelt among us". Which is *exactly* what transpired at the River Jordan when Jesus was baptized by his cousin John. For it was there in front of a host of witnesses that the Logos entered into Jesus. In that instant, Jesus became *the Christ. That* is your sacred mystery!' he exclaimed, forcefully underlining the Greek inscription before turning to face his inquisitor. 'And, by God, what a bloody mystery it is! Absolutely astounding that a mortal man could conjoin with the divine Logos.'

As he spoke, Cædmon heard the roar of thunder in the near distance. So forceful, the chalkboard rattled in the aftermath.

As though God himself was participating in the debate.

'That is pure fiction! Heresy of the worst sort!' the cardinal snarled contemptuously.

'Or it is the truth of the matter. Because of the immaculate planning involved in Jesus' conception and the eighteen years of intense purification of his mind, body and spirit, the Logos was able to enter into him. When that happened, Jesus became the bridge between mankind and the Almighty. An intermediary. So while he was not born divine, his ministry was divinely inspired.' An incredible notion that had not previously occurred to Cædmon.

Edie, clearly awestruck, said, 'That's because Jesus was conjoined or enfleshed with the Logos during the whole of his ministry.'

'Precisely. And, as Gaspar makes clear, at some point during the crucifixion, the Logos left Jesus. One can only presume that the horror of his tortures somehow corrupted what had been, up to that point, a pure vessel for the Logos to reside within. When the Logos fled, I imagine that it amounted to a death of sorts,' Cædmon added, beginning to see the events of that tragic day in a whole new light.

'Lies! All lies!' Spittle misted the air, the cardinal having turned rabid with rage. 'Jesus Christ *is* the Son of God. His divinity is, was and has always been pre-existent to his birth. This is the foundational truth of the Roman Catholic Church. The *Evangelium Gaspar* seeks to discredit that truth by putting forth the Great Heresy!'

Cædmon stared at his inquisitor. Torn between derision and morbid curiosity, he pondered which of the twin peaks to scale first.

'Jesus made it very clear in Gaspar's gospel that he did not want a religion established in his name.' Relishing the opportunity to shove the cardinal's face in his so-called *mysterion*, Cædmon then said, 'Yet that is exactly what you and your power-hungry cohorts insist that he did want; presumably to include all of the rituals and Latin mumbo-jumbo.'

The cardinal's chest heaved, the tightly clutched gun toggling from side to side. 'You are very clever at distorting the truth.'

'So you say, but one doesn't have to be a biblical

scholar to know that the contents of the *Evangelium Gaspar* may prove the most staggering find in the history of Christianity.'

'The Holy See has survived for two thousand years. There is nothing in our house that we can't fix,' the cardinal shot back.

'Your Eminence, might I point out the bloody obvious: that *no one* can renovate when the house is on fire.'

Suddenly catching a flash of movement in his peripheral vision, Cædmon turned his head.

Good God!

As if on cue, Father Gracián Santos stood in the doorway grasping a red fire extinguisher in his bloodied hands. *Resurrected from the dead.*

83

Cædmon wasn't the only person in the room stunned by the priest's unexpected appearance; Cardinal Fiorio appeared downright apoplectic.

'What are you doing here?' he demanded to know, aiming the Beretta at Father Santos. 'I thought you were dead.'

Barely able to stand upright, the priest weaved unsteadily, his black shirt and trousers soaked through with blood. Gasping raggedly, as though each inhalation was a painful ordeal, Father Santos glared at the cardinal.

'*You . . . are . . . an . . . evil man!*' Accusation hurled, the priest then raised the nozzle on the fire extinguisher and, taking aim, blasted a wide spray of white foam in Cardinal Fiorio's direction.

Completely covering the cleric in a thick layer of fire retardant.

Blinded, Cardinal Fiorio writhed violently, arms, legs and torso all jerking spasmodically. Whether by accident or design, he fired the Beretta, a chunk of plaster plummeting from the ceiling.

Cædmon immediately charged forward and manacled a hand around the cardinal's right wrist. Shoving his shoulder into the other man's chest, he slammed the cleric's hand against the chalkboard, attempting to jar the gun loose.

Instead, the impact caused another bullet to discharge; this one ricocheting off a light fixture.

Like a feral animal, the cardinal instinctively tried to pull his right hand free of Cædmon's grasp, foamy spit spewing from his mouth.

Seeking to end the bout posthaste, Cædmon pummelled a fist into Cardinal Fiorio's face, the man howling in pain, his nose broken on contact. Cædmon grunted as the cartilage-shattering blow sent an agonized burst from his balled fist to his battered jaw. The Beretta clattered to the floor, the tenacious little bastard finally letting go of it.

Having disarmed the cardinal, he stepped back, the man in too much pain to launch a counter-attack.

Odious little prick.

'Don't think for one instant that I'm not tempted to kick him in the crystal balls,' Edie said in a nakedly vicious tone of voice. 'I don't care if he *is* a cardinal.'

'I'm a Prince of the Church!' Fiorio wailed loudly, bracing either side of his nose with his middle fingers. 'How dare you treat me as —'

'Spare us the dirge,' Cædmon interjected, cutting the cleric off in mid-lament. 'It sickens me to hear you drone on as though *you* were the victim.'

'More like a devil in a cassock,' Anala remarked. To Cædmon's surprise, she capably held the Beretta pistol, having retrieved it from the floor.

Stepping over to where Father Santos had collapsed in the doorway, Cædmon went down on bent knee and put a finger to the priest's neck. Just as he feared, there was no pulse.

'I don't know if Gracián Santos was an evil man or one

who was terribly misguided,' he said quietly as he stood up. 'Regardless, I'm indebted to him.'

'Hey, look what I found in teacher's desk.' Holding up a thick roll of strapping tape, Edie ripped a long length and handed it to him.

'Excellent.' Cædmon slapped the piece of tape over the cardinal's mouth and wrapped the ends completely around his head. Mummifying the bastard.

With Edie's help, he then secured the cardinal's wrists and ankles, wrapping his limbs in enough tape to have shipped him on air freight.

'That should keep him until the authorities arrive. Speaking of which, you'll need to find a landline telephone,' Cædmon said to Edie, their mobiles having been confiscated. 'Tell the police that they're urgently needed at Sanguis Christi.'

Hearing that, the cardinal's face betrayed an animal fear. No doubt he'd just realized that not only was the contest lost, but he would have to make restitution for his crimes.

'"In dubious battle on the plains of Heaven"',' Cædmon quoted from Milton, unable to summon an ounce of sympathy for a man who had the ambition and guile of a bloodthirsty Borgia.

Anala glanced at the hobbled cardinal. 'I was going to say, "Britain, of course, always wins one battle – the last."'

'Not quite. Unfortunately, Cardinal Fiorio was merely the dragon master. I now have to slay the beast.' *Or, at the very least, capture him.*

A fearful look instantly crept on to Edie's face. 'You mean Hector Calzada?'

Cædmon nodded wordlessly.

'Do you have to?'

'He's a nasty piece of work. Far too dangerous to be released into the wild,' Cædmon said, taking custody of the Beretta. Popping the magazine, he checked the ammo, counting three bullets. He jammed the magazine back into place. 'I want both of you to stay inside Mercy Hall until the police arrive.'

A reckoning in order, he rushed out of the classroom.

84

As Cædmon dashed through the stormy torrent, a silver-glazed bolt suddenly broke free from the sky, pulverizing a towering maple and snapping the heavy-limbed sentry in half. The stentorian boom that accompanied the horrific act sent a pulsing shock wave across the school grounds, as though a cannon had just gone off on yonder field.

Momentarily stunned, he stared, wide-eyed, at the smoking flames that burst up from the severed bole.

Hoping it wasn't a dark omen, he continued running towards the stone chapel.

A few moments later, he arrived, out of breath and soaking wet. The door to the chapel was open. Inside, he could hear a steady thumping.

What the bloody hell was Calzada doing?

Cædmon removed the Beretta from his waistband and stepped through the open doorway into the chapel. Standing near a stone font filled with holy water, he scanned the dimly lit environs. *Wooden pews. Marble altar. Black and white chequerboard flooring. Stained-glass windows.* Typical church fare.

Circumspect, he crept forward a few feet, his footfall muffled by the resounding thuds. Catching sight of Calzada near the front pew, he paused, taken aback to see that the man was in the process of breaking the marble floor tiles with a sledgehammer. Searching for the hidden cache that didn't exist.

Unwilling to move closer, afraid that Calzada would catch sight of him and open fire with the Uzi, Cædmon ducked behind a marble pillar. He considered his options, wanting to take down the beast without any bloodshed. He'd spilled enough already.

I need a decoy. Something to momentarily distract the Bête Noire.

Cædmon scoured the near vicinity, his gaze landing on a small framed oil painting of the martyred St Sebastian, his body pierced with arrows. Removing the painting from the panelled wall, he chose a spot on the other side of the chapel and – waiting for Calzada's next swing – hurled the framed work of art through the air.

Just as he'd hoped, Calzada dropped the hammer and lunged for his Uzi. Having already moved into a shooter's stance, Cædmon quickly fired a round. His aim true, he managed to blow the Uzi out of the Bête Noire's hand, the sub-machine gun skittering across the marble floor.

Calzada bellowed with rage as he moved to retrieve the weapon.

Seizing his chance, Cædmon rushed forward and, going for the soft target, he kicked Calzada in the lower belly. So hard, he felt the satisfying mush of abdominal wall. Felled, Calzada dropped to his knees, braying like a donkey. Unable to stop himself, Cædmon kneed him under the chin, hurling his foe on to his back. For a brief instant, the brute's torso arched before he went completely slack, limbs splayed.

'*Finally*,' he muttered as he stared dispassionately at the unconscious man sprawled at his feet. He felt a singular lack of remorse, convinced that in this one instance, evolution's arrow had gone astray, Hector Calzada more beast than man.

Barely able to stand, Cædmon shambled towards the exit, stopping to pick up the Uzi along the way. As he stepped through the doorway, he heard the welcome blare of sirens. The rain had stopped, the air laden with a fine mist that felt oddly refreshing.

Edie and Anala both ran towards him.

'We heard a gunshot! Did he hurt you?' Edie asked anxiously as she threw herself at his chest and wrapped her arms around his waist.

'I'm all right, love.' Wobbling slightly, he held her, not entirely certain who supported who.

They'd survived! All three of them!

Standing a few feet away, Anala smiled shyly at him. His emotions in a jumble, Cædmon stared into eyes that were hauntingly similar to his own.

'You need to ring your mother.'

'I did. Soon after we called the police,' Anala informed him.

'Right. Of course you did. I didn't mean to sound like a –' *Father.* He shook his head, stymied.

'Look!' Edie pointed to the sky. 'There's a rainbow.'

For several moments, Cædmon stared at the shimmering bands of colour that arced across the eastern horizon. 'It's like peering through Newton's prism,' he murmured.

'Don't you know what that is?' As she spoke, Anala sidled closer to him and Edie. Still smiling, she said, 'Indra, the Hindu god of thunder, used a rainbow arrow to destroy Asura Vrta, the demon serpent.'

Edie gently nudged him. 'Did you hear that?'

Shoulders relaxing, Cædmon pushed out a cathartic sigh.

I did.

Epilogue

Paris, France

Two Weeks Later

'*Ravissant!*' Cædmon enthused, kissing his fingertips *à la française* as Edie entered the study. Attired in a cream-coloured halter dress that showed off her toned arms and legs, she was stunning.

Smiling cheekily, Edie perched herself on the edge of his desk, leaned over and kissed him full on the lips. 'Right back at ya, Big Red.'

He chortled, amused. 'If you don't mind, I prefer "dashing".'

'That you are. Particularly since the nasty bruise on your jaw has *finally* faded. I think the chartreuse stage was the worst.' Extending a bare arm, Edie snatched the desk calendar that he'd just finished marking before she walked in. 'I see that you've blocked off the first week in October.'

'That's the week before Michaelmas terms begins at Oxford.' Cædmon stared at the calendar in Edie's hands, hoping that he'd not bitten off too much. 'Because I've never envisioned myself playing the role of father, I'm admittedly out of my bailiwick.'

Edie returned the calendar to him. 'First of all, stop

thinking of it as a role. Just be yourself. And don't be afraid to let Anala know that you're nervous. Trust me. She'll be charmed. And you have a clear advantage . . .' She paused, a mischievous glint in her brown eyes. 'Not every father can lay claim to having a quiverful of rainbow arrows.'

'Lucky for all of us that I did,' he muttered. Discomfited, he changed the subject. 'Did I mention that I got us tickets for *Rigoletto* at the Paris Opéra?'

'No, you did not.' Edie clapped her hands, clearly pleased with the announcement. 'Ooh-la-la! How I love the gilded splendour of Palais Garnier. This is an outing that most definitely requires a new dress. Champs-Elysées, here I come.'

'Unfortunately, all of the orchestra tickets were sold out. The best I could manage was the second balcony.'

'*Quelle horreur!*'

'Yes, well, the good news is that our seats are in the same box,' he deadpanned.

'My hero.' Grinning, Edie patted her heart, miming a fluttering heartbeat.

Delighted by her playful reaction, Cædmon stared at his lady love, Edie Miller, the source of all his bliss. And an astonishing gift that he wasn't altogether certain that he deserved.

'Stop the presses,' Edie whispered, returning his stare. 'I think that I'm in love.'

'Speaking of the press, I thought you'd be interested to see this.' Rifling through a stack of newspapers that he'd picked up earlier at the corner kiosk, he plucked a day-old edition of the *New York Times* out of the pile. 'Franco

Fiorio didn't make the headlines, but he is front-page news,' he remarked, handing Edie the paper.

'"Cardinal Fiorio Faces Uphill Legal Battle",' she read aloud. 'Good. I'm glad that the district attorney is pressing forward with the criminal case. Although I think it's a shame that she can only charge him with being an accessory to murder and kidnapping. He was, after all, the mastermind.' Wearing a sly grin, Edie lowered the newspaper. 'I wonder if he and Hector will share a jail cell.'

'A fitting punishment for both of them,' Cædmon muttered uncharitably. He glanced at his wristwatch. 'It's getting rather late in the morning. If you like, I can whip together something in the kitchen.'

Putting a hand to her lower belly, Edie said, 'Please, not another one of those egg and sausage fry-ups that you love to "whip together". And is the black pudding and baked beans *really* necessary? Just thinking about it is causing my cholesterol level to escalate.'

'The heart dies, but the breakfast lives on,' he declared in a booming voice.

'I have a better idea. How about we stroll down to the patisserie? I'm in the mood for a gooey éclair. The one that's covered in caramel, what's that called?'

'That would be a bâton de Jacob.'

Edie laughed; a full, throaty sound that was utterly contagious. 'Sounds biblical. In a naughty kinda way.'

'Ah! That reminds me; I received an email from the Reverend Doctor Geevarghese Mar Paulos. He received the third copper plate.'

'And . . . ?'

'And the Nazrani bishops will meet later this month at which time they'll decide whether or not to release the plate to the public,' he informed her, hitting the highlights of the email. 'So, we shall have to wait and see what happens on that front.'

'I know you're convinced that it was the right thing to do, but I'm not so –'

'Need I remind you that Fortes de Pinós did steal the *Evangelium Gaspar* from the Nazrani,' he interjected.

'All right. I surrender,' Edie said with an exasperated shake of the head. 'But I still hope that the Nazrani decide to go public. People *need* to know what's contained in the *Evangelium Gaspar*. They need to know the truth.'

'I suspect that the truth, if it's ever made public, will trigger a violent religious upheaval followed by a painful detoxification.' That was the reason why he'd given the Nazrani custody of the third plate, unwilling to be the person responsible for putting the Christians of the world through a bloody Twelve Step Programme.

As to the current whereabouts of the first two plates, Cædmon suspected that Cardinal Fiorio had done one of two things: he'd cached the plates in the Vatican Secret Archives or he'd stashed them in a personal safe deposit box. Either way, he presumed that the plates were lost to history.

'At least we have digital copies of all three plates,' Edie said, having correctly intuited the direction of his thoughts.

'Which I find more fascinating with each reading. And it makes me wonder about other secrets that the Templars may have unearthed at Mount Carmel.' From the onset, Cædmon had suspected that the Order had discovered scrolls or texts at the ancient monastery that ultimately led them to India.

'Personally, I'm intrigued by the notion that, after the crucifixion, Jesus left his apostles so that he could seek out the lost tribes of Israel. Which begs the question: where did he go? And what happened to him once he got there?'

'Provocative questions, indeed.'

Convinced that there was more to the tale, Cædmon got up from his desk and walked over to the globe prominently situated in the corner of his study. An early nineteenth-century terrestrial globe, it was an impressive bit of cartography. Somewhat idly, he spun the orb before his index finger landed on a particular locale, stopping the globe in mid-spin.

For several moments he stared at the sacred parcel of land known during the Middle Ages as the *Axis Mundi*, the centre of the world. It was the hallowed place that reputedly connected heaven and earth. One to the other.

There were secrets hidden there. Of that he was certain.

Glancing up from the globe, Cædmon smiled broadly at his lady love. 'Fancy a trip to the Holy Land?'

He just wanted a decent book to read ...

Not too much to ask, is it? It was in 1935 when Allen Lane, Managing Director of Bodley Head Publishers, stood on a platform at Exeter railway station looking for something good to read on his journey back to London. His choice was limited to popular magazines and poor-quality paperbacks – the same choice faced every day by the vast majority of readers, few of whom could afford hardbacks. Lane's disappointment and subsequent anger at the range of books generally available led him to found a company – and change the world.

'We believed in the existence in this country of a vast reading public for intelligent books at a low price, and staked everything on it'
Sir Allen Lane, 1902–1970, founder of Penguin Books

The quality paperback had arrived – and not just in bookshops. Lane was adamant that his Penguins should appear in chain stores and tobacconists, and should cost no more than a packet of cigarettes.

Reading habits (and cigarette prices) have changed since 1935, but Penguin still believes in publishing the best books for everybody to enjoy. We still believe that good design costs no more than bad design, and we still believe that quality books published passionately and responsibly make the world a better place.

So wherever you see the little bird – whether it's on a piece of prize-winning literary fiction or a celebrity autobiography, political tour de force or historical masterpiece, a serial-killer thriller, reference book, world classic or a piece of pure escapism – you can bet that it represents the very best that the genre has to offer.

Whatever you like to read – trust Penguin.

read more
www.penguin.co.uk